...and political ...ipping tale'

The it... The Times

'O'Brien is a terrific storyteller'
Daily Telegraph

'A gripping story of love, heartache and political intrigue'
Woman & Home

'One of the best writers around...she
outdoes even Philippa Gregory'
Sun

'The characters are larger than life...and the
author a compulsive storyteller'
Sunday Express

'A fast-paced historical novel'
Good Housekeeping

'This book has everything – royalty, scandal,
fascinating historical politics'
Cosmopolitan

'O'Brien's page-turner vividly brings to life the
restriction of women, and the compassion and strength
of this real-life figure from medieval times'
Woman

'A gripping historical drama'
Bella

Anne O'Brien was born in the West Riding of Yorkshire. After gaining a BA Honours degree in History at Manchester University and a Master's in Education at Hull, she lived in the East Riding for many years as a teacher of history.

Today she has sold nearly half a million copies of her books worldwide. She lives with her husband in an eighteenth-century timber-framed cottage in the depths of the Welsh Marches in Herefordshire on the borders between England and Wales. The area provides endless inspiration for her novels about the forgotten women of history.

Visit Anne online at www.anneobrienbooks.com.

@anneobrienbooks
@anne_obrien

Also by
ANNE O'BRIEN

THE VIRGIN WIDOW
DEVIL'S CONSORT
THE KING'S CONCUBINE
THE FORBIDDEN QUEEN
THE SCANDALOUS DUCHESS
THE KING'S SISTER
THE QUEEN'S CHOICE
THE SHADOW QUEEN
QUEEN OF THE NORTH
A TAPESTRY OF TREASON

The
Queen's
Rival

ANNE
O'BRIEN

ONE PLACE. MANY STORIES

HQ
An imprint of HarperCollins*Publishers* Ltd
1 London Bridge Street
London SE1 9GF

www.harpercollins.co.uk

HarperCollins*Publishers*
1st Floor, Watermarque Building, Ringsend Road
Dublin 4, Ireland

This edition 2021

1
First published in Great Britain by
HQ, an imprint of HarperCollins*Publishers* Ltd 2020

Copyright © Anne O'Brien 2020

ISBN:
PB: 978-0-00-822553-7

MIX
Paper from
responsible sources
FSC™ C007454

This book is produced from independently certified FSC™ paper to ensure responsible forest management.

For more information visit: www.harpercollins.co.uk/green

This book is set in 10.9/15.5 pt. Bembo by Type-it AS, Norway

Printed and bound in Great Britain by
CPI Group (UK) Ltd, Croydon, CR0 4YY

With all my love, as always, to my husband George.
He has accompanied me in my close companionship with
Cecily Neville, Duchess of York (whether he wished to or not).

'Dame Cecily, sir, whose daughter was she?
Of the Earl of Westmorland, I believe the youngest
and in grace her fortune to be the highest'
CLARE ROLL

'Cecily, wife unto the right noble Prince Richard, late
Duke of York, father unto the most Christian Prince my
lord and son King Edward IV...bequeath and surrender my
soul to the merciful hands of Almighty God my maker'
CECILY'S WILL

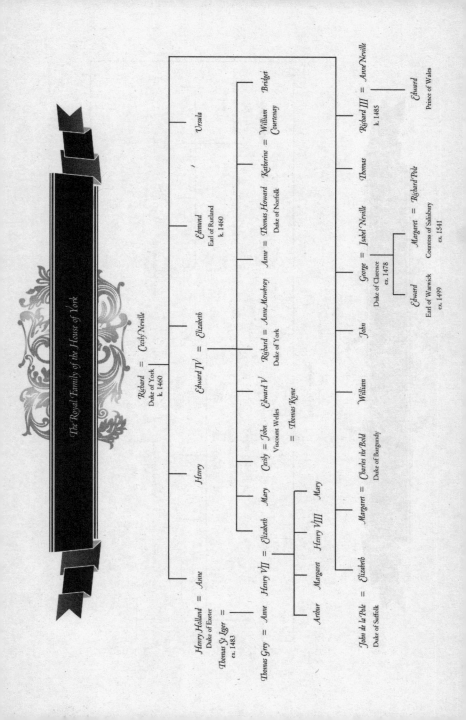

The Royal Family of the House of York

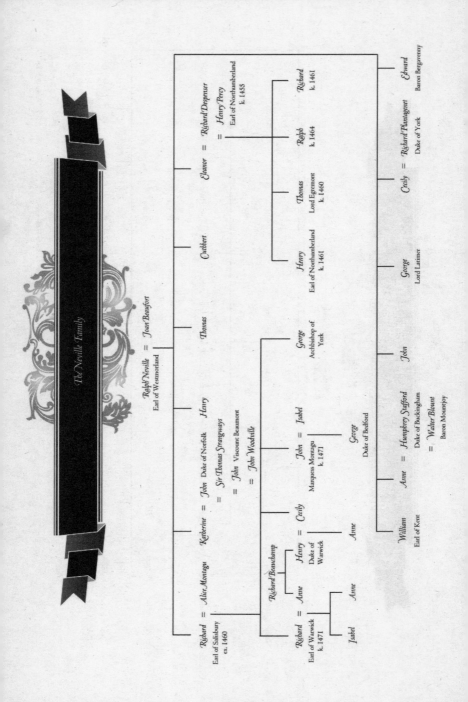

The Neville Family

Ralph Neville = Joan Beaufort
Earl of Westmorland

Richard = Alice Montagu
Earl of Salisbury
ex. 1460

Katherine = John Duke of Norfolk
= Sir Thomas Strangways
= John Viscount Beaumont
= John Woodville

Henry

Thomas

Cuthbert

Eleanor = Richard Despenser
= Henry Percy
Earl of Northumberland
k. 1455

Richard Beauchamp

Henry = Cecily
Duke of Warwick

Anne

Cecily

John = Isabel
Marquess Montagu
k. 1471

George
Archbishop of York

Henry
Earl of Northumberland
k. 1461

Thomas
Lord Egremont
k. 1460

Ralph
k. 1464

Richard
k. 1461

Anne = Richard
Earl of Warwick
k. 1471

Isabel   Anne

George
Duke of Bedford

William
Earl of Kent

Anne = Humphrey Stafford
Duke of Buckingham
= Walter Blount
Baron Mountjoy

John

George
Lord Latimer

Cecily = Richard Plantagenet
Duke of York

Edward
Baron Bergavenny

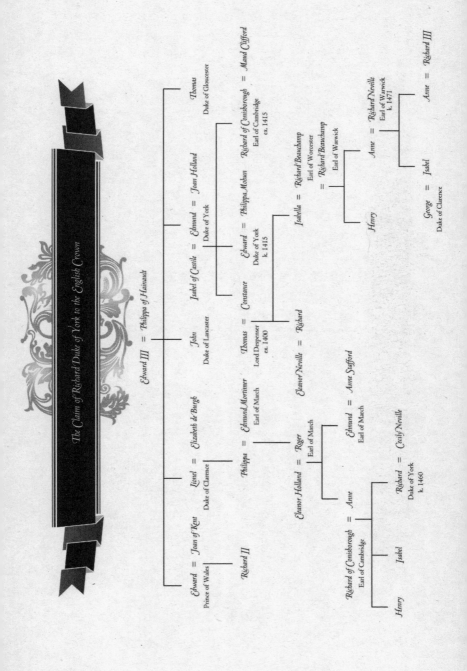

The Claim of Richard Duke of York to the English Crown

Prologue

A Domestic Interlude in the Most Loyal House of York

Cecily, Duchess of York, to my youngest son Diccon, on the occasion of his seventh birthday celebrated here at Ludlow, on the second day of October in the year 1459

Today, my son, we mark the day of your birth.

You will have unwrapped your gifts by now, among them a fine dagger from your father with a damascened blade. He persuades me that you are old enough to own such a weapon. It belonged to him when he was a boy. He has the scars to prove it. Ask him to show you them when he has a moment of leisure. It is not a bauble and you should treat it with respect. I will confiscate it if you use it unwisely.

From me you will have discovered the book of stories of Greek heroes which you are now able to read. They all use their swords and daggers with care.

Enjoy the special day, with all the family here together, although you will be disappointed that the promised tournament will not happen. Your father has much on his mind with so many of our soldiers billeted in the castle and in the town, but your brothers have something planned so that the day does not go unmarked. The cook will make your favourite Payn Ragoun to be served at the end of dinner; it is the day of your birth so I will accept a little indulgence.

Remember to thank the Blessed Virgin Mary for your life and health.

Remember your duty to God and to the King, whatever happens in the coming days.

Remember your duty to your family of York.

Do not forget to attend Mass.

I have also given you an illuminated Book of Hours that belonged to me when I was a young girl. I know that you will be tempted to write in your own birth-date in the page of October. Do not do so. It is a masterpiece of clerkish work and will not benefit from your scrawl in the margins.

From your loving mother,

Cecily, Duchess of York

To my Lady Mother, Duchess Cecily, on the evening of this second day of October 1459

My tutor says that I must give you gracious thanks for the gifts, and prove that I can write well.

My father showed me the scar where his first dagger hacked into his wrist when he was skinning a rabbit. I promise I will not do that. My father said that he was too busy to show me the rest. I have not written in my Book of Hours. But one day I will. One day I think it will be important to me to mark the day of my birth. I promise I will write it neatly.

I have started to read the book of Greek heroes. I have decided I would wish to be like Achilles, to live bravely and to die well, even if I am not very old when I meet my doom.

I enjoyed the Payn Ragoun, although George ate more than I did. He says it is his right because he is three years older than I am.

I hope it makes his teeth drop out.

I have also had to hide my new dagger from him.

From your dutiful son,

Diccon

Cecily, Duchess of York, to her son George

I wish to see you in my chamber immediately after Mass.

It has come to my notice that you have not yet learned the lessons of either generosity or humility, or family affection. Gluttony, I must warn you, is also a sin.

Do not put me to the trouble of coming to find you in the stables. You will not enjoy the consequences.

Because I know that you will take heed and learn from your mistakes, I remain your loving mother.

Cecily, Duchess of York

Cecily, Duchess of York, for the immediate attention of the Duke of York

Richard,

I warned you that Diccon was too young for such a gift. George is suffering from a severe attack of envy so that Diccon has already had to fight to keep possession of his dagger. They have both been blooded and show signs of battle, but our younger son has emerged victorious. He might lack the physical bulk of George but his spirit is strong.

I advise you to make no mention of their colourful afflictions when you next see them. Do not praise them for any false courage. I have dealt with the matter.

I think this will find you before I do, when you at last return to the castle.

I know that you have much on your mind and that you will say, rightly, that it is my role to supervise the education of our sons, but sometimes a word of paternal admonishing would not go amiss.

In exasperation,

Your loving wife,

Cis

Chapter One

The Death of Loyalty

**Duchess Cecily teaches a lesson in
Ludlow Castle, October 1459**

We were in occupation of one of the corner chambers in the
old gatehouse keep at Ludlow Castle because it was a good
vantage point from which to detect approaching marauders.
Despite the lack of light and the all-pervasive reek of damp,
I lit candles then unrolled the precious scroll with a flourish. It
was a line of succession, drawn as a tree with thorny branches,
all the way from the first man and woman on earth, Adam
and Eve, enclosed in leaves and flowers in the Garden of Eden,
to King Henry the Sixth, our present crowned and anointed
King of England.

'Hold down the corners,' I said to my children.

My two elder sons already knew this lesson well, as did my
elder daughters, Anne and Elizabeth, who were wed and living
in their own households. Here with me were my three younger
offspring. Margaret, more frequently called Meg, at twelve years
was adept at reading and could work it out for herself. George at

ten, and Richard, known to all as Diccon to avoid unnecessary complications in our domestic dealings, the youngest of my sons who had not yet achieved eight years, were still in the process of gleaning information on old alliances. It was time they knew of their profound inheritance. Indeed, in the circumstances, it had become an urgent affair.

George slouched over the table edge, pressing down hard with his whole hand, while Meg applied her fingertips with neat precision. Diccon had his elbows splayed along one edge, leaning close to survey the pattern of lines and names.

'Do you see the roundels, painted next to each name?' I pointed to some of them, the closest to us today and the most highly coloured, all capped or crowned with gold. 'The scribe has included a picture of each King, and his heraldic symbol so that you might recognise him.'

They peered over the document, sufficiently engrossed, even George who preferred weapons to books.

'Our King Henry.' George pointed. 'Our cousin.'

Meg placed her finger on a sword-wielding figure, two branches above. 'That is the fourth King Henry.'

'He was my mother's – your grandmother Joan's – half-brother.' I traced my finger down from that fourth Henry to his son, the fifth Henry, and then his grandson, the sixth, our present King. 'These Kings – all three Henrys – are from the House of Lancaster.'

'Why is the fourth Henry the only one with a sword?' Diccon asked.

'Because he used the sword to slice through the branches of the tree. There.' I pointed to the break in the branches. 'Henry cut the order of succession and deposed King Richard.' I watched as a frown furrowed George's brow. 'The fourth Henry is what we would call a usurper.'

'What happened to Richard?' George asked.

'He died. In Pontefract Castle.'

'Did Henry have him killed?' Meg asked.

'No one knows.'

'I wager he did. He is fierce in the picture.' Diccon looked impressed.

'What do you learn from this?' I asked.

'They are all branches of the same tree, from father to son. Except there, when the Lancastrian Kings took over.' Meg regarded me with her solemn stare. Her eyes were forthright, her chin stubborn, her countenance often firm-lipped and unsmiling, but I thought she would grow into a handsome woman. My husband said that of them all she was most like me, and perhaps he was right. She was developing a strong will. 'Would it have been better to keep Richard, whatever his faults?' she asked.

'The Lancastrian Henrys have brought us a peaceful and strong country,' I stated. 'Victory abroad in battles against the French. Richard may not have done so. And Richard had no son to follow him. It is important to have sons.'

'Is our King Henry a good King?' Diccon asked.

'Sometimes he is not well,' I suggested. 'Sometimes he needs good advisors.'

'Like our father?'

I regarded Diccon. My other sons would be as tall and broad and fair as the painted angels on the walls of my private chapel. Diccon would be neither tall nor broad, and his hair was the dark of a raven's wing. He was the image of his father, who had more wiry strength than powerful muscle.

'Yes, like your father.'

But King Henry's worthiness was not a subject for discussion. We were stepping on the quivering ground of a morass that had recently begun to weaken the solid foundations of our vast, far-flung family.

'But where does our father fit on the branches?' George asked.

I pointed further back than the deposed King Richard, to the great third King Edward who had won battles at Crécy and Poitiers and thus defeated the French.

'We come here, from the sons of this King Edward. He had five sons. Your father is descended from one of those sons, the Duke of York.'

'I know that I will not inherit my father's title, even though I have his name,' Diccon said.

His acceptance rather than childish wistfulness made me smile. 'You are named for him, but it is Ned who will be Duke of York. You will have your own title when you have grown a little more.'

My eldest son Edward – still Ned in his adolescence – would make an exemplary Duke of York.

I replaced the scroll, locked the coffer and returned the key to the purse, appropriately embroidered with our emblems of falcons and fetterlocks, at my girdle.

'So our father is royal. We are royal.' Diccon's mind was still absorbed in the multi-layered branches of the tree as we left the chamber, even as he hopped with an excess of energy. George raced ahead down the narrow stairway, his voice echoing in a strident farewell, and I let him go. Meg walked with grace at my side.

'You have Plantagenet blood in your veins, just as King Henry does. From your father and from me.' It was never too early to instil some sense of pride in their inheritance, as I had learned it at my mother's knee. My mother Joan, as one of John of Gaunt's Beaufort children with Katherine Swynford, once disgracefully illegitimate before being restored to respectability, had more than her fair share of pride when she was wed to Ralph Neville, Earl of Westmorland.

'Why are we not on the tree as well, if we are all descended from the great King Edward?' Diccon was asking.

I dropped my hand lightly on his head, ruffling his already ruffled hair.

'Because we do not rule.'

'Even though the fourth Henry was a usurper?'

He had remembered the word well.

'Even though he was a usurper. We do not have the right to rule, and we never will.'

'To think otherwise would be treason,' Meg stated with all the smooth assurance of youth and untried loyalties.

Diccon looked to me for confirmation.

'That is true. We are loyal subjects to the House of Lancaster. The House of York will always be so.' I spoke what were to become fateful words. 'Whatever you hear to the contrary, we are loyal subjects.'

There were storm clouds building on our immediate horizon. It was a simple thing to make this declaration of fealty. It was becoming increasingly difficult to hold it as a truth.

At this moment there was an army outside our gates, almost within our sights across the river. It was led by Marguerite, Queen of England, who would be quick to cry me false.

Cecily, Duchess of York, to her grace the
Queen Marguerite, late of Anjou

Written from Ludlow Castle, on this tenth day of October 1459
Sent by the Duchess's personal courier, claiming safe conduct for
his return with the Queen's reply

Your grace,

I regret this need to write to you. My lord the Duke of York forbids it, but I cannot ignore the desperate situation in which we find ourselves. Do our armies not face each other, about to engage in battle, on the fields beside Ludford Bridge?

I fear for the outcome, as I am certain you do also. Was there not enough bloodshed less than a month ago at Blore Heath, when two thousand of your Lancastrian troops were slain, including your commander Lord Audley?

It stains my conscience. It must also weigh heavy on yours, your grace.

You will call us traitors, but you must know in your heart that the Duke of York has never been moved by thoughts of treason. Your most royal husband Henry is our King. Nothing can change that. We do not seek his overthrow, no matter what poison the Duke of Somerset might drop in your ear. He may be my Beaufort cousin, but there is much bad blood between the Beauforts and my husband and I would counsel you to beware his advice. Somerset's only interest is to wipe out York as a rival to his own position as the most influential of royal counsellors.

Because of this, I need to remind you that I have always proved to be a friend to you in the trials of your early days as Henry's wife, when you were anxious and alone in Rouen, a new bride laid low with illness. Remember when, in your pregnancy, you asked for and received advice because, with children of my own, I was able to give it four-fold. And I gave it willingly, and with much affection and respect for your dignity as a somewhat neglected young wife.

Now those we love and esteem are brought together, by fate, on a battlefield.

As women we can change that outcome. We are not without influence. We should not waste our days in devising vengeance for past slights.

I beg you, your grace, use sweet words to draw our King back from the brink. As I will use mine with my lord the Duke of York.

Your defeat at Blore Heath at the hands of my brother, the Earl of Salisbury, will sit ill with you, but now is the time to negotiate and heal the wounds. If we cannot extricate ourselves from this tangled mess, the fields beside Ludford Bridge may well be soaked in English blood before nightfall tomorrow.

With all humble reverence,
Your lowly servant
Cecily, Duchess of York

Marguerite, Queen of England, to Cecily, Duchess of York
Written from the royal pavilion at Ludford Bridge, on this tenth day of October 1459

Madam

Your empty words carry no weight with me. When the Duke of York takes up arms against my lord the King on a battlefield, it is treason. I recall your kindness in the past, but those days are long gone, drowned in Lord Audley's blood. Further death can only be prevented if York is prepared to bow the knee and sue for mercy.

Somerset remains my most cherished advisor. York will do well to remember that.

I have no pity for your present situation.

Marguerite, Queen of England

England's Chronicle, *October 1459*

Blood and death on a battlefield, Englishman facing Englishman.

How have we been dragged into this fine goblet of disaster?

Is there anyone alive in this unfortunate country who does not know?

We have a King whose mind is not to be relied upon.

We have a Queen who sees the lure of power for herself and her young son.

We have a royal cousin, the Duke of York, whose views are ambivalent. Does he wish to be an efficient Protector and Counsellor to our sad King? Or does he desire the crown for himself?

Our noble Duke is haunted by a vast array of enemies who will undermine his reputation for honesty and hard work on behalf of the King. The Beaufort Duke of Somerset is the most dangerous. So much for the Love Day travesty of renewed friendship last year, when all erstwhile antagonists walked hand in hand, arm in arm. An event that we would all happily forget since it achieved nothing but a mockery of our King's attempts to heal the enmity between his most powerful magnates.

Now it seems that the adherents of York and Lancaster will face each other on a battlefield at Ludford Bridge.

We advise you to pray for a fast resolution. For which side you will pray is a matter for your own conscience. Duchess Cecily will be praying hard for her husband, despite the array of Neville relatives who still cleave to King Henry and the Lancastrians.

Cecily, Duchess of York, to her estranged sister Anne, Duchess of Buckingham
   Written from our castle at Ludlow, on this tenth day of October 1459

Sister, written in haste so excuse the scrawl and blots,

Do not give up on my letter and consign it to the flames before reading past the first sentence. I am writing to tell you that by the end of tomorrow your sister and her closest family may well be dead in a ditch or taken prisoner as traitors.

I can hear your thoughts already, loud and clear from distant Kent, accusing Richard of desiring the crown for his own supreme ennoblement. Unfair, Anne! That is and never was Richard's desire, no matter what Queen Marguerite might announce to the world.

The King's army is outside our gates. I do not know what information you have, but it would be remiss of you if you allowed yourself to become cut off from these dangerous developments. I feel it my duty to write in warning for we will not emerge from this unscathed, although who will suffer most – you or I – cannot yet be determined.

When we were children, who would ever have predicted that, through marriage, we would have become enemies, cleaving to opposing sides in battle, you for Lancaster, me for York. It wounds my heart, but what is done, is done.

I am presuming that your misguided husband Humphrey Stafford, Duke of Buckingham, is at this very moment within shouting distance of us here in Ludlow, with the Lancastrian army at King Henry's side. I can only hope that Henry is not the man for waging war, that he will withdraw and agree to parley, but as Richard says, the King is not always in command of himself, much less his armies.

Neither one of us, Anne, can deny that Henry has proved dilatory in recent years, even when he appears to be in control of his senses.

Richard is confident there will be no battle. He says that we are as well prepared as we could be with ditches and palisades of stakes, with well-set ambushes and traps. We have cannon set in place. Nor will Richard fight, unless provoked beyond reason.

This was Richard's final reassurance as he left me to inspect the soldiery that inhabit, like a plague of rats, every corner of the town and castle. Which should comfort me, but it does not. Do you think Buckingham might use his considerable weight to persuade Henry to negotiate? I know he is a man of good sense and moderation, if he can but capture the King's flea-hopping attention from my cousin Somerset's constant aggression. You should know that Marguerite has refused any kindly intervention. She stands like a beacon on a hill-top, agleam with regal authority and vicious recrimination. All of our past closeness is buried under acrimony and fear.

I am afraid, Anne. My sons Ned and Edmund are with Richard on the battlefield. I know they are of an age to be there, but I fear for them, particularly Edmund who is not as robust as his brother. Meg, George, and Diccon remain here with me at the castle, although George claims he should fight beside his father. He is already almost as tall as I, but then it has to be admitted that I cannot boast of any degree of stature. At this moment he is polishing his weapons.

Oh, Anne, do we not both know what it is to lose children to death? I cannot imagine your grief at the loss of your only son and Buckingham's heir, from his wounds from a Yorkist sword after the Battle of St Albans. At least you and Buckingham could be consoled that he had a son of his own, your grandson, to inherit the dukedom.

I cannot even consider the loss of my sons to Lancastrian swords, on my own doorstep here in Ludlow.

I do not expect compassion from you. The political rifts have been dug too deep. All I can ask is that you petition the Blessed Virgin and Holy Mother for a peaceful outcome, and understand that it was never my intention to be at odds with you. It is the way the world works when men have ambitions.

From your sister who, despite all, loves you as much as she ever did.

Cecily

Duchess Cecily's intercession to the Blessed Virgin Mary

Hail Mary full of Grace, the Lord is with thee.

Blessed art thou among women

And blessed is the fruit of thy womb Jesus.

Holy Mary, Mother of God,

Pray for us sinners now and at the hour of our death.

I raise before you the names of those dear to me, who even now stand at the forefront of their forces on the battlefield. In your blessed mercy, preserve them, keep them safe, nurture them in their decisions and bring them safe home. If they must face death, give them courage and fortitude.

I pray that you do not give credence to anything my cousin,

Henry Beaufort, the Duke of Somerset, might offer up in his prayers. He has proved, in all his dealings with the House of York, to be nothing less than a serpent in the royal grass. He would perjure his soul before telling the honest truth.

Amen

Richard, Duke of York, to Cecily, Duchess of York
Written from Ludford Bridge

Cecily,

Marguerite encourages the King to break out his banners and don armour, as if he were a true soldier and leader in battle, which we know he is not. The King would rather sit in his pavilion and read his missal, but the Queen has him firmly under her heel. I fear that the mummery of the King in full battle array is having the desired effect, filling our troops with awe. There is much desertion, our soldiers abandoning the battlefield to flee or skulk in the streets of Ludlow.

I will negotiate with the King, but never on Somerset's terms.

Whatever the outcome, never doubt the esteem in which I hold you, nor my dedication to the future of our children. You are the one shining candle in the present darkness.

Richard

Chapter Two

Disaster Threatens the House of York

Duchess Cecily faces her worst fears in Ludlow Castle, the twelfth day of October 1459

It was midnight, the darkest hour when barn-owls called and bats flitted noiselessly, caught as black shadows in the gleam of the guards' lanterns. I was sitting on my bed, sleepless, book in hand, but the *Life of St Maude* with her piety and charitable works did not keep my attention, not even her clever involvement in the tenth-century politics of Bavaria. The children were asleep, exhausted by the excitement and tensions in the coming and going of mounted men and cart-loads of supplies.

All my senses leaped into nervous life when there came the distant clatter of a disturbance at the main gate which provided access into the town. I had already cast aside the book by the time a servant, who had been given instruction to keep me abreast of all events, no matter how trivial they might seem, tapped on my door. I dragged a heavy robe over my shift to follow him down the stairs. If it was an opportunistic attack from the royal army I would trust our watchmen to keep the barbican gate closed. But how had a hostile force managed to circumvent Richard's careful defences and reach the centre of Ludlow? Forcing myself not to run, I climbed to the vantage point at the top of the old gatehouse keep, pulling up my hood over my braided hair.

My throat was dry with fear.

What I saw made my heart thud in a heavy beat, for the barbican gate was already open, distant figures moving in the outer bailey, our guards offering no resistance to these incomers with their escort. There were no banners, no visible heraldic symbols to indicate who they might be.

The beat of my heart thudded loudly in my ears.

A small group, tight-knit, rode across the expanse towards the inner gateway below me. I leaned forward, my fingers curled hard around the coping stones. But then my heart slowed at what I saw. I remained where I was, as they rode beneath me into the inner bailey. I knew exactly who my late-night visitors were in spite of dark enveloping cloaks.

By the time I had descended they had all dismounted, allowing me to pick out a quintet of strained faces as hoods were pushed back or helms removed. A potent mix of Nevilles and Plantagenets. My brother Richard Neville, Earl of Salisbury, my nephew, another Richard, Earl of Warwick. My sons Edward and Edmund. And Richard, my Richard, Duke of York. Already in urgent and low-voiced conversation, before I could even ask what was happening, Richard left the group, took my arm and pulled me into the guards' antechamber, dispatching its only occupant with a tilt of his chin.

'What's happened?'

My fingers dug into the cloth of his cloak as they had dug into the stone revetment. I could read nothing in his face in the light of the single torch.

'Disaster.' His voice was a croak.

'Why are you all here? Has there been a battle?'

For if it was a disaster, where was the rest of the army? We had heard no noise of conflict or conflagration. For the first time I noted the groove between Richard's dark brows as he leaned close, his voice low. This was not meant to be overheard.

'A pardon came, apparently from the King, if we would lay down our arms, a pardon I thought not to be trusted. It had the imprint of Somerset all over it. Or perhaps the Queen, to lure us into surrender and so into a trap. But Andrew Trollope, God damn his soul to hell, the man in command of Warwick's main force from the Calais garrison, accepted it, declaiming to his troops that he had never wanted to fight the King in person.'

'Could he not be persuaded?'

We were both whispering. Whatever had occurred was worse than I could imagine, nor should it be spread abroad.

'He gave me no chance. The last we saw of Trollope was a retreating cloud of dust, taking his men with him. I took the only decision I thought left to us. I sent a letter to the King, asking for a parley. The reply came back, almost immediately, that he would not. He would do his negotiating with arms and battle in the field.'

'Did he write it? It doesn't sound like Henry. Marguerite perhaps.'

'Who's to know?' For a moment he sounded so weary. 'It will be a battle and without Trollope's men we are lost. There will be no mercy. I misjudged it, Cis. How could I misjudge it so badly?' Richard rubbed his gloved hands over his face as if to clear his vision. 'Henry looked every inch a warrior, standing proudly tricked out in armour under his royal banner. Even his thinning hair managed to gleam in a kingly fashion beneath his crown. Our troops were weak at the knee at the sight. And there it is. We daren't risk a battle. They'll all go over to him as their King within seconds of a Lancastrian call to arms.'

I could see defeat, engraved deep in the lines from nose to mouth. His familiar features had become a bleak map of failure.

'What will you do?' I knew without asking, but dreaded the reply.

'We have no choices left. It must be flight.'

I could not hide the horror in my face. 'You have abandoned your men?'

This was no time for my censure. Many would say it was not the place of a woman to express disparagement, for what developed on a battlefield was man's work. But this was a step beyond treason against the King. For the puissant Duke of York to abandon his troops was anathema. These were our men, our tenants, our soldiery, born and bred in loyalty to their Plantagenet lord.

'Have you disbanded them and sent them home?' I persisted.

I could almost see his face flush in the shadows, but his voice was edged with his own righteousness, his own belief in what must be. 'No. I have not. We need time, and to disband the army would give Henry freedom of action to pursue us here to the gate of our castle. The army remains in place until tomorrow. I have told our officers that we have retired here for the night, and that we will return at dawn. The Lancastrians will see nothing amiss until we have gone.'

'Richard...' I did not like it. I did not like it at all, but could think of nothing to say. He had made the decision.

He sensed the tenor of my silence, as he would after more than thirty years of marriage, through good times and worse. 'I know. It's bad, but we must redeem what we can from a desperate situation. Henry will not wage war on common soldiers. It's us he wants. If we stay we will be taken prisoner, if not killed outright. That will be the end of our cause.'

I thought that he was trying to convince himself that our men would not be obliterated by his decision to escape. I held his hands, willing him to tell me that flight was not the only possibility, but I knew, as clearly as he, that they must get out of England before the royal hounds were slavering at their heels.

'We'll go in different directions,' he was explaining, already planning, while I had moved no further than the despair that he would leave me. 'I'll take Edmund with me into Wales and from the coast we'll take ship to Ireland where I know I'll be welcomed. My years as King's Lieutenant in Ireland will stand me in good stead. I'll make my base in Dublin.'

How confident he was, or at least sounded – possibly for my sake – that this journey would not entrap him into the hands of his enemies.

'Salisbury and Warwick will go south and they have agreed to take Edward with them. When they reach the coast, they'll take ship and join us in Dublin or make for Calais. Either move will be safe. With the boys travelling separately, there is at least the chance that one of them will survive to continue to lead the House of York.'

My family stripped from me in this one momentous decision, in which I had had no voice at all. I had considered the outcome of battle. I had not accepted that I might be abandoned to face the Lancastrians alone.

'When do you go?' I asked, my voice steady.

'I can't stay any longer than this hour.' He was as calm as I in the circumstances. 'We must go immediately before anyone can raise any sort of alarm.'

'I understand.'

And I did. But surely there was one question I must ask.

What of me? What of those three young children asleep in their beds?

My lips parted to ask it, only to be prevented by an embrace and a hasty kiss before he put me from him.

At the door he turned, his voice breaking in bitter self-condemnation, full of despair.

'I abandoned my army, Cecily. I abandoned my banners. They are lying there to be trampled on, come the day. All the pride and glory of York to be buried in mud and ignominy.' His eyes, wide and despairing, held mine. 'And now I must abandon you. You did not ask. I honour you for it. But I cannot take you and the children with me. Time is too short, and I must get our sons away before they fall into Lancastrian hands. Oh, Cis, my dear love. What have I done?'

He strode back towards me, enveloping me in his arms as he had done so often, in cold departing or joyful arrival. At the same time he whispered in my ear. I replied in kind, but then placed my fingers on his lips to silence him. No time, in this chill guard-room with dawn fast approaching, to express what might be in our hearts.

They were sentiments that I would remember for ever.

And then: 'Keep the gates bolted, your guards set,' he commanded, returning to practicality. 'They'll not get in and they'll not harm a woman and children. Whatever his weaknesses, Henry has more chivalry than to do that.'

But what about Marguerite? What of her chivalry?

Another question I dare not ask.

'I have no doubt of the quality of your courage. The Nevilles were all bred up in adversity and pride. Keep faith with our people here. Will you promise me?'

'I promise.'

'You will never know the depth of my gratitude.'

Now his kiss was deep and wretched indeed. I clung to him for a second, absorbing the essence of him, for what might be the final time.

'Go, Richard. Go before the huntsman sounds the three long motes for the hounds to seek the hart. You will be hunted most fervently by the Duke of Somerset.'

'But by God's will, we will escape and take refuge.'

'Amen.'

Out into the cold air of the inner bailey, there was one more burden to lie heavily on my heart. I must bid farewell to my two sons, for how long I could not imagine.

'May the Blessed Virgin keep you safe from harm,' I said, a soft benediction as all was clamour and activity around us.

A grip of hands, a light kiss of farewell, cheek against cheek. This was no time for excess emotion. Ned was eager to be away, his gaze already straying towards the impressive bulk of his cousin of Warwick, but Edmund remained and shivered under my grip. There was only a year between them but Edmund still had much growing to do, in confidence as well as in height and breadth of shoulder.

'You will bear yourself nobly as a son of York,' I encouraged him. I would worry over this son more than I would over Ned.

'Yes, madam.'

'You will be the first to tell me that you have no time for

accepting maternal advice on your conduct, but pay heed to your father's instructions. Be strong in the faith that I have instilled in you and in your duty to your proud name.'

Edmund bowed his head as if taking a solemn vow before an altar. I felt him straighten, his spine stiffen. He was already taller than I.

'I swear that I will, madam. I swear that you will be proud of me.'

'It is time to go. I look for the day when we will be reunited.'

I was pleased to see him walk with more assurance as I pushed him in Richard's direction. A woman's tears or anxieties would bring nothing to this emotional occasion.

'Farewell, my love.' My final words to Richard. 'God keep you and bring you home.'

'Uphold the honour of the House of York,' he replied, 'the honour which I have this night all but buried. I will keep you in my mind and my heart.'

'As you will remain in mine.'

Surprising me, he drew me close in the darkness, running the pads of his thumbs over my brows, my cheekbones, my lips, along the line of my jaw.

'Just so that I can remember you,' he said, 'when time and distance between us seem too vast.'

The last I saw of my warlike family, they were riding for the outer gate, supplied with money and food for what could be a long journey.

I was beyond tears. I could not imagine when I would see Richard again, or any one of them. I returned to my chamber where, with deliberate self-control, I dressed for the coming day when I must face the Lancastrians. I would stay here in Ludlow, as I promised Richard that I would. I would hold firm to that promise and protect our people with every remaining breath in my body.

Recorded by the private hand of Cecily, Duchess of York

I am alone and Richard has gone, fled from Ludford Bridge, leaving me to record the manner of his flight. Cowardly. Dishonourable. Contemptible. Despicable. The denunciation of my lord clamours in my head.

That is what they will say of Richard. These words will be written in history, in my husband's blood. Richard of York, the great lord who betrayed his wife and children to the marauding Lancastrian army to save his own neck. Who abandoned his army and relinquished his banners on the battlefield because he dared not face his King. The chroniclers will look to me for condemnation, for would I not join my diatribe to theirs? The Duchess of York must surely disavow her loyalties to an ambitious husband who left her behind.

What had he said in those final minutes together, when we could have merely spoken of our love for each other? I record his words here, for my own encouragement in future times of despair, when hope dies within me. *Do not let them turn you against me*, he said. *We have lived and fought side by side for so many years. I need you to believe in me.*

Oh, Richard, how could I not believe in you? But why leave me to face the enemy alone? We were capable of riding as hard and as fast as the rest. Why not take us out of danger, for our safety?

And why had I not, in the end, voiced my fears? Why had

I not demanded to be rescued from what would become a second battlefield, here in the streets of Ludlow?

I had not asked because I knew all the answers and I already understood all the thoughts that had not been spoken between us. The questions I had wanted to ask and had not because time was too short. Who would know Richard and the working of his mind better than I?

If he had remained to face the royal army, it would have been more than the carefully worked and gilded flags that suffered. It would have been catastrophic defeat, leading to almost inevitable capture and death by the edge of the axe. Flight might save his life and that of our sons. And life meant hope of return, to put wrongs right.

But what if, in the process of flight, they were recaptured? A fast beheading outside the walls of our own castle? There would be no trial, no recourse to the King's mercy. Even now Richard might be in Lancastrian hands, facing death.

All is quiet both within and without the castle. But so is death silent. Silent as the grave. Richard and my two eldest sons might already be bodies, stripped and humiliated on public display.

Why had he not taken me with him?

I trust my courage will run as freely as this ink on my pen.

I am here alone because I am the keystone. I am the one firm guiding hand to hold all in place until better times. Easy to fly like a mallard from the nest when a fox comes prowling. Richard trusts me to remain to care for those in need, to speak out for our people's interests. If I had ridden with him, if we had all fallen into enemy hands, the House of York would have been obliterated in the blink of an eye, in a fit of mad revenge for the bloodshed at the battles of St Albans and Blore Heath. What if we had made it to the coast to take ship? Any whirlwind storm to sink our vessel and we would all lie, bones stripped of flesh by fish, at the bottom of the sea.

Now I must brace myself, forcing my shoulders to bear the burden placed on them. Here are the remaining children who are the hope of York, under my care. Meg, who will grow to make a profitable alliance with a European Prince, George who will be the heir to the dukedom if his brothers suffer misadventure, Diccon with all his fervour.

And here am I, to guard and guide them. I must pray that in their youth they will not be held responsible for their father's sins.

Nor, I pray, will I.

I cannot take you with me because you are needed here, Richard had whispered at the end, answering the question that I had never asked. *I have trusted you all my life. You are my heart and my soul and my right hand. I need you to stay here to hold all I have of value. I need you to hold fast to all that I am forced to abandon. I swear that I will return and take up my heritage once more, but I need you to keep the name of York alive in the minds of our friends and allies. And our enemies. Our heritage must not be allowed to die through lack of tending. Will you do it for me?*

I had placed my fingers on his mouth to still his words. Such faith he had in me, and I would hold fast to it. There would be no further destruction of the House of York under my watch.

A record of the sons and daughters of Richard, Duke of York, and Cecily Neville

I have instructed my clerk to make this record. His hand is more legible than mine. In these days of uncertainty, our marriage and the fruits of it must be put on record. For those who may wish to know, I give my signature and my solemn oath before our priest, here at Ludlow, that these are the true offspring of Richard Plantagenet Duke of York and myself, Cecily Neville.

The document will be kept in the sacred safety of the Church of St Mary the Virgin at my beloved Fotheringhay.

★

Anne   born at Fotheringhay on the tenth day of August in the year 1439

Henry   born at Hatfield on the tenth day of February in the year 1441; *died*

Edward   born at Rouen on the twenty-eighth day of April in the year 1442

Edmund   born at Rouen on the seventeenth day of May in the year 1443

Elizabeth born at Rouen on the twenty-second day of April in the year 1444

Margaret born at Fotheringhay on the third day of May in the year 1446

William born at Fotheringhay on the seventh day of July in the year 1447; *died*

John   born at Neyte on the seventh day of November in the year 1448; *died*

George   born at Dublin on twenty-first day of October in the year 1449

Thomas   born at Dublin on fourteenth January in the year 1451; *died*

Richard   born at Fotheringhay on second day of October in
the year 1452

Ursula   born at Fotheringhay on twentieth July in the year
1455; *died*

★

How much joy and sorrow is recorded here. The joy I may acknowledge in my sons and daughters who grow with health and vigour to enter into their own marriages, to raise their own children for the future greatness of England.

The sorrow I keep hidden close in my own heart. Richard knows of it, but it is not to be discussed since it brings grief to both of us. So many dead within a year of their birth.

There will be no more children now. Age has placed its withering hand on my womb.

Here is my testimony to my love for Richard and his love for me.

It is a testimony also to my sorrow.

The last will and testament of Cecily, Duchess of Neville
*Made and witnessed by our priest, this twelfth day of October in
the year 1459*

In the event of my death (I pray that it will not happen) in the aftermath of the battle that never came to pass at Ludford Bridge:

I give the care of my younger children, Margaret, George and Richard, into the safe hands of Humphrey, Duke of Buckingham, my sister's husband. He is a man of integrity who will guard and guide them until their father is able to return. I ask that he will protect them from the waspish tongue of my sister. They do not deserve any degradation.

To my sister Anne, Duchess of Buckingham, I bequeath the rosary-beads that she covets made with white-amber gold and coral. There are two strings. I pray that she uses them well to make petition for my soul.

To my serving women I give my jewels to be distributed amongst them in my memory. I owe them much for their past loyalties. They will find them buried beneath the floor in the stables, placed there in case of a Lancastrian sack. My Steward knows of their whereabouts.

I give all the remaining property belonging to me in Ludlow Castle, including all my books if they survive the coming pillage, which is debatable, to the parish church of St Laurence in Ludlow, to be sold and the money given to the poor who I fear will suffer greatly when the Lancastrian troops are let loose on them.

Finally, to the Queen I give a silver pyx containing the flesh of Saint Christopher. I pray that the Queen's eyes will be opened by this Holy Martyr who, patiently, gave his life to the service of Christ. I pray for her selfless devotion to the needs of this war-torn land. She will need more patience than I have to manage her increasingly fragile husband.

I wish my body to be buried in the Church of St Mary at Fotheringhay, and leave money for that purpose. No other place will do, whatever my family might say.

Signed and witnessed on this day,

Cecily, Duchess of York

Duchess Cecily faces the sack of Ludlow, the thirteenth day of October 1459

I rose with the dawn, knowing in my head and in my heart that this would be a day of danger. As soon as the final blessing was administered by my priest at Mass, I had my sons and daughter stand with me before the altar in the chapel. Hastily clad in funereal severity, this was a time for utmost respect and solemnity; no jewels, no outward show, no ostentation. We could be in dark-clothed mourning, as black as the clouds that seemed to enwrap the Ludlow towers.

'Whatever happens today, you will remember that you are my children. You are the figureheads of the House of York.' I spoke calmly, sternly. Here was no occasion to stir panic. 'Any man who looks at you, whatever his status, whatever his standing in life or the state of his soul, he will see honour and pride and duty to a noble cause. He will see your royal blood shining through whatever trials we are called upon to face. Do you understand me?'

They were so young, but they could still carry out this task. Whatever befell us I would have them stalwart in their demeanour. I tried not to imagine the effects of a marauding army in the town. It might not come to that, but to be forewarned was to be forearmed, and I would have no weakness.

'You will do what I say. If I send you on an errand you will go without question.' I could think of any number of eventualities when I would need them to be obedient.

'Has Father left us?' asked George.

'He has gone because he must. He will return with help to rescue us if we need rescuing. Until then we will hold this castle in our proud name. You will all be very brave.'

31

I saw to it that they broke their fast and drank a cup of ale. I kissed each one.

'Never forget that you are well loved.'

Then we waited. Beyond our sight our army would discover the disaffection of their leaders, their empty tents, the abandoned banners. In the cold light of day it was hard to make an excuse for it but I understood. I must understand. As for my own strategy, it was difficult to construct since the next few hours would be as formless as a shadow in a deep well. It would depend on the outcome of King Henry's response. I returned to the question. What would happen when Richard's army found itself leaderless?

Kneel for mercy if it had any sense.

Three hours after dawn the noise of a rampaging force began as a distant threatening hum, growing in strength until I could not deny it. Henry had loosed his troops to take revenge on a town that would have stood in defiance. But our walls and towers and gates would hold. To the north the River Teme and steep crags and the Mortimer Tower would protect us. Leaving the children in the sanctuary of the chapel, I climbed to the top of the great keep, to look down between the crenellations. The sight stunned me.

There were soldiers, an unruly mass of them.

They were running across the outer bailey. The gates from the town had been opened. Word had spread, as it assuredly would, that the Duke of York had betrayed the men of our garrison. Demoralised, some of our troops had opened the gates and let in the royal army. Below me I heard the sound of the bars on the inner gates being lifted too, to allow access into the private chambers. Within minutes this mob would be occupying my castle, my home. I could do nothing to stop them.

Face them? I must. But could I protect any one of my household from a howling mob? I knew the limitations of my own authority when authority had been cut off at the knees. I descended, taking little account of the steepness of the stairs, until at the bottom my path was barred by one of our garrison. But where were his loyalties now?

'Let me pass,' I commanded, as if I had all the confidence in the world.

'I have come to find you, my lady. Though where would be best for your protection, I know not.'

He was loyal. I felt my momentary terror subside.

'Do you know what happened to our army?'

'The King demanded their obedience, my lady. They knelt before him and asked for mercy, which he gave well enough, his quarrel not with ordinary soldiers. By God, any number of them have joined the royal troops that are laying waste to the town.'

'And to my castle. Get me through this rabble to the chapel where the children wait.'

There, beneath the arch of the chapel door, we stood at bay. I could not stop them; I did not try. These were the memories that would haunt me for ever, battering at me as I held the hands of Diccon and George, Meg standing with her fingers clasped on George's shoulders to pre-empt any courageous idiocy. All my senses seemed to be drenched in icy cold, but I would stand firm as I watched the destruction of my home.

Some captain of the King's army beat a knot of soldiers away.

'No reprisal against her,' he ordered.

'She's the Duchess. Wife of a traitor. Those are traitor's brats.'

'We don't wage war on the Duchess of York. King's orders.'

A momentary relief laid its hand on me, but how long such chivalry would last I knew not.

'I advise you not to draw attention to yourselves,' the captain growled. 'Go into the chapel.'

'I will not. If my home is to be made a ruin around me, I will bear witness to it.'

'You're a brave woman, lady.'

I did not feel brave.

As the rape of our castle raged on, I turned my sight inwards so I might not see my property, my clothing, my furniture, my finely stitched tapestries, all the precious items of my personal existence, being carried past me. The vestments and chalices from the chapel followed, clutched in filthy and disrespectful hands. But I did see them, anger building within me. Everything I had loved and cherished and valued was stripped away. All I could think as the morning passed: would they fire the buildings? They were too intent on looting. They were too drunk on their success, but when their rapaciousness was sated, might they not light their torches and burn my home to the ground? Had the London mob not destroyed my grandfather's Savoy Palace until not one stone was left standing on another?

All that day it went on, a seething mass of hatred and greed, until they trickled out to join their fellows in the town. While I, wearing a heavy cloak cast over all, prayed that it would disguise the fact that I was shivering with a fear I dare not show. My sons must learn to face adversity with a strong heart.

Leaving my despoiled home, I went out into the town where I stood at the market cross to see the fate of Ludlow for myself. The children were still with me. They must see and experience the terror of an army, frenzied and without discipline, tearing itself and its fellow citizens apart.

The sight stopped my breath. The boys drew close. Margaret

slid her hand within mine. The horrors of a sack were beyond words, the town robbed to the bare walls, pillaged and befouled. The streets stank with drink and vomit that seemed to lap against my shoes and soak my hem. Houses of merchants had been raided, broken items of furniture and pottery shards littering the streets.

No one touched me or my children. We stood there in that monstrous voicelessness of a town shattered beyond repair. Even the birds were stricken silent. Then the evening was rent by the wailing of a child, followed by voices raised in fear and despair. There had been no inordinate death, unless by chance, no full-scale slaughter, but the anguish could be tasted on the air.

'Where is the King?' I asked a man who was rounding up drunken soldiers.

'Gone to Coventry with the Queen. They will hold a parliament.'

So Henry had given them the freedom to do this, allowing them in their bloodless victory to take revenge. But we had done no better. Not one of our leaders was here to give our people the promise of sustenance and recompense. No one except me.

Anne, Duchess of Buckingham, to Cecily, Duchess of York
Written from Tonbridge Castle, Kent

Cis,

Rumours are flying in vast flocks, thick and mindless as starlings in winter. I cannot detect what is true or false since I have heard little from Humphrey. All I know is that York lost his courage when the sun set, abandoned his troops and fled. And so did our brother Salisbury. An incomparable betrayal. Leaving you to pick up the pieces of their treachery.

I'll not mince my words. Do not be arrogant, or a martyr for a cause that is lost for all of you. Did Duke Richard tell you to stay in Ludlow? Do not tell me that you obeyed him without question. His flight might have been ignominious, but surely it would have been better if you had all gone with him.

I trust that I do not hear of your death. All I can do is promise to care for your children if their mother is cut down by an undisciplined mob or executed for treason. If you make a will, be sure to leave me the white-amber rosary-beads spaced with gold and coral which belonged to our mother. I have always coveted them. Or perhaps they were two separate sets of beads, I cannot recall. I will happily have them both, in your memory.

Your judgemental sister,
Anne

Cecily, Duchess of York, to Katherine, Dowager Duchess of Norfolk
Written from Ludlow Castle

My dearest sister Katherine,

To whom can I open my heart, if not to you? Not to our sister Anne who has abandoned compassion. Because of the fifteen years that you have lived longer than I, and through three marriages, I know that you have the experience to understand the terrible humiliation that has laid me low. Anxiety I have known, inordinate worry when Richard has been engaged in dangerous affairs in his French campaigns, but nothing like the attack that assailed me in my own home after Ludford Bridge.

What was the worst of it? It has struck at my pride. Nevilles were not born to relinquish their pride, or to surrender, but I have been forced to do so. I have not told Richard; I could not burden him with the full scale of it when he has enough to bear. I will not tell my priest since he will simply preach that pride is a sin. I will tell you. I need to write it down to absorb the enormity of what happened, so you must be the sufferer.

Perhaps you will know of the ravages from your present husband, Viscount Beaumont, parroting the self-congratulatory voices of King Henry's Court. Somerset's is the loudest and most unforgivable, full of self-adulation for the victory as if he had driven Richard from the battlefield with his own sword. Was your husband at Ludford Bridge? Close as Viscount Beaumont is to the King and Queen, I expect that he was. If so, he made no attempt to rescue his sister by marriage, but then I would expect no less. He has been remarkably two-faced in his loyalties. He might once have been a friend of York, but now he kneels to the Queen.

Despite my courage that day, it failed me at the end. I could not immediately enter the Great Chamber to view the depredations for myself. I knew it would be heartbreaking. When I eventually did step across the threshold it was as bad as I had expected, my private chambers stained, robbed, and defiled. The grim outrage of it, the rank stench of destruction and squalor, will remain forever engraved in my mind like the scrolls on my crucifix.

Do you know what hurt me most?

My books, Kat, my precious books, their leather covers fouled unspeakably by the trample of feet, scattered across my chamber in rude disharmony. My fury at such sacrilege was momentarily more painful than all the rest, yet there they were for me to reclaim. The rabble had no need for them, not even to burn them in revenge. I thank the Blessed Virgin that they are left to me.

There, Kat, as you see, I am indeed guilty of vanity, of

selfish acquisitiveness, regretting the state of my books when all around me our people have lost everything. I am ashamed. I should rejoice that we are alive and unharmed, but where do we go from here? I think travel would be dangerous, if I should be recognised. I await a message from the King. And from Richard, of course.

I should tell you that I have made my will. I think I have nothing to leave you. Anne will get her rosaries because I am wearing both of them beneath my shift.

No one laid a finger on me or the children. At least we were spared that, even if the King's troops consider Richard to be a traitor and a coward. It is a comfort, if a meagre one, that Richard was not here to see the wilful desecration of his Mortimer inheritance. I have not told him of it, nor will I. I do not yet know where he is.

I am suffering from an excess of exhaustion. I have no time to be exhausted. I wish you were here with me to give me the benefit of your clear sight and caustic tongue.

Your sister,
Cecily

England's Chronicle, *October 1459*

Blood, rape and rampage. Have we not written these desperate words before?

Troubled times for those living in the Welsh March.

The prosperous town of Ludlow has been sacked by royal forces.

Where was the Duke of York? Fled in fear of his life.

We must have compassion for the townsfolk who suffered bloody violence and mistreatment. Reports say it was nought but a drunken frenzy, houses raided, possessions stolen, even down to the cooking pots from the hearths.

We consider it a disgrace that in this fair land, soldiery should have been allowed to run riot and harm our merchants and townsfolk who had no part in the hostilities. Who can defend the assault and rape suffered by the women of the town? But there appears to have been little morality in this event on either side. How many of the mob were Yorkist soldiers, summarily abandoned by their commanders on the battlefield? We must put some of the blame at the feet of the Duke of York and the Earls of Salisbury and Warwick.

We are told that the Duchess of York herself appeared in the centre of it all as witness to the foul event, refusing to allow her people to suffer alone, with all the diligence of the incomparable lady that she is. We commend her to your sympathies.

But will the Queen feel the same compassion? We doubt it and fear for the Duchess's future. Will the Queen put her on trial for treason in her husband's absence? We hear that those townsfolk arrested suffered no further punishment but to their gold coffers when they were allowed to buy their release. No such good fortune for the Duchess, we fear.

But where is the Duke?

A question certain to be asked when parliament meets with the King in Coventry.

Chapter Three

A Bitter Humiliation

**Humphrey, Duke of Buckingham, to his
sister by law Cecily, Duchess of York**
Written from Coventry, October 1459

My dear Cecily,

I send you a warning.

Since I have no news of your imprisonment or death I must
presume that, despite the despoiling of the town and your castle,
you are still in Ludlow and at liberty. It is expected that King
Henry's new parliament, which he has summoned to meet with
him here in Coventry, will declare all involved with the House
of York in the inexcusable stand-off at Ludford Bridge as traitors
and deal with them accordingly.

Even though I too find it impossible to condone York's behaviour in battle or in flight, I write in a spirit of compromise. I urge
you to throw yourself on Henry's mercy.

Come to Coventry and plead your innocence. Bring the children with you. I am certain that you will be given safe conduct.

Beg for royal mercy on your younger children, your household and your people. If you do not, things will go ill for them.

I believe that it is what York would want you to do.

This is no time for Neville or Plantagenet self-conceit. The Queen is not leaning towards mercy, but Henry has a kind heart.

Your servant,

Humphrey, Duke of Buckingham

Cecily, Duchess of York, to Humphrey, Duke of Buckingham

Written from Ludlow Castle, October 1459

Humphrey,

As you see, I am still alive and at liberty.

Do I need you to advise me of the need for compromise? I wake with it every morning, chew it through every meal and take it to my pillow every night. It is a bitter mouthful, giving me no sustenance but despair.

Do you even know that Henry will have mercy? Can you rely on his being in control of his wits from one month's end to the next? Yet you advise me to put my head into the lion's mouth.

Do not talk to me about Richard's dishonourable behaviour in taking flight. I know at first hand the humiliation of having to plead for my life with the ravaging hordes who invaded my own home. Yet if my family had stayed at Ludford Bridge to debate the issue, my husband, brother, nephew and two sons would be dead or on trial for treason.

I will consider your advice. I see the value of my coming to Coventry, but I will not put my young children into the hands of the Coventry parliament. That would be a denial of my duty and care as their mother.

You should know, Humphrey, that I wrote a will before we were invaded, leaving Meg, George and Diccon to your immediate care if I were done to death by a howling mob, since I know you for a man of honour. I have destroyed that will. Perhaps I should have kept it in case Marguerite decides to send me to my death.

With thanks for your thoughtful but ill-timed advice,
Cecily, Duchess of York

**Katherine, Dowager Duchess of Norfolk,
to Cecily, Duchess of York**
Written from Epworth, Lincolnshire

Cis,

Your experience at Ludlow is diabolical. I will restrain myself from adding to your heartbreak by addressing some harsh words towards your husband. What was he doing to leave you to face this alone?

I would suggest that you come and stay with me. But that would be comfortable for neither of us. As you say, my husband, John Beaumont, is as closely in bed with the Queen as it is possible to be without committing a sin. He might once have been a close friend to York but now he sees his ambitions in Marguerite's camp. Being a participant in the Council of the young Prince of Wales suits his pomposity very well.

I fear you would not find a welcome here.

If you could tolerate her, it might be best to cut your losses and go south to Kent and beg sister Anne's charity. Humphrey might be a King's man but he is the most equable and honest man I know. And of course we must allow Anne some compassion, losing her son so tragically last year when they must have hoped the wounds suffered at St Albans had healed. I suppose that she will always lay the blame for her son's death at the door of York.

Do keep me informed of your predicament.

I suggest that you say nothing to your eldest daughter Anne, to forestall any sensitive information from reaching her despicable husband's ears. But you know this, of course, and must eternally regret the marriage that united her with Henry Holland, Duke of Exeter. The Hollands never were trustworthy. I suppose his willingness to support the Lancastrians was not then an issue, and his close relationship with the King as his cousin would have seemed highly desirable when we were all at peace. I know that York dipped well into his coffers to buy that marriage.

Poor Anne, saddled with Exeter as a husband.

But back to your problems.

If you are persuaded to go to Coventry I could arrange to meet with you there for some support, particularly against the Queen. I expect John Beaumont will be more than vocal against you and yours in the parliament.

I will happily thwart him and argue your case of innocence and wifely duty. Which are traits that John has never witnessed in me.

Your loving sister,

Katherine

Humphrey, Duke of Buckingham, to Cecily, Duchess of York

Cecily,

Events move on apace. Henry, as we expected, summoned a parliament to meet here in St Mary's Priory. It had more to do with Queen Marguerite's desire to stamp her will on the situation than Henry's muddled plans for the future. Sometimes it is impossible to know what he thinks and hopes for.

The outcome is no surprise. Those with a voice to raise against York and the Nevilles did so, loudly and viciously, with the result that the whole of your family – the Duke of York, the Earl of Salisbury, the Earl of Warwick and your two young sons, March and Rutland – are all attainted. Their lives are under threat if they ever fall into the hands of Marguerite and her supporters, their lands are confiscated to the use of the crown. If they return, they will die.

In effect you are now homeless, penniless, powerless: wife of a traitor.

The Queen has achieved your legal and financial ruin. You are stripped of everything: estates, honours and dignities.

I know that this will hurt you. You once had a close and loving relationship with the young woman who has since become bellicose and vengeful. Sadly the atmosphere in this parliament has erupted into one of vicious family division. Viscount Beaumont, your brother by law and one-time fervent supporter of York, was one of those most outspoken in the destruction of York and the Nevilles. It is no surprise that parliament is named the Parliament of Devils.

I have no notion whether King Henry agreed with this wholesale condemnation of his cousin of York. Whether he did or not,

44

whether it was Marguerite's guiding hand, or even the malign influence of Somerset, Henry's royal seal was put to it.

The immediate anxiety for you is whether you will be attainted, too. If you are branded traitor, what will be the future for your three youngest children? Your household, tenants and retainers also deserve your immediate consideration. They will suffer for their loyalty to the House of York unless you grasp your duty to them.

Get yourself here to Coventry. Put on your finery as Duchess of York, jog the King's memory of the Love Day parade, and remind him of your royal blood. I'll do what I can for you, but as you know full well, my loyalties remain with Lancaster. I will not desert my fealty to the King.

You can't stay in Ludlow behind your walls in the face of this disaster.

Your concerned brother by law,

Humphrey, Duke of Buckingham

Duchess Cecily's intercession to the Blessed Virgin Mary

Hail Mary, full of Grace, Our Lord is with thee.

Holy Virgin, guide my steps. Give your blessing to my decisions. Soothe my fears.

Keep safe my beloved Richard and my sons. And my brother and nephew.

You are the only source of help in this time of need.

What do I do?

I know it will entail much bending of the knees and a severe attack on my dignity. It is, I suspect, the price I must pay. I must accept the blame showered by the Queen on my bent head. Better that than an axe to my neck.

In gracious thanks for your mercy,

Amen

To Henry, his most noble grace, my Sovereign Lord the King, from his unworthy subject Cecily, Duchess of York
Written from Ludlow Castle

I regret, your grace, the terrible rift that has opened up between our families.

I ask permission to approach you to beg mercy, for myself and all those dear to me who would profess their sworn allegiance.

I call on the Plantagenet blood that binds us together.

Your most loyal subject,

Cecily, Duchess of York

Henry, King of England, to Cecily, Duchess of York
Written from St Mary's Priory, Coventry

To Cecily, my well-loved cousin,

We will be pleased to welcome you here at our Court in Coventry, small as it is.

I have tender memories of the past, when you and your family were the counsellors to whom I turned, before the sad circumstances that afflict us at present.

I will listen to your plea for mercy and respond as you would hope.

You need not fear for your own safety or that of your young children whom you may bring with you. You will be made welcome and given suitable accommodation.

Henry

Marguerite, Princess of Anjou, Queen of England, to Cecily, Duchess of York

Madam,

My lord Henry and I have spoken of this together. He will be guided by me, whatever the tone of his reply to you.

What is it that you require from us? There can be no mercy for Richard, Duke of York. Nor for Salisbury or Warwick. Their flight is true evidence of their guilt. The same applies to your sons.

Did they not raise arms against us? Will the fair realm of England be forever torn apart by York and his minions?

Do not mention the fiasco of the Love Day in my hearing.

Unless you can deliver the guilty menfolk of your family, and particularly your husband, into our hands I see no value for your journey to Coventry.

Where is Duke Richard? I expect that you will say that you do not know. I find it hard to believe that you have not had word of him. Where are your sons? Unless we deal with them now in their early years, they too will grow to be traitors to the realm.

What a troublesome family you have, Duchess Cecily.

Unless you can bring them to royal justice, you will not be welcome. You will put your own freedom in jeopardy if you come to my lord's Court at Coventry. If he has offered you safety in your travelling, I would advise you that he is not in a position to guarantee it.

I neither expect nor need a reply to these instructions.

Marguerite, Queen of England

Cecily, Duchess of York, to Humphrey, Duke of Buckingham
Written from Ludlow Castle

Dear Humphrey,

I dare not travel to Coventry.

I confess to you, where I would not speak of it elsewhere, to cowardice. I see no hope from Marguerite who regards me as some species of vermin, warning me against travelling. She has developed a surfeit of Angevin pride of late, although perhaps it was always there, waiting to emerge.

Unless the situation changes, I stay in Ludlow. If I come to Coventry I think I would find myself incarcerated at royal pleasure.

Do you have any news of Richard? Or of my brother and his family? I have none.

I feel that I am ensconced on an island in the middle of a hostile sea.

I have plenty to occupy my time here. The sack of Ludlow has left many in need. The state of my castle is beyond my description.

Your sister by law, in fear,

Cecily

Humphrey, Duke of Buckingham,
to Cecily, Duchess of York
Written from St Mary's Priory, Coventry

Cecily,

Here could be the answer to all your prayers, although it will not help Richard or your sons. I enclose a copy with my courier. Please reply by return.

Humphrey, Duke of Buckingham

Hoping to give you some encouragement on your island.

Royal Proclamation

By the hand of the King

Appertaining to those traitors who raised their standards against me at the Battle of Ludford Bridge

Issued by me on the last day of November 1459

In a fervent desire to restore peace to this unsteady country

By my royal will and pleasure

A royal pardon will be granted to all rebels willing to submit before me, in my royal presence in Coventry, within eight days of the issuing of the proclamation

Henry R

Cecily, Duchess of York, to Humphrey, Duke of Buckingham

Written from Ludlow, by the hand of your exhausted courier

Humphrey,

I am coming to Coventry.

I put myself in your safekeeping if this pardon proves false and it is a trap. I will also consign your Lancastrian soul to the Devil!

Cecily, Duchess of York

Chapter Four

Confrontation between York and Lancaster

Cecily, Duchess of York, to Richard, Duke of York
Written from St Mary's Priory, Coventry, November 1459

I am in Coventry, at Henry's Court, and the children are with me.

Before you explode in righteous fury that I should leave the safety of Ludlow, I am gambling our safety, the whole of our future, on Henry's promise of a pardon. Buckingham says it is worth the risk, and I must believe him.

Will I ever see you? Once again I am sending this letter in pure unsubstantiated hope that you and Edmund are safe in Dublin. I have had no word of you, or of Salisbury, Warwick and Ned. For all I know you might be at the bottom of the sea in a chance storm, but I must hold fast to the fact that you are not and are ensconced in some degree of luxury in the old apartments in Dublin where we enjoyed happier times.

I live in a constant state of alarm, Richard. Every day Henry's revenge hangs over us, but we knew that, didn't we, when we stood firm against the royal favourites?

I have done all I can by claiming Henry's pardon at Coventry before the given day. Did you know that he had done this? I fear it is the Queen's influence that the time is deliberately too short for you and my brother and nephew to return and claim their grace. I do not know how efficient your couriers might be in bringing news.

If you are employing them, perhaps you might find time to contact me. I would value, more than you might imagine, some communication with you.

When I arrived at Coventry, at Humphrey's urging, Henry was seated in some degree of state in the bishop's chair, backed by tapestries most aptly chosen to fill me with dread, stitched with the detail of blood and pain of Christ's suffering at the crucifixion. The setting might be one of wealth and power, but it has to be said that Henry's garments left much to be desired for a King: plain and drab, more monkish than regal and with much scuffing around the hem. Open on his lap was a missal, as if he would rather be reading the holy words than dealing with recalcitrant subjects. Unfortunately for me, Marguerite was by his side, clearly in queenly mode, with Somerset smirking behind her shoulder. Henry smiled in greeting. When Marguerite did not, I knew that this would be a difficult meeting. I concentrated on the King for therein lay my redemption.

I sank to my knees, submitting to his mercy, claiming the pardon he had offered, for you, for Ned and Edmund. Henry's smile widened as if he would truly welcome me. He tilted his head, then opened his mouth to reply. He was still smiling when Marguerite's hand moved to overlie his where it rested on the carved arm of the chair. The touch immediately silenced whatever he might have said. His eyes slid to her face then back to me, his brow furrowed as he spoke at last, his voice hesitant as he rejected any hope of mercy for you. How could he pardon a man who had raised arms against him? He spoke the words as tritely as a well-trained popinjay. Marguerite nodded her approval, while I began what I knew, deep within me, would be a negotiation that would bear no fruit. I had considered my approach, summoning all my wit and persuasive skills. There had been no bloodshed at Ludford Bridge. There had been no battle. The King must never doubt the Duke of York's ultimate loyalty.

Henry still frowned at me, yet he raised his free hand, the one not gripped by his wife, to beckon me to rise. Only to be denied by Marguerite who insisted, in tones as cold as the stones on which I knelt, that, if you, Richard, wish to achieve a pardon, you must appear in person to bow the knee.

So there you have it. It is an invitation to return and sue for mercy, but not one I think you will clasp to your bosom. I would trust Henry but Marguerite will not be moved. You would assuredly be cast into a cell.

Fearful of wearing out the royal patience, I could not petition for my brother and nephew. But for myself and my children I must. It seemed that Marguerite would keep me kneeling until the clap of doom, yet still I kept my spine rigid, my chin raised.

I asked what I knew you would need me to ask. Mercy for myself and our young children, who are entirely innocent. I raised my hand to indicate the small figures where they stood behind me, where I had left them just within the door, surrounded by royal guards as if they might leap to attack the royal party. I begged a pardon for the people of our household who are under my orders and have never proven ill-motivated to the King. Thus I threw all of us onto the insecure lap of Henry's infinite mercy.

I had never begged so much in my life. In that day I subsumed all my pride to need. And even as I asked I knew that all would rest with Marguerite. Still less than thirty years to her name, still slight of build, but she has gained an uncompromising maturity since I last set eyes on her. She holds the life of so many in her pretty hands, sparkling with royal gems. Would she allow them to be covered with blood, our blood?

Throughout the whole, the Queen remained silent and intractable, her dark eyes gleaming with the hardness of frost, but at least Henry was moved so that he stood, tucked the missal under his arm and came to lift me to my feet, promising to consider my plea, offering me hospitality until it has been decided what to do with us.

I can give you no hope, Richard. Marguerite's influence will reign supreme, and I have stepped on the hornets' nest, dragging the children with me into peril. Somerset merely basks in an air of satisfaction. There has been no opportunity to speak with Henry alone. If Marguerite is not with him, then Somerset will be.

Meanwhile I am comfortably ensconced in a room in the Bishop's Palace, hoping for an opportunity to get this letter to you. I think I have found a discreet Yorkist supporter in the Bishop's household, a priest who can be trusted if my letter is accompanied, extortionately, by a gold noble. There is no lock or bolt on the door but there is a man posted outside it, and he is no priest; he bristles with weapons, as if I might fight my way out.

My final advice: don't come back. Not yet. To do so would be your death. Marguerite is not to be trusted.

The children are in health. My love for you needs no expression. You behold me driven by a determination to plead our cause in the face of rank hostility.

Cecily

Cecily, Duchess of York, to Richard, Duke of York
Written from St Mary's Priory, Coventry

Following hotfoot after my previous letter. If they both arrive with you at the same time, the vagaries of travel being what they are, read this one first.

This morning I was requested to attend an audience in Henry's private chamber, utterly relieved to discover he was alone except for a discreet body servant who retreated to some minor task. Henry walked towards me, his hands were warm around mine. I knew that he had decided. Regrettably he was at his most loquacious, intent on discussing the weather, his reading from his missal, and what he had eaten to break his fast.

And I am wasting time in not telling you the whole!

You, my dear love, and our sons, Ned and Edmund, remain disastrously attainted, because you have threatened Henry's sovereignty too highly. I doubt it will come as much surprise to you. To raise arms against an anointed King is treason for all to see, and thus Henry has been advised that you must be punished. Our Neville relatives, also. Salisbury and Warwick are attainted, too. The pardon offered was an empty one and can never apply to you.

But I, thank God, am blessed. I and our youngest children are deemed innocent of all such treason. Henry was gracious and noble enough to grant me a pardon. And although our estates remain sequestered and in royal hands, I am granted the sum of one thousand marks paid to me yearly from those lands.

So there it is. A pardon and a more than respectable income for me, but a traitor's reputation for you. I would not leave Coventry empty-handed; the time spent on my knees had won a specious victory. But when the King abjured me, his precious cousin, to remain a loyal subject, when I silently bent my head as if in agreement, I discovered that I could not embroil myself in such a lie. If I must take the path of traitor, too, so that we might be united, I will willingly do it. I will work steadfastly to do all in my power to smooth your return. By the by, it seems that there will be no restrictions on my movement, which loosened the tight knots of fear that I might be put under some restraint at Court and have to live out my days under Marguerite's hostile eye. It is in my mind, if I can gain royal permission, to travel to Middleham and do what I can for our household. Our people have been granted life and limb, even if their lands and possessions have been confiscated, which is as much as I could hope for.

Oh, Richard! Was this mess truly of our own making? Was it all worth it?

And why would I not decide to settle my household at Fotheringhay? Because Henry Holland, Duke of Exeter, God rot his soul, even though I must claim him as a son by law, has been handed our forfeited castle at Fotheringhay for his own use. I hope that he falls from the battlements. You must return soon, if only to get it back from him.

I still don't know where you are! Have pity on me, Richard! Send me word.

Your loving wife,
Cecily

Duchess Cecily faces Queen Marguerite's retribution in St Mary's Priory, Coventry, November 1459

'The King is too trusting; you should not believe all that he says. I am come here to make all plain to you.'

Words to cut through the vestige of relief that had settled over

55

me. No sooner had I dispatched my letter with another substantial bribe than the door of my chamber opened to a rustle of rich cloth, a light footstep and an intense aroma of musk from her habitual perfume. There, dominating the room with her presence, stood the Queen, accompanied by the King. With a bleak twist of her lips that masqueraded as a smile, she drew me aside towards the window, away from Henry, who picked up a well-worn book, leafing through the pages, divorced from any further communication. His shoulders were hunched, his gaze vague, his face devoid of any emotion that might indicate a knowledge of what his wife intended. I doubted that he would have understood anything that was said, even if he had been standing beside me.

Marguerite regarded me with the attention of a hungry raptor. She had grown into a handsome woman, her dark hair now covered by a beaded and embroidered roll, resting flatteringly low over her forehead, although her high-bridged nose spoke volumes of a dominant will. She was not a woman to relish being thwarted. At least she did not have the advantage of height. Neither of us could boast an impressive stature.

'The King is generous,' the Queen advised in the softest of cadences as if she would accept the pardon Henry had just granted me, but then the edge hardened and her lips, smiling no longer, were tight with recrimination. 'Sometimes he is too naive in giving his trust. You are not entirely free to determine your own future, madam. We are concerned that, given your freedom, you will use it unwisely.'

'How could I, my lady?' I queried, instantly wary of what she was planning. 'I have three young children to care for. I have only the grant so kindly given by the King, as you know. I have no lands, no rents. No title, even.'

I could read her hatred of the House of York in every gesture as she swept her skirts and moved to stand beside Henry as if to protect him from unseen danger. 'Given your freedom, what would prevent you from leaving England and joining the arch traitor? The money for the comfort of your young children must not fall into your husband's hand to be used against us. I know that you still have powerful friends, powerful families in England who would help you. There are Bourchiers and Nevilles who will flock to your banners if they should ever be raised again. It would be better for all if you remained in England, with no contact of any description with Richard Plantagenet.'

A little rush of panic forced me to stiffen my knees. To have no contact, no letters? I kept my silence as she delivered her sentence.

'We have agreed that you will be kept under strict surveillance.'

'Am I to be incarcerated?'

It came as a shock, although I should have expected it. I glanced at Henry who had turned away towards the window, the book held close as if he had difficulty in reading it without a stronger light.

'The King knows what he needs to know,' the Queen replied to my unspoken query. 'I will make the decisions here, and inform my lord if I consider it necessary.' Marguerite continued in the same soft accents, 'All has been arranged. You will be sent to live in the custody of your sister, the Duchess of Buckingham. I imagine she will not be persuaded to allow you a free hand in your conspiracies against the crown. Her husband is one of our most loyal supporters.'

I remained calm. 'Do I have a choice in this, my lady?'

'None.'

Which was plain enough. Any hope of my aiding Richard's return was fast dissipating like autumn mist before the rising sun.

'And how long will it be, that I must I bear my sister company?'

'Until we are certain of the loyalty of the House of York. It may be until death takes a hand to rob us of our traitors.' The returning smile on her lips was not a friendly one. 'It may be a long sojourn if the Duke of York remains alive and in exile. You must bend your mind to it, madam. We have arranged that you will travel there tomorrow.'

'And my children?'

'They will stay with you, of course, under your guidance. Have we not offered you mercy with a lavish hand? I would be the last woman to separate a mother from her children of such tender years. You will merely live quietly in retirement until better days.'

So that was what she had planned. As long as I was quiet and biddable and my family remained in powerless exile, I would be punished no further. In that moment I wished that I had fled to join Richard in Ireland.

'I have arranged your travel in one of my own equipages, madam. All that remains is for me to wish you farewell and a safe journey.'

Her expression held the hardness of granite as, at the last, she offered me her hand to salute, whereupon I responded as Court manners demanded. The Queen had deliberately, acrimoniously, thwarted Henry's infinite mercy. I was aflame with rage, but at least she could not reach the exiles, wherever they might be.

'Once,' I said, releasing her cold fingers, 'we would have found a better spirit of conciliation. We would not have parted on these terms. I was a friend to you when you were in need.'

'Now I have no need of your friendship. I do not believe it exists. There will be no conciliation, now or ever. Godspeed to Tonbridge Castle, madam.'

From Anne, Duchess of Buckingham, to Cecily, one-time Duchess of York

Written from Tonbridge Castle

Cecily,

It seems, my sister, that I can no longer address you as Duchess. What a humiliation for you, Cis! You have my sympathy. Marguerite is a vengeful woman, brimful of bile. My advice is not to tread further on her delicate toes.

I am informed that you are to be a long-term guest.

I will give you accommodation because I have been commanded to do so. I expect that you will be bringing your children with you. I trust that they will settle in quietly. I would not want them to disturb the running of the household or to have an adverse influence over my grandsons who are both young enough to be swayed by strong or wayward characters. I remember George being a wilful child, reluctant to accept admonishment. There was the incident of a dead chicken, as I recall, and a broken window on your last visit.

There must be no plotting on behalf of your treacherous husband under my roof.

Do not expect a friendly greeting. You should have known better than to support your husband in his stand against our rightful King.

Your aggrieved sister,

Anne

Cecily Neville to Anne, Duchess of Buckingham
From St Mary's Priory, Coventry

I am coming to you because I have been ordered to do so and for no other reason. I have been given an escort by the Queen in case I am tempted to flee the country.

My children are always well mannered. They will be no burden on you. I recall nothing about a chicken, dead or alive.

I will be with you soon. I am ordered to travel without heraldic achievements. Nothing to denote my connection to the Duke of York or my own Neville forebears. Anonymity, it seems, is to be the order of the day. I am sure that you will work hard to achieve the same within your household. Have you decided how they will address me? Am I to play the role of a poor relation? My new income will certainly match such a role.

You will be relieved at my anonymity so that your Lancastrian neighbours do not associate your visitors with the traitors of York. It would not do for the Duchess of Buckingham to come under suspicion of conspiring with the enemy, would it?

Your sister,

Cecily

Cecily, Duchess of York, to Elizabeth, Duchess of Suffolk
Written from St Mary's Priory, Coventry

My dearest daughter,

I write to you with regret. Your connection with your father's so-called treachery has cost you dear. I am told that your husband John de la Pole has been demoted from Duke to Earl of Suffolk, merely because he is wed to you, even though he has kept clear of the military disturbances of past years. This is not a reproof of his reluctance to declare for York on the battlefield. I know that his heart is with us in our fight to remove the hostile counsellors from Henry's Court.

You will have to become used to being a Countess rather than a Duchess. It is not too difficult. I am stripped of all titles and must not bemoan the fact.

I will be ensconced in Tonbridge Castle with your Aunt Anne for the foreseeable future. I trust that we will be kept from each other's throats.

If you could perhaps encourage your husband John to declare for York with fire and sword rather than with mild promises, I would be very grateful. A woman has many skills, in bed and at board. Have I not taught you that, from the days of your childhood? If you are your mother's daughter, drop wisdom in his ear and get him to do something. I know that he avoids a battle like the plague. Tell him that when York returns to England, and takes his rightful place in government, he will find the opportunity to restore the dukedom to him. There might also be financial remuneration. That might persuade him, if nothing else does! I have never known a man complain so often or so loudly of his poverty as John de la Pole. How do you tolerate it?

Your loving mother,
Cecily

**Anne, Duchess of Exeter, to her mother,
Cecily, Duchess of York**

Written from Dartington, Devon

My dearest mother,

I have heard the news from my husband Exeter who is rejoicing at the defeat of York and Salisbury, and particularly Warwick with whom he enjoys a great enmity. This is in the manner of a warning that Exeter has been granted a commission of array to raise a force to put down my father's rebellion. He is also smugly delighted to be appointed Constable of your much-loved castle at Fotheringhay.

I can only imagine your fury.

Is there no end to my misery in this marriage? There are some days, when he is at his most disparaging against my family, that I consider the benefit of adding the berries of *Atropa Belladonna* to his morning bowl of frumenty. They grow profusely in Devon.

I have not yet done so. You would be proud of the depth of patience that I have developed. I despise him, however illustrious his Holland name and forebears.

I pray for you and my father, of course. I am not as self-centred as I might appear.

Your unhappy, but resilient daughter,

Anne

England's Chronicle, *November 1459*

Do our readers recall the Love Day, that marvellous celebration of reconciliation, held in London a mere year ago? When all bad blood was put to rest? When the Duke of York and his supporters made reparation for the bloody events at the Battle of St Albans? It was a momentous coup on behalf of King Henry who had visions of a heavenly peace descending on the realm.

It was the procession through the streets to St Paul's that drew the eye.

King Henry walking alone, urbane and beaming, richly robed and crowned, jewels shining in the sun, led the way.

Behind him – can anyone forget the sight? – two by two, hand in hand, arm in arm, walked the previous foresworn enemies, smiling in complete amity. The most bitter enemies in the land forced to clasp hands in false friendship.

Such pairings! Men who would rather stick a dagger into the other's ribs.

Somerset and Salisbury.

Exeter and Warwick.

And then, most astonishing of all, the Queen and the Duke of York, stepped formally together, hand in hand, as if in some formal Court dance.

All pomp and glamour. All lies.

Do we readily give credence to the belief that the Duke of York and his Neville allies will accept their banishment, the dread attainder? Do we think that Duchess Cecily will live comfortably without making any attempt to restore her husband to his rightful place in the realm, at King Henry's side?

We offer you a wager if you are of a mind to take it.

Chapter Five

Nevilles Were Not Born to Surrender

**Duchess Cecily settles into her imprisonment
in Tonbridge Castle, December 1459**

'Take the boys to the kitchens. Feed them and escort them to their
chambers.' And then to me: 'You must be fatigued from travel,
Cecily. We will talk privately.'

My sister Anne, come to issue orders and welcome me.

Subdued by the journey and the overpowering stonework of
the high walls and barbican towers, George and Diccon followed
the servant without question, while I assessed our reception. It
was a welcome of sorts, I supposed, but an icy one. I should have
been grateful that my sister had condescended to appear in her
inner bailey for the event, rather than leave it to her Steward.

'Thank you for your hospitality,' I said.

Anne's expression remained unresponsively bleak. She made no
move to approach me; I was stiff and weary, hungry and thirsty,
but I could afford no weakness, and thus I waited, unmoving,
a reluctant guest. There was a vast gulf between us, and no accord.

'Follow me,' she commanded.

And so I did, drawing Meg with me, an encouraging smile in her direction.

Tonbridge Castle, a fortress in Kent, was to be my future home. It was not my first visit, but it struck me anew that it was a castle that demanded respect, with a strength as great if not greater than any in England. Had that been in Marguerite's mind when she sent me here? There would be no escape, no rescue attempt. I was destined to remain at Tonbridge until Marguerite decided otherwise, hemmed in by the great towers at four corners connected by a formidable structure of high curtain walls. A massive keep on a motte where I would be given rooms. A double gatehouse, the walls thick and menacing. Despite the evening glow of the sandstone facings, it did not welcome me. The gates had closed behind me, making it a true imprisonment.

'Don't tarry. It grows cold.' Anne marched ahead of me with her head high and her velvet skirts swishing against the painted tiles.

Thus the chasm between us gleamed as darkly as the approaching night-clouds. Since that terrible day that Richard left me in Ludlow, I had never felt so isolated, not even when I stood alone in the midst of Henry's lawless troops. Not even when I had knelt before the King. Hiding my sense of hopelessness, I followed Anne into the keep, my head as high as hers, and a sharp glance at Meg to do the same.

My sister escorted me up to her solar where candles had been lit, dismissing her women after ale had been brought. I drank. I needed to quench my thirst but even more I needed the strength from its bitter taste, as Anne deliberately occupied the chair with arms and a carved back. For Meg and I, meagre stools were provided.

'I should thank you for receiving me,' I said, to interrupt what was becoming a heavy silence.

'I was given little choice in the matter.'

'Yet still it is good to see you.'

'I find that hard to believe.'

Meg sat silently.

'Is Humphrey with the King?' I asked.

'Of course he is. What would you expect? But then I no longer understand your ambition-driven motives. What does Richard want? The crown for himself? Do you see yourself at his side, wearing a crown?'

I inhaled slowly, taking another sip of ale. 'He does not. I do not. You know that Richard wishes merely to take his rightful role as Henry's counsellor.'

'Why should I believe you?' Anne's fingers were tightly woven together in her lap, when they were not picking at the soft nap of the velvet. 'York raised an army against the King. Our brother Salisbury fought against the King's forces at Blore Heath and killed his commander. With such a history of rebellion, why should I not believe that you are the most disloyal of subjects?'

I held her stare.

'I was never a liar.'

'You could reject him now and regain your freedom. Divorce is possible with support in the right circles.'

'Give me one good reason why I would not remain shackled to him? His ambitions are mine too. I have no love for Somerset and his friends.'

'York has treated you wickedly enough. Why would this not drive you back to where you and all Nevilles belong? Back to Lancaster.'

'What do you mean?'

My weariness had drained away under so personal an attack, against Richard more than against me.

'Everyone has heard the tale of what happened in Ludlow.'

'Then you must tell me.'

'Don't be naive, Cis.' The use of my shortened name was not friendly. 'It has all been repeated delectably in Lancastrian circles — embroidered to make the worst of the Duke of York, I accept, but I would wager there is more than a kernel of truth in it. How he relinquished his wife, abandoning her to face the enemy on her own, allowing her to stand at the market cross, with three small children weeping and clutching at her skirts.' The long-pent-up bitterness flowed on and on. 'Oh, I'll not dispute that the Lancastrian forces behaved like drunken sots, but for York to leave you unprotected, not knowing if they would kill you in drink-fuelled retribution, is too much to tolerate.'

A brief silence fell, as I absorbed the accurate depth of rumour. And how could I put it right?

'But that is not true.' My loyal daughter Meg had found her voice under the onslaught. I had my champion after all.

With a ghost of a smile, I put out my hand to Meg's. 'Your aunt does not mean to place the blame on your father.'

'Yes, she does. It is false.'

'Yes, the tale is false,' I agreed, holding my daughter's infuriated gaze. 'We were not abandoned at the market cross. We were safe in the castle. Except that...'

'Except what?' Anne demanded.

'Except that someone opened the gates,' I admitted.

'Is that any better? That some of your own people betrayed you?'

'Only one disgruntled guard,' Meg said, astonishing me at her summing up of that terrifying event. Until now she had been reticent; in the face of her aunt's attack, she was not. 'No one subjected us to disrespect or lack of care. We did go down into Ludlow, to see what had been done for our people. It was not my father's fault that the royal troops ruined the town. We stood by our duty to him.'

'A brave speech indeed.' Anne's lips twisted in disbelief, dismissing the whole subject. 'What cannot be remedied, Cecily, is that there is no longer a future in England for Richard or for your sons. Accept it. Meanwhile you are to live under my jurisdiction. I do not enjoy this, but it is all your own fault.'

Swift anger swept away my determination to be compliant. I stood, drawing Meg with me, conscious that my brave daughter was wan with fatigue. 'Then since we are here only under sufferance, and to be kept under lock and key, I would be grateful if you would direct me to our chambers. You may then lock the doors after us. Do you release us for meals?'

'There is no call to be frivolous, Cecily. We must strive to not prey on each other's patience.'

'I think you have done quite enough to my patience already.'

When I stood by the door, I turned my head and asked, because I must, for I had still received no firm news of Richard and Edmund, or of Ned and my brother, even after all this time.

'Have you received news of my family?'

'Yes. If you mean the traitors. I know of their whereabouts.'

Did she hesitate deliberately? How vicious political conflict could make us. I turned foursquare, her closed expression a fist below my heart, making me dread her news.

'Will you have me beg for you to tell me? I will kneel at your feet if I must.'

It heightened the colour in her cheeks, I hoped from shame. 'They are all safe and well.'

'Where?'

'Our brother Salisbury, nephew Warwick and Edward in Calais as you would expect. York and Edmund are in Dublin, so I am told.'

I had not realised what a weight this had been on my mind.

'May the Blessed Virgin be praised.'

'Since they are traitors, I doubt the Blessed Virgin is particularly pleased. I imagine She would rather they paid dearly for their sins against an anointed King.'

I was not listening. All my senses were trained on that one surge of utter relief. They were safe. They were alive. Better days would surely come when they returned to England. I even felt more kindly towards my sister who had given me this hope, however small a seed it might be, however reluctantly on her part.

'I advise you not to pray for their return, Cis. The best they can do is to make a life for themselves overseas. If they set foot in England again they will face execution. And you might not come off so lightly if you continue in your loyalty to them.'

'You were not used to be so critical.'

'You were not used to be a traitor.'

'I swear I am not—'

'I do not wish to speak of it. The conspiracy of my brother, my nephew and your husband is not fit conversation for my home. I forbid you to talk of it. I will never be persuaded that what you did was right.'

Which depressed any sentiment I might have had towards reconciliation.

'Furthermore,' Anne continued, 'you will resign yourself to having no communication with the outside world. You are not to be trusted, thus you will receive neither visitors nor correspond-ence.'

I inclined my head and awarded my sister the victory of a brief curtsey. 'I will live here on your terms, because I must. I apologise for the necessity.'

As I walked before her from the room, I thought for a brief moment that I felt the gentle touch of her hand on my shoulder. Turning quickly, I realised I had been mistaken; she was gesturing for Meg to follow.

'Do we speak with no one?' Meg asked in weary horror, when the door to our interconnecting chambers was locked.

'Wait and see,' was all I could say, but I held her close within the circle of my arm, noting that she had grown almost as tall as I.

I had no intention of being separated from the world of Richard and my sons. My sister would not find me a willing captive, however compliant my outward demeanour.

It was dark now beyond the windows so that I could not see the defences that hemmed us in. It was dark within my soul also.

Cecily, one-time Duchess of York, to her grace the Queen, Marguerite of Anjou
Written from Tonbridge Castle

Your grace,

I have a boon to beg of your endless compassion.

You have seen fit to put me into the custody of my sister who is keen to keep me enclosed and unable to send either help or moneys to my treasonous husband. You will be gratified to know that she is pursuing your orders to the letter. And indeed beyond. My correspondence and my visitors have been strictly curtailed.

The Duchess of Buckingham sees it as her duty to lecture me on my sins, also as you would wish, but is not willing to hear my confession of them. Yet, in my acknowledgement of my lord's mistake in raising a force against the King, I am in need of a confidante to point my wayward thoughts in the right direction. That is forbidden me in this household.

I write to ask permission to correspond with my sister in Epworth.

I can think of no better recipient of my burden of regret and failure than Katherine, Dowager Duchess of Norfolk. I ask, gracious lady, your permission to do so, since my sister Anne refuses to allow it. Katherine is no traitor. You will agree that her husband John, Viscount Beaumont, is the most loyal of your subjects. He has already proved that he will do nothing to further the House of York, and I know that my sister Katherine is a most obedient wife.

If you, in your mercy, would allow my sister the Duchess of Buckingham to grant her permission for me to correspond, I would be grateful.

Cecily Neville

Anne, Duchess of Buckingham, to Katherine, Dowager Duchess of Norfolk

Written from Tonbridge Castle

Dear Kat,

I am out of all patience.

She has not been here more than a se'enight and she is already engaged in mischief. Our misguided sister Cecily, balking at the restriction put on her, has requested the Queen's permission

71

to write to you, against my better judgement. She wrote to the Queen behind my back, bribing one of my ostlers, which is certainly in character.

Cecily claims a need to make a confession and receive counsel. Why not confess to my priest? She says that she finds him an intolerant ear. Why would he be tolerant of a woman who came close to being attainted?

I even understand that she signed the letter Cecily Neville, as if she would distance herself from York. I don't believe it for one moment.

However, with the Queen's permission, I now cannot prevent her writing to you. I trust you will reply with admirable stiff-necked advice to lower her pretensions. Don't encourage her in any acts of rebellion. Your husband would certainly not wish it, and neither would I. She sits in her chamber spinning a web like some small malevolent spider, smiling all the while.

It has to be said that she has not changed, despite her recent experiences. No one would think that she had to fend off a violent and carousing mob in Ludlow. I don't know how much she suffered because not one word of it has crossed her lips, but her will is so strong. If she mourns the loss of York, I see no trace of it. Cecily may be clad as if in mourning in black damask, but her veils are miraculously embroidered, transparent as the finest gauze, supported by fine wires into airy confections. And I covet them. Which is of course a sin.

Cecily continues to pluck her brows with marvellous precision.

I will not suggest to her that to care so much for appearance is the sin of pride.

It might be better if you refuse all correspondence; however, since I cannot prevent it, it must be your decision. I threatened to read every letter myself before allowing it beyond my walls. Cis said she could not believe I would be so petty. Would it not be beneath my dignity to treat a sister with such disdain and lack of trust?

I admit to a wave of guilt. I cannot do it, even when I suspect that same sister of arch dissembling. Marks of sleeplessness and anxiety mar her handsome features, blemishes that I have never seen before.

What I can prevent is any communication between Cecily and our neighbours. The less local gossip the better.

I am in need of a recipe for a dish of eels I think you might recall, one that our mother enjoyed. My cook is unable to produce anything edible. I would be grateful if you would send any recipe you have.

Your sister,

Anne

Katherine, Dowager Duchess of Norfolk, to Cecily, once Duchess of York

Written from Epworth

My dear Cis,

How should I address you? Dame Cecily?

Reading between Anne's caustic lines, it seems that I am chosen by you to be a conduit for treasonable communication. Have I read it correctly? I doubt you would need my counsel. Even if I gave it, you would probably ignore it.

Should I agree to be part of your conspiracy? Anne has warned me off any attempt to help you reach out to York or our family in Calais. Did you know they are all safe? Our brother and nephew and of course Ned slipped happily into Calais through an unguarded postern gate, where, as Captain of Calais, Warwick was made very welcome. Richard and Edmund are now safe in Dublin.

Beaumont is furious that the Queen's party cannot get their hands on them. I have commiserated with him, of course. He makes no concession that it is my brother he is condemning. Beaumont is a man without sensitivity.

I await your letters with eager anticipation, even if I have still not decided what I will do about them. My husband would deny me the freedom to comply with any of your wishes. How exciting! How tempting! I rarely refuse an opportunity to put a spoke in Beaumont's wheel. His stand against the House of York at Coventry was deplorably self-interested. But then, are we not all so motivated?

Not least you, Cis.

Please pass the enclosed to Anne. She was desirous of receiving it. I do not recall eating it with any pleasure, but then I am not fond of eels. Nor can I recall our mother the Countess of Westmorland ever being ecstatic when they appeared on the table during Lent.

Anne says that your face is acquiring the prints of old age and worry. I don't believe her, but try a daily decoction of ground lily-root mixed with egg and vinegar to hold the ravages at bay. Let me know if it is efficacious. I may make use of it.

Your loving sister,
Katherine

★

A Recipe of Joan, Countess of Westmorland, for Eels in Gauncelye (Garlic Sauce)

Take eels and skin them and simmer them in water with a little salt.

Take scalded bread, grind it and add it to the broth with a measure of ale.

Take pepper and ginger and saffron and grind together.

Boil onions and parsley together.

Mix altogether and serve it forth.

*

Do not expect much enjoyment from this. I eat it as infrequently as I can.

Chapter Six

A Soft Imprisonment

Duchess Cecily's intercession to the Blessed Virgin Mary

Hail Mary, full of Grace, Our Lord is with thee.

Blessed Virgin, I kneel in utmost gratitude. They are safe. All of them. Alive and far from retribution. I bend my head in thanks. I weep at your feet.

Holy Mother, sustain them.

Do I fear or rejoice? I know they will not be content to remain in exile.

Grant me the patience to live with my sister without recourse to temper when she lectures me on my refusal to see the good qualities in our Beaufort cousin, the Duke of Somerset.

Grant me tolerance of my sister's priest who is a dyed-in-the-wool Lancastrian.

Grant me the imagination to be crafty-clever in my gleaning of information.

Grant me the fortitude to eat my sister Kat's recipe for eels in gauncelye.

Grant me acceptance of the marks of time and anxiety, in spite of my liberal use of Kat's ill-smelling remedy. Forgive the vanity of a woman who dares no longer glance in her looking-glass.

Amen

Cecily, Duchess of York, to her daughter Anne, Duchess of Exeter

Written from Tonbridge Castle

To my dear Anne,

I am allowed to write to you, through the kind permission of your aunt Buckingham (although I begrudge her the right to give me such permission), since Exeter is well known to be hand in glove with the House of Lancaster. There is no hope of aid for York in your household.

What should I write to you, my daughter? Be brave. There is no blame on you for Exeter's deeds. Nor can his commission of array have any effect on those we love. They are all safe, beyond the sea.

Pray for your father and brothers. There is no need for Exeter to know what is said between you and the Blessed Virgin. As your mother I absolve you from total obedience to him. He is a fool and a treacherous one at that. If you should find a need for consolation outside marriage, I cannot blame you. All I would say is, be discreet.

You may consider this to be strange and sinful advice from a mother to her daughter, but life can be very long and lonely without affection in it.

Your loving mother,

Cecily, Duchess of York

You will notice that I retain my title. In my own mind, with my own pen, I refute the right of Queen Marguerite's law to remove it from me.

Cecily, Duchess of York, to Katherine,
Dowager Duchess of Norfolk
Written from Tonbridge Castle, January 1460

My dearest sister,

You may continue to address me as Duchess of York, if you were under any misunderstanding of the situation.

I enclose a letter. Can you see your way to delivering it to Dublin? And to sending his reply to me, when he writes one, with a covering letter? I know that it may tip you into a confrontation with your husband, but I think you will not greatly care. I doubt that Beaumont reads the letters that you receive. Tell him that it is a dispute over rents and he'll gladly assign it to you.

You might even enjoy playing him as a cat plays with a mouse. Although he is a most important mouse, as he will never allow us to forget.

Here's the situation at Tonbridge, enough to drive any woman of intelligence and ambition to tearing her veils. All those great towers connected by a formidable structure of high curtain walls. I feel as enclosed as a hen being fattened in a coop before the Christmas festivities.

Life here is as dull as your taste in antique houppelandes. I am superfluous; the events of the castle flow smoothly around me, like a fast-flowing river around a small stone in its path. I am not necessary. Even where I see possibilities for improvement and itch to apply my fingers to the issue, it is not my problem to alleviate.

All I can do is keep my own counsel and wonder that Anne should not take better care of her household. I suspect that her Steward has his busy fingers in the ducal coffers. Anne spends far too much time with a book in her hands. This week it is *Legenda Sanctorum*, Jacobus de Varagine's lives of the saints. I have not noticed any increased saintliness in her approach to my predicament.

Diccon and George are given into the keeping of the priest and the sergeant at arms to practise with pen and sword. I think young Henry, Anne's grandson, enjoys their company. Meg spends time with Anne's books and the experienced mistress of the still room. Anne is intent on destroying my influence over them in case I turn them into traitors.

For me, my life is bound around and narrowed to the female pursuits of reading, stitching altar cloths and lute playing. The chains, although invisible, are securely in place. My only freedom is in my prayers. Anne will never know the fervency of my pleas for my husband and sons. Will they ever be able to return?

Even my freedom to walk is restricted to the wall-walk and Anne's small garden within the castle, a pleasant plot that has no need of my care. Anne employs servants to prune and plant and gather. All I can do is look out over the crenellations to the south, to the west, hoping for good news. Yet I know that to hear of their return could be the worst possible happening. To return could well mean death.

We celebrated the Feast of the Birth of the Christ Child, swiftly followed by the New Year, but there was no celebration in my heart. So much hostility simmering beneath the false mirth of the mummers and minstrels. It was not a happy time. What would we be without our marriages, Kat? Would we still be the same sisters who enjoyed each other's company, who played and sang and rejoiced together at New Year as children, although you were so much older than I? Not one of us Nevilles chose the husband we would wed. We must live with the life we were assigned by our ambitious parents.

I am desolate, Kat.

Do write to me, even if you have nothing to send me from Richard. I need your encouragement in this house of rancour. You would be astonished at how polite and amenable I am become.

Your loving sister,

Cis

Do send a different recipe for the preparation of eels. Anything to give Anne's cook an idea beyond the use of Lenten fare. What about something to enliven carp? Anne's fishponds have a surfeit of them.

Cecily, Duchess of York, to Richard, Duke of York, by the hand of Katherine, Dowager Duchess of Norfolk
Written from Tonbridge Castle

My most well-beloved Richard,

How difficult it is to begin this letter.

So much to say – the words clamour in my mind and in my heart – but so little to say of value. I am a prisoner at Tonbridge Castle under my sister Anne's aegis. I expect that you can imagine the strained atmosphere. Humphrey is away from home so not available to keep the peace between us with his good sense.

You are safe in Dublin, I know. You are alive. There had always been that fear that your ship had foundered in the waters off Ireland. Better days will surely come when you return to England. I anticipate it with a fervour that you cannot imagine.

As you see, I have already circumvented the curtailment imposed by Anne with the aid of Katherine. I have arranged that through my letters to her — with royal permission due to Beaumont's excellence in licking the royal boots — I will write to you, and you can return them using the same route. A convoluted arrangement but the best I can do. Katherine has decided that she will enjoy thwarting her husband.

Here is what you should know, my dear Richard, if it has not reached you by other means. Following hard on the attainder, our lands have been split and apportioned to friends of the King. We are truly landless. Exeter has got Fotheringhay in his tight fist. All those who have danced attendance on Henry have been rewarded with gifts of great value.

Thus by a stroke of a pen you have been stripped of land, title, power, and made a penniless outlaw. It is too vast to contemplate. Every title, every castle, every piece of land that you owned, all part of your proud inheritance, all gone.

You would not believe the accusations made against you at Coventry. All Marguerite's doing. She sees you as her most bitter enemy, believing that your whole life has been spent in wretched manoeuvrings to take the throne from Henry. She will blacken your name beyond salvation.

I cannot bear to contemplate the destruction of your heritage and the inheritance of our sons. You, I trust, will be more stalwart. Meanwhile, I am learning to guard my tongue for the first time in my life.

Living at Tonbridge, despite all the comfort, drives home for me just what it is that I have lost. Not to any casual observer, of course. If such an unbiased creature existed in this turbulent time, they would say that I am leniently served in the light of my family's clear-cut treason. I might be dispossessed of lands and title, but I am still Duchess of York to my sister's household, treated with every respect. I am not penniless and my sister, with the air of a martyr, is unstinting in her physical care of me and my children.

But that is merely the pretty pattern of shadows on the surface of the pool. Below it is a maelstrom of great loss. Anne's household might be respectful but only within what I might ask or require.

Beyond that I am closely guarded, with a subtlety that sets my teeth on edge. It is rare that there is no guard to accompany me whenever I step beyond my chamber or the solar. What if I order a horse and an escort to ride into freedom beyond the gates? Will they be so accommodating? They would refuse me. I am forbidden to receive private visitors. Marguerite fears that if I am allowed freedom I will work to bring your return. Of course she knows me well. I will do it, if and when I can. You know that your reinstatement at the King's side occupies my thoughts every day.

Tell Edmund that I think of him. Ensure that he continues to apply himself to his reading and writing. Perhaps you should find him a tutor. He will neglect such skills if you do not watch him. Here at Tonbridge Meg continues to be a solemn witness of events in this world. George is noisy and Richard contemplative. They are children of whom you should be proud. Did I not instil them with honour and pride and a duty to the noble cause of York, that terrible day in Ludlow? I swear that their royal blood will shine through whatever trials we are called upon to face.

I have told Anne that I am considering repentance, of making a confession of my sins. She does not believe me.

Here I make my oath, my dear love.

I will never turn from you. I will never abandon what we have worked for. Our love will last for all time. I pray for your safekeeping and your swift return when affairs are more stable. Commissions of array have been given, to prevent any further rebellion by you or your allies. I doubt you will be surprised that our son by marriage, the diabolical Exeter, is one of those so blessed.

You know my love for you. I cannot write it here.

I would ask you to rescue me, but I know that I must withstand the storms and torrents of our ill fortune. When will you find the need to write to me, to tell me of how you go on? By the Blessed Virgin, Richard. Surely you can employ a clerk if your energies are demanded elsewhere. Do you not have a dozen scribes at your command? I dislike being encumbered by this abhorrent silence.

Your most loving wife,

Cecily

Richard, Duke of York, to Cecily, Duchess of York
Written from Dublin Castle

My most-beloved wife,

I read your anger between the words – indeed you have not exactly made an attempt to mask it, which tells me that you are still in good heart and very much the woman I admire. I acknowledge my fault in this, that I have been lax in sending word to you. It has been too dangerous to commit my plans to pen and ink. I accept your reprimand. It is good to know that you have retained your spirit despite the attack on your dignity and your skirmishes with your sister. It means everything to me when the world I knew is shaking on its foundations.

I have little news for you, except that we are alive and safe in Dublin where I am made most welcome as Lord Lieutenant. It is a relief not to have every action and thought picked over for hidden motives. The Irish will never hand me over to the enemy. It is my intention to summon a parliament in Dublin in early February. I am promised that if we work together to allow Ireland autonomy from England, I will receive finance, protection and an army of archers. All I could hope for. My allies from the days when we lived here have proved most generous and accommodating.

I know it will be high in your mind, but I must not yet speak of the future. Nothing is written clearly, nor would I wish for any plans to fall into the wrong hands. I accept your advice and agree that all is not advantageous for my return. I must rely on your patience and good sense to keep your faith strong. Our history, my dearest Cis, is not yet complete. One day we will be together again. One day our inheritance will be returned to us, I swear it.

I cannot write what is in my heart, but I know that I do not need to do so. You are aware of all I am, all I have ever been, and all I hope to be.

Hoping this reaches you safely through Katherine's kindness. When secrecy no longer matters, I will write more.

You may take satisfaction from the castle here in Dublin being as inconvenient and draughty as it was when we were in residence. The walls still drip with damp and every wooden panel grows its own species of mould. It will be my punishment, while you are in luxury in Tonbridge.

Your most loving husband, in spite of all appearances to the contrary,

Richard

Edmund, Earl of Rutland, to Cecily, Duchess of York
Written from Dublin Castle

To my most revered Mother,

My father says that I must write and tell you how I spend my days, to set your mind at ease. I am in good health now that we are settled in Dublin. I did not enjoy the sea crossing.

It will please you to know that I have at last been installed as Chancellor of Ireland, a position that has been mine since I was eight years old.

Do not expect me to write too often. The hunting here is very good, with fast runs after the deer. I have received a gift of my own wolfhound, called Cuchulain after the Hound of Ulster, the proud Irish hero. I have read about him. I do not have time for much reading.

I do not know when we will return to England.

Your affectionate and obedient son,

Edmund

Cecily, Duchess of York, to Katherine, Dowager Duchess of Norfolk
Written from Tonbridge Castle

My dear Kat,

Here you have a letter from an aggrieved wife.

I am not sure what I expected from Richard. A plan of action? A letter expressing his undying love? Even the briefest comment to relieve my concerns over his good health? I received none of those. I know no more than before his letter arrived. For all the personal touches it could have been written by his clerk. I would say it had been, if it were not for Richard's instantly recognisable scrawl.

Richard seems comfortable taking up the reins of Lieutenant. Edmund has been confirmed as Chancellor. Shall I say what worries me? That my husband might be tempted to remain there and carve out a new realm for himself. Do you suppose that he sees himself as King of Ireland?

Meanwhile, I live in hope of better things. The temperature here is as cold inside as it is out. My sister Anne has handed the *Legenda Sanctorum* to me. She has taken up a French translation of Lucan's epic poem *Bellum Civile*. In the circumstances I would much rather enjoy the warlike exploits of Julius Caesar and Pompey than the endless prosing of saints but Anne thinks Caesar and Pompey unsuitable for calming my mind.

My embroidery is improving, Anne tells me.

Diccon wishes to write to Edmund, so I have included this. George has no inclination to write to anyone. Please send it on when you are next in communication.

What is Beaumont doing? Still working hard to remain a recipient of Queen Marguerite's smiles?

To do justice to Richard, he left me in no doubt of his affections, and his desire to be reunited with me. It's just that I cannot see when it can ever happen.

Your affectionate but thwarted sister,
Cecily

Richard, youngest son of the Duke of York, to Edmund, Earl of Rutland
Written from Tonbridge Castle

Brother!

I wish I were there in Dublin with you. We are at Tonbridge Castle which is all very well but we are kept closely confined.

I would like a wolfhound. Could you send me one? I don't suppose that would be possible.

If I cannot be with you in Dublin, I would wish to be with our cousin of Warwick. His fleet is raiding along the south coast of England, stealing ships and ravaging towns. It sounds like a pirate's life and very exciting.

Our Lady Mother has helped me to write this. She says that my hand with a pen is lamentable. She hopes I will be better with a sword.

Your envious brother,

Diccon

Anne, Duchess of Buckingham, to her sister Katherine, Dowager Duchess of Norfolk

Written from Tonbridge Castle

Sister,

I mislike that Cecily writes to you so frequently. I do not approve of the tally of correspondence and I have threatened to read the contents. Cecily challenged me to do it, but I could not, in the face of her utter disgust.

I could shake Cecily! Does she not realise that York's bid for power is well and truly dead? Her temper grows shorter by the day.

By the by. Do you have our mother's remedy for the ague? I am suffering.

Your affectionate sister,

Anne

Katherine, Dowager Duchess of Norfolk, to
her sister Anne, Duchess of Buckingham
Written from Folkingham Castle

Sister,

Do you accuse me of deceit? Of collaboration with my sister for the good of the Yorkist cause? Save your ink and your parchment. We agreed that I would not encourage Cecily in her passions. I have not done so. If she wishes to write to me because she finds me a more sympathetic ear than any to be found in Tonbridge Castle, then that is entirely your own doing.

In God's name, give Cecily something cheerful to read. Something that is not sermons and saintly encouragement. The never-ending virtues of the Saints can be quite overpowering, not to say lowering to the spirits. And something other than in Latin. It was never her strong point. She is very anxious, as you would be if you lost your husband. She worries that Richard might not return. Cecily will soon come round to the reality of life.

I have no remedy against the ague. Our mother never suffered an ague in her life. With ten children to raise to adulthood she had no time for agues. Neither have I suffered such an inconvenience.

As always, your affectionate and always honourable sister.

I still resent your accusations.

Katherine

Cecily says that you are in need of a method of making carp interesting. My cook says to try this. Substitute carp for tench if you have a taste for it. It is not one of my favourite recipes.

★

A Recipe of Joan, Countess of Westmorland, for Tench in Sauce

Take a tench, scald it and roast it.
Grind pepper and saffron, bread and ale, and mix it all together.
Take onions, chop them and fry them in oil and mix them in.
Serve it forth.

★

Better than the eels, I would say.

Chapter Seven

The House of York Begins to Stir Again

Cecily, Duchess of York, to Katherine,
Dowager Duchess of Norfolk
Written from Tonbridge Castle, March 1460

My dearest Kat,

All I hear is rumour.

The Neville Earls in Calais are taking up arms.

Salisbury and March and Warwick are plotting a return.

There'll be an invasion from Calais before the year's out.

As far as I can tell, there is no proof that anyone plans to do anything, much less put to sea. What Richard might be doing is shrouded in impenetrable fog.

George is becoming an expert collector of gossip, informing me that Ned is coming home because Sim, one of the grooms in the stable here, tells him so.

Perhaps it is true. What are we coming to, when the grooms know more than me? And what if they returned and were met with strong resistance from a royal army under Sir Richard Woodville and his son who are proving fervent supporters of the

King and Queen? Would you care to write to Richard and warn him that my spirits are fast descending into hell?

My main concern is for Meg, for I see where her thoughts are straying. Who will she marry? She is of an age to have a husband chosen for her. Were not her sisters much sought after?

The problem now is who will look to the disinherited House of York for a bride? No one. My heart weeps for her. As it is, Meg is destined to remain a spinster and I, through default, a widow.

Your anguished sister,

Cecily

**Katherine, Dowager Duchess of Norfolk,
to Cecily, Duchess of York**

Written from Epworth

Stop that, Cis!

This is all a product of isolation and self-pity! There is more than rumour to all this, even here in Lincolnshire. Every house talks of it, a ripple of excitement from those with Yorkist sympathies, and fear of what it might threaten from those who wish the impending invasion would simply go away.

I hear from Beaumont that Somerset, empowered by the Queen, is building a fleet in Sandwich, to invade Calais, put down the rebels, and take the Captaincy of Calais for himself. Not much chance of that, I'd say. March and Warwick have already poked Somerset's nose. They've raided the port of Sandwich, then escaped back to Calais without harm. My guess is they'll wait until Somerset's fleet is rebuilt. Then strike again. Somerset remains bullish, but he must be cursing Warwick to the heavens.

Ned would seem to be finding his feet at sea under his cousin Warwick's command.

Of your errant Richard I hear nothing. I don't see that my writing to him will have any effect. It looks as if he may in all truth be considering a permanent position as King of Ireland. Could you not be resigned to living out your days in Dublin with an Irish crown to wear?

I'll see if I can get any truth out of our brother Salisbury.

Tell Meg not to worry. One day she will be a much-desired bride. Have not I managed three husbands? And I have no call on either intellect or beauty, whereas she has the promise of both. She is very much your daughter, Cis. I wager that one day she will make a fine marriage.

Your hopeful sister,

Katherine

I have included a nostrum for guarding against headaches and melancholia. I use it when Beaumont becomes too Lancastrian for my Yorkist principles, although I advise you to administer it sparingly. It can be very powerful in its after-effects. I speak from experience.

As for your late slur on my liking for the 'antique' houppelandes, they are comfortable. I am too old to be dealing with close-fitting bodices, high girdles and bared shoulders.

A Nostrum of Wild Valerian:
A most potent herb of Mercury

Collect the root in summer in moonlight.

Hang it to dry in the Still Room.

Powder the dried root and stir into a cup of heated wine.

Drink morning and evening.

Excellent against the trembling and palpitations.

Richard Neville, Earl of Salisbury,
to Cecily, Duchess of York

Written from Calais, March 1460

Cis,

I write care of Katherine as she tells me I must. Our plans to return to England from Calais come on apace and I can promise that there will be an invasion before the year is out. Our feet will be back on English soil again. My son and nephew are already making life difficult for Somerset. It is Warwick's pleasure to thwart his plans at every opportunity, destroying his ships almost before they are built.

Even better, my son has sailed along the west coast, avoiding Exeter, to make contact with York in Waterford where, so he says, plans for his return are being laid. Warwick says there is little sign of such preparations but we must trust in York's ambitions. Unless there is truth in the talk that he sees himself as King of Ireland.

Be patient and sit tight, Cis. You always were the most restless of my sisters. There is nothing to be gained from worrying over things that you cannot change.

Your brother,

Salisbury

Edmund, Earl of Rutland, to Cecily, Duchess of York
Written from Dublin Castle

To my Lady Mother,

My father is still mightily occupied and so am I. My appointment as Chancellor of Ireland takes much of my time. We are safe and have much support here. When William Overey arrived from the Queen with writs for our arrest following our attainder, he was arrested instead, tried by my father, found guilty of inciting rebellion and disobedience, and promptly executed for treason. It was the first execution I have seen. It was not pleasant but necessary, so my father said.

The Queen has no sway here. The Irish are keen on their independence and they hope my father will remain. Did you know that we have our own Great Seal?

Rest assured, my father says that we will take no action that will endanger you, since you are the only one under the Queen's hand who can be punished for our actions.

We are enjoying the hunting in the forests around the city.

We are in no danger. Every man of property has now to keep a mounted archer within his household to ride at a moment's notice to defend Ireland against any English invasion.

I can think of no more that will interest you.

Your obedient son,

Edmund

Cecily, Duchess of York, to Katherine,
Dowager Duchess of Norfolk
Written from Tonbridge Castle

Oh, Kat,

What an unsettling letter this is from Edmund. It gives me

no comfort at all. It seems more and more possible that Richard will remain in Ireland, creating a kingdom. Perhaps there never was a plan for him to return.

What do I do? Wait here in vain, or try to escape this bleak confinement to follow him?

Ignominiously, it appears that I am his weak spot in his planning, as I am the one under the control of the English crown, and so can be used as a pawn against him.

Richard is being wretchedly silent about it all.

The Wild Valerian does not help either.

Your increasingly desperate sister,

Cecily

Katherine, Dowager Duchess of Norfolk, to Cecily, Duchess of York

Written from Epworth

Well, you ask my opinion, Cis. Do you truly need it? Living in adversity with Anne has robbed you of your strength of will. How can you be so indecisive!

You know what you must do.

Ask him, Cecily. Ask him plainly. Tell him what it is that you fear. What have you got to lose? The letter might fall into the wrong hands, but it's not going to say anything the political world is not chattering about. It is not some Court secret that you are divulging. All the world is wondering if Ireland will have a King Richard in the near future.

Do it!

Or no. *I* will. I will take him to task for you. How can he leave you in permanent ignorance? You should expect a fast reply from Richard.

Katherine

I regret the inefficacy of the Valerian. Try instead an infusion of the new-grown leaves of the Greater Periwinkle. It is excellent in warding off nightmares and hysteria. You sound to be much in need.

Richard, Duke of York, to Cecily, Duchess of York
Written from Dublin Castle

My dearest long-suffering Cecily,

God's Blood! Your sister has a sharp tongue, even through the medium of her pen.

Once again, I have been remiss. I acknowledge it. It would be dishonest of me to claim my preoccupation with matters of power. Katherine rightly says that my silence is alarming. Surely my fear of any future plans falling into the hands of the Lancastrians does not preclude a letter to my wife. She suggests that the gossip is more damaging than the truth. Edmund, I understand, has been surprisingly informative.

I have no master strategy as yet, but this I can say. It is not my plan to remain in Ireland. It might be safer here for the health of my neck, but my future is in England.

My future is with you.

I will return.

Look for news before the end of August. I know this will be less than satisfying but I am in good heart and I understand that you are, too. I have given Edmund a brief but effective lesson in discretion when addressing his mother. I have also enclosed with this a gift to reassure you that you remain with me, in my heart and mind, at my rising and at my final prayers at the end of the day. I know that you will make use of it.

Your loving but repentant husband,
Richard

Anne, Duchess of Buckingham, to Katherine, Dowager Duchess of Norfolk
Written from Tonbridge Castle

To my dear Katherine,

If you were under the impression that York was neglecting our sister, then it is necessary to revise such an opinion. She has received a letter and a package. She has shown me neither. She keeps one in the bosom of her gown, so its content must be of value to her. The other, the package, she has safe-stowed in her jewel coffer.

I have investigated that package. I have no shame. It is a finely wrought gold crucifix, heavily bejewelled and set over-all with diamonds. If affection can be judged from the weight of bullion and precious stones, then Cecily is well loved. I could wish that Humphrey remembered me in similar glittering terms when he is long absent. As he is at present.

As for our sister, there is also a brightness about her, a liveliness that had become lacking. It is as if an inner candle has been lit, the lines on her brow smoothed out. She was always the most handsome of us all, and now it is evident, despite the passage of years.

I could wish that if York was not going to return, he would have left her alone. Disappointment will only restore her to desolation.

I do care for her, regardless of her political malfeasance. She is my sister, after all.

I trust that you remain in good health despite your slippery husband. He might be a staunch Lancastrian, but I cannot like him.

Do I like any of my brothers by law?

Your sister,

Anne

Duchess Cecily experiences a renewal of joy at Tonbridge Castle, June 1460

It was the last day of June, the country somnolent around me with sultry heat, when I sat alone in Anne's garden, destroying a spire of lavender which I should have been harvesting under my sister's direction.

'Idle hands find malicious tasks,' she informed me as she handed me the basket and shears.

Now bees were busy around me, but I was not. I could hear Anne, distantly engaged in conversation with a delegation of merchants demanding her support over some local squabble. Meg was stitching a new gown in the solar with Anne's women. Our clothing much depleted, she was delighted with a bolt of velvet from Anne's store even though her opportunities to wear it were limited.

Running footsteps and loud voices shattered my retreat. George and Diccon. They stood before me and bowed.

'Mother. Sim says that you must come to the stables.'

'Sim says?' It was hard not to be imperious. 'The mythical Sim again.'

There was a cunning slant to George's eye. 'He says it is impera-tive.'

'What do you say, Diccon?' He usually proved to be a solemn fount of knowledge, if not always impartial; Diccon had a young-est child's eye to his own survival.

'I say to come. There is a new horse, a huge bay, like Father's. It needs a name.' His smile was ingenuous yet still I suspected some youthful plotting, particularly when George nudged his brother with an elbow.

When did I ever obey the dictates of a groom? With no urgent demand on my time, and a curiosity, I stood, brushed the lavender heads from my skirts and followed as they raced ahead. It was too hot for running but I admired their enthusiasm. They were laughing.

Into the warm shadows of the stable, pungent of horse and new-laid straw.

'So where is Sim? And where is this magnificent animal that I must immediately admire?'

A soft laugh to my left. 'Here he is, my Lady Mother.'

How would a mother not recognise the voice of her eldest son? I froze. Waiting. All my senses warned me that this was not possible.

'I hoped you would welcome me,' he said. I could hear the smile in his voice.

I turned slowly, unable to smile in return, unable to even touch him. I realised that in my hands I still clasped the lavender-basket and shears. My first words were unforgivably as sharp as the blades.

'What are you doing? No supporter of York is safe here. Buckingham has a commission to assemble every man of Kent capable of fighting, as soon as even one rebel sets foot in England.'

'Which is why I'm dressed as plain as the merest groom, rather than a son of York.' All of his father's confidence.

The basket and shears now fell unnoticed from my hands, the lavender scattering.

'Oh, Ned.' At last I embraced him, then put him from me to take stock, my hands gripping his arms. I was forced to look up to survey his face. Had he grown in the months since Ludford Bridge? In that moment he filled my whole world.

'Are you well? You look well.' The words tumbled from my tongue. He was vivid with good health. And then, as I absorbed the implication of his presence in Tonbridge Castle's stable, I felt a surge of joy bubble up inside me: 'Is this an invasion?'

'Yes.'

Immediately all my anxiety was back, three-fold. 'Then even more dangerous.'

I drew him further into the stable, into an empty stall. 'Did you truly bring a horse?'

'Of course. I needed an excuse to get me through the gates. One of your neighbours who is quietly Yorkist wrote me a note to guarantee my authenticity. I am bringing the animal for Humphrey's consideration.'

How young he was. It was naught but an adventure for him, delivering a warhorse into an enemy camp. I did not know where to start with my questions.

'Tell me. Tell me what has befallen you since Ludford Bridge.'

I pulled him to sit on a heap of straw, regardless of the damage to the high nap of my velvet.

'We escaped to the Dorset coast, but found it impossible to get to Ireland, so we took ship to Calais where we knew we would have a friendly welcome. From there we've been attacking the English coast—'

'So I've heard—'

'We landed in Sandwich a week ago.'

'Have you much support?' I could not wait for Ned to lay his plans out for me to see, my emotions torn between maternal delight, fear for the future, and anticipation for the political manoeuvring which I had so critically missed. 'What do you intend?' Suddenly, in my mind, a battle loomed, with all its dangers. 'Have you come back with an army?'

'Will you wait, and just listen, madam? I'll tell you all.' There was tolerance of my love for him. Waving away his brothers, he spoke fast, low-voiced, with a marked maturity in his choice of words, his clipped delivery reminiscent of Warwick. I felt his dominance, his control of the meeting, with surprise, and not a little alarm.

'I have scant time.' Already he was watching the movement of the sun, the creep of the bars of shadow across the floor as the minutes rushed by. 'This is what you need to know.'

George and Diccon had retreated no distance at all, until I turned my eye on them and they vanished into another stall. I expected that they were still listening.

'From Sandwich we marched to Canterbury. Warwick was right. He said the men of Kent would be pleased to welcome us, despite royal orders to repulse us.' His eyes were alight. 'Ha! They opened the gates of Canterbury as soon as they saw us on the horizon. Warwick is popular hereabouts.' I smiled, detecting a note of hero worship in my son for his thirty-one-year-old much-experienced cousin. 'Welcoming verses had been pinned to the city gates. Some local wordsmith had put pen to parchment.'

He laughed, struck an attitude with chin raised and fists on hips. *'Edward, Earl of March, whose fame the earth shall spread.* I liked the sound of it. We came with two thousand men and we are collecting more along the way. Warwick says it will top ten thousand by the time we are in London.'

I wondered how often I would hear the phrase 'Warwick says'.

'The thing is,' I said when Ned drew breath, 'what will you do when you get to London? Is this more treason that you are plotting? Will you challenge the King?'

His voice, supremely confident, fell again.

'No. We have talked of this. We'll not take up arms against the King.'

So easy to say, so difficult to accomplish if Marguerite pushed for a confrontation, which she undoubtedly would. My brother and nephew must know this. But Ned was explaining.

'We have published a list of what we hope to achieve, to win men to our cause. We do not attack the King but rather his disreputable counsellors who tell him that good is evil and evil is good. Henry is being persuaded to hate and destroy his friends.' I could hear my brother Salisbury's words here. 'We'll be in London by the first week in July – next week, in fact. It is all happening so quickly. We offered prayers at the shrine of Saint Thomas Becket and received the blessing of Archbishop Bourchier who agreed to ride with us. It helps to have family in high office. My Neville uncle and cousin are already marching on to Rochester and Dartmouth. I came here first.'

He took my hands in his. How large they were, like small hams, dwarfing mine. In a moment of softness I lifted our joined hands to my cheek, before releasing him and returning to hard planning.

'What will you do when you get there? What are Salisbury and Warwick planning?'

I did not know how far they would be prepared to go. A shadow of uncertainty momentarily crossed Ned's face but his reply was assured.

'We will negotiate with Henry. Loosen the ties to his so-called friends. We will become the most loyal subjects that he has, and so we will be restored to the King's right hand.'

It sounded like my brother. But what about Warwick? Would he be ambitious for more? There was an undeniable strength in him. I suspected that leading a flotilla of piratical ships against Somerset was not the height of his ambition.

'Do you give us your blessing, my Lady Mother?'

'Of course. But take care. Be sure to winnow your friends from your enemies,' was all I could say. 'And thank you. That you found time to think of me. Should I ask why you must make a twenty-mile detour, when Warwick is by now in Rochester?'

'To see if you needed rescuing, of course. My aunt can be a severe taskmaster.'

It made me laugh, imagining my son insisting to my sister that I should escape with him and join what she would see as a rebel army, riding with them to London, intending to bring down the King's vicious friends. Who would win the battle of wills? I thought that it might just be Ned.

In that moment in the stable, gilded with dust motes, his hair transformed into a golden cap, his once-broad cheekbones sharpened with maturity, I had the image of riding into London beside my son. Plantagenets and Nevilles returned in glory to put right the attack on their inheritance. It was a breathtaking vision of all I could hope for, a vision I would wish to be part of as Duchess of York. But I shook my head. I would be no help to him at this stage in his journey to adulthood, and perhaps a hindrance.

'I am safe enough here. Your aunt has no designs on my life and we have come to terms over the extent of my freedom. You must expend all your energies on coming to some agreement with Henry. When you have done that, then send for me.' My heart lurched at what had not been said through all of our exchange of words. I held even tighter to his hands. 'What of your father? Are you in communication? Will he join you?'

'We hear nothing.' Ned was untroubled. 'But of course he will come back. All our success hangs with him. He must protest his innocence and loyalty so that our lands and our titles are restored to us. He will return. Do you not believe it?'

He thought me a weak woman prey to fears and rumour.

'He will return,' I repeated. I stood, my moments of maternal weakness past. 'It is time you left, before your aunt has finished with her merchants. Will you be safe? Are you alone?'

'No, I have a small escort waiting for me beyond the village. I wager I'll be back soon enough, to open the gates for you. What a dour place this is. How do you stand it? I might just lay claim to the horse, too. It's one of Warwick's. No one will know if I take it with me. If challenged I'll argue that it is unexpectedly lame and no use in battle.'

We were standing. I wished that Ned had not resurrected the thought of battle. Reaching up, I drew his head down and kissed his brow.

'God keep you safe, my son. May the Blessed Holy Mother walk beside you and give you good counsel.'

He surprised me by sinking to his knees and kissing my hands. His fervent dedication, almost a vow, moved me unbearably.

'And may She walk with you, too. God grant the day when all will be put right in this turbulent nation and we are reunited.

I will fight for the restoration of the House of York, as my father would wish me to do. We will become once more King Henry's most trusted cousins.'

I watched him go. He bent a little, shuffled a little, transforming himself into a faceless, nameless ostler. No, he was no son of York in that disguise.

'Will he come and see us again?' Diccon asked, watching him go.

'Will there be a battle?' George added.

All they had received was their brother's heavy hand clapped to their shoulder in farewell.

'Perhaps and perhaps.' I collected the forgotten shears and basket, abandoning the lavender spires on the floor. 'Now show me this animal that has earned your brother's admiration.'

Ned had not taken it with him, after all.

Cecily, Duchess of York, to Katherine,
Dowager Duchess of Norfolk

Written from Tonbridge Castle

My dear long-suffering sister,

I have seen Ned. I have spoken with him. I have held him in my arms.

Such a change in him. He has become as impressive as one of the old Plantagenets, burnished with a gloss of knightly glamour.

Perhaps now Richard will come home.

Suddenly all is falling back into place, but we may not come out of this unharmed. It is so easy to forget that the evil counsellors are our own cousins. The lines of family through Neville blood and marriage are very tight, yet we would sever them without compunction. Sometimes it worries me that we can be so unthinkingly zealous. Blood will assuredly be shed.

And then I recall that we are fighting for our own survival and our rightful place in this realm, which they would deny us.

Your sister, renewed by hope,
Cecily

Chapter Eight

Beleaguered by Blood and Death

Cecily, Duchess of York, to Katherine,
Dowager Duchess of Norfolk
Written from Tonbridge Castle, July 1460

After St Albans I hoped never to say this again in my lifetime,
but here it is.

There is to be, or perhaps by this time there has been, a battle,
to the north of London. News filters through by the usual means
of merchants, pedlars and groups of minstrels. Anne has had
a letter from Humphrey, which was written to her before any
conflict. She is still anxious. She graciously allowed me to read
the letter, because Humphrey instructed her to do so.

What a kind man he is. I wish Richard were as considerate.
Does Beaumont keep you informed?

You should know. Salisbury and Warwick have identified
your husband as one of their three mortal and extreme enemies.
Their words, not mine. Once he was so closely aligned to Yorkist
interests, but then was enticed by royal office, I suppose. He was
the obvious ally for Marguerite with her dower lands, centred

in Leicester and Kenilworth and Tutbury, close to Beaumont's acres. It is to be hoped that Beaumont never falls into Yorkist hands.

It is fortunate that you have no deep affection for him.

Here's what I know.

When Salisbury and Warwick landed at Sandwich, they were quick to proclaim their absolute loyalty to Henry. All their anger is directed at Wiltshire, Shrewsbury and, of course, Beaumont. They are the ones seen to be bolstering the Queen's power. I expect Somerset's name will be added to the list before long. With Salisbury is Bishop Coppini, a tame papal legate who, since he is no friend of Marguerite, will give them the support of the church.

Salisbury is left in charge of the siege of the Tower of London which is holding out strongly. Warwick and my son have marched north.

Richard was expected to be returned for this battle, so they say. Did he arrive? Surely I would have heard if he had.

It has crossed my mind to make a bid for freedom, to insist on some transport, even if a mere horse, and ride to London. It appeals in my weaker moments, but common sense will prevail. What if Warwick loses the battle? If so, King Henry and the Queen will once more be in the ascendant and I would be returned to my sister's threshold in all ignominy. Or I would have to become a fugitive in the wilds of Scotland.

We all live in fear of what will happen on the battlefield. If you hear anything, even if it is only imperfect rumour, please send word. I am in silent distress.

Would it not be better if there can be a reconciliation before they meet in a passage of arms? I fear we have reached an impasse that will only be breached by the spilling of blood.

Your sister,

Cis

England's Chronicle, *the tenth day of July in the year 1460*

War! Bloodshed! Death!

Once more we have to report a battle that has stained the fair fields of England near the town of Northampton, on the banks of the River Nene in the sacred environs of Delapre Abbey.

Those who hoped that the flight of York and the Nevilles after Ludford Bridge, and the subsequent attainder of this treasonous family, would bring an end to any conflict were misguided. Those who hoped that King Henry would be left to rule in peace were misled. We understand that many of you care little who rules, as long as you are safe from lawless mobs, and your properties are not despoiled in battle or siege. For those of you who have an interest, the Neville Earls of Salisbury and Warwick are back in force with the youthful Earl of March.

What do we see on the field of conflict?

Well over a thousand men dead. A defeat for the Lancastrians. Their army is destroyed, their captains hunted down and hacked to death. The ground sodden with rain, the gunpowder of the Lancastrian guns rendered useless, the whole lasted no more than a half-hour when Grey of Ruthin turned from Lancaster to York, betraying the royal forces by helping the Yorkist troops to find a way through the royal defences. Those Lancastrian soldiers who tried to escape across the swollen River Nene drowned in the deluge.

A disaster! Unless you are a supporter of York.

What happens now?

Where is the King?

We do not know. The Queen took him to the battlefield, but we have no news of his fate.

Nor was the Duke of York seen in the heat of the conflict. Was he even there?

By the time you read this, we may be better informed.

We pray for the King's good health.

**Richard Neville, Earl of Salisbury,
to Cecily, Duchess of York**
Written from the Yorkist camp in London

We have a victory!

Before all else, Cis. For your comfort. Your family all survived the battle and fought with courage. Any rumour to the contrary is false. Warwick sent a fast courier from the battlefield.

King Henry was taken captive in his tent, where he was discovered on his knees in prayer. Marguerite and the young Prince have fled to Wales to take refuge in Harlech Castle which is under the control of Jasper Tudor, Earl of Pembroke. We will deal with that later. The Great Seal of England has been placed in the hands of my son George Neville, Bishop of Exeter.

We are in control, Cis. We will command the future.

I regret that the Queen was allowed to escape. For now we must rejoice at justice being seen to be done.

The King is being brought to London, a prisoner, under Warwick's aegis, where some form of government will be made with Henry's agreement, willing or otherwise. It gives me hope that the bloodshed might end and the rights of inheritance of

York and Neville be recognised. In that royal pavilion on the battlefield, Warwick was exemplary in his efforts to smooth over past differences, kneeling before King Henry, asking forgiveness, as he restated our loyalty to him. Ned, because of his young age, had not yet sworn his fealty to the King. There on the battlefield, full of solemn dignity, he took the oath.

I would ask you one question, Cis, although I fear that you are in the dark as much as I. Where is York? All we had planned, to join forces to demand restitution from Henry, has collapsed. York has not, as far as I know, left Ireland.

What in God's name is he thinking?

All we have achieved, all we have fought for, was done without him. London was taken in the name of York. The rotting heads of Yorkist supporters have been removed from their ignominy on London Bridge. But where is he? God's Blood, Cecily! Why is he not here, fighting at our side? Why is he not here to remind our citizens of his name and his face, his rightful heritage beside the King?

It drives me to improper language, and I ask your pardon.

On a calmer note, wherever he is, whatever devious plotting is engaging his mind, you are now free to return to London. There is no longer any compulsion for you to remain at Tonbridge Castle with our sister.

I do not yet know the names of the Lancastrian dead. I think in some quarters it will not be good news. The common soldiery was spared, but not the commanders, which was Warwick's policy from the start.

Be prepared for some sad losses. It is all part of the terrible aftermath of the battlefield.

Your brother,

Salisbury

Duchess Cecily faces death at Tonbridge Castle, July 1460

My sister Anne looked as if she had been struck on the head with a poleaxe.

I did not know who had informed her, but by the time I found her it had been done. Nor was it done with any compassion. Probably announced to her by a harassed courier, as bleakly as any death on a battlefield might be reported. She had dismissed her women. Spine straight, shoulders firm, Anne stood at the window and looked out to the north. She might have been listening to some voice, which was not audible to me, or perusing some distant scene that only she could see. There was no expression on her face. Like all Nevilles she had an inner strength to weather storms and torments.

She had loved him. She had not made great fuss by it, but I knew that over the years he had grown to be the very centre of her life. Now her husband, the powerful Duke of Buckingham, was dead. A man of integrity, of honour; a man of high temper, it is true, but also of humour and compassion. He was cut down as he attempted to protect our worthless King, who had not even emerged from his pavilion to face the enemy.

'I did not love him,' she informed me no sooner had I opened her door, her face still angled away from me. 'Not as you love Richard. But he had all my respect. And affection.' She swallowed, now covering her face with her hands in despair. 'I think that I did indeed love him.'

I walked to stand beside her. I did not touch her. I thought she might disintegrate if I did. All the animosity that had built between us melted away into a useless puddle at our feet. She was my sister, the most beloved, and she needed me.

Slowly, allowing her hands to fall away, Anne turned her head to look at me.

'Humphrey is dead.' Tears that she made no effort to control spilled down her cheeks. 'Cut down in the battle,' she said, her voice flat as if recording an event which was of little account to her. 'He was defending the King who had taken refuge in his tent.'

How I wished, with some savage response to my sister's misery, that Humphrey had lost his life, if so he must, in defence of a worthier man.

'He's dead, Cecily.'

The tears dripped faster, marking the fine velvet and fur edging of her bodice. Her hair was pleated and pinned but still uncovered, tendrils damp against her cheeks.

It broke my heart.

'Oh, my dear.'

I put my arms around her and she wept as if her heart were broken, too. As perhaps it was.

Regardless of dignity, of the stuff of our garments, we sank to the floor, my arms around her, her face buried against my shoulder, reconciled at last through her loss and grief. I stroked her hair that was fast becoming unpinned, murmuring useless words of comfort, trying to imagine my own mourning if the news had been that Richard had been cut down on the battlefield. When one of her women knocked softly and opened the door, I shook my head so that it was closed again, equally quietly. All I could do was allow Anne to weep. There was nothing I could say in comfort, nothing I could do but pray for her ease of heart.

This was her moment of sorrow. She must offer it up alone, through her tears, for her dead husband.

At last the sobs quieted until they were no more than a hitch of breath and Anne applied a square of linen, which I had pushed into her hand, to mop up the ravages. She began to talk.

'When they fought in France, it was always easy to fear the worst. You must know that, Cis. How often was Richard away on campaign when you were settled in Rouen? Months at a time. And you were so young. In Ireland, too. But we never expected conflict on our own soil, did we? It seems so much worse; family against family, English lord against English lord. At least when the enemy is French we can justifiably detest them. But these are my own people. The campaign plotted by my own nephew Warwick was responsible for Humphrey's death.' Another sob threatened. 'I lost my son in the aftermath of St Albans. Now I lose my husband. I know not whose hand it was that cut him down. I don't think I wish to know.'

'It is said that it was done by a force of Kentishmen, under Warwick's command,' I said. I thought she might indeed wish to know, being so close to home.

She might have sobbed again, but controlled it.

'I am so sorry, Anne,' I offered, pushing her hair from her cheeks and throat, realising for the first time that the soft brown hue was now marked with strands of grey. How the years passed by without our realising it. It made me grip her hands hard, as if to anchor us both to this moment.

Anne's gaze sharpened, she pushed herself from my embrace. Her voice had acquired a sharp edge, too. 'Our brother and nephew, and your son, are unscathed. It was a victory for the House of York. The King is in Yorkist hands and the Queen is fled with the Prince. All due to Warwick's bloody strategy.'

'I know.'

I could make no excuses. Nor would I even try. The Queen

had, equally callously, condemned the menfolk of our family to death. But one piece of news she should know. I gripped her hands once more, to still them on her lap.

'Katherine's husband, John Beaumont, met his end on the battlefield. I imagine that Warwick had no intention of allowing him to live.'

'I doubt she'll miss him,' Anne replied with vicious lack of compassion. 'She had no love for him.'

'No.'

'Three husbands dead and buried.' Bitterness still spiked her tongue. 'Will she look for a fourth to share her old age?' But then the grief returned, the overwhelming sorrow for all we had lost. 'Where will it end?' Anne wailed. 'Who will be the next to die? Our family is ripping itself into shreds.' Then her tone hardened. 'No need for you to weep yet, Cis. But one day I swear that you will.'

It was like the clang of the mourning bell. It struck home, as she knew it would, and my hands fell away from hers.

'Oh, you have lost children,' she continued. 'All so young, barely before they drew breath. I am not lacking in pity for you. To lose infants before they have lived to the end of their first year is tragic. But it's not like losing a son and husband on a battlefield, hacked down by an enemy who is of your own blood. Was your husband York even there?'

'No,' I admitted. I had heard nothing of Richard.

'Perhaps you should give thanks that he was not. At least he is alive.'

And then, her face twisted in anguish: 'Listen to me. I am wishing death on the Yorkists. Am I no better? It is like a disease, a plague that infiltrates every nook and cranny and drags us all down. I swear that I have been as much your enemy as the most fervent Lancastrian, even the Queen. And I am ashamed.'

I stroked her arm, relieved when she did not flinch. 'My heart weeps for you, Anne,' I said. 'How can we take opposite sides?'

But Anne was now distracted by the terrible practicalities. 'The new Duke will be our grandson Henry. He is four years old. It is too great a burden for such a young age.' Wiping her tears on her sleeve, she closed her fingers into my sleeves like a raptor's claw. 'Shall I live to see him die on a battlefield, too?'

I sat with her as she fell into restless dreams, incapable of offering her any comfort. Anne had enough living sons and daughters to give her consolation, enough to keep any woman busy, but that was no solace for her loss. She was right. We had lived with war for so long, in France, in Ireland. But here on English soil it is so much worse. I wondered if Katherine had after all wept for John Beaumont. I did not think so.

I could not contemplate Richard's death.

I allowed my rosary to slip through my fingers, bead after bead, as I lifted all whom I loved into the Blessed Virgin's care. How accurate Anne had been in her grief. We were tearing our family and England apart.

The rosary prayers came to their allotted end with the final coral bead. It was the rosary that Anne had coveted. I had not expected to use it in her household to mark the death of one so close to her.

Prayers complete, I began to make plans.

Chapter Nine

The Restoration of the House of York Gains Momentum

Cecily, Duchess of York, to Edward, Earl of March
Written from Tonbridge Castle, September 1460

Ned!

Drag your mind from battles and conquest for one moment and listen to me.

I have a need to return to London.

Find me somewhere to stay. Is there any reason why I should not leave Tonbridge, since King Henry no longer has jurisdiction over me? I think not. I have had my fill of captivity.

Are you still outlawed, or has the attainder been reversed now that the King is no longer in control? I have not heard, but since Salisbury has broken the siege of the Tower of London, the residents preferring surrender to starvation, what is to keep me here?

I am bringing Anne with me. I think that she might wish to go on to pay her respects to Humphrey at his grave in the Church of the Grey Friars in Northampton. You might send for Katherine to join us, too. Three sisters together; it is many years since that was so. I regret it is to fulfil such a melancholy task.

It is my preference to stay at Baynard's Castle. It is comfortable and large enough to accommodate any visitors. I would be grateful if you could have it arranged and all put in order for me.

Have you heard from your father? I have no idea where he is or what he is doing.

Your affectionate mother,

Cecily, Duchess of York

I am of course relieved beyond measure that you survived the battlefield at Northampton. Did I need to say that?

England's Chronicle, *September 1460*

For those who are interested in the bellicose movements of the families of Neville and York: our Duchess Cecily of York is on the move.

Where will she take up residence? We understand at Fastolf Place on the banks of the Thames in Southwark, a very comfortable and secure dwelling, all enclosed with a buttressed wall of new bricks. The Duchess of York wished to go immediately to Baynard's Castle, but her son the Earl of March insisted on Fastolf Place as easy to defend with two gatehouses, its own inlet from the river and a private dock. He is obviously concerned with keeping his mother safe from Lancastrian reprisals.

Meanwhile the Yorkists tighten their hold on the capital. George Neville, a wily cleric and brother to the Earl of Warwick, the priest who opened the gates of London to his father's troops, has been created Lord Chancellor and given the care of the Privy Seal. A neat little Neville coup d'état.

What of King Henry?

All is quiet on that front.

We look forward to welcoming Duchess Cecily to the capital.

Will the Duke of York return now that all the excitement is over? Perhaps his wife knows more than we do.

Richard, Duke of York, to Cecily, Duchess of York
Written from Dublin to Fastolf Place, September 1460

To my well-beloved Cecily,

The time is right. All is now in place for my return.

When you read this, Edmund and I will have landed, near Chester if the winds and tides are in our favour.

Here are my immediate commands. I require you to join me. I will travel to Ludlow. And then on to Hereford, before turning my face towards London and my true inheritance.

Come to me in Hereford.

Time is of the essence. Arrange your travel forthwith. I enclose instructions for you to give to Ned's Steward. Tell him to obey it to the letter. You will not arrive here in the Welsh March unnoticed.

Of course you have my love and admiration, as always.

Forgive the brevity of this. There is much demand on my time. My courier carries money to pay for your journey. There is nothing for you to do but set out.

In anticipation of our being united after so many months apart.

Wear the jewel that I have enclosed.

I regret Buckingham's death.

He is a loss to England. I could have worked with him. Was he not of our own blood through his mother, granddaughter of the third King Edward? Buckingham was a true Plantagenet. Express my consolation to your sister.

Your affectionate husband,

Richard, Duke of York

Cecily, Duchess of York, to Richard, Duke of York
Written from Fastolf Place to Ludlow Castle

My lord,

In some haste to settle the care of our children before I make my leave. Which you, of course, found no time to consider.

Now it has been done, I have made arrangements.

The Steward's grizzled brows met above his formidable nose when I handed over the instructions. He said he had seen nothing like it in all the years of service to our family. The last I saw of him he was issuing orders, loud enough to wake the Devil. His minions were scampering while George and Diccon were getting under his feet.

I will travel with all the panoply that you have demanded.

I will be with you forthwith.

Why Hereford? I can think of better accommodations. Nor do I comprehend why you should need me there. If you have returned, why not just come to London and meet me here?

I expect there will be a reason. I will come, a perfect image of wifely obedience, wearing the jewel.

Cecily

**Anne, Dowager Duchess of Buckingham,
to Cecily, Duchess of York**
Written from the Palace of Westminster

I regret that you cannot travel with me to Northampton. I had hoped for your stalwart if acerbic company, now that we are to some degree reunited in spirit.

Before I left Fastolf Place, I saw the arrangements taking shape. I am astonished at the level of ostentation. What was wrong with the litter we used to bring us there from Tonbridge? I dare not estimate the cost of all this. Some would say that it is an outrage. What sort of statement is this to be, from a traitor's family?

I wish you well. I regret our last months. It does not help when families are pulled apart, does it?

I look for your return. May the Blessed Virgin keep you safe from harm, and from the sin of pride. It worries me. What might Richard have in mind? Nor do I think that you will always be a calming influence.

In all honesty, I had hoped that you would accompany me to Northampton as a safeguard. No one will dare attack the Duchess of York, while the widowed Duchess of Buckingham will be fair game for vindictive Yorkists. I will spend the journey looking over my shoulder.

Your sister in mourning,
Anne

Cecily, Duchess of York, to Edward, Earl of March
Written from Fastolf Place

Ned,

I leave George and Diccon here at Fastolf House. And Meg

also. Their household is to be trusted and they are well guarded, but I ask you to keep a brotherly eye on them until I return. They should be no trouble to you, but George has an adventurous mind. Both he and Diccon were not anxious to stay behind while I travelled into the west.

I have warned them that they must not disobey you. If you can take them with you into the City sometimes, it might help, but do not under any circumstances allow them to neglect their lessons. I am sure that you are well acquainted with all the ruses available to a young boy. You and Edmund used them effectively at Ludlow, to drive your governor to distraction.

Only allow them to go hunting if under your supervision.

Meg will not be a burden to you.

When I return, your father will be with me. May the Blessed Virgin be praised. Then we will take our revenge for the humiliation that we all suffered at Ludlow.

Do not forget that all eyes in London will be on you, as your father's heir. Do not participate in youthful extravagance that will draw scowls down on the House of York. I wish to hear no news of your frequenting the stews and brothels in the environs of the Thames.

Your loving mother,

Cecily, Duchess of York

Edward, Earl of March, to Cecily, Duchess of York
Written somewhere between Baynard's Castle and the Tower of London

To my Lady Mother,

I promise to visit them daily at Fastolf Place, even at the cost to my own convenience. Warwick and I are working together to restore peace in London now that Salisbury has ended the siege of the Tower. Warwick has ambitious plans for the future although he does not tell me the detail of them. I admire him. His reputation blazes like the rising sun on our horizon. He will be the strongest ally we have when my father returns.

We are aware of the need to make a good impression. I promise there will be no surfeit of ale or flirting with women of ill repute. Any youthful extravagance on my part will be kept well hidden from the townsfolk. We plan a public pilgrimage to Canterbury, taking King Henry with us, to give thanks for the lasting peace. That should do the trick.

Godspeed, my lady, in your own endeavours.

You will assuredly blind everyone you meet on the road with the quantity of the gilding on your equipage and the polish on your horses.

Tell my father that we await him without much patience. It will be good to see Edmund again. The House of York will be united once more.

Your dutiful son,
Ned

Anne, Dowager Duchess of Buckingham, to Katherine, Dowager Duchess of Norfolk
Written from the Palace of Westminster

Dearest Katherine,

I was right about York buying our sister's compliance. Another piece of hefty jewellery, this one to hang around her throat, more suitable for a bishop's regalia. Not that she doesn't deserve it, after

123

being abandoned so disgracefully at Ludlow, but why would she be deluded by so obvious a ploy? It would need more than a sacred reliquary to make me travel the breadth of the country, when there really seems to be no need.

Who knows what plans are afoot in York's mind?

Do you come to Northampton to join with me in my memorial? Two ageing widows, suffering similar loss.

Your sister,

Anne

Katherine, Dowager Duchess of Norfolk, to Anne, Dowager Duchess of Buckingham

Written from Epworth

Dear Anne,

Leave Cecily be.

She knows what she is doing, and if she doesn't she'll not thank you for advice. Give it to her when she asks for it, if she ever does. Even you must see that to wear a reliquary containing a piece of the true cross, along every mile between London and Hereford, will give York's return to England more than a holy blessing. He is, if nothing else, a cunning man.

I have no plans to come to Northampton. I see little similarity in our loss.

Keep me informed as to when you are intending to wed again. I never will.

Your sister,

Katherine

Who would have believed it? Can we give credence to what our eyes have seen?

For those of you who are of a curious nature, it has been noted that a certain lady, of notable royal birth, a lady no longer in confinement, is once again on the move, this time out of London.

Where could she be going?

Since she travels west, alone except for a considerable entourage, we can only presume that she intends to make contact with her still absent husband. We hear that he is newly returned from Ireland. A husband who is still an outlaw and attainted for treason.

Is this indeed the Duchess of York? When last she was travelling into London, hard on the heels of her Neville brother, her son and her nephew, together with their armies, it was in an unassuming litter, noted for much wear.

Not so now. Here we have a superb show of wealth and magnificence, even regality. Mayhap it is not the Duchess at all, but the Queen herself? Ah, but we hear that the Queen is adrift in Wales, with neither wealth nor magnificence, and very little regality left to her name.

What would you have seen if you were out and about at an early hour, on the road leading westward?

Four pairs of fine horses to pull a wheeled travelling-litter.

But that is not the half of it. All the splendour of blue velvet curtains, of blue cushions, of gilded tassels. It should be pointed out that the particular shade of blue, vibrant in the morning sunshine, has not been chosen by chance. It is one of York's livery colours. No livery motifs as far as we could see but the ownership was unmistakeable, as was the ostentation.

Thus our regal traveller is most certainly the Duchess of York.

Since her husband, brother and son were stripped of their estates as well as their titles, it is interesting to speculate where the money for such aggrandisement came from. Irish coffers, we presume, containing Irish gold.

Duchess Cecily is also clad in blue. It becomes her. As does the velvet and ermine cloak which bears the York insignia with a smattering of regal heraldic motifs to enhance the whole. Her hair might be confined in a gilded and jewelled roll, draped over by a short veil, but it might as well have been a crown.

The writer of this chronicle, who claims lack of bias towards either York or Lancaster, would not suggest any underhand intent by the said Duke and Duchess of York. We will keep you informed of the progress of their return journey to London, so that you might bear witness to this grandeur for yourselves.

Chapter Ten

The House of York Is Reunited

Recorded by the private hand of Cecily,
Duchess of York, September 1460

My heart leaps inordinately as I begin my journey to the west. I am full of hope for we will be reunited at last after almost a year apart.

Hereford surprises me since its state of readiness for occupation is not good. I expect the linen will need airing if nothing else. I imagine that I can write my name in the dust on coffers and panelling. I doubt that our Steward has taken issue with the rodents in my absence. Why Hereford, of all places? Doubtless Richard has his reasons, to which I am not to be made privy.

After a year's absence, Richard is not allowing grass to grow under his feet. So I must travel immediately, without knowledge of what is being planned. He has clearly become used to unquestioned command while in Dublin, demanding my participation in his new campaign.

Richard is still officially an outlaw, living under an attainder. Should I allow my mind to worry over this? I think not. There is a sea-change in this country. Henry is a prisoner in everything but shackles. Salisbury and Warwick control the capital. My nephew George Neville is Lord Chancellor. A parliament is summoned for October to ratify these changes.

No harm can come to Richard – to us – now.

I feel joy, pure as new season's honey, as my hand writes the words. Richard wants me in Hereford, so I will go to Hereford. I need no persuasion. And I shall see Edmund again.

If my designated mode of travel is unnervingly close to regal, then so be it. Richard left no detail unconsidered. It assuredly unnerved Ned at what must be accomplished in so short a time, with not one item being changed.

It is fortunate that I am an adherent of the colour blue.

What are Richard's intentions?

It will not be the first question I ask him. But probably it will be the second.

I cannot imagine the intensity of our reconciliation. In all our early years apart when he was on campaign, it was never like this. There were times in the last months when I feared that we would not meet again on this earth.

The miles pass so slowly. I could wish that my horse's hooves were winged, as Pegasus, to draw me fast to Hereford through the clouds.

Duchess Cecily is reunited with the Duke of York in Hereford Castle, late September 1460

The azure curtains were drawn back with a sharp snap of the cloth and slide of their rail-attachments.

He was here. He stood beside the carriage, within touching

distance if he stretched out his hand. His eyes met mine, and in them I read a silent but heartfelt welcome. Around us, all seemed to pause, to be held in readiness for the outcome of our reunion. I realised that I was holding my breath. Slowly I exhaled.

My entourage had drawn to a standstill in the familiar bailey of Hereford Castle, on the flat expanse above the River Wye, but it was Richard who filled my sight and my mind to the exclusion of all else. The anticipation of the discomforts and rodents of Hereford had paled.

Instead of helping me to extricate my skirts and my veils, he turned to thank my escort, liberally dispensing coin, leaving my women to help me to alight, allowing me freedom to acknowledge so many faces I knew, both from Ireland and from the Welsh March. One instruction caught my attention. Worthy of note, but not unexpected. Within two days we would be gone from Hereford.

As the horses were led away, he walked beside me and we mounted the steps into the Great Hall, where servants were waiting to divest me of my hood and cloak and gloves, dispensing wine, ushering me towards the fire that did little to warm the vast space. Only after what seemed an age of greeting and acknowledgement was Richard able to dismiss the servants.

We faced each other. Just a little distance between us, yet it seemed so great. He had not yet touched me, nor I him. The air was full of tension, as if a single plucked lute string, not quite in tune, vibrated softly.

Richard.

Had I thought that I would not remember him? All was newborn in my mind, bright with immediate recognition. Not tall, not excessively broad in shoulder or thigh; indeed many would say slight of build. His hair was still as dark as the jackdaws that flocked in the trees beside the cathedral with none of the grey curse of age. Every turn of his head was familiar, every gesture with his fine-boned hands; the lift of his chin, the flattening of his brow when in thought. The sojourn in Ireland had left no legacy on him that I could see.

I realised that I was staring at him, as he was at me.

'Is Edmund here?' I asked, in what was undoubtedly a croak.

'Yes.'

Such a simple exchange of news, and quite unnecessary, but it broke the ice. He smiled. I felt my face relax in return.

'Cecily.'

'Richard.'

'My wife, of more years than I can count.'

'I can count them.'

So foolish, as if we needed a reintroduction, like young people in the early days of a betrothal. We were still smiling. We had been aware of nothing but each other since the moment I had arrived in the bailey.

'You have had adventures,' he said.

'As have you. More dangerous ones than I, I suspect.'

'Not if even half of what I have heard is true. Ludlow was an appalling humiliation.'

I did not deny it.

Now he took my hands, lightly kissed one palm and then the other, before he drew me to the window that looked down over the river far below. The scene did not interest either of us. Light fell on his face, so that now I could see the effect of a year's enforced exile. Lines I did not recall, evidence of anxieties I could only guess at. What did he see in me? What signs of age?

Very gently, he stroked one finger down my cheek.

'I swear you have not changed to any degree.'

'I would like to believe it.'

Would not any woman seek flattery, and enjoy it?

'I have not seen you for so long,' he said, quietly as if we might be overheard, as if these were thoughts that had long been in his mind, 'but I have not forgotten one inch of you. I honour you for staying behind. I honour you for speaking for our people. I fled. I know what was said of me, that I acted with neither honour nor courage and abandoned you. But you, my dearest Cecily, had the audacity to withstand every danger. I know what you did for me, for us.'

My throat was tight with emotion.

'It was my duty. Was I not raised to protect those who gave us their oaths of fealty? I only did what had to be done.'

'More than that. Far more, and to the danger of your own life. How many times did my conscience tell me that I should have taken you with me?'

I laughed a little, but softly. It was what I had wanted to hear.

'When I stood in our home at Ludlow and was forced to face an invading rabble of soldiers, I thought so, too,' I admitted. 'And when I had to beg for mercy from Henry and Marguerite.'

'All I can do is beg your forgiveness.'

To my astonishment, he sank to his knees before me, holding my hands flat against his chest so that I could feel the beat of his heart beneath the rich cloth. Would the Duke of York kneel to me? In all the years of our marriage, he had been the dominant figure, the one who laid down the pattern of our lives together. Here he was, in subservient recognition of his faults, if faults they had been. His eyes were dark with a desire for confession, and for absolution.

'No...' I said. 'You do not need to do this.'

The heartbeat was firm and sure. I felt it spread through my own flesh, my own blood.

'It is necessary. I have a great debt to repay.'

'You have repaid it by coming home, although I'll never forgive the deplorable lack of correspondence. Such excuses you could make for picking up a pen.' I bent to kiss his brow, aware of the curve of his lips. 'I was afraid you would stay and make your own kingdom in Ireland. But now you are here, nothing else is important.'

I turned my hands to lace my fingers with his. 'Stand up, my love.'

Which he did, the reliquary latched to my bodice with its heavy chain immediately attracting his gaze. 'Superb,' he said, running his thumb over the gold mounts. 'It makes exactly the statement of holy power that I had hoped for.'

'And I am wearing it, as you instructed, although I thought it foolhardy.'

'No footpad would attack you with such a powerful escort.'

'I understood that I was to make an impression.'

'Which you have. I received news of your approach two days before you arrived.'

He drew me into the circle of his arms, the sacred reliquary a symbol between us. For a long moment I simply rested there, my brow pressed against his shoulder. Here was the answer to my prayers over so many days and weeks. And then reality once more fought its way into my consciousness.

'I have to ask. What are you going to do next? Why did I need to be here with you, if you will travel to London within two days? Why do I need to wear a King's ransom in diamonds?'

Richard shook his head. 'My plans can wait, other than to

say that I have come to claim my inheritance of York. Now, my dearest Cecily, I find a need to become reacquainted with you.'

He linked his fingers with mine and drew me towards the door to the private chambers. Yes. It would wait after all.

We discovered our chamber, made ready with fine linen and sweet-smelling herbs of lavender and rosemary, where all proved to be familiar and welcoming as, with deep affection, Richard once more enclosed me in his arms. We kissed and we talked and eventually we disrobed. Youth was not on our side, nor was agility, yet we found that no detriment. Did we not know each other so well? Had we not shared a passion, a union of heart and mind? Of ambition? The memory of every scar and memento of battle, every mark of the passage of time, was reclaimed and acknowledged. Thus we lingered with laughter and the softest of touches, until Richard's patience abandoned him. His knowledge of an effective siege was without comparison. It was the greatest pleasure, for both of us, to spend much time in our reuniting.

We had two days in which to make restitution for a whole year.

**Cecily, Duchess of York, to Anne,
Dowager Duchess of Buckingham**

Written from Hereford Castle

My dear Anne,

I am reunited with Richard.

It was unnerving at first. All was so familiar, and yet it was as if I needed to reacquaint myself with his face, his manner of speech, the sort of man he is. Without saying more, it was a reunion much enjoyed by both of us. Richard's sojourn in Ireland has not changed the man I love.

I pray that there will be no need for us to be parted again, but I doubt that life will be so placid, with Marguerite at large. All I can say is that I do not yet know what his plans might be.

Will you bring Humphrey home to Tonbridge, or will you leave him where he was buried in the Church of the Grey Friars in Northampton? I imagine that if Richard died in battle, God forbid, that I would want him to lie in the place he loved best, not where he met his death.

If you return to London before I do, I would be grateful if you would call at Fastolf Place. Ned promises to look in on the children daily, but what weight would you put on such a promise from a young man of seventeen years, full of ambition and energy?

Your affectionate sister,

Cecily

Recorded by the private hand of Cecily, Duchess of York, Hereford Castle, September 1460

I have discovered in the muniment chamber a document of high treason.

Not that I had any suspicion of such when I recognised the little carved coffer that contained the scroll of the lines of descent of the Kings of England that I had shown to Meg and George and Diccon at Ludlow. I considered the sword-bearing figure of the fourth Henry, my mother's brother, so different from the others as he cleaved through the line of succession to take the crown for Lancaster.

But a new section has been added, an extra sheet of vellum, softer and whiter in its newness. A line of descent from the mighty third King Edward, quite separate from the line of Lancaster. It portrays clearly the five sons of King Edward, with my Richard descended from both the second and the fourth son. And I was there, too, joined to him in wedlock, with my own Beaufort descent from John of Gaunt and his mistress, later legitimate Duchess, Katherine Swynford. Our children had been added, with all the weight of their complex but undoubtedly royal Plantagenet blood.

Whose work is this? There is only one possible source for something so inherently treasonable. This is Richard's claim to the throne of England, exhibiting his descent from the second son, Lionel of Clarence, more potent than the Lancastrian claim of hapless Henry, from King Edward's third son. More potent, as long as we are prepared to ignore Richard's descent through a female line, Philippa of Clarence, Lionel's daughter. If this is admissible, then Richard's claim is supreme. One day, if this is proved to be a presentiment of the future, Richard and then Ned will wear the crown of England.

What's more, it is clear to me that I have been summoned here to be a part of the conspiracy. Here is treason on a far more dangerous level than facing King Henry on the battlefield at Ludford Bridge, when our quarrel was not with the King but with his counsellors. Far more dangerous than attempting to win back the position of Lord Protector, to hold the realm together until the young Prince Edward is of an age to rule in his father's stead.

There is one critical omission in that newly designed chart of royal descent; the name of Prince Edward, son and heir of King Henry and Queen Marguerite, around whose birth there has been so much discussion. Given Henry's fragile mind and incapability, how could this child be his legitimate son? Rumour has not been slow to question the Queen's chastity within her marriage. Here

Richard is denying the young Prince his birth and inheritance as Prince of Wales.

I record here that Richard has made a life-changing decision, for both of us, for our children, which will put us at odds with the magnates at Henry's Court and with our own family.

I am afraid.

Duchess Cecily accepts the seeds of treason in Hereford Castle, September 1460

Without a word, I placed the coffer on the table, slid it in front of him, opened the lid.

'Do I understand this?'

I had not intended it to be a challenge, but it undoubtedly was. Richard knew it was.

'I am sure that you do,' he replied, pushing back in his chair, 'since I expect you have already investigated the contents.'

'It is treason, Richard.'

'It has been treason since we raised arms and banners against King Henry. Am I not declared traitor? Am I not disinherited? And my sons after me?'

Suddenly we were both drenched in the bitterness that he had so far hidden from me.

'Is claiming your inheritance not enough?'

Richard's hands clenched hard around the edge of the table but he fought to keep his voice equable. 'No. How can it be enough? How can we trust Henry to keep his word? We cannot trust the state of his mind from one day to the next. We are fortunate if he actually recognises who we are. Marguerite's influence is too strong. Demanding the restoration of my inheritance is no longer enough. It is my right, my right through my Plantagenet blood, to be one of the King's trusted counsellors. If I cannot be assured of that, then why should I not rule? Henry has proved time and time again that he is incapable of holding England together. He wavers from one counsellor to another. I would spend my days looking over my shoulder for a dagger in my back, most likely wielded by Somerset's hand, or even one of your disaffected Neville and Percy relatives. Do you not see that?'

'Yes. I do see it but...'

'But it is treason. Yes it is treason, but the man who is successful is no longer treasonous.'

'You would be a usurper, as was Henry Bolingbroke.'

'He made an effective King, far more so than the second Richard. He was able to pass a stable country to his son. A son who, in Europe, made a name second to none at the battle of Agincourt.'

I moved to perch on the edge of the table beside him, curling my fingers around one of his wrists. Aware of the heavy beat of his pulse, as I had felt it the previous day. Today, as I called into question his vision of the future, the throb was irregular.

'Is this what you wish to do? Usurp Henry and wear the crown, to make England strong and admired again?'

'Yes.'

I inhaled slowly, trying to absorb all that it would mean.

'Don't tell me that you don't have the belly for it, Cis. Will you support me?'

Releasing him, once again I lifted and unrolled the new, final section by the clerkish hand, studying the lines that ran down the page to Richard and our sons. There was the little gilded crown adorning Richard's name.

Ambition flared. There was no doubt that we had a claim. Did we have the right? I looked up at Richard, still uncertain.

'Is this what you wish to do?'

'Yes. Who would be a better King? Henry of Lancaster? Or Richard of York?'

'But Henry of Lancaster has been anointed and crowned.'

'Henry of Lancaster is no longer fit to be King. Moreover I would question his son's legitimacy. How he could have got a child on Marguerite, when he was victim of a mute and uncomprehending state of stupefaction, I can barely imagine. Is it not true that he had no understanding that a son had been born to him?' Richard slammed his hand down onto the wooden surface in a sudden burst of irritation. 'Can you deny the legitimacy of my claim to the throne?'

'No.'

'Can you deny the claim of our sons? Made doubly acceptable through your own royal bloodline.'

'No, I cannot.'

He stood, and drew me to stand also, hands firm on my shoulders, as he might draw forward a young knight who was making his first oath of loyalty. Between us, the scroll rested in my hands, full of potential for glory and tragedy.

'Are you with me or against me, Cis?'

And indeed, that was what he wanted. My loyalty, my fealty. As if I were that young, untried knight. But it did not need him to put that question to me.

'Do you have to ask?'

'I need you to say it.'

'Then this is what I will say. In the name of the Blessed Virgin, I give you my absolute fidelity.'

I saw him exhale slowly, the little grooves beside his mouth flattening. Had he ever thought I would stand against him?

'Then will you ride at my side?' he asked with a sudden urgency. 'To London.'

'Yes.'

'You will stand with me when I put forward my claim?'

'I will. When did a Neville and a Plantagenet retreat from what is honest and just?'

'Never. Particularly a Neville.' He took the scroll from me and re-rolled it, replacing it in its case. 'Did you not suspect what was in my mind?'

'No.' And indeed I had not. 'I thought you would make a bid to oust Somerset and Exeter and rule as Lord Protector again.'

'Once, that is what I would have done. Now I have had too much of uncertainty and exile. I wish to return, to settle again, with full reinstatement and recognition of who I am. And if it means that I challenge Henry for the throne, then I will do it.'

An uncomfortable thought crossed my mind.

'Does Warwick know? You met with him in Shrewsbury.'

He shook his head. 'You are the only one to know my mind. I need you with me. You are essential to my cause. Be with me, Cecily. In mind and heart as well as body.'

'I will be with you. In mind and heart and body.'

Thus I committed myself to whatever the following days would bring. Thus I gave my complete and utter allegiance into the hands of my husband. And yet...

'I see a frown in your eyes,' Richard observed.

'Perhaps there is.'

'And you will tell me.'

'I think it would be dangerous to risk pushing Salisbury and

Warwick into opposition. I think you should be circumspect in how you handle the Nevilles when you arrive in London.'

'In what manner?'

'You may not wish to hear.'

'But you will say it anyway.'

And because I knew him so well: 'Don't cast your hood to the floor in a challenge as soon as you arrive. Be patient. Make a bid for authority at Henry's right hand to begin with. Don't rush in to snatch the crown before you have sounded the attitude of parliament. Don't threaten their power before they have barely taken their seats. Be gentle with Henry.'

'What good would that do? He'll make any promise demanded of him, then break it within an hour of Marguerite's return, as soon as she tells him otherwise. Is that not so?'

'Yes.' I sighed, accepting the truth. 'But promise me that you will be careful. We have loyal friends, but too much arrogance would stir revolt. If you claim the throne, not all will smile on us. Salisbury and Warwick might just resent your presumption. They have worked and fought hard for you in your absence. Don't push them aside as if they no longer have a role in your plans.'

He thought about it, head bent, studying the scuffed tiles at his feet.

'You speak sense, as always, Cis. I will be discretion itself.'

'You won't antagonise parliament or the Nevilles.'

'I will be the perfect example of courteous, well-mannered conciliation.'

I did not believe a word of it, but I had made my promise. I would follow him into the depths of hell if necessary.

Cecily, Duchess of York, to Margaret of York
Written from Hereford Castle

To my dear Meg,

We expect to be in London by the second week of October if the Duke's travel plans fall out as expected. It will please you to know that your father has some bolts of Irish cloth for you in his luggage.

It will please you even more that your father is considering a betrothal for you. If his planning comes to fruition, there will be a string of suitors, as many disreputable as suitable. Don Pedro of Aragon is one possibility, a young man who is a contender for that throne.

As a daughter of York, newly reinstated and absolved from past sins, we anticipate that there will no longer be an obstacle in your path to a good marriage.

You have not been forgotten in your father's absence. You will always have our love, and our burden of care. You have become a young woman of beauty, intelligence and piety.

Your father has a litter of Irish wolfhound puppies. I expect he will give you one, whether you wish it or not. George and Diccon will enjoy the prospect more than you, my dearest daughter. I trust that your brothers are in good heart since I have had no urgent letter from Ned to the contrary.

Your loving mother,

Cecily, Duchess of York

Duchess Cecily's intercession to the Blessed Virgin Mary

Hail Mary, full of Grace, Our Lord is with thee.

Blessed Virgin, Holy Mother. I am in need of your guidance and your infinite understanding.

This is a dangerous path. Guilt and ambition war within me. I accept that I have little control over Richard's plans. I fear for the impression he will make when we leave Hereford. Here we are still anonymous, even if ostentatious. Anonymity will not last long when the Duke of York shakes out his banners. Already he resents my suggestion of discretion.

Give me strength, Holy Mother.

Be with me, he said.

Of course I will. He owns my loyalty, as his wife and as his love. Give me strength and forgiveness when I put his wishes before all else.

It is the power of love.

If we are to be indiscreet, then so be it.

Still my heart quails a little at what we are about to do.

Queen of England. Am I worthy of a crown? I believe that I am. As worthy as any woman in England.

Blessed Virgin have mercy.

Cecily, Duchess of York, to Richard Neville, Earl of Salisbury

Written from Hereford Castle

Brother,

It is essential that you know what is afoot in my lord's mind. This should reach you by fast courier before we do. Do not speak of this to Ned or to Warwick, although Warwick might already have more than an inkling of the way the wind is blowing. Still, I am of a mind to say that the fewer to know of this the better.

Richard intends to make a bid for the crown. Not as Lord Protector, but as King.

If he does, we will all be called on to make our loyalties known.

I see nothing but more trouble, but he does not always accept my opinions when so much is at stake. Sadly, women have the habit of merging with the tapestries when matters of high politics take precedence.

Ambition is a fine thing, but also a deadly one.

My loyalties are committed. You may yet have to decide on yours.

I fear it will take more than a holy reliquary to bring this venture to a successful conclusion.

Your sister,

Cecily

Chapter Eleven

The Wheel of Fortune Begins to Spin

Cecily, Duchess of York, to her son Richard
Written from Gloucester, on the second day of October 1460

To my well-beloved son Diccon,

Today is the commemorative day of your birth and we are not together to celebrate. Do you remember this day, one year ago, when we were all in Ludlow and managed some festivity even with an army at our door? It was the last time that you saw your father. Now he travels home with me. Soon you will see him again.

Give thanks to God for your life and health.

When we are reunited, we will mark this auspicious day, however late it might be.

Do not give any weight to rumours of unrest in the City or your father's continuing perfidy. All will be well.

Your father sends his affection.

Your loving mother,

Cecily

For those of you uncommonly interested in the travels of a certain noble lady earlier in the year, it is our duty to inform you that she is returned to London. Of even greater significance to every man in England, her husband, traitor and outlaw, is riding with her.

Sufficient to record here that the Duke of York is making a progress, accompanied by an army in everything but name. And what takes our attention, apart from the size of the retinue? The fact that the mustered company might be promoting the falcon and fetterlock, York's own heraldic symbol, but the banners, shaken out in Abingdon for all to see, display the royal arms of England, the royal devices outlined in gold over the bright red and blue. And yes, the crowds are cheering. Duchess Cecily is smiling, bowing her head in gracious style. On her breast can be noted the jewelled reliquary. The value of the gems cannot be disputed. Nor its contents. A piece of the true cross, so we are told.

We foresee the Duke being present for the summoning of the parliament. Which might be acceptable if the Duke merely wishes to make a genuflection to the government that has King Henry within its control. We believe that York has returned with more than his reinstatement in mind.

Does Duchess Cecily realise how great an asset she is?

If you wish to make comparisons:

Our present absent Queen has only managed to produce one son, and that birth is open to question if you are a gleaner of gossip. Duchess Cecily has four strong sons, with no question of her faithfulness and honesty within her marriage.

Duchess Cecily is proven to be an obedient wife, rushing to be at her husband's side when he called. Her piety is beyond question. Who can say that of Queen Marguerite? When is she ever guided by her husband? She abandoned him on the battlefield at Northampton, leaving him to Warwick's tender mercies.

So make your comparisons as you ask the question:

What does the Duke of York seek when he returns to London?

These royal arms that are so prominently displayed are York's arms too, as a royal son with legitimate descent. He has every right to display them. Even more disquieting, before York in the procession is borne his sword, upright, as if it were the Sword of State carried before the King himself.

The message is clear to all: 'Let England know that the Duke of York is back.'

Beware, mighty Duke. Is it the role of Lord Protector that you seek, or do you make a bid for the throne itself? Who will smile on you in your ambitions, other than your Duchess?

Duchess Cecily returns in triumph to London, October 1460

We rode into London on the tenth day of October, with all the panoply that Richard had been devising over the last twelve months. Parliament had been meeting for three days.

'Which is perfect timing for me,' Richard said. 'All the tedious business of taxes and corruption and the frequency of highway robberies will have been swept out of the way.'

All we had talked of on that long journey remained a fervent desire for both of us. That Richard should indeed be proclaimed King of England. But how it would be achieved remained firmly in Richard's hands. Securely locked in his fertile brain.

What an impression we must have made. I in my blue-velvet-hung carriage which had suffered little from its recent travels over the autumn roads. Nothing that a thorough clean could not put right in the night before our arrival. The horses had been groomed to gleam as bright as any for a tournament. But that was not the height or depth of it. With us rode a retinue, of eight hundred horsemen, Richard said. The trumpeters of Abingdon were in fine tune.

Now I understood why I had been ordered to Hereford. Richard wanted to shout his royal credentials far and wide, from the border-lands of Wales to London, to as many who would throng the route to watch us pass by.

Even as I rode, the curtains of my litter drawn back so that I might see and be seen, I felt fear building in me until it all but choked me. Should the end result of our return not be achieved through negotiation, through careful manoeuvring? Should we not bend our Yorkist knee before the King, brought forth from the Tower for this occasion?

'You look anxious,' Richard said as he drew abreast of me when the mass of people slowed our pace. 'You are in no danger. There'll be no more imprisonment for you.'

'I don't fear that. This is what I fear.'

I swept a wide gesture with my arm.

Here was no subtlety. Here was no negotiation. Here were the beginnings of insurgency. I had already seen the shocked expressions, even as the masses cheered with raucous voices.

'It's too precipitate, Richard,' I censured, something I had privately sworn I would not do. But I could not support this explosive aggrandisement of York power.

'They have to know what I fight for.' Unperturbed, his face creased in a smile, albeit severe. 'Besides, the crowds will cheer such a display. No one welcomes a weak leader.'

And they did cheer. I remembered the old stories of the Londoners cheering the return of Bolingbroke. But any crowds would cheer when primed with ale and a colourful event to enliven their day. At Bolingbroke's coronation he had set fountains running with red wine in Cheapside.

A brusque movement of horseflesh brought me back to the present. Richard was about to ride off to the front of our procession.

'Do you go on to Baynard's Castle?' I called after him, still unsure of his immediate destination.

He turned his horse, returned, leaning down to address me. 'I go straight to Westminster Hall. I have not come this far to hesitate now.'

I put out my hand to touch his sleeve, then curled my fingers into the rich cloth as if I could still prevent the plans that were fomenting in his mind.

'Just remember, Richard, that you are not yet King.'

'Can you give me one reason why I should not be King? Have we not already wrung every drop of blood from this discussion?'

'But until you are...'

I had not thought that he would drive the claim home so urgently. Had Richard not agreed that he would take no undue risks? It would be far better to step carefully, to remake old connections, to reaffirm old friendships. He had been absent from the political manoeuvrings for a whole year.

He must have seen the anxiety in my face. 'What advice will you give me, Cis?'

'Exactly the same as I offer every time we speak of this meeting at Westminster. Be careful not to tread on magnate toes. They'll not thank you for it. Get my brother Salisbury on your side. Warwick too.'

'I'll be as circumspect as you would hope for, Cis, but I will make my case whether they like it or not.'

Pride was stamped over every inch of him from his azure-and-gold-patterned chaperon to his costly thigh-length boots. How had I ever thought that I could influence the manner in which he would announce the right of his royal blood? The year in exile had honed his temper, which had always been unpredictable when his pride had been challenged. I had seen only flashes of it, when the journey was hampered by organising such a major force, but I feared the worst. They would turn on him like a pack of hunting dogs bringing down a tined stag. The mob in the streets might acclaim him with his royal banners but these men in parliament, used to wielding power with the ear of King Henry, were of different calibre.

I could not even be there, in parliament, to see my worst fears unfold.

**Richard Neville, Earl of Salisbury,
to Cecily, Duchess of York**
Written from the Palace of Westminster

Cecily,

This is a disaster! Has he lost his wits? Well, you did warn me, but I had not expected this. No one could have expected this. York will make excuses for the outcome. Of course he will. He has an argument, full of fervour, to cover every eventuality. I'll tell you the truth, even if no one else will.

I was already in Westminster Hall when he arrived. So were March and Warwick. A family affair. It had been a busy session, but at least the atmosphere was one of calm achievement, set to welcome the returned Duke of York. There was no animosity, rather a degree of compassion for a man who had suffered exile and disinheritance.

Compassion? Understanding? York set a burning brand to

it, stoking up anger and hostility. The Hall shook on its ancient foundations. He marched in as if he owned the place, daring any man present to object.

Could you not have stopped him? You had the whole journey from Hereford to London to talk some sense into him.

Well, the end result was a scene that will be engraved on my mind for all time. York strode directly to the dais at the far end of the Hall where the King would sit. But Henry was not there. The throne, under the canopy of state, was empty. Yet still it was a sacred space, untouchable, impregnable.

York should have known that. Should I have stretched out my arm to stop him as he strode past? How could I? I never thought that he would do it.

He was undeterred by the cautious inhaling of breath as he marched through the midst. He bowed to the throng. Then, as if all had been planned, even to his gesture, he placed his hand on the arm of the empty throne, at the same time turning to face the Hall and its assembly.

It was as if he had cried out:

This is mine. I will have it.

I swear every man there held his breath. I felt March stiffen. Warwick looked less than impressed but not altogether surprised. The whole assembly was transfixed as if awaiting the next step. No one was persuaded to respond or reply. Every face, every expression was set in stone, rigid in disbelief.

As for York, did I detect a moment of surprise, of uncertainty? After your victorious progress through England he had expected voices raised in welcome and support. What he had not expected was the slide of an eye. A silence. An embarrassment that could be tasted like bitter herbs on the tongue.

Slowly he removed his hand from the gilded chair. Every breath was held as tight as a drawn bow-string.

York took one step away from the dais, stepping out from the shadow of the canopy. From my close proximity, I could see the anger simmering within him, his mouth tightened into a line of fury.

His voice rang out in a claim that the throne and the crown were his by right as the true heir of King Richard the Second. You will not be surprised to know that it was followed by a murmuring of dissent, low at first like a distant hum of bees, then growing in intensity. York raised his hand to throw down another challenge, only curtailed when the Archbishop stepped forward with a suggestion that York should seek an audience with the King. His brow heavy with frustration, York strode back through the length of the Hall, retracing his steps, ignoring the shiver of noise behind him. The only wise action of the day, to my mind. What he will say to King Henry I have no idea, nor what the King will say to him.

I cannot foresee the outcome. Speak to him, Cis. Tell him that he must not pursue this outrageous course. He is digging a pit into which we will all be cast if he claims the throne as his own.

If he thought that he had such a strong right to rule, why wait until now to shout it from the roof beams like a cock on a dunghill?

York has become a danger to himself and to the rest of the family.

Use any influence you have. I think he will not listen to me. I doubt he will listen to anyone other than the voice in his head and the conviction in his heart that tells him he should be King.

Your brother,
Salisbury

Cecily, Duchess of York, to Richard Neville, Earl of Salisbury

Written from Fastolf Place

I suppose I should thank you for this account of what happened. I suppose I should have expected it. Well, I did, but not quite in so brutal a fashion.

No, I could not stop him. I have already placed your arguments before him but to no avail. You know him well enough. Who could alter his direction, once he has the bit between his teeth like a high-mettled warhorse with spurs applied? He might wear a fetterlock emblem to proclaim his name, but I have yet to see one that could shackle him to less than a gallop when the road is clear.

Do you think he will listen to me if I tell him that the throne can never be his? The year in exile, humiliated and disinherited, has spiked his temper. Besides, his claim to the crown is as strong as any, and does he not have the strength and ability to hold it and bring this sad country to peace?

Try to keep faith. All might not be yet lost.

Besides, have you considered that I might agree with him? I may regret the manner of his challenge, but what do I think of his claim of legitimate inheritance? You have not asked me that question, dear brother.

Cecily

Richard, Duke of York, to Cecily, Duchess of York

Written from the Palace of Westminster

Cecily,

You will hear soon enough and I doubt you will enjoy the telling of it.

I was driven to do it.

You would say I should have hugged diplomacy to my breast. That if I see myself as King, I should be able to exercise self-control when dealing with these pompous magnates. Instead I allowed my desire for justice to overwhelm my political sense. It is done. Now we must await the outcome.

I am sending this to Fastolf Place since I presume you have gone to be with our daughter and young sons. Ned and Edmund are with me.

I need you to come to Westminster, where I have taken occupation of the King's chambers. Henry has moved into those put aside for the Queen. I am expecting a delegation from Salisbury and Warwick. From their concerted frowns when I walked out from the seething parliament, I don't expect it to be a friendly one. You must come to pour oil on troubled waters for me.

Did I not say at Hereford that I would have a crucial role for you to play?

Come soon.

Richard

Duchess Cecily experiences a hostile family reunion in the Palace of Westminster

What a desperately angry half-hour it proved to be. What a tumultuous clash of opinion and antagonisms, when Richard returned to our accommodations, fast followed by my brother Salisbury and nephew Warwick. My chamber in the palace, cramped and confined in this rabbit warren of accommodation, hung about with dusty tapestries, seemed to be full of angry men. The only blessing was that their armed escorts were left outside, but there was still a surfeit of weaponry to hand if tempers frayed too far.

As I realised from the start, there was no place for a woman in this conflagration.

There was Richard, fists braced on hips, standing at one end of the chamber, our Neville kin smouldering side by side at the other, my sons Ned and Edmund hovering somewhere between. I, firmly ensconced at Richard's side, could have laughed at the incongruity of it all, but this was no laughing matter. Richard has stirred up a hot-buzzing hornets' nest, and here were the principal Neville hornets, prepared to sting.

I imagined the raised voices could be heard in St Stephen's Chapel, providing an uncomfortable background to Compline.

'So you met with King Henry in a private conversation,' Salisbury accused.

'Yes I did,' Richard replied, all belligerence.

'I doubt you got much support from him. Or sense. He would hardly agree to handing over his crown to you.'

'No, he did not.'

'Then where does that leave you? Leave us?' Salisbury's expression was heavy-browed with disapproval. 'Or do you plan to keep your conspiracy to gain power a secret?'

'Why would I? Are we not family?' At last, in reply to my tug on his sleeve, Richard had relaxed a little, his fists falling to his sides, his hands flexing open as if to dispel some of the aggression. 'Henry stated the rights of his inheritance, descended from his father the fifth Henry. He assured me that you – and I – had all sworn featly to him, if we chanced to have forgotten. At least he recalled that much of our past history. He then asked, how could his right be then disputed after almost forty years of ruling? As I told him, it could, quite easily. Furthermore…'

All I could do was open the door to allow servants to enter, bearing ewers and cups. An edgy silence fell on the room as they proceeded to fill the vessels and dispense them to our guests. It would not soothe the passions, but it would at least give a moment for reflection.

'I swear that the lords will oppose it,' announced Salisbury into the silence.

'There was no great opposition from the lords when King Richard was deposed by Henry of Lancaster,' Richard retaliated.

'King Richard threatened the power of his lords,' Warwick replied, admitting what would be the key concern of every magnate in the country. 'Our King Henry, even in his madness, has never been a threat. What advantage is there to us in removing him? What we saw today was an upheaval that could topple all power into your hands. Name me one magnate who will hand over his own power to a man who has just marched into London with an army?'

Richard's reply flared once more with heat.

'Do you accuse me of threatening you? Of abandoning my friends with whom I have struggled and fought against adversity? Would I put power before family loyalty?'

Which was exactly what Warwick was saying. What they saw before them, what they had seen in Westminster Hall, was a man of power, of unbridled ambition, belted and booted, vibrant in fur-trimmed blue and black and gold damask. A man who had marched through London to wide acclaim with an army at his back and royal banners above his head. Salisbury and Warwick might have their own loyal forces, but these were insufficient to challenge Richard on a field of battle, if it ever came to that.

'I say that you are presumptuous in your claims. What happens if we do not support you?' Salisbury asked, his thoughts running in a similar pattern to mine. 'Do you turn your army on us? Better for us the weak King we have than a tyrant who might just shed our blood in his own cause.'

Tyrant. An ill-chosen word, I thought.

Richard picked it up too. 'I am no tyrant. Do you not know me better than that?'

'I thought that I did.' Warwick waded into the quagmire of dispute once more. 'But now you are urging us to break our oaths to Henry. It is a sin. It is blasphemy.'

'And it wasn't a sin and blasphemy when we faced him at Ludford Bridge? Your oaths to Henry had no weight with you then. Are you saying that you had no thought that I would return one day to claim what was mine? When we met at Shrewsbury, I made all plain.'

'I don't recall your telling me that you would snatch the crown,' Warwick replied.

An accusation that Richard simply ignored, which made me presume it to be true as he continued in his fierce denial. 'Now you accuse me of threatening to use my army against you. I see no threat. Who planted that despicable seed? Was it my brother of Salisbury?'

He glowered at my brother. I held my breath for the inevitable outburst from Warwick in defence of his father. To my amazement it was Edmund who replied, stepping forward, less combative in figure, far less aggressive in voice and face.

'Speak peace, cousin Warwick, not war. There is no force here. We all know that my father has the right to the crown. Why should he not claim it? Why should we not support him?'

But Warwick swept Edmund's suggestion aside with the flat of his hand as if it were a troublesome gnat.

'I'll stand by my oath of allegiance to King Henry, as my father will stand by his. And so will the rest of the lords. Answer me this, York: if you are so certain of your claim to the throne, why have you waited until now to fly it like a new falcon?'

I realised that I was holding my breath. Richard had indeed kept silent on this for all the years of his manhood.

'The fact that I did not does not make my claim less true,' Richard snapped.

'I like not your ambition, York.'

'I like not your accusations, Warwick.'

Warwick placed his cup on the table with a sharp sound, deliberately turning his back on Richard. I knew it would be dangerous to allow him to leave in this mood. I nudged Ned with a nod in Warwick's direction, while I moved to talk with Richard.

'You cannot afford to antagonise my family,' I suggested sotto voce.

'They cannot afford to antagonise me. Warwick talks of my ambition. I like not his.'

I looked across to where Ned was in deep conversation with my nephew of Warwick.

'All shall be well,' I heard Ned say. I could not hear the reply.

Edmund and Salisbury were in conversation, my brother's face as uncompromising as a dish of cold pottage.

I could only hope that the rift would be patched, even if the patching remained evident with clumsy stitching. As I stepped forward to add my own sisterly soothing to my brother's mood, with barely an acknowledgement of farewell, the Nevilles strode out of the chamber in a cloud of prickly animosity.

'What a pleasurable family reunion that was,' I declaimed to anyone who would take note. 'I see that we will soon be at war with the Nevilles as well as the House of Lancaster.'

And I took myself to discover a refuge in King Henry's private chapel, my only company the frescoed angels benignly clutching their harps, with no ruffled tempers to be seen or heard. I was too weary, too dispirited, to do more, unable to see the future clearly. My only solace was my deep satisfaction in my sons, of their attempts at conciliation. All I could hope was that Ned understood exactly what it was that his father had taken in hand, the inherent danger of it all. As the heir to York he needed to know.

Cecily, Duchess of York, to Richard Neville, Earl of Salisbury
Written from Westminster Palace

Salisbury,

I trust you were satisfied last night. I thought it to be a disgraceful show of hostility on your part. A deplorable antagonism. All you did was stoke the flames even higher than the initial conflagration.

There has to be conciliation, for both our families. Are you really content with Marguerite wielding power in the name of her incapable husband?

I will work on York. You take Warwick in hand. He is your son, so you must be responsible for his recalcitrance.

I know the strain of family loyalties very well. I put it on your shoulders to heal this breach.

Your sister,
Cecily

Richard Neville, Earl of Salisbury, to Cecily, Duchess of York

From the Palace of Westminster

This breach is not of my making.

Look to your husband whose ambitions run amok.

Do you believe in signs and portents? Nothing like a cloud in the form of a dragon to give rise to rumours of upheaval and insurrection. No malformed clouds here, but did you know? At the precise moment that York claimed the crown for himself, a gilded crown that decorated one of the candle sconces in Westminster Hall became, by some means, mystical or otherwise, detached. It clattered to the floor, to lie, dented on one side, on the tiles.

You can imagine the reaction. The portents spoke clearly. Henry of Lancaster's kingship had toppled, irreparably damaged, crashing to earth like the crown. It must be replaced by a stronger claimant.

I am astonished that York is not making more use of such a prediction. Is not the House of York pragmatic in all things? I should remind you that I have no belief whatsoever is such chance occurrences. Nor I suspect do you, although that will not deter you from making political use of it.

Salisbury

Anne, Dowager Duchess of Buckingham, to Katherine, Dowager Duchess of Norfolk

Written from the Palace of Westminster

Dear Kat,

As you might expect, Cecily is weathering the political storm with much aplomb. And what a tumultuous storm it is. She spends her time scurrying between one obstinate man and the next, trying to keep Warwick and Salisbury in harmony with York.

Before you take me to task, I do her a disservice. Cecily does not scurry. She retains her dignity even in the midst of a furious anger.

Cecily's present exceptional piety is something I do not quite recognise. Nor the fact that she wears what I can only describe as the height of Court fashion with tight fur-cuffed sleeves and a surprising décolletage that our mother would have frowned upon.

I do not know what will come of all this. I am of a mind to retire to Tonbridge or Maxstoke. I like not the atmosphere here in London. It could erupt into violence at any moment.

Your unsettled sister,

Anne

I could not imagine coping with a hennin as Cecily did when she rode into London. She will send you the pattern if you ask her. I wish you well of all the pins and wires and length of veiling.

Recorded by the private hand of Cecily, Duchess of York, October 1460

Animosity. Rancour. Loathing.

Call it what you will. All as sharp as a new-edged sword, it continues amongst the Lords. I see no hope of a change of mind.

Thus Richard, depressed by disappointment, needled by his lack of judgement, goes about with a thick scowl lodged on his brow. Ned and Edmund step round him as if he were a wild boar, unpredictable, his temper chancy. His claim to the throne is rejected because he is descended from the second son, Lionel of

Clarence, through the royal blood of women, Edward III's female descendant, rather than male.

It was a weakness, as we both knew.

Had Richard not planned for this? It was the arms of Edmund of Langley, Duke of York, the fourth son, that he wore as his own when we entered London.

Another weakness that we had acknowledged. Richard's claim through the fourth son was cast into shadow by King Henry's legitimate descent through the third.

It is all now beyond the decision-making of the Lords. The men of law in conference at the Black Friars say that Richard must meet with King Henry and decide between them, which is just a deceitful way of abandoning the whole argument.

Henry will never abdicate. Nor will Marguerite. Nor will Richard be prepared to compromise. All Richard can hope for is to take up the position of Lord Protector again if Henry should slide into mental turmoil. But how is it possible to uncover such a rats' nest of claim and counter-claim, then re-cover it, allowing it to linger and fester, the rats to grow in strength? A rats' nest must be destroyed by a fierce ratter, for the good of all but the rats.

But who are we? Is our House of York a family of rats in the nest? Or are we the ratters set on to kill the vicious pests who would undermine the King's power?

I know not the answer to this conundrum.

Cecily, Duchess of York, to Anne,
Dowager Duchess of Buckingham

Written from Baynard's Castle

My dear sister Anne,

I think that you are now settled back at Tonbridge.

All, as you might guess, is at sixes and sevens. You are well out of it.

I know this will concern you since you were always anxious for King Henry's condition. There is no need for you to have a concern for him. He is treated well, even though he may not appreciate it. Henry has been removed from Westminster to the house of the Bishop of London. Richard has visited him there. Henry will discuss nothing but his descent from the third King Edward and the state of his soul. There is no moving him.

I was surprised that Richard thought there would be. There is a streak of stubbornness in our King as wide as the sea between us and France, and twice as dangerous when he sets his mind to something. If God speaks to him, what hope does any man have of his voice being heard?

Our puissant King Henry refuses to have any interest in arrangements for his future. Instead he proclaims his dislike of the tapestries on the walls of his chambers. He says the Bishop of London is a heathen to have nothing but hunting and hawking scenes, full of blood and death. He says that he would rather have Saint Sebastian transfixed by arrows to keep him company.

I moved into Baynard's Castle, thus reunited with the younger children, but my mind remains entirely at Westminster.

It is Richard's rightful inheritance that we seek. You will not agree, of course. I understand why so many would deny it when the matter has never been raised before. It is opportunistic, they say; a selfish grasping of personal power, twisting the family connection to suit the mighty Duke of York. And they fear his power. But would not England sleep more easily with a strong man at the helm rather than the unreliable mind of King Henry?

Even you must give a vestige of a nod to this.

But here is a thought that I will plant in your mind. One I know you will detest. That I would be a more appropriate Queen of England than Marguerite.

There. The word had sprung for the first time from my pen. If Richard pushes his claim with any success, I will be Queen of England. Am I not Queen by right?

If that drives you to sleepless nights, don't let it. There seems no possibility of it happening. The main problem for most of our lords is the oath that they all took to Henry. Some are more ready to abandon it than others, but even our brother Salisbury feels the oath is sacrosanct. That is, until self-interest persuades him otherwise.

Richard says that if he sees one more yellowing, curled-edged sheet of royal genealogy being passed around, he'll send in his troops and clear the Hall of the lot of them.

Which may not be the best policy.

Your sister,

Cecily

Chapter Twelve

Queen in Waiting

Cecily, Duchess of York, to Richard, Duke of York
Written from Baynard's Castle, October 1460

Richard.

Is there no news?

There is rumour and gossip aplenty but it would be good to hear it from the horse's mouth, preferably an identifiably Yorkist horse. I suppose the legal men are still proving squeamish in coming to a decision.

The children would value a visit from you. They will think that you no longer exist except in my imagination. I too would value an hour in your company.

Do you want my advice? I'll give it anyway. Remember to keep your arguments calm and mild. Nothing will be gained by becoming overheated. Accept the office of Lord Protector. Then you can keep the sheets of genealogy for another day.

I expect that you have had quite enough advice and will consign this to the fire. Do not be provoked into sending in your troops.

Cecily

Richard, Duke of York, to Cecily, Duchess of York
Written from Westminster to Baynard's Castle, sent by return of courier

They've done it, Cis.

They've agreed.

At last, against all the odds, since the lawyers amongst them slithered out of the decision-making like snakes heading for long grass.

It has been decided. My claim is stronger than that of Henry of Lancaster. The crown will be mine.

It is a compromise, of course. It is a compromise, but not a weighty one after all. No one was prepared to make a change in the dynasty now. After well-nigh forty years as King, it was thought that Henry was owed some loyalty, so the crown will remain his until the day of his death. And I will accept the legality of their decision.

Has Henry agreed to this? Yes. It could not be done without. Do we believe him? Will he keep his word? Was he put under pressure to agree? Certainly, but persuasion was easy enough when the Lords who visited him urged him to comply. I had no part in it. I was, whatever my enemies might claim, no heavy-handed bully.

Now that Henry has given his consent, it will become official, through an Act of Accord. My claim will be beyond question, supported by the law of the land. Is that not all we had hoped and planned for?

'What of Marguerite?' you may well ask.

She is ordered to return to London, and to bring her son with her. She has been assured that they will be treated well.

Does she not have an army to call on? Another crucial question.

It will have to be seen. We do not yet know if she has managed to raise a force in Scotland to augment her English followers. But I too have an army.

All we have to do now is hope they speed up the Accord and all can be settled. Then we need not worry that Marguerite will return and persuade Henry to change his mind all over again.

I will come to Baynard's Castle when the Act is passed. Until then I still feel that all hangs in the balance and it would not be good policy for me to be absent from the centre of events.

I did not burn your letter. I am always receptive of your advice, even when I do not act on it. I did not send in my troops.

Richard

England's Chronicle, *the thirty-first day of October 1460*

It is the talk of the City, from lord to merchant to the beggar outside Westminster Palace.

What is it? The return of Queen Marguerite? The sanity of King Henry? Another unsettling Love Day Festival?

The passing of the Act of Accord.

Here, for those who have slept through the last se'nnight, is the gist of what is decided.

We are pleased to announce that the King Henry, the sixth of that name and of the House of Lancaster, will remain King of England, untroubled by any claims to that position, until the day of his death.

On his death, in the fullness of time, his heir is Richard Plantagenet, Duke of York. He will be followed in that inheritance by his two sons of York, Edward, Earl of March, and Edmund, Earl of Rutland.

Edward, Prince of Wales, is thus duly disinherited.

Richard Plantagenet, as he styles himself, Duke of York, is acknowledged as Prince of Wales, Duke of Cornwall, Earl of Chester. All royal titles that are now his to claim as heir to the throne.

During the lifetime of King Henry, York will bear the title Lord Protector. He will enjoy an annual income of ten thousand pounds.

Thus it is decided. The Lords, met together in our parliament, after much fractious debate, have sworn to support and protect the Duke of York as heir to the throne.

It is now declared treason to plot against him.

Queen Marguerite has been commanded to return to London. In her predictable absence with her young son, all has been celebrated in a formal reconciliation between the King and his new heir in St Paul's Cathedral, in the sight of God. Henry wore his crown, led in procession by the nobility of the kingdom who could persuade themselves to forgo their previous oaths of allegiance and attend. It was a mighty procession of hypocrisy. When York knelt before the King and received a blessing from the royal hands, Henry smiled. It was, you might say, an exceptional symbol of concord. Whether anyone believed it is quite another matter.

What will Duchess Cecily say to this promotion for her family? Her sons are now in direct line to the English throne. On Henry's death she will be Queen of England.

Of even greater interest, will Queen Marguerite be touched by any spirit of concord?

We doubt it. We watch and wait in anticipation.

Oath of Accord

In the name of God, amen. I, Richard Duke of York, promise and swear by the faith and truth that I owe to Almighty God that I shall never do, agree, instigate or incite, directly or indirectly, in private or in public, nor as far as I can or shall be able, allow to be done, agreed, instigated or incited, anything which may cause or lead to the shortening of the natural life of King Henry VI, or the harm or injury of his reign or royal dignity, by violence or in any other way, against his freedom and liberty;

So help me God, and these holy gospels.

Anne, Dowager Duchess of Buckingham, to Katherine, Dowager Duchess of Norfolk
Written from Tonbridge Castle

What can I write, that you cannot already guess?

But perhaps this is so extravagant that you would deny it.

You should have been here. It was truly a sight to behold. Plantagenets and Nevilles en masse, as well as those sycophants who hang on the sleeves of families who are in the ascendant. All in celebration together of their marvellous change of fortune. All circling around Richard and Cecily. Richard is now Lord Protector, ruling England in the name of Henry, with a legal hold on the crown when Henry is dead.

How long will Henry live? By the nature of things, and the span of years, he must outlive Richard, but who's to tell? His health is not strong. And then we'll have King Richard with the York boys to follow. They are not short of heirs, and when they wed, we'll have a whole warren of Plantagenets.

Don't misunderstand me. I don't suggest that Henry will die an untimely death. That is not what I intend to say.

I have yet to decide what I think about all this. Humphrey would have said: 'Smile, bow, and keep your mouth shut.' But Humphrey is dead, in the cause of King Henry.

I have to admit that Henry becomes more ineffectual by the day, his grasp on reality waning.

There is, of course, Queen Marguerite lurking on the periphery of this new scene. What she will have to say about all of this, we have yet to discover. Her voice will be loud and clear. So will that of her army, I fear.

Back to the revels. Richard was at appalling ease, urbanely confident, moving between groups, conversing, winning friends. It seems that the rifts have been healed within the family, at least to all outward show. Our brother of Salisbury was amenable, and so was our nephew of Warwick, although I suspect that Warwick has an ambition to match that of Richard. He is young and powerful. Who knows how high his sights are set?

How fortune changes. There they are, basking in regal glory. Did I rejoice? I am a widow, and so are you, our husbands done to death by this celebrating throng.

I found it wearying.

Do come and join me. I am in need of a sympathetic ear. Cecily sees nothing but Richard crowned in gold. Are you still mourning Beaumont's death? I doubt it. I think that you need some levity in your life.

At least these unsettling developments have taken my mind from my ailments. I have found myself no longer in need of tincture of bryony (perhaps a herb too powerful for its own good and only to be used in moderation!) to soothe my aching joints. Even so, my predilection for standing at royal receptions (whether real or false) are long gone.

Although Richard has not the inches and breadth of a King, Ned will be perfect. A golden youth from the old legends. I expect he will make a mighty King if Marguerite fails to stop him.

Your suffering sister,

Anne

Before you warn me, I am not overdosing on bryony. I know full well that it can bring a painful death for those careless enough to take too much.

Cecily, Duchess of York, to Katherine, Dowager Duchess of Norfolk

Written from Baynard's Castle

Dearest Kat,

I expect Anne has written to you, bemoaning my perceived sins. Her mouth was pursed as if I had forced her to eat a dish of sour apple throughout our family gathering.

I can barely believe the change in fortune. Richard is all but King of England. All that stands between him and that power is Henry, thirty-nine years old and undoubtedly afflicted in body and mind.

God's grace shines on us with the brilliance of a summer sun. The attainders against us and our followers are lifted. Our titles, lands and possessions restored. It is now treason to speak ill of Richard, of myself and of our children. We are truly protected.

When Richard takes the crown, I will be Queen of England.

Is it wrong of me to rejoice in our achievements?

And yet, I must be wise to the fact that not all who concur with the changes today will continue to do so tomorrow.

I am not blind. I surveyed those under my roof at Baynard's Castle.

What emotions could I read there? A whirlpool of ambition that might well drag us all down to drown in its depth. With the House of York ascending to the throne, there would be power for our widespread family, pleasing to all. But was there envy, too? I detected a belief that we had stepped too far. A fear that Richard might not permit the same freedom of power as Henry had allowed. An even stronger fear that the days of royal patronage flowing into the magnate coffers was at an end. That was the immediate fear of Salisbury and Warwick. I think them to be misguided. Richard would be fair and honourable. As would my son Ned after him.

There is danger, though; I cannot pretend otherwise. When the Accord was signed, there were some difficult absences. Somerset and Wiltshire and Lord Clifford, of course, as well as my nephews, the Percy Earl of Northumberland and the Earl of Westmorland, but also our brother Baron Latimer. They might be Nevilles but they remain bound to Lancaster. And my predictable son by law the Duke of Exeter. I expect their troops will be mustering with those of the Queen.

How long do you think Henry will live?

On that day in St Paul's when Henry gave his assent to what had been done in his name, I swear it was in everyone's mind.

Richard assures me that Henry will live out the years allotted to him by God and we will prove to be loyal subjects. If that means that Richard will never see the crown, then so be it. Henry will live as long as his breath and his heart allow.

Has Richard not sworn the oath that he will do nothing to threaten the life of Henry or hurt his reign or his royal dignity, an oath designed to win support from those who thought he might have an interest in Henry's premature death? My two sons,

Ned and Edmund, young as they are, have sworn a similar oath. The House of York will not be seen as a threat to the stability of the realm, although there are those supporters of Lancaster who will never accept what has been done. Already there are signs of discontent and destruction of property of Yorkist friends and allies in the north.

Marguerite will never obey the command to return to London, bringing her son with her into certain imprisonment. Her son will always be Prince of Wales in her eyes. She remains in the north, under the safeguarding of our Scottish enemies.

I have pity for her. If I were in her gilded shoes I would do the same.

I will continue to put on a brave face, but sometimes, in the dark hours of morning when thoughts always dive into dread, I foresee hostility and blood.

I pray that we can keep our family safe.

Do visit with us, Katherine. You'll hear more truth from me than from our sister Anne. I expect that you will say that you must remain to protect your lands from the northern hordes. Perhaps you are right.

Your affectionate sister,
Cecily

Richard, youngest son of the Duke of York, to Cecily, Duchess of York
Written from Baynard's Castle

To my Lady Mother,

Does this mean that one day I will be King of England? George says not, that he will be King before me.

I think I would make a better King than George. He does not know how to behave to people with courtesy. He struck out at his groom because he said it was the groom's fault that George's horse fell lame. It was George's fault for riding him too hard. George will never admit that he is in the wrong.

I do not think that it is a good trait in a King.

Will I be King?

Your obedient son,

Diccon

Cecily, Duchess of York, to her youngest son Richard
Written from Baynard's Castle

To my most well-beloved son,

I found your note tucked into my missal. You should have asked me after Mass. Perhaps I know why you did not. Some things are best kept silent in your own heart.

You are the youngest of all my sons and much loved. But no, you will not be King, and neither will George.

Your father will be followed by your eldest brother Ned. When he marries and has his own sons, they will become King after him. That does not mean that you are not valuable in our family. Your brother, when he is King of England, will look to you for loyalty and support in the coming years. You will be well rewarded for that loyalty.

Enjoy your childhood before such onerous duties fall on your shoulders.

Your tutor tells me that you can read and write almost as well as he.

Your affectionate mother,

Cecily, Duchess of York

Cecily, Duchess of York, to her son George
Written from Baynard's Castle

To make all plain, you will never be King of England, my son. You will be a loyal support and counsellor to your brother Ned. It is important that you realise that the crown will never come to you. If Ned should die, God forbid, then Edmund will step into his shoes as the heir after your father.

I forbid you to tease Diccon.

You will treat your horses with respect. You will never see your father ride his horse until it is lame. Also your groom deserves your civility. Our servants are part of our household and we have a duty to them in courtesy.

You will kneel beside me at Mass tomorrow and ask the Blessed Virgin Mary's forgiveness for your selfishness.

I believe the best in you as a son of the House of York.

Your affectionate mother,

Cecily

Duchess Cecily experiences fears and hopes for the future at Baynard's Castle, November 1460

The wall-walk at Baynard's Castle was a chilly place to be on a November morning, but it was where I discovered Richard who was leaning on the coping and looking along the river towards the Palace of Westminster. The light was slow to brighten, a sharp warning of the coming winter. All was quiet, but I could imagine the teeming life beginning to stir along the Thames. The boatmen who ferried travellers from one side of the river to the other were already plying their trade. As always the rank aroma of mud and refuse assailed us; we were too used to it to flinch or even comment.

'Well?' I asked. I leaned beside him. It reminded me of our days in Rouen, that precious moment of intimacy before he rode off to a campaign which would keep him from home for months at a time.

'I could not sleep.'

'I know. It was like sharing a bed with a hurricane. Most of the bed covers slid to the floor. I am here because I was cold.' I stood on my toes to run the fingers of one hand through his tousled hair. My other hand clutched my fur-lined cloak to my throat.

'Look at it,' he said with a lift of his chin.

'London. This is not new to us.' I smiled. 'What is it that disturbs you?'

'The enormity of what we have done. What can be ours. What will be Ned's inheritance. Sometimes it takes my breath.'

'When you are not using it to harry royal counsellors!'

'Sometimes it is hard to be conciliatory.'

He was in contemplative mood, something uncommon in Richard who was a man of action rather than deep thought. Today there was a groove between his brows.

'I think you will need to save your breath for the battles ahead,' I suggested.

'But not today.' The groove smoothed out a little. 'Henry is content, Marguerite is in Scotland, and the Lancastrians lie low.'

I would not think of the Wheel of Fortune as I tucked my hand within his arm, and yet I must, for in the midst of all our rejoicing there was a malignant worm inserting its way into my heart.

'What are you thinking?' he asked, turning to look at me, as if he could read the direction of my mind.

'That it is cold, and you should be wearing a hood.'

'Tell me true, fair Cecily!'

And so I did. 'The Wheel of Fortune,' I said. 'I came across it again yesterday, inscribed into one of my books, rescued and brought here from Ludlow. I know it well, but now it seems horribly pertinent.'

Smiling, he tucked my hair within my hood with calloused fingers.

'The Wheel of Fortune always tells the same tale, Cis. The King sits in glory, but as the Wheel turns, he slides, losing crown and sceptre and royal robes until his ermine is quite vanished and he crawls in the earth at the base of the Wheel. It is assuredly a lesson in the fragility of earthly power. It is true that with the turn of the Wheel, the King can climb back to his allotted place. Is that what worries you?'

'One up, one down,' I tried to explain, the raw inevitability of the Wheel's movement holding me in thrall. 'One moment in heaven, the next in hell. Fate is all chance. What will lie in store for us, Richard?'

'It is in God's hands. At this moment it is all good.'

I looked away towards Westminster where Henry continued his earthly existence behind a locked door. One day I might be Queen of England.

'Anne says I am proud,' I said.

'You are. You have much to be proud about.'

'But am I the ambitious harpy of the *English Chronicle*'s writing?' I glanced up at him. 'Am I?'

'I'll not say!'

'How fortunate! And your plans for today?'

His mood had softened. He planted a kiss on my temple.

'Come, Queen Cecily, with all your pride. The day is ours. We will hear Mass and then we will break our fast. Then we will talk, of hopes and fears and family, like any married couple of advancing years.'

Keeping my arm pinioned, he laced his fingers through mine and we walked down to where our household was astir, the scent of wood-smoke promising warmth and welcome. Richard knew as well as I that until Marguerite could be brought to terms and forced to lay down her arms, nothing for us was certain.

Chapter Thirteen

The Wheel of Fortune Spins Awry

England's Chronicle, *December 1460*

Here's a development to chill our souls.

Did we not anticipate it?

Whilst our newly appointed Lord Protector, together with his Duchess and his august family engage in revels at Baynard's Castle, and King Henry lives quietly with the Bishop of London, what is Queen Marguerite doing?

She is planning an invasion.

It has come to our notice that a letter has been written in Prince Edward's name (now simply Duke of Lancaster, of course). Did he write it himself? He is seven years old. We would wager a gold hanap that this is his mother's hand.

The letter warns of foul deeds to come.

Will we be called upon to face bloodshed, mayhem and destruction in the streets of our fair City of London? Can our Lord Protector actually protect us?

Where will be our loyalty then? York or Lancaster?

Nothing like blood and destruction to concentrate one's allegiance.

Edward, Prince of Wales, addressing the Mayor and Aldermen and people of the fair City of London

You have been tricked.

The Duke of York is a false traitor who is spreading rumours that I and my Lady Mother intend to bring in strangers who will despoil, rob, and utterly destroy your City in an attempt to rescue my father, the true King of the line of Lancaster.

The rumour is false.

I would never destroy London. It is of great value to me, as the rightful heir to the throne. I know that I can call on the loyalty of all our subjects to rise up and free my lord King Henry from York's vile grasp.

Richard, Duke of York, is a forsworn traitor and mortal enemy to my lord the King, to my Lady Mother the Queen, and to us, the rightful heir. York is promoting an untrue pretended claim to the crown of England.

Rise up and restore your rightful King! Reject the Act of Accord!

Edward, Prince of Wales

Anne, Dowager Duchess of Buckingham, to Cecily, Duchess of York

Written from Tonbridge Castle

I smell war in the air, even though this is assuredly not campaigning weather.

Can we not stop this? There has been too much blood spilt. I feel Humphrey hovering at my shoulder, advising compromise. Can you not draw on all your past friendship with Marguerite to negotiate for the good of the realm?

But even as I write this, I know that it is impossible. How can there be compromise now, unless Richard is willing to abandon all he has achieved? How can there be compromise unless Marguerite is willing to accept Richard as Lord Protector during the King's infirmity?

I am afraid. I expect that you are, too.

Anne

**Cecily, Duchess of York, to Anne,
Dowager Duchess of Buckingham**
Written from Baynard's Castle

Sister,

No. Of course I cannot urge Marguerite to negotiation. How can I dislodge the Queen from her crusade to restore her son? We have gone far beyond that. Marguerite refused my overtures at Ludford Bridge, when there had been no battle and Henry was still King. Now there is so much more to fight for. Marguerite will never come to any terms but her own. And, I have to say, neither will we.

Richard's dedication to the cause is as strong as Marguerite's. We have held what can only be described as a Council of War at Baynard's Castle. How different the mood and tone from the last time we called a gathering here. Then we rejoiced, with good food and wine and at least a fragile layer of unity. Now it was sour with the unpleasant tang of incipient violence.

A storm cloud hung low over all of us.

Marguerite may be in Scotland but we know that she has been in touch with the Lords Somerset and Devon, whilst her ally Northumberland and the northern magnates are raising an army, whether it is the campaigning season or not. All those you would expect. Northumberland and Dacre. Clifford and Neville, Latimer and Roos. Marguerite has ordered her troops to muster at Hull.

We are not without strategy, although I had no part in it, merely as an interested observer with much to gain and much to lose. Nor do I need to say anything in such gatherings. Richard knows my mind. Here is the plan of his campaign.

Our nephew Warwick will stay in London to guard the King. Ned will go to Wales and rouse support in his own lands in the Marches, and hold the Lancastrian Earl of Pembroke at bay. Richard will head north with Salisbury and Edmund. He plans to make Sandal Castle his base. Once there he will await the Queen and see what transpires.

I remain here at Baynard's Castle. With good fortune we will emerge with some sort of settlement. Although I would not speak this openly, I have little hope for it. All I can hope for is that Marguerite will retire when she sees the opposition ranged against her.

What point in offering prayers? The Blessed Virgin will be forced to choose between the rights of two beleaguered women.

Your sister,

Cecily

Duchess Cecily experiences a parting at Baynard's Castle, December 1460

I had done this before. I could do this again. It would tear my heart asunder but I would not allow Richard to sense the terror that chilled my blood and closed a tight hand around my throat.

He would know, because after so many years I could hide nothing from him, but he too would play the game.

I smoothed the velvet of his gambeson, letting my palms rest there, flat to the thick pile so that I could sense his every breath, and the metal strips below that would ward off any casual sword blow.

'Do not go into battle without breaking your fast first. Do not neglect to wear every piece of armour laid out for you by your squire. Do not, under any circumstances, remove your helm on the battlefield. Try not to take any unnecessary risks. Keep an eye on Edmund. Pray to the Blessed Virgin before battle. When there is even a whiff of a battle, tell me so that I do not have to find out by rumour.'

After years of campaigning, I knew my instructions and warnings by heart.

Richard was a master at farewells, reining in all emotion. He placed his gauntleted hands over mine.

'I promise all of those things. Do not wear yourself away with worry. Do not look for a courier with the sunrise of every day. I will be too busy. Make Christmas a joyful time for Meg and the boys. Have faith in me. Edward will be safe in the west and Warwick will keep you informed.'

There. It was done. As much as it was necessary to say. Except...

'How many times do we have to part?' I studied his face, the soft tolerance in his expression. He knew well what it was like for a woman at home.

'We've done it before. We can withstand this.'

'Every day at dusk I swear I will stand on the wall-walk here and think of you,' I said.

And I would do it.

'And I of you, on the battlements at Sandal.'

I knew that he would forget.

'My heart is sore, Richard, and you have not yet left.'

'There is no need. I will return to heal your heart.'

'It gets no easier with the years.'

'But we have experience and knowledge to weather any storm. What we have once done can be repeated. I will go on campaign and return to the abundance of your welcome.' The twist of his lips was wry. 'You mean more to me than all the jewels in King Henry's crown.'

His words were flattering, and yet I knew that he coveted that crown more than anything else in life.

'May God smile on you,' was all I could say.

'As He keeps you safe in His arms.'

Don't go, was what my heart wished to say. *Don't leave me.* But I could not. I must not.

Richard kissed my hands, and then my lips in a final acknowledgement.

I watched them ride out, York and Rutland, faces turned to the north. Ned had already marched west. There would be little rejoicing over the Birth of the Christ Child or the coming of the New Year with our families so distant.

Blessed Virgin, Holy Mother, preserve them from harm.

Richard, Duke of York, to Cecily, Duchess of York
Written from Sandal Castle, Yorkshire, on the ninth day of December 1460

My most well-beloved Cecily,

We are settled in Sandal Castle, and expect a lengthy stay.

Despite all my assurances before I left you, I think we will not come out of this clash of wills without a battle. I wish our path was smooth and easy to follow. It is not. Your one consolation must be that Sandal is a superbly defensive site which is to my advantage. Marguerite has challenged me to settle the matter by force of arms. She is marching south with an army to take London and rescue the King from his enemies. If I stand in her way, she will fight. She has also finally persuaded the Scottish Queen Regent to aid her.

How big a force does she have?

Ten thousand men, so they say. Most of them a rabble more intent on plunder and destruction than settling the right to the throne, but it is still a dangerous army. I cannot match them in number, but I trust I can in discipline and loyalty, and hopefully guile.

I am hopeful that Warwick can make use of his persuasive tongue, offering a vile image of the savage northern hordes descending on London. The City won't like it, and if persuaded they will refuse the loan Marguerite has demanded from them. If Warwick can offer a blood-soaked picture of the ungovernable Scots running amok through the streets, the City will offer the loan to us fast enough. Warwick can also make the most of our control of the royal arsenal in the Tower. Marguerite's troops might decide to be less brave when staring down the mouths of a dozen primed guns.

You will be in no danger in Baynard's Castle, my dear love.

But first Marguerite must face me in the north.

Some bad news, but not entirely unexpected. Her forces have laid waste the lands of our tenants hereabouts, and those of your brother Salisbury. She has told her forces that as they march south they can plunder all the English towns in their path in lieu of wages.

Before you ask, I will keep a fatherly eye on Edmund, whereas Ned is quite capable of controlling his own campaign in the west, supported by some experienced captains. I told George and Diccon that their task while I am at Sandal is to keep you and their sister safe. I think they were not convinced but you will find ways to occupy them.

My love for you remains as strong as it was when we were first man and wife, when we were both little more than children. I value you even more now as a helpmeet and counsellor.

I fear that you may be spending Christmas alone without me. When you celebrate, think of me in Sandal, watching over the crenellations for Marguerite's armies to loom out of a winter mist with frost on the ground. I know that we will be in your prayers.

One day we will be reunited, and we can put all this behind us. It will be a glorious unity.

Richard

Chapter Fourteen

The Wheel of Fortune Becomes Fickle Indeed

Cecily, Duchess of York, to Richard, Duke of York
Written from Baynard's Castle, Christmas 1460

To my beloved Richard,

By the time this reaches you, depending on the state of the roads and my courier's enthusiasm despite my generosity with gold coin, it may well be into the New Year. We have celebrated with everything you love best, even though our gathering is small. Even though it has not been the happiest of times; I cannot put out of my mind that Marguerite is breathing fire in the north.

God be with you and keep you in His abundant care. May He bring you safe home to me. If you were ever in any doubt, know that I believe in your cause. In our cause, for it is as much mine as it is yours. I pray constantly for your return, fancifully with the wreath of victory on your brow, like one of the champions of ancient Rome.

I feel my isolation, but this is a fine place of refuge for me. I will always love Fotheringhay best of all, but Baynard's Castle shelters me with its strength, wraps me around with its beauty. The gardens and terraces – too cold to enjoy at present – are protected by high walls. It has been a home, but also a fortress. I will think of you in spartan Sandal and wish you were here for the festivities and the feasting. Eating rich dishes of roast venison and fricassee of game birds – which you enjoy to excess – all but choked me as I imagined your presence at the meal. The scents of herbs and spices, and of the evergreen boughs that decorated the chambers, still pervade the place.

At my invitation, Warwick has made his base here, which keeps me in touch with the mood in London. I show myself frequently in the streets around Westminster, and by barge along the Thames, to reassure those who ask that you have their safety at heart. They fear the Queen's northern hordes. I do not dissuade them in their fear. Warwick merely stokes the flames.

Don't forget to dispense our traditional Christmas coin amongst our household at Sandal. Arrange a gift for Edmund, from both of us. I expect that he needs a new gambeson. He has grown much in the past year.

There is a great loss within me, until we can be reunited, but I have smiled with fierce tenacity throughout the enforced merriment. My cheeks ache with the effort. Margaret suspects my anxieties, and has tried to direct my mind with a gift of the *Lais of Marie de France*, touchingly romantic poems with their themes of love and courtliness amongst knights and aristocratic ladies. They are pretty but do not anchor my mind. The boys, however, are easily distracted. Warwick took them to Westminster for a few days. I do not wish to know what they got up to but they are now back under my discipline.

Meanwhile King Henry keeps the festivities quietly. I visited him. He spends his time in prayer and conversation with his priest. He knew me, and called me by name, but he had little concern for events to the north. I took him a basket of sugared plums but he handed them to his body servant. He is quite gaunt and has no interest in any matter other than that to be found within the covers of his books.

I hold fast to the memories of our days in Rouen, when you were absent on campaign for weeks and months, but still returned unharmed. How young we were, how full of optimism for the future.

I live for news of you.

I fear the Wheel of Fortune's malicious spinning.

Your devoted wife,

Cecily

England's Chronicle, *the second day of January 1461*

Hush! Listen!

We hear the first news, soft as a breath, that there has been a battle in the north on the thirtieth day of December. Queen Marguerite's forces led by the Duke of Somerset have met with those of the Duke of York, our Lord Protector, at Wakefield.

News is slow to trickle through.

We will report when we know more. It seems that it was no minor skirmish.

Who has won? York or Lancaster?

For those of you who have a concern, not having seen him for a number of days, King Henry is still safe and well in London under the care of the Earl of Warwick. He was seen at Mass this morning in St Stephen's Chapel and spoke cheerfully to the courtiers present.

Cecily, Duchess of York, to Richard Neville, Earl of Warwick
Written from Baynard's Castle to the Palace of Westminster

I have heard there has been a battle but have no reliable facts. It seems that Richard rode out, leaving the security of Sandal Castle.

Do you know more? It may come to you before it reaches me. Please reply by return.

Is Ned safe in the west? I have heard nothing from that quarter.

I am wrung with anxiety.

Your aunt,

Cecily

Richard Neville, Earl of Warwick, to Cecily, Duchess of York
Written from the Palace of Westminster, by return of courier

I know no more than you, Aunt. A battle, certainly, but the outcome is still in doubt. I will return to Baynard's Castle from Westminster tonight. We can worry together, although I have no sense of bad news. We must trust in York's skills on the battlefield.

I have heard nothing but good out of the west. Your son March has all in hand to stop the Lancastrians from pushing east towards London.

Keep the faith, as do we all.

Warwick

Duchess Cecily's intercession to the Blessed Virgin Mary

Hail Mary, full of Grace, Our Lord is with thee.

Keep my husband Richard, Duke of York, safe in your blessed arms.

And Edmund, my son, I lift him before you.

My tears fall at your feet.

I cannot imagine the true horror of a battlefield.

May they return to me without harm.

Have pity on my fears.

Amen

England's Chronicle, *first week of January 1461*

Blood and death!

As we predicted, there has been a major conflict at Wakefield.

On the thirtieth day of December the Duke of York, together with his son the Earl of Rutland, and his brother by law the Earl of Salisbury, led the Yorkist army from the shelter of Sandal Castle to engage with the Queen's army, which proved to be vastly superior in numbers. The result was a foregone conclusion. We are told that York, Rutland and Salisbury are all dead, as well as Salisbury's son, Sir Thomas Neville.

The flower of the Yorkist cause is dead.

Thus the Queen has had her revenge in devastating fashion.

She is marching south, with her son, to take possession of King and capital. The tales of her northern troops, raping and pillaging as they go, are ones of horror. Will we soon suffer the rape of London?

Where is our Lord Protector now, in this hour of our need?

Dead in the north.

We are told that it was his own mistake, his own lack of judgement, that brought him to death on the battlefield. Should we be surprised? Have we not seen it for ourselves, that when the claws of ambition gripped, the Duke of York was lured into extreme actions.

We expect that the Duchess of York will be not so proud this morning. Will she weep real tears? Some say that she is incapable of it.

Our advice! Lock your doors and hide your valuables. Take your weapons from your closets. The Queen is coming and her troops are out of control.

Anne, Dowager Duchess of Buckingham, to Cecily, Duchess of York

Written from Tonbridge Castle

To my dear sister,

I know you will be inconsolable if what I hear is true. Shall I come to you?

You allowed me to weep on your shoulder when Humphrey died. I can offer the same. And then we can both grieve for our brother and our nephew.

Humphrey and I did not share the deep love that was abiding between you and Richard, but I know what it is to lose a son to the ravages of war.

How can our family have been so devastated?

Your wretched sister,

Anne

Cecily, Duchess of York, to Anne,
Dowager Duchess of Buckingham

Written from Baynard's Castle

No. Don't come.

I cannot bear to be around people. Every conversation clamours in my mind like a cracked bell.

I told Richard to have a new gambeson made for Edmund. Now he will never wear it. My last letter to Richard was full of such inconsequential chatter. His favourite dishes and King Henry's foolishness. Such a terrible waste.

When he stood on that desperate battlefield, did he know that I loved him?

I still don't know what happened, to bring him to his death. And Edmund. Our brother Salisbury. I cannot write of it. Every sense is overwhelmed by inconsolable grief.

Leave me alone, I beg of you.

But I love you no less.

Cecily

Richard Neville, Earl of Warwick,
to Cecily, Duchess of York

Written from the Palace of Westminster

My most revered aunt,

Better to come from my pen than from callous rumour or the trouble-stirring *England's Chronicle*. I'll not spare you but tell you the truth you desire.

It was carnage, both on the field at Wakefield and in the aftermath. All our fears are realised. York and Rutland are both dead. My father Salisbury is dead. My brother Thomas is dead too.

How easy it is to write the names. How difficult it is to believe it. I mourn with you.

The Yorkist cause at Wakefield has been obliterated and Marguerite marches south to make her revenge complete by taking control of London.

I cannot tell you why York should have left the secure walls of Sandal to face so vast an enemy. One day we will know.

What will you do?

You might consider flight, but my advice is to stay at Baynard's Castle and keep your defences strong. I will use my retainers and my allies to keep Marguerite at bay. I think the citizens of London will not be willing to open the gates to her when they see – and hear – the quality of her army baying outside their walls.

I can say nothing to give you ease in your distress. All I can say is that York will not have died in vain, nor my father. March and I will pursue your husband's desire to have a Yorkist claimant on the throne of England.

I swear it on my honour.

Richard Neville, Earl of Warwick

Cecily, Duchess of York, to Edward, Earl of March, now Duke of York
Written from Baynard's Castle to Shrewsbury

To my well-beloved son,

I cannot yet talk or write of it. What you must now realise is that you are my hope, and England's hope, for the future. As your father's heir, England needs you to restore firm and impartial government. To restore peace. We have torn each other apart for too long. The Queen has no thought of healing, merely of victory and the restoration of her son as Prince of Wales and heir to his father.

That must not be. You, my dear son, are the heir to the power that your father won in the Act of Accord.

I trust this letter finds you on your way back to London. We need you here to restore faith in the citizens. All is panic. The Queen is expected to arrive and allow her troops to overrun the City. Warwick is still here but we need you too to stand as figurehead of the House of York.

I am told that the Lancastrian Earl of Pembroke and his Welsh forces may be a threat to your freedom of movement.

Travel with care. I cannot lose you as well as Edmund.

Your devoted mother,

Cecily

Recorded by the private hand of Cecily, Duchess of York

I have held my emotions together to do what must be done.

Now I make a record, a simple note-making of what occurred at Wakefield and in the aftermath, for those in the future who need to know. For me it is a place that will for ever drip with blood and merciless cruelty. I will never go to Sandal Castle again.

Why do I not give this heavy task to my clerk?

Because to write it myself will make it real to me in cold hard words. My family. The heart of my existence. Destroyed on one field of battle.

Richard Plantagenet, Duke of York, my husband, cut down in the melee of the battlefield, his dead body mutilated, executed.

Edmund, Earl of Rutland, my son, seventeen years, caught in

flight after the battle, cut down and executed on Wakefield Bridge by Lord Clifford to avenge his own father's death at St Albans.

Sir Thomas Neville, son of the Earl of Salisbury and my nephew, killed on the battlefield.

Richard Neville, Earl of Salisbury, my brother, captured after the battle and executed at Pontefract Castle.

Such loss for me cannot be quantified. And the vicious revenge for past deeds. I have lost husband, son, brother, nephew. All on one day.

Will I weep? Of course I will weep. It cannot be a simple record, after all. I weep over it, however much I promised I would not. Tears blur my writing. How can I tolerate such pain and grief? Richard said that we would weather any storm. Here is a vicious tempest that I will never weather. He will not return to me. He will not come back to the abundance of my welcome. My heart is broken. It will never be healed.

**Cecily, Dowager Duchess of York, to
Katherine, Dowager Duchess of Norfolk**
Written from Baynard's Castle

To my sister,

My mind is full of one question. I cannot get past it. It meets me when waking, it slides into my restless sleep and keeps me ill company during the dark hours. A question to which there will never be an answer, for who would know but Richard and those of our family who died with him? What persuaded him to march out from his safe vantage point in Sandal Castle when he knew the Queen's forces were far greater than his? I know what is being said of him, and none of it honourable.

The *English Chronicle* accuses him of being taunted for his cowardice in refusing to fight. It is said that he thought it dishonour to remain behind the walls in Sandal Castle for dread of a scolding woman, whose only weapons were her tongue and her nails. They say a Lancastrian herald provoked him into taking dangerous offensive, fearful of being tamely defeated by a woman.

Blessed Virgin! I cannot believe it. That is not the Richard I know.

The Richard that I knew.

The only reason to which I can give any credence is that he was incautious, engaging with the Queen's forces before he had rallied his own strength, but I will deny to my final hour that he was a coward.

Outrageous ambition could lead him to unexpected aggression, an accusation that I must in all honesty accept, but surely never on a battlefield when the lives of his men were in his hand. Had he indeed ventured from the safety of Sandal's walls to rescue Edmund who was out with a foraging party? Another empty suggestion that has crossed my path. All I would say – would they have sent out a foraging party if the arrival of the Queen's army was imminent?

I can find no answers, and now Richard will never give them to me.

They say that two thousand of our soldiers died with Richard on that dread field.

Marguerite was not even there. She did not leave Scotland until the battle was over. She wore a robe of black and silver lent to her by the Scottish Queen and rode a silver jennet. How is it that I can relate such unimportant facts, yet be ignorant of what it was that took Richard to his death?

How the Wheel of Fortune turns, and with such cruelty.

You will regret our brother Salisbury's death. He was closer to you since as children you were of an age and raised together. There were fifteen years between us. He was adult and far from home when I was a child in the north. And yet still I remember his kindness.

My thoughts return again and again to Richard. How can I live without him? How can I live, never hearing his voice?

Cecily

**Katherine, Dowager Duchess of Norfolk,
to Cecily, Dowager Duchess of York**

Written from Epworth

To my dear Cecily,

I can do nothing to assuage your grief. You must survive it as best you can. I tell you from what I know that it will not destroy you. Grief such as this is an emotion to be borne and gloried in, not to be gulped down as if it is poison. Use it to honour Richard Plantagenet's life.

If you want my advice, then this is it:

Banish your grief.

Attack those who would defile York's name.

Support your living sons.

You can do this so well.

Destroy the rumours. Demolish the stories that make Richard a coward, and his leaving the safety of Sandal nothing more than a rash impulse to gain fame on the battlefield. Their father will live in the memory of your children, particularly the young ones. Make his name great. Ned will remember him, but the young boys need an image to carry into their manhood. Make for them what men will call a myth, if you will. But you will know in your heart that it is the truth.

This is what you can do for his memorial. York will live in men's memories as the King who never was. He rode at the head of his troops, away from the staunch walls of Sandal, to right a great wrong.

He is a heroic figure, Cecily. Courage and bravery are his.

My thoughts are with you in your campaign. For so it is a battle for you to engage in. Marguerite will hamper you at every step.

Your sister in adversity,

Katherine

Duchess Cecily experiences an overwhelming grief at Baynard's Castle, January 1461

A courier arrived and was shown into the room where I sat with my women, Katherine's words heavy in my mind, the tiniest flicker of a candle-flame on the horizon of my grief. I had a campaign to fight, as vicious as that faced by Richard against the Lancastrians. I would fight it and fight it well.

The courier approached, bowed. He held out a letter, his face raw with effort. I knew him. He was one of Richard's own men.

The chatter around me died away. The lute stilled when the courier fell to his knees, his head bowed in exhaustion and respect. With the barest gesture I waved my women to depart. This was my time. The letter, still in the courier's hand, lay between us.

'Who wrote it?' I asked.

I took the letter. How astonishingly unmarred it was by time and travel, as if it had been written yesterday. It all but burned my fingertips.

'My lord the Duke. On the day before the battle, my lady.'

'So you escaped, when so many brave men perished.'

His face flushed as if I had struck him. 'It was not my choice, my lady. The Duke wished this to be delivered to you immediately, if it seemed that the battle was lost. I rode south when he gave me the order.'

'I would not impugn your courage, sir. You have my thanks.' I raised him with my own hand to his arm. It was as if I watched my actions from a great distance. 'There is ale. Drink and sit.'

I walked to the window where the light fell on the superscription:

To Cecily, Duchess of York at Baynard's Castle
Written from Sandal Castle

The packet was bulky with something hard enclosed in the centre. Breaking the seal, unfolding it, I caught the brown petals in the palm of my left hand as I lifted the single sheet to read. I had to catch my breath.

*

To my well-beloved Cecily,

If this finds its way to your hand, then affairs have gone badly for us in the north. We face a vast force. Who knows what the outcome will be since neither side is prepared to compromise. If I see a chance of success, I will lead my troops out of the fortress here at Sandal and join in battle with the Queen's forces. I believe in the strength and dedication of our mighty cause.

I swear that I will take no untoward risk.

What of me, when you read this?

Probably the Queen has me imprisoned in one of my own castles, to make an example of me, while she takes Henry back into her authority and rules for her son's future as King of England. I expect that Edmund is here with me. I think she will demand a high ransom for my freedom, as well as my oath that I will reject the Accord.

If I am a prisoner I will have no choice but to give my consent.

All I can hope is that I will be reunited with you and that we will live to wait for better times for the House of York.

The token of my regard that I have enclosed has certainly seen better days. It was flowering bravely in a sheltered corner of the pleasance here at Sandal. Any frost would have killed it so I thought I would send it on to you, with my everlasting love, as a New Year's gift.

I arranged the gambeson for Edmund. He looks well in it. Whatever happens on the battlefield, he will be a credit to us. There is nothing wrong with his courage.

I send you my thoughts at this difficult time, and my love, knowing that I can leave all my affairs in your more than capable hands. I know that Warwick is still in London if unrest breaks out, and that Ned is based at Shrewsbury in the west.

I pray for a happy reunion, for all of us. If I should take victory in the coming battle, I will be with you before the end of the month.

If aught should happen to me, our son Edward will pick up my mantle and my sword to carry on the battle. But for you, my dearest Cecily, for you will be the hardest task. You are the keeper of the flame. The rock and foundation of the House of York. So much for your slight shoulders but no more than you can bear.

I do not believe that it will come to this. I will return and we will fight the good fight together.

Keep me for ever in your thoughts, as I keep you in mine.

Richard

★

Slowly I refolded the single sheet. Strangely I felt no emotion at all. It was as if a hand had tightened around my heart. The words written by my dead love, who had hoped for release from imprisonment even if he lost the battle. There never was such a hope. Marguerite, for the sake of her son's inheritance, would never have let him live.

I regarded the sad remains of the white rose, withered and dry in the palm of my hand. Once white, the emblem of York. I sent the courier away. There was no one to whom I had any wish to send reply.

You are the keeper of the flame.

I would accept it. I would tend it and carry it aloft until the day of my own death.

Chapter Fifteen

The Wheel of Fortune Spins Madly

Recorded by the private hand of Cecily,
Dowager Duchess of York, January 1461

They lie to me, those who tell me that time will bring relief. They lie to me who tell me that time will ease my pain. They lie who say that with every day I will feel a softening of the great loss in my heart. I miss him in the rise of the sun, in the soft rain, in the harsh frosts. I miss him in the scent of burning apple-wood, the music of the shawm and lute and timbrel. I want him, and cannot have him.

I am told that Richard is buried at the Priory of St John the Evangelist at Pontefract with Edmund and my Neville family. Buried by those who killed him. I should rejoice that honest burial was not denied them, although I know nothing of the memorial. Perhaps there is none. Perhaps it was wiser to allow discretion, to prevent their graves being desecrated by the supporters of Lancaster.

I cannot make my pilgrimage there, as my heart wishes. Marguerite hovers, a malicious shadow growing ever closer. One day, I swear it, I will make a memorial to last for all time and tell the history of the brave life of Richard Plantagenet, Duke of York. Am I not keeper of the flame? At present it is a pale thing that barely flickers into life.

Where will this memorial be?

At our beloved Fotheringhay, of course.

It will not be in Pontefract!

I am awash with restlessness, with indecision. It seems to me that this is no longer my story. The pages on which my life would have been written have been torn from the ledger. It is for my sons now to make their imprint on life and on this country.

I will never be Queen, as was my right.

I find no inner will to be involved. All is in the hands now of my nephew Warwick. And Ned, if he returns to me. Perhaps my future is as a widow in a nunnery, a world of prayer and contemplation. Or to live in this world but as a vowess, like a nun in isolation within my own household.

I wish that I could carry another child for Richard. Another son. We lost so many, who were conceived but could not withstand the trials of birth.

I remember when our last child was born. Ursula, who was born, lived and died at Fotheringhay within a twelve-month.

I must not think of such sadness.

Anne, Dowager Duchess of Buckingham, to Katherine, Dowager Duchess of Norfolk
Written from the Palace of Westminster

Sister!

Order up your horses and escort and come to London!

Why are you not already here? I can see no good reason.

Your argument holds no more water than a leaking bucket. If the Queen's troops are allowed freedom to attack your estates, what good can you do, sitting on them like an immobile toad in a pond? Give your orders to your Steward and come to London. Besides, if the Queen issues any commands that some properties must be safeguarded from attack, it will assuredly be the castles and lands of Lord John Beaumont. She cannot question his loyalty.

We have far greater need of you here.

Cecily refuses to reply to my letters, or to see me. Her household at Baynard's Castle is well trained. They tell me that she is unwell and receiving no visitors. She was always so strong-willed and has now shut herself away, except for occasionally gleaning news from Warwick. He is no help, but then his concentration is firmly on the advancing Lancastrian army.

Cecily must drag herself out of this despond. Things are critical and the House of York's future is not assured. Will she sit in Baynard's Castle and wait until the Queen's army is camped on her doorstep?

Do you suppose that she knows about the ultimate fate of Richard and Edmund? And our brother and nephew? I can hardly stand at the gate and shout my question over the walls. Nor can I deliver the terrible news in the same manner. Do come, Kat. You can stay with me at Westminster and we can plan an assault to bring her back to life.

Anne

Katherine, Dowager Duchess of Norfolk, to Anne, Dowager Duchess of Buckingham

Written from Epworth

Sister,

I admire your confidence in my abilities, but I am not coming to London.

Do you suppose the Queen's rabble can distinguish between a Lancastrian and a Yorkist estate? I doubt they'll respond to the fact that John Beaumont was on their side. I'll stay here to supervise the manning of our defences. I may be old, within a breath of my sixty-second year, but I am not dead yet.

Write again to Cecily. Tell her that she is being selfish, that her Neville and Beaufort ancestors will never forgive her if she declines into melancholy. Tell her that Richard will haunt her if she abandons their cause.

If all else fails, summon up her daughters to come to stay at Baynard's Castle. After she has discussed the treachery of the despicable Exeter with Anne for more than a day, she will be glad to emerge again into the real world.

You did not ask, but I am well.

Being a widow suits me. I have now practised it three times.

I would be grateful if you would organise the following. My garrisons are short of a number of crossbows and pole-axes. Could you arrange for some to be sent north? I am also in need of the following, if the prices are good. I have written a list for you and I trust your Steward to drive a hard bargain with your tight-fisted London merchants.

Your hopeful sister,
Katherine

Household Necessities for Katherine, Dowager Duchess of Norfolk

Pepper	Cloves
Mace	Ginger
Cinnamon	Almonds
Rice	Saffron
Galingal	And two sugar loaves

Anne, Dowager Duchess of Buckingham, to Katherine, Dowager Duchess of Norfolk
Written from the Palace of Westminster

I have given the task of supplying armaments to our nephew Warwick, and your kitchen supplies to my cook. Do you not have a Steward who can deal with such trivia? My cook will do as well as he can with the cost, but do not expect it all to come cheap.

I do not have time for such things. We are living with much anxiety here.

Your sister, still in despair,

Anne

Cecily, Dowager Duchess of York, to Anne, Dowager Duchess of Buckingham
Written from Baynard's Castle

Dear Anne,

Thank you for your kind but quite unnecessary letter. I think that makes six since the news at Wakefield, all of them asking what I am doing in my desolation.

I am doing nothing. I am clad in black. I am mourning. I see the world through a single dark prism of loss and grief. I do not need you hammering on my door.

I presume from your discreet but clumsy query that you are trying to discern if I am aware of the atrocity acted out on Richard's body.

Of course I am. I have been told all the macabre details by our nephew of Warwick, who thought it would be better that I knew. I suppose he was right, but I cannot bear the images it creates in my dreams.

To put it cruelly, my husband, son and brother were decapitated. Then their heads were exhibited on the spikes of Micklegate Bar in York, so that York could look down on York, so it is recorded. Even worse, a paper crown was set on my lord's head, a mockery of vast and disgusting proportions. Such humiliation, even of an enemy, is beyond my encompassing.

I have known and loved him for three decades. How can I turn my mind to the politics of the day?

I am as bitter as unripe sloes.

I know that the Queen was not there at York to give the command, but I suspect the orders came from her. I don't think I will ever be able to forgive Marguerite for this.

I think I will retire from public life and become a vowess, a nun in all but name.

Cecily

England's Chronicle, *February 1461*

Battle in the west!

A terrible prophecy!

Do we believe in such miraculous signs and wonders?

Three suns appearing together on the morn of battle, on the Feast of Candlemas, in some distant field named Mortimer's Cross in the Welsh Marches where the Lancastrian Earl of Pembroke's forces met with those of the Yorkist Earl of March.

Who has the victory?

Who will claim the three suns as God's grace? Pembroke or March? Lancaster or York?

Has another scion of the House of York been laid low on the battlefield in blood and gore? Is this to be another reaping of the sons of York?

We advise the citizens of London to change their allegiance from the white rose to the red, without delay.

Anne, Dowager Duchess of Buckingham, to Katherine, Dowager Duchess of Norfolk
Written from the Palace of Westminster

My dear Kat,

Your strategy was to no avail.

Cecily can see nothing beyond her loss of Richard and Edmund. How formidable is the army led against Ned by Pembroke and Owen Tudor? We know that the Welsh fight with great ferocity. If we have lost Ned on the battlefield, within six weeks of Richard and Edmund, I don't have much hope for our sister's taking up her role in this life. Or for her soundness of mind.

All I can do is leave her alone, and pray for her strength of will. She must not be allowed to retire.

Your resigned sister,

Anne

Duchess Cecily's intercession to the Blessed Virgin Mary

Hail Mary, full of Grace, Our Lord is with thee.

Blessed Virgin, who knows what it is to lose a son, in your mercy, grant me fortitude.

I cannot rest. I cling to my faith but it is so hard to accept another blow.

Keep my son Edward from death. Preserve him from all harm. Send him home to me to take up his father's royal mantle.

Stop him from launching a foolish attack against an army of vast numbers. A holy vision of yourself on the battlefield might do it.

Give me the inner spirit, I beg of you, to drag myself out of the trough of despond.

Amen

Edward, Earl of March, to Cecily, Dowager Duchess of York

Written from Croft Castle, Herefordshire

To my Lady Mother,

How terrible a blow is the death of my father and brother at Wakefield? I know that you will be frozen in grief.

I have had my revenge, and in that you must rejoice.

At Mortimer's Cross, a short distance from this castle, I met the Welsh forces led by the Earl of Pembroke in the name of the Lancastrian Queen. It was a superb victory. Pembroke fled, which I regret for I hoped to bring him to justice, but his father Owen Tudor was taken prisoner and executed in Hereford. I had his head placed on the market cross for all to see.

I have been bloodied on the battlefield and blessed with victory. I am truly my father's son. Were we not granted a heavenly image of three suns in the sky on the morning of the battle? I made good use of it. The three remaining sons of York will, one day, be united to take control of this realm and end the bloodshed.

I am marching towards London where I will join up with Warwick to thwart Queen Marguerite and secure King Henry's person.

One day I will fulfil all that my father dreamed of. One day the crown will be mine. I will be King of England and the House of York will come into its own.

I need your support, my Lady Mother. I need your knowledge of men and allegiances, and your ability to reach out to the citizens of London. I will make my base at Baynard's Castle on my return, where we will plan for the future.

Your loving and obedient son,
Ned

Cecily, Dowager Duchess of York, to Anne, Duchess of Buckingham

Written from Baynard's Castle

My dear Anne,

Behold me in abject apology.

I have not been amenable to all your attempts to rouse me from my misery. My conscience troubles me, particularly when I returned the book you sent to me. An interesting subject, I see. The Life of Saint Catherine of Siena, a humble woman who worked for her family of weavers, and for God, to become a saint. You were never subtle, Anne. If you would consider sending it again, I will read it and try hard to learn the lessons of humility and service. Although I have no intention of taking up weaving.

Perhaps you could deliver it yourself and I can make my apologies in person. I find that I am in need of conversation.

My prayers to the Blessed Virgin are answered and I am overflowing with pride and gratitude. It fills me to the brim and more. So would Richard rejoice at this momentous victory of his son.

Is it wrong to experience such exhilaration, all because of the deaths of more men on the battlefield? All I can think is that Ned is safe and well and victorious. And Richard avenged. I fear there is a strong streak of retribution in me, for which I should be ashamed.

I think the three suns was indeed a sign from the Blessed Virgin. If not merely a trick of light through mist.

I must repent of my lack of faith. My family will live again. It is Ned who will rule on Henry's death.

As long as we can defend ourselves against the Queen.

I know it and must put my trust in Ned and in Warwick.

I will continue to wear sombre garments in Richard's honour, but my days of mourning are over in support of my beloved son.

I understand that Warwick has marched north to take issue with the Queen's forces. I know that he will be successful. After Ned's victory, what can stop us now?

Cecily

England's Chronicle, *the seventeenth day of February 1461*

Dust off your red roses, citizens!

More disaster, if you are of a Yorkist disposition and have a white rose pinned to your cap. It might be politic to remove it and wear a red one for the coming days.

Our pens are indeed dipped in blood.

For those of our readers who thought that the Battle of Mortimer's Cross, only two weeks since, would draw the conflict to a close, with victory for York, their hopes must be dashed. The Queen's forces were closer than we thought, meeting with the Earl of Warwick at St Albans.

The results are still unclear, but we suspect a Yorkist reversal. Who rules England now?

We may see the value of dissociating ourselves from the ambitions of the Earls of March and Warwick. We advised the citizens of London to be prepared to hop from York to Lancaster speedily, if the news is bad for that ambitious family.

Richard Neville, Earl of Warwick, to
Cecily, Dowager Duchess of York

Written from St Albans

To my revered aunt,

Our cause has suffered badly at St Albans. No time to write more, only to say that my army is defeated and King Henry has fallen into the hands of the Queen and her son. In retrospect it was not good policy to take the King with us to give my army royal authority.

I have no choice but to leave the field and venture west to try to make contact with March near Oxford.

If the Queen takes control of London – and who is to stop her? – she will have no compassion for you or on your children. Henry was persuaded to issue a proclamation against plundering, but Marguerite's army ignored it. Her treatment of prisoners was bloody and without justice.

I cannot give you advice, unless you wish to flee to Ireland where your safety will be assured. It might be good policy in the circumstances.

Richard Neville, Earl of Warwick

**Anne, Dowager Duchess of Buckingham,
to Cecily, Dowager Duchess of York**
Written from the Palace of Westminster

Cis!

Do you have plans for your safety? The Queen will not look kindly on you. Henry's guards were executed on the spot at St Albans, as an example to all who cross her. She allowed her eight-year-old son to pronounce the sentence.

Do you flee?

Anne

**Cecily, Dowager Duchess of York, to Anne,
Dowager Duchess of Buckingham**
Written from Baynard's Castle

I remain here at Baynard's Castle. I do not flee.

Even if the Queen stands outside my gates, I will remain and I will face her. My children remain here with me. I trust in the strength of my walls and towers.

If you fear for me, use your past loyalties and beg for her mercy for me, in Humphrey's name. Although I doubt she will be receptive.

Cecily

England's Chronicle, *February 1461*

The Queen is outside our gates.

Panic ensues in our streets.

Do we open them and welcome our Lancastrian King and Queen once more?

What will Queen Marguerite ask of us? Will it be retribution for our support for York?

Lock your doors, brave citizens. Lock your doors!

Cecily, Dowager Duchess of York, to Anne, Dowager Duchess of Buckingham

Written from Baynard's Castle

What?

I cannot believe you would ask it of me. Do I understand you correctly? Will I lend my authority to a delegation of women, to carry Queen Marguerite's demands to the Mayor of London? Will I intercede between the Queen and the citizens of London, so that she might march in and take control with no opposition?

No and no and no.

Not even if it prevents bloodshed. Not that I trust any promises that the Queen might make. Ned is Richard's heir to the throne, not her young son. The Act of Accord makes that more than plain. The citizens must put themselves in order to protect their own rights.

I advise you to have nothing to do with it, Anne. All Marguerite needs is a handful of pawns who will do her bidding. Or puppets who will dance as she pulls the strings. I will not be one of them. In the present crisis I have other carp from my fishpond to fry.

I have two letters to write. One to give some advice that I know will not be welcome and will probably be rejected out of hand. The other is to call in a most royal debt, shaking my Plantagenet begging bowl.

Henry is no longer fit to rule England. I hear he was sitting, singing and laughing, under a tree on the battlefield, when he was snatched from Warwick at St Albans. Only a fool would work for his restoration.

Your defiant sister,
Cecily

England's Chronicle, *February 1461*

Exciting times! Desperate times!

The Queen devised a scheme to get herself and her forces through the gates of London without conflict. A delegation of three noble ladies agreed to carry terms from the Queen to the Mayor.

Who were they? Noble ladies indeed. Jacquetta, once the powerful Dowager Duchess of Bedford and now wife of Sir Richard Woodville. That notable heiress Elizabeth, Lady Scales. And Anne, Dowager Duchess of Buckingham. All three with reputations for being strong proponents of the House of Lancaster.

It has to be noted that Duchess Cecily refused to be one of these noble petitioners. She is quoted as saying: 'I would spit at her feet first.'

The petition: *The Queen promises no harm will come to you and your City if you will profess your loyalty. In recognition of that loyalty, the Queen requests food and supplies due to her and her army.*

Requests? Demands more like.

The Mayor panicked. Assured the Queen of his loyalty. And when a skirmish between citizens and soldiers left some for dead at the City gates, he packed a number of carts with money and food to conciliate the royal anger. Which might have calmed the situation, but the citizens refused to let the carts pass through. Instead the worthy citizens took the keys of the City gates, locked them and divided what they found in the carts between themselves.

Upon which we were all left to tremble at the prospect of a long-drawn-out siege.

Ah, but the Queen went into retreat.

We would have expected the Queen to have more backbone. Not the King, but why would the Queen decide to retreat, taking King Henry and the young Prince with her?

What persuaded her?

Who persuaded her?

Perhaps she decided she had enough on her golden plate with Henry, without a full-scale siege. We hear that the royal party has retreated as far north as York. Do we heave a sigh of relief, or wish that they had taken up residence in London and dispatched our Yorkist usurpers about their business?

What now?

Where is the Earl of Warwick? Where is the Earl of March?

What colour roses do we wear for the next week?

Marguerite, Queen of England, to Cecily, Dowager Duchess of York

Written from York

Madam,

I received your courier to my pavilion outside the gates of London with some surprise. I read your letter. It was stark in its reading of the situation. I would, of course, have expected no less.

You ask for compassion. I have none.

You offer me advice. To this I must give some passing consideration.

It is difficult to feel compassion for a family that has inflicted so much damage on mine. I feel nothing but antipathy. I have been hurt too deeply. Yet because of past associations, and because I saw the political sense of it, I will take heed.

It goes against the grain but my counsellors agree with me and consider it unwise to engage in a siege in this cold and uncertain weather. The City of London is not welcoming, nor do I see much hope of a change. I know that you are in residence at Baynard's Castle, from where I have my suspicions that you are stirring revolt in the name of your son and the Earl of Warwick.

It is a bitter decision but we have retired north to regroup in the city of York. I swear it has better memories for me than it will for you. I have not given up my fight. My son is the rightful King when Henry comes to the end of his mortal struggle, and I will support him until my dying breath leaves my body.

You should be warned. If your two youngest sons ever fall into my hands, I will ensure they suffer the same fate as their brother Rutland after the battle of Wakefield. March and Warwick do not control this country. Thus you and your children remain in danger.

There is room for more heads on Micklegate Bar.

Marguerite, Queen of England

Cecily, Dowager Duchess of York, to
Philip, Duke of Burgundy
Written from Baynard's Castle, February 1461

Your grace,

When you read this, my gracious lord, you will be confronted by two small boys, probably almost dead on their feet from exhaustion and anxious about their future. They are my sons. They are the sons of Richard, Duke of York, brothers of Edward, Earl of March, who will, by right, be King of England in the fullness of time.

I have sent them to you because I know you for a man of solicitude towards us and our cause. Here in England any son of York will be in danger from the vengeance of Queen Marguerite. I dare not keep them with me after the despicable treatment of my husband and son, and my brother.

I had no time to request your kindness, or that of your Duchess, Isabella, who is my cousin and will not be without compassion. Thus I am presuming, by sending them without warning, that you will not turn your back on me.

All I can ask is that you will offer them sanctuary in Burgundy until times change and all is safe for their return.

Until my son March returns, I stand as figurehead of the House of York in London. I have a duty to do so. I can do this if I know my young sons are safe. I considered sending my daughter Margaret with them but she will stay with me. I think the Queen will never loose her vengeance on a young woman.

I beg on your charity, take my sons under your care until the Wheel of Fortune turns once more. Treat them gently for they have had much to suffer in their young lives, even though I suspect that you are reluctant to nail your flag openly to the Yorkist masthead.

It will relieve my mind of a burden that is almost too great for me to bear.

Cecily, Dowager Duchess of York

Cecily, Dowager Duchess of York, to Edward, Earl of March

Written from Baynard's Castle

I wait to greet you, in your father's name and mine.

I know what you will hope for when you march with Warwick into London. Allow the citizens their moment of welcome. It will be vociferous for they feel wantonly betrayed by King Henry, as they feel hostility towards the Queen for her selfish demands. There was a real fear in the streets when she stood outside our gates, threatening us with her unmanageable forces. It will be a good lesson for you to learn. It is vital that you have the support of London. If the City turns against you, you are in danger.

Will you take some of these words from your mother? And a warning. All can still so easily slide into disaster for you.

When your father marched into London from Hereford, he was too rough, too demanding. Too presumptuous of his power. You were there and you saw it. You tasted the sour response. Your father would be the first to admit that he handled it badly. He would be the first to admit that he rejected my advice to act in a spirit of compromise.

You need to plan carefully and thoroughly, my son, and with patience. Come to Baynard's Castle, wait here in isolation, and let others pave the way for you.

Do not, under any circumstances, march on Westminster to take what you consider to be yours, because to do so might push the Lords into reigniting their loyalty to King Henry, or his son the Prince of Wales.

You came of age at the Battle of Mortimer's Cross. Now you must become politically astute too, despite your lack of years, casting aside the restlessness that is akin to youth. Come to Baynard's Castle and we will work together to write the history of the House of York. Leave your troops camped outside the City walls in Clerkenwell Fields. It will make a good impression.

The time passes slowly until I see you again, after all the fear of recent weeks. I have sent George and Diccon to the safe hands of the Duke of Burgundy. You are my only son with feet on English soil. I was advised to flee with them but I will risk imprisonment and humiliation to proclaim the name of York in this capital in your absence.

I miss your father more than I can tell you. We will work together to see his dream realised. I expect you at Baynard's Castle within the week.

Your devoted mother,

Cecily, Dowager Duchess of York

England's Chronicle, *the twenty-sixth day of February 1461*

What a joyous return! White roses to the fore!

Here's a fact that no citizen of London will need telling. Were you not all out in the streets, cheering him on? Edward, Earl of March, now Edward, Duke of York, has marched into London with twenty thousand knights and thirty thousand foot soldiers behind him. At his side rides the Earl of Warwick.

You might cheer this resurrection of the House of York, but the question that should be on every man's lips is:

'What will this new Duke of York do with such a force?'

Do we not all recall his father, demanding more power than was his right? With the Queen and King Henry, far to the north, all is open to possibilities. If King Henry is not here to wear his crown, then others might take it from him and give it elsewhere, and not wait until his death.

They say our King Henry was discovered sitting witless beneath a tree during the Battle at St Albans. Does that sound like the action of a King when his soldiers are fighting for their lives and his future?

What is Duchess Cecily doing? We know she is in Baynard's Castle. Will she encourage her son to steal the crown? Or will she advise him to keep to the letter of the Act of Accord and await King Henry's death?

By the by, we note the absence of two of the younger members of Duchess Cecily's household. Her two young sons are enjoying the luxury of the Court of Duke Philip of Burgundy. How can we blame her for sending them to safety?

Why would she not go with them? The humiliation of being taken captive into the presence of the Queen would be enough to spur anyone into flight.

Chapter Sixteen

A New King Is Crowned

**Cecily, Dowager Duchess of York, to
Richard Neville, Earl of Warwick**
Written from Baynard's Castle, March 1461

Nephew,

I don't trust Ned's common sense to hold sway over his enthusiasms. He will listen to you, whereas he might consider his mother's words those of a weak woman. He should know better. He will soon learn.

Meanwhile, I turn to you.

Stop Ned from going straight to Westminster. It would be a mistake. You were there a year ago and saw the repercussions when York claimed the throne. Bring my son here to me.

Then we wait. And plot.

Cecily, Dowager Duchess of York

Cecily, Dowager Duchess of York, to
George Neville, Bishop of Exeter

Written from Baynard's Castle

To my clerical nephew,

I write in haste. Here is where you will come into your own in the service of your Neville family, and particularly your young cousin of York.

You have a way with words and enjoy the sound of your own voice. Some would say that you have a pomposity and a love of self-aggrandisement. I would agree. You have also shown acumen in dealing with legal matters. I require you to make use of your many and various skills.

Make a case for Ned to be acclaimed King. To be acclaimed now. Not when King Henry has passed from this life. By then Marguerite will be well entrenched with the Scots as her allies, promoting her young son in the role of heir, whatever the Act of Accord might say. I am convinced that it would be wrong to wait. It would leave England without sails or anchor.

If you need help from me, you know where I am based. I am sure that you can do it on your own, with due recourse to the law.

From your aunt,

Cecily, Dowager Duchess of York

George Neville, Bishop of Exeter, to
Cecily, Dowager Duchess of York

Written from the Palace of Westminster, on the first day of March 1461

To my esteemed and perspicacious Aunt.

I have fulfilled your wishes with great promptitude, and I have to say with even greater acumen. I enjoyed your praise of my skills and will overlook your animadversions on my character. What the outcome of my interventions will be, that is a matter for fate to decide. It is a hard task to push the Lords into action against their better judgement. Every last one of them is conscious solely of his own power and prestige. Will they, en masse, support Ned? I have no clear idea.

The uncertainty aside, I take exception, Aunt, to the idea that I should need direction. Nevilles have always been quick to adopt a pragmatic approach, when they were not waving swords and uttering battle-cries.

Shall I tell you the gist of my masterpiece of a speech?

Edward, Earl of March, now Duke of York, is here in London awaiting on your pleasure and your decision. It is yours to make, my lords. Is it not true that King Henry and Queen Marguerite violated the Act of Accord, an Act of your own making, by attacking the Duke of York and his family? Can this not be read as treason? How can any man here present not accept that Henry of Lancaster is too weak to hold the throne with any authority? Is it not time that we implemented the Act of Accord and recognised a new King?

There is such a man, a man well proven on the battlefield, at this moment awaiting your decision at Baynard's Castle. The royal blood in his veins runs thick and true. He will be a King to bring peace and stability back to this fair land.

No need to remind them that they were reluctant to make the Act of Accord in the first place. If they agree, I expect an apology from you over an excellent cup of Bordeaux. If Ned becomes King I look for further promotions. I would like to be confirmed as Chancellor of England.

When I asked the citizens of London who came to listen to my sermon if they believed Edward of York was their rightful King of England, they replied to a man:

'Yae! Yae! King Edward.'

They clapped their hands and the soldiers drummed on their armour.

I could not have done any better, whether they hold to their enthusiasms or not. Is a man not worthy of his hire? Do I not deserve a promotion? I have in mind a more important bishopric than Exeter.

Don't forget that I too mourn the death of a father and brother at the Battle of Wakefield. My loyalties to Plantagenet and Neville are unimpeachable.

If I fail it is not through want of trying.

George Neville, Exeter

Cecily, Dowager Duchess of York, to George Neville, Bishop of Exeter

Written from Baynard's Castle

Nephew,

My thanks, and my apologies if you think them necessary. I do not. I leave nothing to chance where this family is concerned.

Thank you for the warning that the Lords may not comply.

I put no blame on you.

They are capricious.

I will await the outcome. I was impressed with your speech.

Cecily, Dowager Duchess of York

Cecily to Richard, Duke of York: Memento Mori: A Reflection on Mortality

To my most beloved husband,

I received your last letter written from Sandal, many days after you had fallen on the battlefield at Wakefield. Now I will reply. Even though it is a letter that I will never send and I know will never be answered, I have a compulsion to write it and place it in the records of our family.

You would be so very proud of your eldest son. His achievements fulfil all our hopes and dreams. That you could not have lived to claim the honour for yourself is the one grief I hold fast in my heart, but here is our son taking hold of the culmination of all your work for himself.

Hail to the Rose of Rouen!

That is what they called when he rode through the streets of London to attend Mass at St Paul's. What a superb King our son Edward will make. Where had he learned such ability to draw every eye, wringing approval from every man in that crowd? His smile was a blessing, bright as the sun. Jewels glinted on his fingers. They loved his felt cap with the peacock feather that brushed his shoulders. And yet here was a warrior, come to save them from further warfare, for he had not put aside his sword.

A deputation came to Baynard's Castle of all the great and the good. They offered him the crown. Thus it is done. I could feel your presence beside me, a ripple of air, the cast of a shadow.

I must not weep for what is lost, but rejoice for what is to come.

Ned is still to be crowned and we fear another conflagration in the north. It is essential that Ned and Warwick win a great victory against the Lancastrians that will end their claim to the throne once and for all. Only then will Ned be able to take this crown with conviction. It seems I have a role here in this new England. It will please you to know that our son will listen to advice.

I feel a need to tell you. Sometimes I recall such inconsequential details which drive me to a renewal of grief. The soft hollow below your collarbone. The hard ridges on the palm of your right hand from a surfeit of sword-wielding. The scar along your ribs from the Rouen campaigning. You are as much part of my life as you ever were. I swear you always will be. And I swear that I will not leave you interred in Pontefract for ever. I will bring you home to Fotheringhay.

Your grief-stricken wife,

Cecily

Cecily, Dowager Duchess of York, to George Neville, Bishop of Exeter

Written from Baynard's Castle, on the third day of March 1461

Nephew,

All has worked out to perfection. Ned is here and so is the deputation from the City. It pleased me to sit and listen to their requests.

The cup of Bordeaux awaits when you have time in your busy day to claim it.

I have spoken with Ned. You will be confirmed as Lord Chancellor.

A more important bishopric? Throw your dice well, my clever nephew, and I think you might even look as high as Archbishop of York. Plantagenets are never slow to reward those who support them. Ned will be grateful to have his two Neville cousins at his side.

Cecily, Dowager Duchess of York

Richard Plantagenet to Cecily, Dowager Duchess of York
Written from Utrecht, March 1461

To my Lady Mother,

We are now well settled in Utrecht, with our books and tutors. We are told that we will not be taken to Bruges to the Court of Duke Philip of Burgundy because the fortune of our family is still in doubt. The servants say that the Duke has no desire to receive us if we are of no value to him. His merchants have good trade with England and he does not intend to put it in danger. If King Henry returns to power, the Duke will probably send us home by the first ship. It would not be in his interests to keep us. So the rumours say. We are surrounded by rumours.

We are well treated and in good health. Our tutor allows us little time to explore. George says that we should try and escape.

When can we return home?

Your obedient son,

Diccon

Cecily, Dowager Duchess of York, to Richard Plantagenet
Written from Baynard's Castle, March 1461

My importunate son,

You may not return. Do not even think of it. It is not suitable. Your brother has been accepted as King but he is not yet crowned, so I fear there will be more battles before all is settled. Only when Ned wears the crown will I bring you home.

Apply yourselves to your lessons until the Duke decides that you are worthy of an official reception. Even if the time hangs heavy on your hands, do not disobey your governor. He knows what is good for you. I do not wish to hear that you have been disobedient.

George has not yet written to me. Tell him that I expect him to do so. On no account must you write it for him.

May the Blessed Virgin keep you in her love and care.

Your loving mother,

Cecily, Dowager Duchess of York

Richard Plantagenet to Cecily, Dowager Duchess of York
Written from Utrecht, March 1461

To my Lady Mother,

We are still here in Utrecht. We have still not yet seen the Duke.

You will be pleased that we spend time with our books. I am not so pleased. I would like to visit Bruges where the Duke lives, but there is no prospect of that.

I am told, madam, that my father was not the heroic figure who fought and died with great courage at Wakefield, as you led us to believe. Why would he have left a safe castle, to face an army so much greater? They say it was pride, that he could not bear to be subjected to humiliation by a woman. Is this true? Did my father make a bad decision? I would be grateful if you could let me know in your next reply. We are not unhappy.

May we come home?

Diccon

Cecily, Dowager Duchess of York, to Richard Plantagenet
Written from Baynard's Castle, March 1461

My son,

I forbid you to set foot in England. Under pain of my utmost displeasure if you disobey me. Stay where you are in safety.

The situation here is critical and all is in the hands of fate and Almighty God. Your brother has marched out of London to the north, with the Earl of Warwick, to destroy the Lancastrian threat to our family.

Pray for him. When your father and brother marched north to confront the Queen, they never returned. Pray for Ned's success.

As for your father, there is no question of his bravery. He would never have risked his life for pure pride. Nor did he make a bad decision. He was betrayed by one of our own Neville family, a cousin of mine, who promised to support him then changed sides.

The lesson here, my son, is always to know who is your friend and who is your foe, no matter what promises they make.

Your affectionate mother,

Cecily, Dowager Duchess of York

Duchess Cecily's intercession to the Blessed Virgin Mary

Hail Mary, full of Grace, Our Lord is with thee.

My faith is compromised. I kneel at your feet with the petition of any mother. Once again I fear for my son's life, this time on some blood-drenched battlefield of the north.

Forgive the sad repetition of my prayers. You know the cruelty of men when they sent your son to his death. Protect Edward. Grant him victory. I am sleepless with despair.

Once again I watched my closest family ride out from London, bright with banners and confidence in their cause, whilst I was forced to accept that I might never see them again.

I cannot weep. My tears are frozen in fear.

Forgive my untruths, if such they were, in keeping the flame of Richard's courage and leadership alive for his young son. I am certain it was the Neville betrayal that brought him to his death. That is what Diccon must believe. My lord Richard's honour must be upheld for his sons, and I will do it.

Amen

England's Chronicle, *March 1461*

It is said that York and Lancaster will face each other once again on a battlefield.

Is there no end to it?

Have we not suffered enough? It is said that the conflict will be at Towton, a village outside York that no one has ever heard of. If it occurs on Palm Sunday, when Christ rode into Jerusalem, what a terrible day that will be for both sides. The weather is not fit for battle. The Queen and her son, and Henry of Lancaster whom we may no longer call King, have taken refuge in York to await news. Here at Baynard's Castle our Duchess Cecily will, hourly, be demanding couriers with news from her son Edward, the new but as yet uncrowned King.

Were you aware? Edward of York, soon to be crowned King if he returns with a victory in his hands, has instructed the illustrious Mayor and Aldermen of the City of London that in his absence it is his Lady Mother who is named by him as his representative? It is the Duchess who presides over our new king's household. We swear she will do it with superb efficiency.

Such power for the lady who never wore the crown.

When will battle be? Who will come away with victory? White rose or red?

We wager it will be white. But who's to know? We have been wrong before.

The Bishop of Elphin to Bishop Francesco Coppini of Terni, one-time Papal Legate
Written from Baynard's Castle, Easter Monday 1461

Your Grace,

An event of some moment that may be to your advantage.

We had just heard Vespers. The Duchess has been fraught all day, and our spirits were low with lack of news from the north, although the Duchess's demeanour was as always exemplary. She has marvellous self-control, even when racked with fear. Except when she dropped her Missal during the raising of the Host.

And then, after Vespers, her control deserted her completely.

The Lord Treasurer, waiting for us in the Great Hall, carried a letter to our blessed Duchess of York. She read the letter. Her face paled. Her hand trembled as she passed the misused Missal to me, her other hand clenched like a claw around the document. It had taken her naught but a moment to read the news, fair or foul. Her face was as white as the snow falling outside the window. Or as colourless as a death-mask. I might have thought there were tears on her cheeks, if I did not know her better.

I feared the worst and took her arm, offering my assistance in what I considered to be her overwhelming grief. She clung, fingers digging into my sleeve, but only for a fraction of time, before she turned on her heel, climbed the staircase to re-enter her chapel, beckoning for me and her two chaplains to follow. There she fell to her knees before the image of the Blessed Virgin and buried her face in her hands.

I did not know whether I should begin a Requiem Mass or start to sing a *Te Deum*, so silently distressed was the Duchess.

You will know the answer by now, I expect.

I imagine that you are praying hard for a Yorkist victory. The family is close to your heart and you will have your eye on the papal legate's promotion again. You should also pray that your enemies (Queen Marguerite and France) do not speak out against you.

Elphin

England's Chronicle, *April 1461*

The Battle of Towton was fought on Easter Eve.

The longest and bloodiest battle on English soil, the conflict bitter and vicious, repaying old scores.

Fought through a snow-storm, impossible to see friend from foe. The snow and Cock Brook ran red with blood.

How many lost? Hundreds. Nay, thousands. Enough to need mass graves where all were tumbled.

Who claimed the victory?

The House of York.

Anne, Dowager Duchess of Buckingham, to
Katherine, Dowager Duchess of Norfolk
Written from the Palace of Westminster

My dear sister,

Do I mourn or do I rejoice?

I fear that Cecily will become unbearable in her pride for the achievements of her son. As if in imitation of the brave and noble heroes of old who fill my books, Ned has asserted his hold on England's crown on the battlefield of Towton.

Cecily already acts the role of Dowager Queen. She has set about making preparations for the coronation. I wish you would come and give me strength to support it.

A Queen does not need to be crowned in order to rule, Cecily says if I dare to take her to task for her peremptory commands throughout her household.

I am pleased for her, of course, but I cannot help but remember my husband and son, dead on battlefields or in the aftermath. Nor can Cecily be cold to the onslaught of death on both sides. We have lost nephews in the terrible carnage at Towton. Lord John Neville and Henry Percy, Earl of Northumberland, add to the number of our family dead.

I feel wrung out with mourning.

Perhaps the outward jollity of a coronation will do us all some good!

Anne

Cecily, Dowager Duchess of York, to Edward, Duke of York, King in Waiting
Written from Baynard's Castle

To my well-beloved son,

This is why I write to you.

I would commission you with a task before you leave the north.

Have the heads, those terrible mementoes of Wakefield, removed from Micklegate Bar. Have them carried to Pontefract to be reunited with those we love. It would be a double humiliation to leave them longer for public view and despoliation from time and weather.

You will be feted in York, of that I am certain. It is your task to tighten the bonds of friendship with this important northern base.

I will ensure that all is prepared for your return to London.

Your affectionate mother,

Cecily, Dowager Duchess of York

Richard Plantagenet to Cecily, Dowager Duchess of York
Written from Bruges

To my Lady Mother,

At last! We have been escorted to Bruges to the Court of Duke Philip. We knew there had been a battle which Ned won.

You are now deemed worthy of recognition, we were informed by one of the Duke's household, who bowed to us. Few servants have bowed to us before.

It would be good to be worthy of recognition for our own sakes, George says. Are we not sons of the Duke of York? Why have we been shuffled off to a garret in Utrecht in the first place?

The Duke came to visit us in Bruges because Ned won, and

now life has become very exciting. We have seen his library with more books than I could count. We were not allowed to touch them because of the gilding and the fine leather. Did you know? We have been allowed to go to a fete at the castle of Hesdin. I liked the fountains and waterfalls, and the hunting is good too.

May we come home?

George says that he is too busy to write, but that I should say that he is well too.

Your obedient son,

Diccon

Cecily, Dowager Duchess of York, to Richard Plantagenet
Written from Baynard's Castle

To my obedient son,

Still not yet.

Ned is not crowned. There are uprisings in the north that he must deal with first. I promise that you will be here in London when the celebrations begin and you will play a part in them at his side.

Inform George that I will personally supervise the progress he has made in his education on his return to England.

Your affectionate mother,

Cecily, Dowager Duchess of York

George Plantagenet to Cecily, Dowager Duchess of York
Written from Bruges

To my Lady Mother,

I am well and minding our governor.

We have visited the Duke's estate at Hesdin. What a marvellous place it is. It has lots of tricks and traps for those who are unwary. There are secret trap-doors to fall through, and sacks full of feathers that burst over our heads. Corridors sprinkle you with rain and snow and statues spray paint on you as you pass.

Not everyone is pleased, but I enjoyed the fun.

I would like to build a castle like Hesdin in England when we come home.

We are not unhappy.

Your son,

George

Cecily, Dowager Duchess of York, to George Plantagenet
Written from Baynard's Castle

My son,

It pleased me to know that you are withstanding your exile with fortitude. I hope that it will not last long.

I do not think it a good idea to build a Hesdin here in England. We have enough tricks, traps and shocks to keep us on our toes without creating more. I can think of none of our magnates who would respond kindly to being sprayed with paint.

Your affectionate mother,

Cecily, Duchess of York

Cecily, Dowager Duchess of York, to Katherine, Dowager Duchess of Norfolk
Written from Baynard's Castle

Dearest Kat,

All that Richard and I had striven for is now achieved, and my heart burns with gratitude and God's grace.

Henry, Marguerite and their son were seen bound for Scotland when I last heard, Somerset in unholy alliance with them. I pray that they might stay there for a lengthy sojourn. Or even that Marguerite will return to France, taking her troublesome family with her. Now I can look to the future. Ned will be crowned.

And I? Am I not Queen Dowager? Richard never wore the crown that was stolen from him at Wakefield. It was I and my family who brought my son to the throne, so do I not have an interest is this new reign? Ned has not quite yet nineteen years, and so will need advice and counselling. Who better to give it than I? Rest assured that I know that it is my son who is King. I will never do more than support that honour. I have made that promise to myself.

I expect Anne has already complained to you about the authority given to me in my handling the reins of power. She is bitter, I think, that her attempt at reconciliation between the Queen and the City went so wrong. I told her that she should not have got herself involved.

Do you come to London for the coronation?

I will be relieved when Ned has returned to London. The terrible fear remains with me that, having survived the bloody deeds at Towton, he will be cut down in some minor skirmish on the roadside somewhere in the north. He is not a man to hide his consequence or his person. Instead he displays it, much like the proud peacock whose tail feather he sported in his cap when he last rode into London.

I suppose I must now consider him to be a man. Until such a short time ago he was my son and a mere boy.

Your sister,
Cecily

Cecily, Dowager Duchess of York, to
George and Richard Plantagenet

Written from Baynard's Castle

To my most well-loved sons,

Come home now.

I have sent a courier and entourage to escort you to London. Make your grateful thanks to the Duke of Burgundy, as I will too. I have sent gifts to mark his generosity to you.

Don't waste time. You will give thanks in Canterbury Cathedral for your safe journey, then come on to me at Baynard's Castle. You are young men of significant importance. You, George, until your brother Edward weds and has sons of his own, are heir to the throne of England.

You will behave accordingly.

Your affectionate mother,

Cecily, Dowager Duchess of York

Chapter Seventeen

The Stark Reality of Ruling

Duchess Cecily offers advice at Baynard's Castle, the twenty-ninth day of June 1461

'You wished to speak with me, madam.'

My son, the new King, come from the Palace of Westminster, without too much haste. I could forgive him that, but he must not make a habit of it when I express a desire to speak with him. On this occasion I would forgive him; he would have much to do during these crucial weeks.

Ned bowed, while I surveyed the changes that his victory at Mortimer's Cross had wrought. The sun falling through the high window gilded a bright new maturity. His garments were rich, his face fair, his hair, newly trimmed and curling about his ears, the hue of new-minted gold coin. His movements were confident, hammered with an assurance that power had vested in him. His formality also amused me, at odds with his flamboyantly hanging sleeves and the feather that depended from his felt cap. Ned had discovered the importance of adopting the eye-catching style of a ruler. I must accept that he was now King and should be treated as such.

'This will not take long, my son. Come and sit with me,' I invited, gesturing to the window embrasure with its familiar view over the busy life on the Thames, the coming and going of craft large and small.

Placing a bulky package on a coffer by the door, Ned sat, his legs stretched before him, his fingers smoothing the carving on the arms of the cushioned chair. However great his regal authority, however lacking in years he might be, Ned was at ease. His feathered hat had been cast on the floor at his feet, with his gloves.

'I have barely had time to draw breath,' he said.

'Then I am grateful that you found one moment in all that occupies you to respond to my invitation.'

He did not rise to my gentle bait.

'As you see, madam. But I cannot stay long.'

'Then here is your mother's counsel,' I began. 'As a new King, with no experience of the art of government to draw upon, you will need strong supporters and knowledgeable counsellors. My advice is to use your family, your closest allies and friends.'

'Yes, madam.'

'Then here, from my own experience, are my suggestions.' I held out to him a document, on which I had written a comprehensive list of the men whom I considered essential to the success of my son's reign. Ned took it, glancing idly down as if it were of little account.

'Reward them for their past allegiance, and they will continue to remain loyal,' I urged, turning fully towards him to hold his gaze with mine. 'Promote your Neville relatives as well as the powerful Herbert family in the west.' Ned's gaze had strayed beyond me, to the window. 'Do you hear me, Ned? You must keep the Nevilles with you. Raise George Neville, most valuable in swaying London in your favour, to be Archbishop of York.'

'I can see the value of that.'

He folded the document, and made to rise.

'I have not yet finished.' I stretched out a hand and gripped his wrist to keep him still. 'There are your two brothers, newly returned in time for your coronation. Young still, but they will grow and their loyalty will be of inestimable worth to you. Ennoble them, Ned. Use the royal titles which have become obsolete. It will make a grand impression on the whole realm. Make George Duke of Clarence. Make Richard Duke of Gloucester. I think they will both benefit from being placed in the household of the Archbishop of Canterbury until a more permanent settlement can be arranged. It will be good for their souls and for their education. Their maturity while in Burgundy is significant, although I have to say more so for Diccon than George.'

'Of course. I will not neglect my brothers.'

Did I detect a faint sigh? I allowed my hand to fall away. Ned instantly sprang to his feet, to patrol the length of the chamber with all the excess energy that I recalled.

'You must also consider our enemies, the Lancastrians,' I said.

'What do I do with them?' He had come to a halt before me. 'An axe to each Lancastrian neck seems appropriate.'

'Do not be too quick to punish. Be generous in granting pardons to those who can be won to your side. You may feel bitter, having watched your supporters die on the battlefield, but so did the Lancastrians die in vast numbers. My advice is this.' I proffered another document. 'Pardon some of them. Pardon Sir Richard Woodville and his family. His wife Jacquetta was once an important woman as Duchess of Bedford, and a close friend in our Rouen days, even though they have become supporters of Marguerite. It will do no harm to win over Jacquetta's new family. They may be willing to espouse Yorkist sentiments if the purse of gold is sufficiently large. Their eldest son, Anthony Woodville, is a man of some talent. It might be politic to look for a marriage for him.'

Ned held the document, but made no move to read it.

'I will consider your advice, madam. I am aware of my obligations, and of the need to build support.' He paused, then added, 'Although I would have come to the same conclusions from my own assessments.'

Was this a warning to me not to interfere too closely? Would he reject my advice? Ned's face had suddenly acquired an austerity, as if he would announce some policy that I would not like.

'I should tell you this, madam, before you hear it from Court gossip. I will keep the Earl of Warwick as my chief counsellor. My cousin has been my rock and my strength.'

'Which is good policy.' I could see nothing wrong here. My hands, that had tensed in my lap at the hint of Ned's insurrection, once more relaxed.

'It is also my intention to appoint him Great Chamberlain of England. Also Admiral of England, as well as Warden of the Cinque Ports and Dover Castle for life.'

My hands re-clasped, fingers hard-gripped. I took a breath to reply, but Ned continued, as if in a confessional.

'I will give him the Wardenship of both east and west Marches in the north – the old Percy areas of power – as well as the office of Steward of the Duchy of Lancaster, where he can keep his eye on my own lands while I am busy governing.'

I could no longer sit. I pushed myself to my feet, searching for appropriate words.

'I know that you will agree,' my son said. 'He is your nephew, your much-missed brother's son.' For a moment I thought that his eyes were sly, but perhaps it was the angle of the light that caught a gleam. 'Do you think that this enhancement of Warwick's power will keep him firmly chained to my rising star? Do you not approve?'

I abandoned any attempt to be conciliatory. What had he done?

'Before God, Ned! I do not approve!'

'Why not?' His brows rose, but he knew the answer.

'Have you thought about this?' I tried to keep my voice level, to banish any sense of turbulence at what my son was planning. 'How much power are you willing to shower over Warwick's head? A man already the strongest magnate in England. Why not give Warwick the crown as well?'

Ned smiled as if I needed to be soothed. 'But he is such an able man.'

'And his ambitions match his ability.' I was beyond soothing. 'I think that you would live to regret it. I advise you to reconsider concentrating so much influence in the hands of one undoubtedly clever man.'

Ned strode away again, mayhap to escape my disapproval, but then returned as if he had made up his mind.

'How can you question my preferment for my cousin of Warwick? So many of the Nevilles rode beside me all the way to the steps before the throne, when others did not. They deserve to be rewarded with brilliance. And yes, I will make George Neville Archbishop of York. He has the métier for it. He is already planning a great feast to celebrate. I presume that you have no fault to find with that.'

'No. But for Warwick to be handed so much power on a gold platter...'

'He will use it well, in my name.'

I could already sense that I was fighting a losing battle. Ned's admiration for his magnificent cousin had not dimmed with the events of the past year.

'Can I not persuade you to reconsider?' I tried once more.

'No, madam. My decisions are made.'

Thus the King had spoken.

Suddenly Ned grinned, his face alight with joy, and he fell to his knees before me, gathering my hands in his, covering them with extravagant kisses.

'Can we now forget all of this, and simply enjoy my coronation? It seems a hard task, to take on the government of England. I know that I can rely on your strength at my side.' He cocked his chin winningly. 'Will I find any time for hunting? I think I must make time. Wearing the crown must not be all hard work.'

Leaping to his feet, he retrieved his hat and gloves, filched a ripe pear from the dish beside the door, tossing it in the air before sinking his teeth into it, and then he was gone.

The large parcel wrapped in linen, which I now unwrapped, contained a velvet robe, of superb quality, for me to wear for the coronation. I would not myself have chosen violet patterning on a red field, or the weight of bullion at cuff and hem, but the sable trimming was of excellent density.

I laid it aside.

My sharp concern over the Earl of Warwick becoming an all-powerful subject, with my son's blessing, had suddenly taken precedence over the patterning of a gown. So had my failure to bring Ned round to my way of thinking. There it was, writ as clear as a spring morn in Ned's every word, every gesture: Richard's pride, Richard's arrogance, Richard's intolerance of any will but his own. And I loved him for it.

England's Chronicle, *the twenty-ninth day of June 1461*

One final comment on the coronation day before London settles into the normal business of trade and shopping.

We expect that the Duchess of York was present with some degree of sadness. This should have been Richard, Duke of York, wearing the golden coronet. She should have been Queen of England.

Not to be. We expect that she will grow used to being King's Mother, although our young King does not look to be the man to be wound around his mother's fingers.

Will King Edward make a more effective King than King Henry? He looked every part the perfect monarch on this day of his coronation. He wore the ermine and crown as if they were made for him, and not borrowed from a passer-by. He won many hearts.

Are we not all now enthusiastic supporters of this resurrected House of York? King Edward has called parliament. He has stated that he will welcome every man who gives him his loyalty, no matter what his past allegiance. It has won over many who have fought for Lancaster. Although it has to be said that those who resist have been charged with treason. I foresee executions on Tower Hill if they refuse to bend the knee. Our King may be young, but he is not without political foresight. Better a dead enemy than a live one.

Will this now be peace?

We fear not. Marguerite of Anjou, once Queen, will never accept. There are pockets of resistance throughout England, as we know. One day soon we will return to sieges and conflict.

On this happy day, there is one further step which must be taken to make King Edward's hold on the throne a strong one. Perhaps the Duchess is already advising him of it.

Perhaps King Edward has decided he has had enough advice from that quarter.

Anne, Dowager Duchess of Buckingham, to Cecily, King's Mother
Written from the Palace of Westminster

Dearest Cecily,

You will note that I have honoured you with your new title.

I have to say it was a glorious occasion, although the violet hue did not become you.

Since you are not slow in handing out any opinion that crosses your mind, consider this, if you have not already done so. All is still so unstable. If Ned dies without a direct heir, it will be worse than unstable. All will be upheaval. George, as Ned's heir, has a mere twelve years to his name. Dangers threaten from over-powerful magnates when a King is without experience and too young for the office. Did we not see that with King Henry, King before his first birthday?

Ned needs a wife.

A wife will also make his life more regular and worthy of the supreme office he now holds. I hear many rumours of his inordinate love of women and I am sure you have heard tales of these licentious liaisons also. Ned needs a marriage and a legitimate heir.

I am surprised you have not already considered this and placed a stratagem before him.

Your sister who enjoys dabbling her fingers in family marriages,

Anne

Cecily, King's Mother, to Anne, Dowager Duchess of Buckingham

Written from Baynard's Castle

Who's to say that I have not considered it? You know me better than that, Anne. Ned needs a wife and quickly, I think. I consider it to be well-judged policy to look abroad so that any bride will not give too much power to an English noble family. I need an ally to achieve this for me, the seeking out of a suitable bride. I know just the man.

Thank you for your good advice. I know I can always rely on you to relate the obvious.

Have you any thoughts about a husband for Meg? She is of an age. It would all have been arranged if Richard had not met his death at Wakefield.

I am thinking of establishing Meg in her own household in Greenwich, and Ned is in agreement. Now that she is an English Princess she will be much in demand. How high can we look? Please send any ideas.

It was my plan to spend Christmas at Eltham, a quiet occasion, rather than with Ned at Greenwich which will be full of festivity and extravagance. For me this year it will be bitter-sweet indeed, the first since Richard's death. I am in no mood for anything but austerity and mourning.

And before you tell me, I know that I cannot withdraw into

misery. Royal receptions are important, and I must make an impression of wealth and power on Ned's new subjects. I will have to resign myself to feasts and dancing after all, the fuss and fretting over where to buy, what to buy and how to cook it. I remember a detailed recipe for stuffing chickens with the flesh of other fowl, before colouring and glazing them altogether, but have lost it.

Can you recall? If so, please send. Even better, come and oversee the cooking of it. I'll leave my cook in your hands. He tends to grumble when I appear in the kitchens.

Your resigned sister,
Cecily

Anne, Dowager Duchess of Buckingham, to Cecily, King's Mother
Written from the Palace of Westminster

Cis,

The recipe you mention is too time-consuming and not worth the eating at the end. Here is a better one, fit for a feast. Tell your cook to collect the ingredients. I will come and oversee the cooking of it and insist on cleanliness. Your cook can grumble at me all he likes.

Anne

Recipe for a Royal Festive Occasion

Take a capon, scald it and draw it clean. Smite it in two down the middle.

Take a pig, scald it and draw it clean in the same manner and smite it also.

Take a needle and thread and sew the fore part of the capon

to the after part of the pig. And the fore part of the pig to the hinder part of the capon.

Stuff them as you would stuff a pig.

Put them on a spit and roast them.

When they are done enough, glaze them with yolks of eggs and powder of ginger and saffron and juice of parsley.

Serve it forth for a royal meal to impress all.

If it does not, they do not deserve to be invited!

Duchess Cecily arranges the Year's Mind Mass of the late Duke of York in St Paul's Cathedral, thirty-first of December 1461

I arranged it all. It was my right. Wrapped in grief, I left no stone unturned to honour the name of Richard, Duke of York, England's heir.

We gathered in the nave of St Paul's Cathedral, a large congregation of the highest blood in the land, our purpose to process slowly, with great dignity, making our way from the nave, through the chancel towards the high altar. Our garments were dark in mourning but nothing could hide the richness of satin and velvet, or the sigh of the costly cloth as it brushed the painted tiles. Jewels on breast and finger began to throw off their iridescent colour as we approached the banks of candles. All glittering like stars in an evening sky. The spice of incense enveloped us, assuring us of God's presence at this most holy of events.

My sister Anne stood on one side, a stalwart support. On the other was Katherine, Dowager Duchess of Norfolk, as dry and austere as a winter rush, wrapped around in fur and dark veiling, newly come from her lair in the north to give me the support of her presence. My relief at such intimacy from my sisters was palpable.

'Impressive!' Katherine observed softly as we came to a halt before the bier.

'It is meant to be,' I said.

'Will you wed again?' she asked, inconsequentially, as those following shuffled in the cold to achieve the best position.

'Hush!' said Anne.

I ignored the question.

'I will not marry. I am past the age of desiring love and affection or even male companionship,' Katherine mused. 'Nor am I willing to be dangled before some fortune-seeking lord who thinks I will soon die, allowing him to get his hands on my Mowbray lands. How disappointed he would be, since they were granted to me for my lifetime only. Besides, three husbands is enough for any woman.'

'Who knows what the future will hold, for any of us?' I said, holding back the despair.

'I am too old for searching for the future and I am too old to weep,' Katherine continued, at least sotto voce. 'The next tears I shed will, I swear, be on my deathbed.'

Which lugubrious statement cast us all into gloom, as dense as the church beyond the orbit of the candles. Behind me, in a neat row, had gathered my children Meg and George and Diccon, the boys cowed into stern behaviour. Then my daughters: Anne, Duchess of Exeter; Elizabeth, Duchess of Suffolk. Behind them, a powerful sheltering force, stood Ned, King Edward the Fourth of England, who had in his compassion allowed me to walk at the head of this solemn procession.

Who would begrudge me such pre-eminence?

On this day we would hold the formal funeral rites to

commemorate the deaths one year ago in Wakefield, and the scanty funerals held so far away in Pontefract. But now the rites would be repeated with the ostentation that our dead deserved.

I knelt.

I heard the soft hush and rustle and murmur as the congregation followed my example. Then the Requiem Mass began the Year's Mind to bring the beloved dead back into our presence.

'How much did you spend on this?' Anne whispered.

'One hundred and fifty pounds on the candles. As for the rest, I know not,' I replied with a frown to quench her inappropriate nosiness. 'And I would be grateful if you could preserve a melancholy aspect rather than tallying up the outgoings!'

The hearse, black-draped in a pall, sat before the altar. The bodies were still interred at Pontefract but today we would bring their memory forth into the vast space of this cathedral. Candles burned to make of it a living brightness in the shadows of the arches on either side. The solemnity of death pressed down on our shoulders, the finality of death. Not even the violent clap of wings, from a pair of pigeons trapped within the vast space, would draw attention from our purpose.

Hands clasped around my rosary, I concentrated my whole mind on that empty bier as if I could indeed conjure up Richard's body into my presence. Incense filling my mind, drenching my emotions with holy power. As if it was possible, in that moment, Richard was still with me, granting me permission at last to experience more than emotion and distress. I could almost feel the light touch of his hand on my veil as I bent my head, the flutter of his breath against my cheek.

One day, one day not too distant, I would have his remains removed from Pontefract. He did not deserve to remain there.

With final prayers of remembrance, it was over, the spirits of the dead once more dispatched from the realms of the living. The congregation departed, silently, soft-shoed, as a young priest came forward and began to douse the candles. The great building settled into its habitual shadows around me where I remained kneeling, looking back at those years of my marriage. Despite his temper, his faults, it was possible for a woman to love such a man with her heart, her mind, her body.

I, Cecily Neville, had been that woman.

I stayed until the final candle flickered out.

'God be with you, Richard. And God be with you, Edmund. You will live in my heart until its beat stops. May your souls rest on His bosom.'

The light had gone out of my world too, but perhaps it could be relit. I had been wrong to consider shutting myself away. Alone, I stood and made my way to the entrance to the chancel where Ned waited for me. How he shone, gilded with power, even brighter than the jewelled chain that lay across his dark robes.

'It was well done,' he said in confirmation.

'Yes.'

He took my hand.

'We have much to do. You and I.'

'Do I have a part in it?'

'Of a surety. Are you not the King's Mother?'

Ned smiled at me, and it was his father's smile. It left a warmth around my heart, where all had been dark and cold. I had a new life to construct.

Chapter Eighteen

The King Needs a Wife

Cecily, King's Mother, to Edward, King of England
Written from Baynard's Castle, 1463

My son,

This is become an urgent matter since you appear to be ignoring it.

Do not shelve this letter before you have read more than the first line, under the premise that it is only from your mother and so can be ignored while you attend to important kingly business. This is important. It is my duty to advise you, and your duty as a son and the King to at least consider my suggestions.

On the subject of a wife, as you know, I am of the opinion that it is time that you took a bride. Have I not broached this subject on numerous occasions, even on the day of your coronation? Now that you are King of England I advise that you choose a lady with exceptional connections to further an alliance with one of our European neighbours.

We need allies. The Lancastrians may have been defeated

at Towton but no man of sense would regard their threat as moribund. Queen Marguerite will never acknowledge the loss of the throne for her son. From my past acquaintance with her, she will already be sounding out the French King for an alliance. Probably in the form of an invading army.

Thus, to return to your marriage.

Philip the Good, Duke of Burgundy, who was kind enough to shelter George and Diccon through the terrible times, has a niece, the daughter of the Duke of Bourbon. She will make an admirable contract with a powerful neighbour.

Would you have any objection to her as a wife? It will be a popular marriage with the merchants in the City of London who would benefit from Burgundian trade. The lady is also said to be very beautiful, if that is of importance to you. From the rumours that ever circulate, you, my son, have an eye for a fair face. Every comely face that comes within your orbit, from kitchen maid to high nobility.

I think that we should open negotiations. You need a son and heir to the crown. A legitimate heir. If the rumours are only half true you could now have a handful of bastards being raised in your kitchens. I would advise discretion and discernment in your choice of female company. Kitchen maids are not appropriate. A wife would solve the problem.

Your father always treated the female members of his household with respect.

With my brother's reinterment at Bisham Priory, I am reminded that your father's body still remains in isolation in Pontefract. This should not be. I would wish you to take this matter in hand and bring him home to Fotheringhay.

I expect a prompt reply. Not as last time when it took you near on a month to put pen to parchment. I hear far too much of your wasting time in tournaments and dancing.

Your mother,
Cecily

Edward, King of England, to Cecily, King's Mother
Written from the Palace of Westminster

To my Lady Mother,

Here you are – a prompt reply within the week. You cannot rail at me for being dilatory on this occasion.

I honour your suggestion. I will consider Mademoiselle de Bourbon.

At the moment my time is taken up with Lancastrian pockets of insurrection in the country so marriage must be put on hold. After all the upheavals, we are bedevilled with plots, rioting mobs, public disorder, not to mention the new King Louis of France who is casting an eye on our shores and declaring support for Lancaster. An army has landed near Bamburgh Castle, and unfortunately some of our Neville relatives would rather rise in its support than give their oath of allegiance to me. Marguerite and her son are still in Scotland, plotting who knows what.

There is no need for you to be anxious about my marriage. I am far from the age when death claims a man through his natural span. I am aware that I need a son and heir but there is plenty of time. Meanwhile if I should fall in battle or to an assassin's blade, there is George.

Are you planning a marriage for Meg?

This will give you something to think about rather than my nuptials. We must find her a more amenable husband than you managed for my sister Anne, one with unquestionable Yorkist credentials. Anne has had a miserable time with Exeter. I am inclined to support her in her quest for a divorce. Exeter will never be of value to the House of York.

I am told that she has a lover, but of course she does not talk to me about it. She probably thinks that I will disapprove. He is Thomas St Leger, a gentleman from Kent. I expect she is enjoying Exeter's absence in impoverished exile with the Queen. It pleased me to grant my sister a London home near yours at Coldharbour just along the Thames and make the rents from Exeter's lordships available for her use. It is what she deserves.

It is true that I enjoy the company of women. I never treat them with disrespect. Women like me too. I will make no excuses.

Your utterly respectful son,

Ned

I will arrange the reinterment of my father when events are less pressing.

I note with interest your signing with your name alone. Is it not a Queen Regnant who would do that?

**Anne, Dowager Duchess of Buckingham,
to Cecily, King's Mother**

Written from Tonbridge Castle

Dear Cis,

I have been thinking.

It is more than two years now since Richard's death.

Will you wed again?

I think you will not appreciate the question, but you are a mere forty-eight years and a woman of influence. I can think of a number of high-born men who might consider you as a wife. If only to guard your interests, a husband might be good policy. Broken hearts apart, men can be very useful. It does not have to be for love. He does not have to be a man who owns your heart and soul. I even doubt if you have to obey his every word. If nothing else, it would guard against loneliness as the young ones move to their own households.

A new husband might be just the thing.

Your thoughtful sister,

Anne

Cecily, King's Mother, to Anne, Dowager Duchess of Buckingham

Written from Baynard's Castle

Dear Anne,

Do I take it, from your enigmatic letter, that you are considering diving once more into the fraught pool of matrimony? All I would say is this:

Beware of those who have their mind set on your extensive estates and the revenue of your dower lands. You would be an asset to any man's money chests. Beware of those who see you as a stepping stone to the good offices of the King. We will not, at our advanced age, even mention love.

There, my advice that you can take or leave. I have thought about remarriage. Did you think I would not? My heart might belong to Richard until the day I die, but yes I can see loneliness on my personal horizon. Yet I think I will not. A new husband for the King's Mother might expect too much power as the King's Father by Marriage.

I have no wish to be merely a man's wife. Being King's Mother will suit me very well. Any influence over my son will be mine, and mine alone.

I have enough marital problems on my plate as King's Mother without considering my own remarriage.

Besides, who would I wed? Who would be a suitable mate for such as I?

Your sister,

Cecily

Cecily, King's Mother, to Edward, King of England
Written from Baynard's Castle, 1463

I trust you are in health.

More importantly I trust that you make good and regular confession of your sins to God.

Now about your marriage. How many times have I written to you concerning this matter since you took the crown? It has always been a sign of my affection and my concern.

Now it is a sign of my displeasure.

The rumours that flood the Court and the City fill me with nothing but incredulity. Your father and I raised you to be honest and chivalrous, to be respectful in your dealings with women. What I hear is that you are gaining a reputation for lust and lasciviousness. You did not get that from your father who was never promiscuous! Even the chroniclers are aiming their arrows at you.

I can only echo this sentiment.

Men marvel that our sovereign lord is so long without a wife, and were ever afraid that he was not chaste in his living.

What sort of weapon is that to put into the hands of the chroniclers? The reputation of a King should be sacrosanct.

I wish you to come and see me at Baynard's Castle within the week, to continue this discussion. It is time that you showed England that you are prepared to take your duties to the realm seriously.

We will also discuss the possibilities for Meg, since you must have a hand in the decision. If you can find the time... At least you have emerged from your amours to consider the promotion of your brothers. I find the offices most suitable, George as Lieutenant of Ireland to continue our connection there, and Diccon as Admiral of the Sea.

Your mother,
Cecily

Edward, King of England, to Cecily, King's Mother
Written from the Palace of Westminster

To my Lady Mother, with all my love and respect,

I see no discussion here, merely your taking me to task.

Is my life to be all war and duty? I have spent the last two years in nothing but the heaviest of conflict, ensuring that England is now fully under my control. Marguerite and the boy are now fled into exile in France, which could be dangerous. Thus I am closely involved in securing peace with France and Scotland with a promise there will be no more aid offered to Queen Marguerite, as she still styles herself. I am working on an alliance with Burgundy too.

I will not neglect my duty to marry.

Meanwhile I enjoy the company of women. Any rumours you hear that I treat them with disrespect are false.

I will visit you at Baynard's Castle when I have the time.
Your dutiful son,
Edward, King of England

Katherine, Dowager Duchess of Norfolk, to Cecily, King's Mother

Written from Epworth

Dear Cis,

You won't like this, but I will send it anyway.

Ned might be much admired for his exploits on the battlefield and at the negotiating table where he looks every inch a King, but this is what I am hearing, even as far away as Lincolnshire.

Ned has acquired in two short years the reputation of being licentious in the extreme. He is not to be trusted in the company of any woman. He pursues the married and unmarried, the noble and the lowly, with no discrimination. He is addicted to conviviality and excess. He is vain and drunken. He has taken a mistress, flaunting her at Court.

Do I go on? I cannot believe that you are deaf to this. Are you actually refusing to give credence to it? Even if it is not all true, it is not appropriate.

It is time he was taken in hand.

Dear Cis, I love him as a nephew, but this manner of kingship is not what so much blood was shed for. Exert your maternal powers. Pray over him. Or simply take him by the shoulders and shake some sense into him.

If you cannot, get Warwick to take him to task, as one soldier to another. Ned always admired Warwick. Now is the time to make use of this close friendship.

Your very stern elder sister,
Katherine

Cecily, King's Mother, to Edward, King of England
Written from Baynard's Castle

Edward,

On receiving a letter of the appalling scandal surrounding your behaviour from my sister Norfolk, I expect you to be at Baynard's Castle before this day is finished. Travel by river.

Is it true that you have taken a permanent mistress to your bed? A certain Mistress Elizabeth Lucy, by whom you have an illegitimate daughter? Some say that you have actually promised marriage to the woman. I trust that is not true. Even you would have more sense than that.

If I have not made it plain, I wish to see you immediately.

Your mother,
Cecily

Edward, King of England, to Cecily, King's Mother
Written from the Palace of Westminster

I cannot fulfil your request. I am preparing to leave London. Our conversation must wait my convenience.

I have not taken a mistress. I have not promised marriage to Elizabeth Lucy. Not that it is your concern if I had.

Edward, King of England

Cecily, King's Mother, to Edward, King of England
Written from Baynard's Castle

Your convenience? It appears to me that there are too many women pandering to your convenience.

Where are you going, that you cannot spend one hour with your mother?

Cecily

Edward, King of England, to Cecily, King's Mother
Written from the Palace of Westminster

King's business.

Cecily, King's Mother, Duchess of York, to Richard Neville, Earl of Warwick
Written from Baynard's Castle

My nephew of Warwick,

Since my son is lax in this matter, I look to you for aid. I need not tell you that Ned is dilatory in the affair. It is time that he was presented with a fait accompli. If she is pretty enough, well endowed enough, I doubt he'll object.

The matter of a wife for the King. Here are the well-connected young women I have given thought to.

Mademoiselle de Bourbon is still a possibility, with all the advantages to our merchants of a Burgundian alliance. Then there is Isabella, sister and heiress of Henry of Castile. Or even Margaret, sister to the King of Scotland. The latter two are both very young, of course, but we have long held connections with Castile since the marriage of the heiress to John of Gaunt. An alliance with

Scotland would solve the problem of constant treachery beyond our northern border. Any one of these would put a halt to the Lancastrian search for allies against us.

Some mischief-maker has suggested Mary of Guelders. She may be Scottish Regent and mother of King James but her reputation is almost as louche as Ned's and her advanced age is a problem. I think it is not a serious suggestion.

An alliance with the French House of Valois, Louis, a new King looking for a new alliance, might be good policy. Critically it might prevent France from sliding into a dangerous agreement with the House of Lancaster.

I confess I am leaning towards a French bride.

Will you travel for me, and discover the sentiments at the French Court? Is there a suitable lady with impeccable and royal connections to keep my son on the straight and narrow?

But beware of this eleventh King Louis. He is not named as some species of spider for nothing. A weaver of webs and intrigue. He will not make an agreement for no advantage for himself. We also need a guarantee that he will abandon the Lancaster cause for all time.

Do not enter into any final agreement with France until you have spoken to me again.

Your aunt,
Cecily

Richard Neville, Earl of Warwick, to Cecily, King's Mother

Written from Paris, summer 1464

My illustrious aunt,

I am here at the French Court and the news is favourable.

I can think of no better Queen Consort for our King than the lady, Bona of Savoy. She is young, attractive and will shine in Court circles. King Louis is keen on the match, or so he seems, although it is difficult to read behind the wily facade. It is my plan to be present in St Omer in October to consolidate the truce between our two countries which will prevent Louis from engaging in Lancastrian plots. What better culmination than to heal the wounds between us with this fortuitous marriage?

All we have to do then is to bring Edward into the negotiations and ensure that he turns up to meet the bride and grace what would be an ostentatious diplomatic festival. He has been prevaricating for months. I am not sure why, and for once Edward has not been forthcoming with his plans. I thought it might be that he does not to wish to unsettle Burgundy, who will not be in favour of this French marriage.

I hope that my efforts on England's behalf meet with your approval. I return home laden with extravagant gifts from King Louis. There are a number of costly books, enclosed in leather and jewels, gilded throughout, that you might enjoy.

I trust that Edward will comply and bring our efforts to glorious fruition. Do you broach it with him, or do I?

Your nephew,

Warwick

Cecily, King's Mother, to Richard Neville, Earl of Warwick

Written from Baynard's Castle

Warwick,

I have a concern. There is a sting in the tail of my gratitude for your efforts on my behalf.

I expect Louis will reward you handsomely, as I am sure that

265

you deserve for all your efforts to bring my son to his true inheritance, and to bring off this alliance. I have heard as much from the couriers who come and go between Paris and London. That Louis calls you cousin and has promised to make you a sovereign Prince in your own right, with your own European Duchy. I would not begrudge it as an addition to your growing power.

Sadly, my nephew, it has come to my ears that there is a witticism much enjoyed at Court, at Edward's expense. This is what one of the ambassadors who dined with us at Baynard's Castle had the misfortune to chuckle over:

England has but two rulers, Monsieur de Warwick and another whose name I have forgotten.

Not said in Edward's presence, but in mine. The dinner ended on a sour note.

Such light-hearted ripostes can become bitter thrusts and greatly damaging. Beware of self-aggrandisement. I trust you have England's future in your heart, and that of your cousin. I would not like to think that you are overstretching yourself.

As for Edward, the time for his personal feelings or otherwise are long gone. It surely cannot be the attractions of some Court whore that distract him from this important policy. You might have a word with him, man to man, cousin to cousin. I know he values your experience and knowledge of all matters of government. I will pray for a healing in Ned's reputation.

Cecily, King's Mother

Richard Neville, Earl of Warwick,
to Cecily, King's Mother

Written from Paris

To my most conscientious aunt,

I assure you that although I value Louis' offers of recompense
– and what ambitious man would not? – my loyalties lie wholeheartedly with my cousin Edward and this kingdom.

I have worked hard for this alliance. I will take pride in its
completion. I do not deny that I have a love of finery, of display
and personal grandeur. It behoves an English magnate, of old and
illustrious lineage, to advertise his power and prestige, particularly when negotiating with European Princes. I doubt you will
disagree with me here.

I am no threat to your son's authority as King of England.

Warwick

England's Chronicle, *summer 1464*

All is peaceful in this realm of England.

But we are given to understand that a storm of much ferocity
is about to break over the heads of the House of York.

What might be contained in these storm clouds we have as
yet no knowledge.

The return of the exiled House of Lancaster with a French
army? A sudden death? Our King's predilection for the company
of women, whether fair or dark?

We have not yet got to the bottom of it, but the whispers are
becoming louder. A name has been mentioned. Such delicious
scandal.

Chapter Nineteen

Take Heed What Love May Do!

**Cecily, King's Mother, to Richard Neville,
Earl of Warwick, at Reading**
Written from Baynard's Castle, September 1464

Warwick,

I cannot believe my reading of your recent letter, just received from a sweating courier who was himself agog with the news. I thought it was to be further warning of plague rampaging through London, two hundred or more dead every day at the last count, which might force me to move my household to Fotheringhay. This is far worse.

Tell my son that I wish to see him in person.

Tell my son that I have no wish to receive a list of written excuses or trite explanation.

Why did I know nothing of this appalling development?

This is a command from the King's Mother, not a request.

I can barely believe what you have written to me. How could this happen and I not know of it?

Cecily

Richard Neville, Earl of Warwick, to Cecily, King's Mother

Written from Reading, September 1464

My aunt,

I have delivered your command.

It was received with a thin smile and a dismissive tilt of the chin and I see no likelihood of the King responding. He no longer takes kindly to orders and, besides, the damage is now done.

You may claim not to believe it, but it is the truth.

The King seems to have no appreciation of the disaster he has wilfully contrived, not least to me. I find that I have been humiliated beyond bearing. I have had to make my excuses to the King of France that all our plans for an alliance culminating in a marriage between Edward and the Lady Bona are now detritus in the dust. Cast there by Edward himself.

Why did you not know of it? Because it was all accomplished, quite deliberately, under a cloak of desperate secrecy.

The Lords of the Council, met here in Reading, are ablaze with ire.

Edward is now fully engaged in preparing a ceremony for the end of the month in Reading Abbey, where The Woman will be presented to the Court.

I am trying to preserve some vestige of good humour, for the sake of all our past friendships. It is difficult.

Warwick

Cecily, King's Mother, to Edward, King of England
Written from Fotheringhay, September 1464

Edward,

You are refusing to communicate with me.

What possessed you to become involved in this outrageous scheme?

Are you so lacking in political sense? This marriage is a travesty of your birth and your inheritance.

I swear, you are not your father's son.

Cecily

Cecily, King's Mother, to Katherine,
Dowager Duchess of Norfolk
Written from Fotheringhay, September 1464

My dear Katherine,

You behold me enveloped in rage. How do I write it?

My son the King has been married for at least five months.

In secret!

It still takes my breath away that he would engage in an act so reprehensible. I expect you have heard by now. The whole country is talking of it. A scandal to dwarf all others.

I need to unburden myself. I must be careful to whom I speak.

This is the gist of how it all came to public knowledge, when the Council was called for the first week of September in the Abbey Church at Reading. Warwick was hoping to finalise everything for a meeting with the French King at St Omer, long in the planning but now almost complete. Ned was difficult to pin down. Warwick kept up a relentless pressure. It all ended in Ned announcing to the Council that he could not agree to marry the French woman. He was already married, and had been since May.

Edward's complicity in this shameful deceit is beyond my tolerating.

'And who is she?' I hear you ask.

She is no virgin. She is a widow in her middle twenties with two sons by a recently deceased member of the lower nobility. Even worse, from a notoriously Lancastrian family.

She is Elizabeth Woodville, daughter of Jacquetta, once Duchess of Bedford, and her Lancastrian husband Sir Richard Woodville, now Lord Rivers. None of them unknown to either of us.

An appalling misalliance.

So much for my plans. So much for strengthening England's position in Europe, for raising Edward above the struggle for power of our English magnates. A pre-eminent foreign alliance would have been perfect. All obliterated by one thoughtless vow.

Does it have to be said that I have seen neither hide nor hair of my son, nor had any written correspondence? Here are the unfortunate details, according to Warwick. It happened at the Woodville house at Grafton in Northamptonshire, possibly on the first day of May, arranged by her mother Jacquetta, witnessed by two waiting-women, a priest and a boy to help the priest sing the responses. I suppose I should say that at least there was a priest to invest the diabolical proceedings with some sanctity, but that means there is less ground for annulment.

Where did they meet? All is in some doubt, but since her father has been drawn back into the Yorkist fold and became a member of Ned's Council last year it would not be difficult for their paths to cross.

The Council informed Edward that she was not a suitable

match, however good and fair she might be, and he must know that she was no wife for a Prince such as himself.

At present that is as much as I can tell you.

I burn with anger that my eldest son should be guilty of such wretched misjudgement. What's more, he is avoiding me.

Your furious sister,

Cecily

Katherine, Dowager Duchess of Norfolk, to Cecily, King's Mother

Written from Epworth

Is she beautiful? Is it a love match, sweeping Ned off his feet at last? I suppose I have met her but cannot bring her to mind. Not that I have any experience of such an uncomfortable position, of being swept off my feet.

Or is she pregnant? Is that the sticking place? That he was forced into this marriage by an ambitious family to make her child legitimate and heir to the crown?

What a pity that there was a priest. If it was a simple marriage *per verba de praesenti* at least there would be a chance of an annulment, although a slim one.

It seems to me that you will be forced to accept it, Cis.

Do keep me up to date.

I love a good scandal, even though this one appals me.

Katherine

Cecily, King's Mother, to Katherine, Dowager Duchess of Norfolk

Written from Fotheringhay

Sister,

As I recall, Jacquetta and her Woodville husband escorted Marguerite to England as a young bride. It may be that this daughter was taken into the new Queen's household, although I am uncertain. Why should I have taken any note of the girl? Her mother might be from European nobility, but her father is a minor knight, of no importance.

Pregnant? It seems not. The story I hear is that Edward had promised to marry her, to get the woman into his bed. Don't tell me – it is not the first time that my son has used such means. I am not deaf to what goes on at Court. The Woodville widow – she was wed to Sir John Grey of Groby who was killed in the Lancastrian army at St Albans – refused him, it seems. She attempted to defend her honour by threatening Edward with his own dagger, before succumbing to his wiles and charm. As he apparently succumbed to hers.

And before you ask me if I intend to be there when she is presented to the Court as the new Queen of England, and they all bow their knee, no, I will not. It is all a bitter taste in my throat. I will find it hard to be polite to my son, much less his wife.

Yes, yes, I know that I must behave with dignity. Well, I will, but it will be as cold as hoarfrost.

Your beleaguered sister,

Cecily

**Anne, Dowager Duchess of Buckingham,
to Cecily, King's Mother**

Written from Tonbridge Castle

Cis!

So what's the truth of it? The stories are creations of fantasy. Secret ceremonies in a forest on the day of Beltane. Mystery meetings on the side of the road when Edward was hunting in the forest of Wychwood near Grafton. Or beneath an oak tree in Whittlebury Forest, wherever that is, where the widow was standing with a petition, begging to be granted the lands owed to her for her dowry, accompanied by her two little sons, determined to catch Edward's notice.

Why could he not just have made her his concubine?

At least we have proof that she is fecund and will present England with an heir.

Your only hope is that he is already regretting his foolish choice and will pack her off to a nunnery with an annulment and a purse of gold before any more damage is done.

If he does not, you will have to bow before her, as Queen of England.

Oh, dear!

Anne

**Cecily, King's Mother, to Anne, Dowager
Duchess of Buckingham**

Written from Fotheringhay

Dear Sister,

To put you fully in possession of the detail appertaining to my son's terrible misalliance.

She is five years older than Edward.

She is fertile with two sons.

She is inordinately beautiful, by God!

She is not Queen of England yet.

Cecily

England's Chronicle, *September 1464*

We are aware that Cecily, King's Mother, is travelling from Fotheringhay to Reading.

Now why would that be?

We did not think that she would see a need to be there at the meeting of the Royal Council. Perhaps there is another reason.

The Duchess is intending to impress, travelling with jaw-dropping pretension, accompanied by servants, boxes, a train of laden pack animals and a ruffled popinjay chained to a travelling perch.

Does it not remind you of her momentous journey to be reunited with the now dead Duke of York in Hereford? This journey we wager will not end in so pleasurable an event.

Our courier is pleased to inform us of his opinion of the Duchess. All the beauty of her youth is now fading, but she still has a reputation for wit and temper as keen as that finely chiselled nose. Her mind is clearly razor-sharp. Now nearing her fiftieth year, the passage of time has had little more effect on her than to silver her dark hair (so we are told by those privileged to see the Duchess with her hair uncovered) and engrave lines beside eyes and mouth. Spare of flesh she might be, but she possesses a fine-boned elegance. Our informant's eyes were drawn to her slender wrists, her small hands, the jewelled fingers that held tight to her missal.

What will she have to say to her most royal son?

Nothing that he would wish us to hear, I warrant.

We wonder if she is travelling with her new seal, safely cushioned in its velvet pouch. Now there's a symbol of regal power, if ever there was one. Gone are the days when she used the small personal seal, the York arms impaled with the Neville saltire. Now she makes use of a great seal of some size, which includes the royal arms of England.

Cecily has ambitions, of course, as King's Mother.

Could it be that she sees her new daughter by law as a threat?

Duchess Cecily takes the King to task in Reading Abbey, September 1464

The chambers offered to me in Reading Abbey were all that I would expect of a wealthy bishop. I had no interest in the furnishings despite the opulence of the tapestries and the high polish on the wooden accoutrements.

Edward, King of England, stood before me.

'Where is she?'

'Who?'

'Do not be obtuse, Edward.'

I could not address him as Ned. There was no maternal affection within me.

His eyes widened with just the hint of the temper that he rarely showed to me.

'You refer to my wife, Madam.'

A little silence fell, broken only by a squawk from the popinjay that had been consigned to the corner of the room. I ignored the wine poured and presented to me. Rejected the delicacy of fried fig pastries he had ordered to sweeten my mood. There would be no sweetening here.

'What have you done, Edward? What in God's name have you done?'

Replacing the cup on the salver, my son stood foursquare before me. He had known that he would have to face this conversation with me. They said that he was charismatic in his treatment of women. There was no doubting it. His smile could have melted winter ice.

'I have entered into a marriage. Was that not what you had been commanding me to do since the day that I became King?'

The truth of this stirred my anger to a new level of heat.

'I am finding it difficult to choose my words. You have married a commoner, a woman of no connection, a woman already wed, with a family of her own, and so defiled. A Queen of England should be a spotless virgin, not a widow. I can barely believe the truth of it, that you should have embarked on so misguided a policy.'

'I regret that you are so dismissive of my choice of wife.' How smooth he was. How adult. I remembered that he was now two and twenty years old. 'Not one word to wish us happy. I might have hoped for more.'

At least his smile had waned.

'Happy is not a concept for a King when entering into matrimony,' I replied. 'Did you not think? Did you not stop and consider before you committed the deed? As King of England you had your choice of European women of high birth. Bona of Savoy would have been the perfect match. Your children would be magnificently connected to the best blood of England and France. Here was a chance to tie France into an alliance which would defeat the Lancastrians for ever.'

Since, without a reply, Edward picked up his own cup and drank, I continued.

'Instead you have chosen a woman who will give you no advantage, and in so doing you have antagonised Warwick, humiliated King Louis, horrified your Council. And if that were not enough you have angered the bedrock of your Yorkist followers whose blood has been spilt in our cause on the battlefield. They think that you have betrayed them by this marriage. Surely I and your father raised you to see the value of making and keeping friends in political circles. You have destroyed so much goodwill. It will serve you badly if King Louis, feeling thwarted by your inexplicable volte-face, promptly gives his support to Queen Marguerite and furnishes her with French troops to win the throne back for her son. We could have a French army landing on our shores within months, and it will be entirely your own fault.'

Which at last prompted my son into some level of response.

'You take no account of the reason why I asked that she would wed me. It is very clear to anyone who knows me well, and who knows the lady. I fell in love. I wed her because I did not wish to live without her.'

His features were alight with it. I would not be persuaded.

'Love! It is an embarrassment.'

And there again was the flash of temper in his eyes as they held mine without any sense of regret.

'I love her! Did I not appreciate the problems surrounding this marriage? I am neither ignorant nor naive, but the moment I set eyes on Mistress Grey, my heart was hers, as hers was mine. I wed her because I wished to spend my life with her. I know that she will be an unimpeachable Queen.'

His confidence was disquieting.

'You say that you are not naive. This marriage was the opportunity to make that one single irrevocable alliance with a European power through the hand of a foreign Princess. Instead you have thrown it away on a family of little renown. Rivers, a man of meagre nobility. Jacquetta, it is true, the daughter of some distant branch of the family of Luxembourg, but it does not make amends for Woodville's less than glorious birth.'

'I care not.'

'You should care. A King, particularly a new King with a kingdom to take in hand, should wed a virgin, a woman of pure reputation. It is not acceptable for you to wed a widow.'

My son's face was wiped clean of any expression, but he was not lost for words.

'It's always an education to hear your views of my character, Madam.'

I walked the length of the room, to put some distance between us, dismayed that he was unwilling to even recognise the damage he had done. 'Surely my nephew of Warwick must have guided you. And yet you have squandered your options, Edward. Your father would never have done anything so foolhardy.'

When I turned to face him, Edward had taken occupation of a window seat and was considering his reply, watching me over the rim of his cup.

'Would you then have had me wed the Scottish Queen with her amours and insatiable appetite? Simply because it would have secured Scottish friendship and protected the northern border from Scottish inundation?'

'Of course I would not! Don't play the fool with me, Edward.'

'I love Elizabeth.' Restless, angry, he pushed himself upright to stand in my path. 'As you loved my father.'

'It is nothing like my own situation as a bride,' I replied. 'That was a political marriage. Love came later, a mere chance blessing to a union of benefit to both families. Love is of the least importance for one in your position, as it was in mine. Love must have respect or it is nothing, as empty and worthless as the husks after the autumn winnowing. Can you respect this woman who apparently waylaid you on the road to beg a boon of you for her children? Or is it merely lust you feel for her?'

'You dishonour yourself by such an accusation.'

I was losing him. He was his own man on the battlefield. Now he rejected all advice that did not please him.

'Do we speak of dishonour? Rumour credits you with more mistresses than days in the month. Could you not have taken the woman as one more paramour and have done? Did you have to *marry* her? You dishonour your marriage by its secrecy!'

'Elizabeth is virtuous. She is a widow, not a harlot.' My son had stiffened under my onslaught, but now a ghost of a smile touched his lips. 'She would not come to my bed without the sanctity of the church.'

'I find that difficult to believe. Have you lost your skills of persuasion?'

'I don't think I have.'

'What does Warwick say to this misalliance?'

'Ah – Warwick!' Edward's glance slanted to me. 'He was uncomfortably outspoken – but we've found a level of agreement.'

'Beware of him.' For the first time I touched my son, my fingers resting lightly, persuasively, on the hand that held the cup. He did not pull away, but I felt there a furious tension. 'My nephew could be a dangerous man. Do not make an enemy of him. He'll not take humiliation well and he has the power to harm you.'

Even when he pulled away, I continued.

'You enabled him, encouraged him. He has proved his worth on the battlefield. If you would deign to take advice from your mother, it would be unwise of you to antagonise him further than you have already done by rejecting his efforts on your behalf to make a French alliance. If he feels threatened he might consider the need to challenge you. I admire him, but it would be unwise to push him too far. Loyalty is a finite commodity.'

'I am aware that I have angered Warwick but he must accept that I am no longer a child who needs guidance. I am King and have policies of my own. As for Louis, I am of a mind to pursue an alliance with Burgundy, which he is free to accept or reject. If I make a firm undertaking with Burgundy, Louis' espousal of Marguerite's cause will be of no account.'

I heard his voice gain an unaccustomed edge.

'I will not be governed as though I were a minor, bound to marry at the whim of a guardian. I would not be a King if I allowed such a curb on my own liberties, would I?'

A resolute inflexibility marred his good nature for a moment, hardening his face with the glamour of power. Then Edward smiled and once more held out the chased goblet of wine.

'I ask that you will soften towards Elizabeth; I ask that you will play a role in her coronation in Westminster Abbey. I believe that the rest of my family will be willing to show their support. As for my Yorkist followers, I think that they will be won over by a beautiful woman. Is it not also an excellent policy to win Lancastrians to my reign? Her family will be foremost in giving me their loyalty, and others will soon follow. I thought my marriage would please you, Madam.'

'Please me!' I placed the cup on the table with a snap, the

wine slopping onto the surface. He had filled it too full, which strangely fuelled my anger. 'Nothing about this situation pleases me! To wed her in such secrecy seems to me to be a sign of a guilty conscience. Perhaps you knew all the problems, but in a moment of unforgivable blindness and lust chose to ignore them and your duty to England.'

All I received in return was a careless shrug.

'My wife has already proved her worth. She has two healthy sons. I am proved to be fertile. I acknowledge at least one bastard child as my own. Thus each of us has demonstrated the unlikelihood that we will prove barren. We should be more than capable of producing an heir for England. I trust in God that before long my wife will carry a young Prince for you to dote on. That should please you, if nothing else does.'

I suddenly felt weary. More than weary. The deed was done. My son was married and there was no turning the tide back. Nothing I could say would have any effect. I made my way to the door, desperate to seek solitude in the bishop's chapel, until my son's voice stopped me.

'You have not said if you will be present at the coronation. We need to know so that your role in the proceedings can be clarified.'

'I will not be there.'

'I have to decide where Elizabeth will live before the event. Are you willing to give her hospitality at Baynard's Castle?'

I would not be accommodating. I would not have her living under my roof.

'It will not be convenient for your wife to take up residence at Baynard's Castle,' I said. 'Send her to Greenwich Palace. Your sister Margaret and your two brothers are in residence there, to

282

escape the plague. It would do perfectly as a temporary accommodation for your wife.'

Edward, opening the door for me, chose not to respond to my suggestion.

'I hope you will change your mind. In the interest of harmony in my household.'

Before it closed behind me, all I heard was the popinjay's shriek, startled by some reaction from within the room. Edward laughed. The popinjay had more effect on him than I.

All was clear, like iron nails hammered into a coffin. Elizabeth Woodville would be Queen of England. I had been supplanted by a woman for whom I had no respect.

At some point I would have to meet her.

What a game that would be to play out. Queen versus King's Mother.

Chapter Twenty

A Woodville Queen

**Anne, Dowager Duchess of Buckingham,
to Cecily, King's Mother**
Written from Tonbridge Castle, October 1464

Dear sister,

Have you met the Woodville bride? Since the wedding, I mean.

Will I see you at the coronation?

I understand it will be an event of untold magnificence.

I think I will come and stay with you at Baynard's Castle to encourage you into attending.

Your sister, agog with prurient interest,

Anne

**Cecily, King's Mother, to Anne, Dowager
Duchess of Buckingham**
Written from Reading Abbey

Dear Anne,

No, I have not yet met her formally. That pleasure still awaits me. It is one thing to acknowledge a young woman of little importance and quite another to take her into my bosom as my daughter by law.

I have made it clear to Edward that I will not be at the Queen's coronation.

I do not need a description of how superb a ceremony Edward has arranged. I am well aware that he has a gift for showy display.

I find that I cannot be present when the Lancastrian Woodvilles rejoice at their achievement. I suspect that Richard will be turning in his unsuitable shroud. Were you aware that his most precious remains are still in Pontefract?

You will say that I am too selfish and proud, but I find it impossible to give my recognition to such a disastrous political mistake.

You will note that I am now addressing my eldest son as Edward. He has forfeited my affectionate appellation of Ned.

Cecily

**Anne, Dowager Duchess of Buckingham,
to Cecily, King's Mother**
Written from the Palace of Westminster

Dear Cis,

Well, you will get a full description from me, when it happens. I will tell you every succulent detail of how proud the Woodvilles are become.

Will you be the only one of the family not to be at the ceremony and the feasting? I think it good policy to show compliance with Ned's choice. It would not do to announce to the realm with trumpet and herald that you do not approve.

Will you truly allow personal sentiment and pride to overrule political necessity? Would it be wise to allow discord to develop between King and King's Mother?

I need your advice on what I should wear.

He is still Ned to me.

Your sister,

Anne

Duchess Cecily meets the Queen in Reading Abbey, October 1464

Mistress Grey was awaiting me in one of the bishop's sun-filled antechambers. She curtsied as I entered and pressed her lips to the hand that I offered. She was of course not yet Queen, and had been well schooled, either by Jacquetta or Edward himself. Low and formal and elegant, her obeisance to me was perfection itself. Against my inclination, I was impressed.

And by her handsomeness. Was she not gilded with the light? Her finely plucked eyebrows were marvellously arched.

I raised her to her feet.

'Let me look at you.'

She was indeed as comely as they said. I led her to the window, where I was forced to admit to a sharp pain of jealousy. If beauty was in the perfect oval of her face, in the unblemished skin, in those wide lustrous eyes, then this woman was undeniably beautiful. How could my son not be entranced?

The days of my own beauty were long past, and I was never as lovely as this woman.

'You are my son's wife.'

Regrettably, Elizabeth Woodville was taller than I. Height was an advantage with which I had always struggled.

'Yes, my lady.'

I almost asked her if she had connived at their meeting, waylaying him in the forest, but to what value? Her eyes were downcast in seemly respect, yet I sensed a latent power within the low-cut, fur-trimmed bodice.

'It pleases me that I was well received here at Reading, madam,' she observed with a gentle smile. 'Being presented to the Court in the chapel of the Abbey I thought would be difficult. You were not there, of course, to receive me. But Warwick and the King's brother Clarence led me in, to give me royal support.'

I felt my shoulders stiffen. Was this a criticism of my deliberate absence?

'I regret our marriage was without your knowledge, madam,' she continued. 'Your son the King insisted on it.' How impressive was her serenity as she retrieved a small package from her over-sleeve. 'I have a gift for you as a memento of that day when you were unable to be with us. I hope that you will accept it as a token of my regard.'

I opened the little book. It was costly, the work of an expert scribe.

'My thanks.'

'I know that you will have wished for a better marriage, to a lady of rank and connection. I hope that your son and I will be as successful as you in producing sons and daughters. I pray that those born to us will live long lives.'

For the first time my composure was shaken.

'I hope that you will be guided by your husband,' I suggested.

'Of course. And by yourself, my lady. I know that you will advise me most carefully to make a good wife for Edward. He has told me that he has seen the value of your support and advice in the past. I will try to emulate him. As well as giving due honour to my own father and mother, of course.'

Another little sting in the tail.

'I hope that we will both work for the good of the realm, madam.'

There was nothing more to say. She expressed a wish to join me in the chapel to hear Mass, where her behaviour was exemplary. All those political choices torn up and cast in the flames for a lovely face and charming manners.

I could see behind the beauty and the charm. I could not trust the innocence in those softly glowing eyes.

Here, I feared, was a woman of ambition.

Cecily, King's Mother, to Anne, Dowager Duchess of Buckingham

Written from Reading Abbey

Dear Anne,

Is it possible that I have misjudged her?

I have met with Edward's wife.

She proved to be graceful and well mannered. Or at least she had the ability to mask any ill-advised ambitions, other than to become my son's wife in such regrettable secrecy. We managed a frictionless conversation with both of us on our best behaviour. I will never be accused of crude manners, and nor it seems will she, although I detected an unwise wit that might be used at the expense of those whom she dislikes.

She had been urged to come prepared with a gift. It is a pretty psalter and not without value. I will make use of it. Or perhaps I will give it to Meg.

At least they should produce some comely children. A son to inherit the throne.

I may have to be less critical of her and include her in my prayers.

You will be pleased to know this. That I may have been wrong.

Yet I am old enough to wait before casting judgement. She has a very forthright stare. I suspect that the battle has not even begun.

Why am I thinking in terms of war and conflict? You would say that I should know better.

Your sister who is not yet quite won over by the Woodville charm.

Cecily

Cecily, King's Mother, to Edward, King of England
Written from Baynard's Castle, October 1464

Edward,

I am once again displeased.

It has come to my attention that you have made a decision which I consider unwise. I cannot allow it to go unremarked.

I recall suggesting that you allow your new wife to lodge at Greenwich Palace until you could make better accommodation for her than at the Palace of Westminster. Although why she could not occupy some of the royal apartments there, or in the Tower, I could not imagine.

But the matter of Greenwich Palace. It was not my intention to suggest that you grant her the property, for her personal use. It troubles me that you could be so thoughtless, and that she would be so insensitive in taking over an establishment much loved by your brothers and sister Meg, who are in residence there. Do you intend to turn them out so that your wife can rule supreme and probably accommodate her own extensive family? Where do you suggest that Meg and your brothers will live? Do I have to take them back within the walls of Baynard's Castle? You must know that they are of an age to be in possession of their own households.

I hear that you have also granted your wife the use of Ormonde's Inn in Knightrider Street beyond the City walls, presumably for when she needs to retire from the hurly-burly of Court. Is she so fragile?

I will not mention the jointure of four thousand marks every year that you have granted to her.

I await your rapid response.

Cecily, King's Mother

Edward, King of England, to Cecily, King's Mother
Written from the Palace of Westminster

My Lady Mother,

Your disapproval on this matter does you no favour. How could you think so poorly of my care for my family? Would I deprive my family of suitable accommodations?

It is my intention to extend the palace at Greenwich, already much improved at the hand of Queen Marguerite, with its new jetty. I consider it perfect for Elizabeth and our children when God sees fit to bless us. Meanwhile Meg will remain at Greenwich as long as she wishes, or until a marriage is arranged for her. There will also be ample room for George and his ever-increasing household. How does a boy of fifteen years require almost three hundred servants and officials? I will inform him that the number must be curtailed. It will be good for him to practise economy.

As for Diccon, it is my intention to send him north, to learn the skills of knighthood and leadership at the hands of my cousin of Warwick. I expect he will be based in Middleham. You have encouraged me to strengthen my ties with Warwick. Giving him the care of my brother will show him the respect I have for his friendship and loyalty.

As for your own comfort, madam, Baynard's Castle will continue to be yours, and the use of Fotheringhay, which I know remains dear to you. I will also ensure that the accommodations at the Royal Wardrobe will be refurbished for the use of the family.

I trust this all meets with your approval.

Elizabeth has expressed a keen desire for life at Greenwich.

Your dutiful son,

Edward

Cecily, King's Mother, to Katherine, Dowager Duchess of Norfolk

Written from Fotheringhay

Dear Kat,

I am becoming beleaguered. My family is prepared to be welcoming to Edward's new bride, while I am out of step with them. You are the only one to whom I can communicate my anxieties. Except Warwick, and he is so angry I am leaving him alone to work out his personal melancholy.

Am I being too intolerant? I know you will be honest.

Dame Grey might not yet be Queen of England, crowned and anointed, but still it begins. When I met with her, I admit to being beguiled by her smiling face and graceful manners. She almost won me over.

And now? How naive I was, how willing to be seduced by

a mistress of a sweet expression and dulcet tones. Much as my son, I expect. Her father, now promoted to become a member of Edward's Council, is regarded as one of the most important men at Court. His heir, Anthony Woodville, by virtue of being wed to the Scales heiress, is now addressed as Lord Scales.

I think it must have been in her mind when we met at Reading, although nothing was said. Margaret, one of the Woodville sisters, is betrothed to Thomas, Lord Maltravers, son and heir of the Earl of Arundel. How high they look. This may be the first but I fear it will not be the last.

Will Edward see sense and not allow every prominent and useful marriage to be snapped up by this ambitious family? Warwick will advise him to have a care, if he will not attend to me. It would be unwise to antagonise the English nobility by putting all the marriageable eggs into one Woodville basket.

Will you come to Court? I could do with a sympathetic ear. If I continue to express my determination to not set foot in Westminster Abbey when that woman is crowned, I may be the only member of the family to be absent. Perhaps you and I, Katherine, can sit together in Baynard's Castle and enjoy a stripping of the Woodville character.

I always had a suspicion of Jacquetta's motives. She may have married low after Bedford's death, but she certainly intends to make up for it as mother by law to the King of England.

I will not complain again to you about Edward's high-handed encroachment on Greenwich, but I am sure that I will wax long and bitterly about the Woodville family.

You see I am still driven to address my son as Edward.

Your thoroughly irritated sister,

Cecily

**Katherine, Dowager Duchess of Norfolk,
to Cecily, King's Mother**

Written from Epworth, January 1465

My dear and intolerant but wise sister,

I should warn you before you say more, and in a tone of voice that both you and I might regret. I am planning to marry again.

And I advise you to attend the coronation. Much good may come of it.

I have nothing more to say of this impending marriage as yet. And will not until it is all settled.

Your sister,

Katherine

**Cecily, King's Mother, to Katherine,
Dowager Duchess of Norfolk**

Written from Baynard's Castle

What?

Who?

I can think of no man suitable.

And why would you wish to wed for the fourth time?

Who is it that has his greedy eye on your estates and money-bags? He can hardly be wedding you for your youthful beauty.

And why did you not tell me who, in your previous letter? I smell a rat.

My decision about the coronation is made.

Cecily

Katherine, Dowager Duchess of Norfolk, to Cecily, King's Mother

Written from Epworth

I suppose I did not tell you because I know you will despise what has been planned.

My fourth, and very new husband, is a Woodville rat. John Woodville.

Is it worth our wasting ink and our couriers' time and horse-flesh for these missives?

I can already hear your explosion of outrage.

Katherine

Cecily, King's Mother, to Katherine, Dowager Duchess of Norfolk

Written from Baynard's Castle

Katherine!

In the name of the Blessed Virgin!

By the time I received the news at your own hand, the scandal was drenching London. What a wretched fool you have made of yourself.

He is all of nineteen years old. Shall I tell you what they say? That it is a diabolical marriage. That you are a slip of a girl at sixty-seven years, seeking to renew your youth in the bed of a mere boy.

What they say of him is unrepeatable. Power-grabbing and ambitious are the mildest faults.

Who persuaded you? Edward, I presume. All to please his wife and further the Woodville aggrandisement.

I weep for you. I feel the humiliation for you.

He hardly lusts after tumbling you between the sheets. What will you talk about?

Cecily

Katherine, Dowager Duchess of Norfolk, to Cecily, King's Mother

Written from Epworth

Thank you for your compassion.

It was entirely absent, of course, but I do not need it.

Do not weep. John Woodville will be no burden to me. I doubt our paths will cross too often. My life will not change to any degree and I will certainly refuse to be addressed as anything but Duchess of Norfolk. My husband has an ambition to make a name for himself as a knight. I expect him to spend most of his days at Court.

The gossip has no effect on me. When did it ever? The marriage has been consummated sufficiently to please the church and without embarrassment for either of us. Any further intimacies are of no concern to anyone but myself and my Woodville husband. Those who wish to mock and crow their derision are free to do so.

And do not pity me.

He makes me laugh.

Don't cast me off, Cis. I was given little choice in this match. I would hate not hearing the news from your bitter pen.

Katherine

Edward, King of England, to Cecily, King's Mother
Written from the Palace of Westminster

My Lady Mother,

I request that you will be present at Elizabeth's coronation. I will not, of course, as it is tradition that I absent myself. It is her day, but it would be most seemly for you to be there as King's Mother. Elizabeth's own mother will also be there to support her.

I cannot command it. I can ask of your generosity and knowledge of Court matters that you take your place in the celebration. It would not be good for the realm if there appears to be more dissention within the family.

Your dutiful son,

Edward

Cecily, King's Mother, to Edward, King of England
Written from Fotheringhay

Dissention?

I am no creator of dissention.

Perhaps you should look closer to home. Do you think the Court magnates will take kindly towards your plans for promotion of Woodvilles? Your wife must be overjoyed at the sudden preferment of her brothers, even before she is crowned Queen. Lionel Woodville earmarked for the vacant post of Bishop of Salisbury, Edward Woodville destined to be Admiral of the Fleet.

I cannot even put into words my opinion of the marriage of Sir John Woodville with your aunt Norfolk. It is a disgrace and a humiliation.

My mood is not one of rejoicing.

Cecily, King's Mother

Royal Proclamation

On this day, the twenty-sixth day of May in the year 1465
 The crowning of Queen Elizabeth
 In Westminster Abbey
 God bless her
 And God bless King Edward the Fourth our King

England's Chronicle, *May 1465*

Welcome, Queen Elizabeth.

We trust you spent a comfortable night at the Tower before your pageant-filled journey to Westminster. We wonder at the cost of so many peacock feathers to create angels' wings but we are assured by the citizens of London that it made a fine scene. Those starving in the gutters of our City will have been highly entertained.

All in all, a most auspicious day, the sun shining on her golden beauty. So many guests to honour her regal enhancement, too many to mention.

Who was not there?

We will leave you to guess.

As for the Queen, as long as she can curb her Woodville desires to promote her family, the country will welcome her with open arms. Queen Marguerite has dealt a death blow to the popularity of foreign Queens. For our King to take an English woman to wear the royal crown with him is perhaps a wise choice.

Anne, Dowager Duchess of Buckingham,
to Cecily, King's Mother
Written from the Palace of Westminster, the twenty-seventh day of
May 1465

Dear Cecily,

Well, here it is, as promised, and I wager you will read it even if you have sworn to ignore all mention of the Event of the Year. You will wish to know every element of that astonishing day. I thought you would have the courage to attend.

What should I tell you? What will you dislike most? Ned's extravagance in purchasing jewels, cloth of gold, fine silk for her chair and her saddle, and a particularly eye-catching gold cup and basin so that she might wash her hands? Or the purple mantle, the canopy of cloth of gold and the sceptres in both hands as she entered the Abbey, flanked by bishops. Her horse-litter rivalled your own.

Watch your power, Cis! You now have a rival.

We were well represented amongst her attendants when she prostrated herself before the high altar. All very appropriate, although it provided some amusement that the soles of her Woodville bare feet were not altogether clean from the Abbey dust.

What else would you like to know?

It could not help but be noticed that you were absent from the massed ranks of the high-born retinue that accompanied the new Queen.

And then the banquet in Westminster Hall. Trumpets to announce the courses, twenty dishes for each course. Clarence held the basin for the new Queen to wash her pretty fingers. We all were required to do an awful lot of kneeling. Your daughter

Elizabeth's husband Suffolk knelt at her side with Essex throughout the tiresomely lengthy banquet. I suspect they mentally counted every dish in the three separate courses as their knees groaned and creaked for the whole of the three hours it took us to eat our way through it.

The minstrels were better than usual, a procession of mounted knights impressed, and then the whole finished off with a tournament. Altogether a tour de force.

I have to say, she was crowned most regally.

Don't you wish you had been there? I enjoyed the Woodville display. Your daughter Meg also seems to hold our new royal lady in high esteem.

You might be my lady the King's Mother, Cis, but Elizabeth Woodville is now undoubtedly Queen of England.

Anne

Cecily, King's Mother, to Anne, Dowager Duchess of Buckingham

Written from Fotheringhay

Sister,

Thank you, although it was not necessary to drown me in so much irrelevant detail. Can I imagine a smirk? I know what coronations are like. I attended the festivity when Marguerite was crowned – and nothing good came of that.

The effigies of flaxen-wigged virgins in the pageant that welcomed Elizabeth Woodville seemed to me to be inappropriate. Her hair might be fair, but a virgin she is not!

It was not lack of courage that kept me away. It was lack of approval.

Sometimes, Anne, I miss Richard more than I can bear. Sometimes I am still sick with love. Which perhaps should make me more compassionate towards Edward, but it does not.

There is more to consider than coronations and inadvisable love matches. I wish Edward would set his mind to eradicating the threats that loom around him. Marguerite might be in France with her son, but Henry is still in the north. The last I heard he was in Bamburgh Castle before fleeing across the country and taking refuge in Lancashire. It would be best to have him under lock and key.

The Yorkist crown is still not secure, Anne. Taxation is high and resented. All that we achieved through Edward becoming King might well be undermined. Critically, my son must turn his mind to the needs of the country.

We may have a new Queen, but I can never forget: I was Queen by right. If it were not for the horror of Wakefield, I would be wearing the crown and there would be no Woodvilles snapping at Plantagenet heels.

What a terrible stitching this is, and now far too late to unpick. Warwick continues to snarl. King Louis is tossing a French coin to see where he should give his future allegiance.

It breaks my heart. We did not raise Edward to be so deceitful and manipulative.

The Council is not won over. I am full of anger. Ambassadors gossip about it through the courts of Europe.

Elizabeth Woodville has usurped my power. She has usurped my position. She has usurped my son.

Cecily

Chapter Twenty-One

A Surfeit of Marriages

England's Chronicle, *August 1465*

More weddings on our horizon?
  Woodville weddings?
  Oh, yes!
  Prepare to be entertained. Or infuriated.
  Duchess Cecily will not be amused.

**Anne, Dowager Duchess of Buckingham,
to Cecily, King's Mother**
Written from the Palace of Westminster

Dear Cecily,

Well, you warned me. I was loath to believe you. Now I do, but what could I do about it? I don't know whether to be admiring of her ability to outmanoeuvre my royal nephew, or horrified at the result. Horror is uppermost at this moment.

My family is to be part of the Woodville plot to consolidate its power by whatever means possible. By marriage, of course. Has Ned discussed this with you? I doubt it. He seems to have handed all control over to his new wife, simply giving his name and signature to endorse the fait accompli.

This is what has been agreed. Queen Elizabeth's sister Katherine Woodville is to marry my grandson Henry. It was bad enough that his wardship, he still being a minor, was given into the care of the Queen. Would I, his grandmother, not accomplish the task with more skill? Now Henry's marriage is arranged, and what a catch it is for the Woodville girl. She will hop in one brief religious ceremony from being Mistress Woodville to Duchess of Buckingham.

My grandson is not pleased. He was always an outspoken child. I think that I have failed in the schooling of him, to teach him better manners. He states that he will not wed her. That as Duke of Buckingham he will choose a worthier bride from a family of higher rank than a common Woodville.

I felt like dispatching him to the priest to confess the sin of pride, except that I tended to agree.

Anyway the marriage is arranged and will take place at the wish of the Queen.

Have you heard more from Katherine? I hate to hear her ridiculed. She does not deserve it. I think we will all be ridiculed as pawns of this family.

Your desolate sister,

Anne

Cecily, King's Mother, to Anne, Dowager Duchess of Buckingham

Written from Baynard's Castle

My dearest Anne,

You have my sympathies over young Henry, but I have fast come to realise that there is nothing we can do about it. I misjudged the depth of the woman's ambition, and it worries me inordinately.

Have you taken count of all the other marriages snatched up for the promotion of this family? Every unwed scion of aristocratic lineage is now marked to be wed to a Woodville bride. I imagine there are complaints within these families up and down the country to mirror yours.

Except that many will see the value of a marriage alliance with the King's wife.

I am afraid, Anne. I fear the repercussions.

Did you know that Edward has given the Barony of Dunster to the Herbert heir as a wedding gift when he espouses Mary Woodville? It is a barony that Warwick was claiming for himself, as heir to the Montagus who held it. I see trouble brewing there. Where will Warwick look for husbands for his two daughters? It may be that he has to look across the sea. I have not heard his thoughts on this.

Surely it has crossed Edward's mind as well as my own that this is dangerous policy. He was always so politically astute. This infatuation seems to have entirely robbed him of perspicacity.

It is my intention to keep close with Warwick. It would be disastrous if Edward pushed him into any degree of hostility. The Woodvilles are becoming more influential at Court, but I feel that it is Warwick's support that will keep my son strong in his kingship. Warwick helped bring him to the throne. Warwick must help keep him there.

I can only hope that I am merely stirring up a storm in an ale-cup.

Meanwhile, we wait to hear that the bride is carrying a royal child. It would be the only blessing out of this whole maelstrom of bad decision-making.

The other news on the family front is the proposed marriage of my daughter, Meg. Which reminds me that I must tell her the good news, and I think a word of caution.

Cecily

If you choose to wed again, do not under any circumstances wed a Woodville. Are there any left?

Cecily, King's Mother, to Margaret, King's Sister
Written from Baynard's Castle

My most well-beloved daughter,

It is with joy that I write to inform you that at last we have a suitor for your hand in marriage. Don Pedro of Aragon, a contender to the throne of Aragon and claimant of Catalonia, has expressed his wish for the match. Negotiations are already underway between your brother the King and Don Pedro, even to the extent of a description of your betrothal ring, which is very fine. We must now consider your robes for this marriage. I doubt that Edward will be parsimonious in his spending.

I have to say this, dear Meg. There is much support for this marriage from the Queen and the Woodville faction. Do not be swept away by a beautiful face and gracious manners. I know that you admire her, but remain careful and judgemental. Do learn to keep a distance. It will be good practice for when you are the consort of Don Pedro. The wife of a ruler must learn to be selective of where she gives her affections and patronage.

I regret having to give you up to a marriage overseas, but I know it must be.

Your affectionate mother,
Cecily

Cecily, King's Mother, to Richard Neville, Earl of Warwick

Written from Baynard's Castle

Written to you, my nephew, in a spirit of commiseration.

In spite of all that Edward might owe to you, he has served you ill through his Woodville marriage and its aftermath. I regret the loss for you of the Dunster barony, and more importantly the destruction of your negotiations for a firm alliance between England and France.

Humiliation is a hard cross to bear, as I know from my own experience.

I am hoping that my son comes to his senses and sees where his best interests might lie. I beg of you to keep faith with him and this reign might come to no harm. He needs you, as a friend, counsellor, and a strong right arm.

Do not give way to temper. It will do no good.

How is Diccon? I hope that he has settled well into his lessons and his training at Middleham. He was never the strongest of my children, but he has great loyalty and tenacity. I am sure that your Countess will not allow herself to be twisted around his clever fingers.

I imagine that you will have to look abroad for husbands for your two daughters. I wish you well in your search. They will be much sought-after, given their magnificent lineage.

Your affectionate but troubled aunt,
Cecily

**Richard Neville, Earl of Warwick,
to Cecily, King's Mother**
Written from the Palace of Westminster

My thanks, Aunt, for your warning and advice.

I was angry. I cannot deny it, but I have in my political wisdom put aside my anger. Edward and I have too much past history together in bringing him to the throne. Thus we have, to some degree, mended our clash of temperament.

I still have hopes for an alliance between England and France. I am aware that the Woodvilles are pressing for a firm contract with Burgundy, supported by the strong voices of the English merchants, but I believe that I can persuade the King that France would be a move of political wisdom, if only to prevent Louis from throwing in his hand with Marguerite.

Perhaps a French alliance would provide well-born husbands for my daughters.

There is no need for your concern. All will be settled amicably, as I will accept the loss of the Dunster barony.

Diccon is in good spirits. He might lack strength and stature but he is learning the art of swordplay with some skill. My master at arms is impressed with him. He remains ever-loyal to his brother Edward and seems to have discovered a kindred spirit in my daughter Anne. They both have a love of sweetmeats.

I was not blessed with a son. Diccon is a joy in my wife's heart.

I am sanguine about the future, yet I am wary of the growth in Woodville power. It is difficult for a man of my experience to be ignored in Council when the King leans toward Lord Rivers. I will keep my temper equable as long as I am able.

Warwick

Cecily, King's Mother, to Edward, King of England
Written from Baynard's Castle

Edward,

Did I not warn you about the dangers of making Warwick too strong a power in the land? And yet, you did it. To attack him and his family, ignoring his advice, is equally dangerous.

He is like a fast-simmering pot, about to boil over and quench the flames of the warmth and loyalty he still holds for you. The Woodvilles cannot offer you the strength and wisdom that Warwick can. They are too intent on strengthening their own position. If you are thinking of Sir Anthony, Lord Scales, he may well be a fine man, with a reputation for his prowess in the tournament, but he is not the same calibre as Warwick.

Take care how far you insult him in the arrangement of these marriages and the disposing of titles.

Are you quite sure that you wish to follow Woodville advice to achieve a Burgundian alliance, rather than one with France which has Warwick's blessing? It will go ill with Warwick if you do. Equally it would be unwise to topple Louis into a dangerous alliance with Queen Marguerite, as she still styles herself.

What can have possessed you to arrange so humiliating a wedding for your aunt Katherine? She might be phlegmatic about it, but it is a degrading situation for a woman of her history and connections.

I do not enjoy jokes at the expense of my family.

Cecily, King's Mother

Edward, King of England, to Cecily, King's Mother
Written from the Palace of Westminster

To my Lady Mother,

There is nothing to disturb you. As time passes my wife will be accepted, as will be her family. When we have a son, the country will celebrate with ale and dancing.

Meanwhile I will win Warwick to my plans.

My aunt Katherine is a woman of character and will not be disturbed by a political marriage. It surprised me that you have given any mind to what the inhabitants of the London gutter shriek after a surfeit of ale. Why would you care?

I know that you will be receptive of one promotion I have arranged. My cousin, and your nephew, George Neville, will be enthroned as Archbishop of York, followed by a day of feasting and pageant, already commissioned in true extravagant Neville style, in Cawood Castle. I hope I have reinstated myself back into your good books by my promotion of a Neville.

Warwick will like it too.

Your dutiful son (who is not quite without political guile),

Edward

Cecily, King's Mother, to Edward, King of England
Written from Baynard's Castle

Excellent. I approve of all Neville advancement.

You will reinstate yourself even more securely if you can get your wife with child. Perhaps you need to spend more time with her, rather than in the hunting field.

Cecily, King's Mother

Elizabeth, Queen of England, to Cecily, King's Mother
Written from Greenwich Palace, 1465

Madam,

It pleases me to inform you that I am expecting a royal child.

It will be born at the beginning of the new year.

It is my fervent hope that it will be a son.

I know that you will rejoice with me.

Elizabeth

**Cecily, King's Mother, to Katherine,
Dowager Duchess of Norfolk**

Written from Baynard's Castle

Dearest Kat,

May the Blessed Virgin be praised. At last she has fulfilled her role.

We will all pray for a safe travail. And a boy to step into Edward's shoes.

I am even tempted to call him Ned again.

I am feeling in a forgiving mood and will instruct the monks at Westminster Abbey to lend the Virgin's Girdle to her, to give her ease in childbirth. It is my thought to send her a book of the Life of St Margaret. Even if she does not read it, she can have her women read to her. Although unmarried, I suppose being swallowed by a dragon and then spat out would give the Blessed Margaret some knowledge of pain and discomfort in childbed.

I trust that your Woodville husband is making himself useful. I will not wish you happiness.

I am still considering possible betrothals for Meg. We had high hopes of Don Pedro of Aragon. Everything was arranged, including a betrothal ring costing more than two hundred pounds. Sadly, he fell ill and was dead within a week. Meg never did receive the diamond and gold ring.

Our nephew of Warwick is no longer simmering like a pot of stew. I have hopes that all will be well.

Your sister,
Cecily

England's Chronicle, *January 1466*

It has come to our attention that the Queen has gone into seclusion in her chambers in Westminster Palace.

There can be only one reason for this.

We await events with fervent hope and prayers and we have lit votive candles.

We know that the nation will follow our example.

Even Duchess Cecily might be praying for the health of our Queen.

Royal Proclamation

On this day, the eleventh day of February in the year 1466
  Born to King Edward the Fourth and his wife Queen Elizabeth
  At the Palace of Westminster
  A daughter
  Elizabeth

England's Chronicle, *the twelfth day of February 1466*

Today the little Princess was baptised in Westminster Abbey.

She is named Elizabeth, for her mother the Queen. Her lungs are clearly working well. We would have preferred a son but a healthy daughter is no detriment to the making of powerful alliances for England in the future. We think the King is already discussing a possible husband.

The Queen was not present, of course, not having yet been churched.

But here was a situation for all to savour.

Who were the great and the good chosen to stand sponsor for the child?

Jacquetta of Luxembourg, Lady Rivers, once Duchess of Bedford, the child's maternal grandmother.

Richard, Earl of Warwick. One of the mighty Nevilles, cousin to the King.

Cecily, Duchess of York, King's Mother, the child's paternal grandmother. An interesting trio to stand together in harmony to support the little Princess. It is well known that relationships between the Woodvilles and the Duchess are not at their best. Nor is the Earl of Warwick a Woodville friend.

Sword blades seem to have been buried on this occasion. There was no apparent animosity. Everyone heaving a sigh of relief as the child was blessed, named and cradled in the arms of her godmothers. Lady Rivers was aglow with achievement, the Duchess of York resigned, Warwick at his saturnine best.

Expect another Woodville marriage mooted on the horizon. Who will it be? And to whom? Will Duchess Cecily and Warwick approve?

Cecily, King's Mother, to Katherine, Dowager Duchess of Norfolk
Written from Baynard's Castle

My dearest Kat,

Edward is a fool.

Would I ever say that of a son of mine? A son of the mighty Richard, Duke of York?

We have a granddaughter, Elizabeth. A fine healthy child. Edward was disappointed that it was not a son, as were we all, but he has hopes for the future. He awarded the Woodville Queen with a jewel costing over one hundred pounds to mark the birth.

Edward, with utter disregard for the balance of interest at Court, has undone all the latent goodwill. Even worse, he is blind to what he is doing. He listens to no one but the Woodvilles. With one hand he makes George Neville Archbishop of York, which must be some balm to Warwick's wounds, although the King and Queen were not present at the ceremony and feast, which might well be regarded as a slight. Nor was I, but I heard of the flamboyant feasting, typical of our nephew.

And then. What does Edward do? He has ennobled Lord Rivers further. He is now Earl Rivers, would you believe, and what's more, Treasurer of England. Which might not hurt so much except that Edward dismissed Lord Mountjoy, Warwick's uncle, to make way for him.

Warwick is not pleased and wears a permanent frown.

What's more, King Louis is still in negotiation with Warwick. He has lost the marriage but has no intention of allowing England to sign agreements with Burgundy and Brittany.

I live in dread of what I will hear next. When I look in my mirror it seems that I have been keeping vigil for months. The shadows beneath my eyes are as dark as thumbprints.

My family has become the object of common and salacious gossip.

Did you know that Edward has created Thomas Grey – eldest son of the Woodville Queen's first marriage – Marquess of Dorset? An earldom was not good enough for him. *England's Chronicle* is talking of another Woodville marriage. How many of them are there still to marry off? I despair.

Where will it end?

Your sister,

Cecily

England's Chronicle, *October 1466*

More Woodville dealings at Court to spice your daily exchange of news with your neighbour.

Was Duchess Cecily expecting her granddaughter Anne Holland, daughter of the absent Duke and present Duchess of Exeter, to be wedded to her Neville great-nephew, the son of the Earl of Northumberland?

She may live to be disappointed.

And what will the Earl of Warwick have to say, when his brother Northumberland is robbed of this heiress for his son?

Money has changed hands in this dealing, we understand.

Is the King involved? Was it his strategy? Or did he simply allow his wife to have her way?

The Queen, so we are told, is carrying another child. Perhaps this new marriage was a gift from the King to the Queen for her undoubted fertility.

Anne, Duchess of Exeter, to Cecily, King's Mother
Written from Coldharbour, October 1466

To my Lady Mother,

Since *England's Chronicle* is spreading the word, I think I should make my excuses before you descend on me in understandable fury.

My daughter, Anne Holland, who was betrothed in a much sought-after Neville alliance to wed the son of Warwick's brother, the Earl of Northumberland, will no longer do so. She is now the intended bride of Thomas Grey, the Queen's son by her first marriage. The Marquess of Dorset, as he is now styled.

I hear that my husband Henry is attached firmly to Marguerite's side in France. I hope that he stays there.

I really had no choice. And would it be so very bad? It will connect my daughter with the most powerful family in the land.

Your affectionate daughter,

Anne

Cecily, King's Mother, to Anne, Duchess of Exeter
Written from Baynard's Castle

Oh, my daughter!

Yes, it would be so very bad!

Why in the name of the Blessed Virgin did you allow it? That a daughter of mine should be hand in gauntlet with the Woodvilles in their bid for power.

Of course I know why you did it. Perhaps I am wrong to blame you. I should put that at the feet of my son. I have my own sources. I know that Edward paid you four thousand marks to break the Northumberland alliance and allow the marriage with the Grey boy.

Why did you not come and talk to me first?

I can only imagine what Warwick will say, to see his brother's family thrust aside in this manner. The Neville pride will suffer another injurious blow from which it may never recover.

Well, it is done, so no use repining. Another nail to enclose us tightly into the same coffin as the Woodvilles.

I too hope that your husband remains in exile.

Your loving mother,

Cecily

Royal Proclamation

On this day, the eleventh day of this fair month of August in the year 1467

Born to King Edward the Fourth and his wife Queen Elizabeth

At Windsor Castle

A daughter

Mary

For those not caught up in the celebrations for another royal daughter, here are some more movements on the Woodville front to give rise to speculation. None of them will be enjoyed by Duchess Cecily and the Nevilles.

Earl Rivers has been made Constable of England. Which puts him firmly in a position of authority in the Royal Council.

As if that were not enough, George Neville, Archbishop of York, brother to the Earl of Warwick, has been dismissed by his royal nephew from his position of Lord Chancellor. Our King finds his desire to achieve a cardinal's hat a conflict of interest. The Archbishop is also scheming in a marriage that is not to the King's liking. (We are bound to secrecy about it for now!) What if the Neville brothers are driven into an alliance against King Edward?

On a lighter note, Duchess Cecily's sister Anne, once Duchess of Buckingham, has decided to re-enter the state of matrimony.

We wish her well.

We also wish the Lady Margaret, youngest sister of the King, health and happiness in her forthcoming marriage.

Anne, Dowager Duchess of Buckingham,
to Cecily, King's Mother
Written from Tonbridge Castle, September 1467

To my dearest sister,

I have decided to remarry. He is Walter Blount, Lord Mountjoy, and, before you ask, he is no fortune-hunter, nor a Woodville adherent, and has wooed me with great consideration. He already has three sons to inherit his own property. I plan to live in peace with my books and Walter.

If you wish to send me a betrothal gift, I much admire your Book of Hours made by the Master of Wingfield. I can enjoy it as I confess my sin of covetousness.

Your affectionate sister

Anne

Cecily, King's Mother, to Anne, Dowager Duchess of Buckingham

Written from Baynard's Castle

Dear Anne,

If you will be content with the match, then I will wish you every happiness. I know him for a loyal supporter of the House of York, a brave man on the battlefield and a pious one. Nor do I think his ambitions are particularly strong.

Another marriage is not for me.

All is at peace in this kingdom, but until we have a son born of Edward and Elizabeth, the House of York is not as strong as I could wish. Warwick remains a worry when I attend Court and see his restlessness, but I have hopes of reconciliation. Meg's imminent marriage must be pushed forward, although there is no doubt that her suitor, the Duke of Burgundy, is keen to achieve an English alliance against his enemy France. I hope that it will bring her every happiness. Warwick may need to be persuaded to accompany her as regal escort but I think I can do that. It will give him a high profile in the King's favour.

I still need to bring the sacred remains of Richard and Edmund home to Fotheringhay.

Thus I cannot yet retire into solitude with my books, even though the future suddenly seems far more benign for the House of York.

What can go wrong?

Your loving sister,

Cis

I have sent you the Wingfield Book of Hours with all my best wishes. Marriage to Lord Mountjoy will strengthen your allegiance to the House of York, remove your predilection to suffer agues, and give you a more skilled cook who can make masterpieces out of salted meat.

Royal Proclamation

On this day, the third day of July in the year 1468

Graciously escorted across the sea by her cousin the Earl of Warwick

The marriage of the Lady Margaret, King's Sister

To

The Illustrious Charles, Duke of Burgundy

One of the mightiest Princes in the world that weareth no crown

Joined in Holy Matrimony in the City of Bruges

With much celebration and magnificence and priceless jewels

None has been seen to equal it since the days of King Arthur's Court at Camelot

Chapter Twenty-Two

An Eruption of Family Discord

**Duchess Cecily detects a plot at the Palace
of Westminster, summer 1468**

My fears assuaged by the success of Margaret's marriage into the
House of Burgundy, I closed my mind to the ever-widening rifts
created by Edward's marriage and promotion of the Woodvilles.
It was five years since that disastrous meeting in the forest, or
wherever it was. I believed it was a time for healing within the
ranks of the Court.

Until I saw it for myself. The disharmony. The rank disapproval, the sour dislike, the rampant hostility. The whole Court
was awash with it, just below the surface. I could taste it, smell
it, like a miasma from the overused drains, thick as a glaze on
a roast pig.

It was a most unfortunate incident, precipitated by Edward's
clever and witty Fool. I condemned what he did, but I should
have been grateful to him for opening my eyes to reality. At the
time I would have had the despicable little creature torn limb
from limb by Edward's wolfhounds.

Edward's Court was smoothly and expensively dressed and jewelled, united in the endless round of conversation and exchange of views. Even in the height of summer with the heat of London pressing its weight down on us, the Court met and made its patterns under Edward's watchful eye as I steered a gracious course between Plantagenets, Nevilles, and Woodvilles alike. Even Warwick, elegant in dark-patterned damask, seemed not as sombre as his wont, engaged in discourse with Earl Rivers. All was placid, the Queen restored once more to society after the birth of her daughter, resplendent in trailing skirts and extravagant veiling.

An outburst of laughter to my right marked the change in the atmosphere, the rising murmur of voices in response to some unexpected merriment that dragged all attention. It was Rob Woodhouse, Edward's Court Fool, small in stature, agile and impish. Ridiculous in appearance he might be with his skinny limbs and barrel chest but no Fool in understanding, he was making his way across the room as a space opened before him, the vivid Fool's garb with its tassels and bells catching every eye and ear. He lurched to halt in front of the Queen.

I sensed the danger, like wood-smoke on the air. Here was an intent sufficient to stir the sleeping dragon of enmity into open, fire-breathing mockery. Was the Fool not clever with words?

Edward sensed it, too; moving smoothly to the Queen's side, he cocked his chin.

'Master Woodhouse,' Edward rose with humour to the bait cast by the Fool. 'Have you been travelling? And garbed for winter? One of the hottest days of the year and here you are clad in thigh-length boots and with a travelling staff. Is this a jest?'

'No jest, sire.' Rob Woodhouse planted his staff with a thump, looking around for maximum effect, his eyes twinkling in their malice. 'I would never have believed it. Only the first days of September and the summer one of the driest in memory.' His voice had a terrible carrying quality, his gaze moving over the little knot of Woodvilles. 'Dry, I say. Inordinately dry.'

And there was my son Clarence, face alive with equal mischief.

'So why the need for boots and staff, Sir Fool?' he asked.

The Fool smirked.

'Because the *Rivers* run so high it's near impossible for *lesser* mortals to get through them. I had to search the depth with my staff for safe-footing.' He thumped the staff forcefully to the floor again between his two booted feet. 'How will it be come February, I ask myself, when the *Rivers* are in spate?' He giggled unpleasantly. 'All those not of a *watery* connection will surely be swept away in the deluge.' His stare was turned on me. 'Did my lady the King's Mother not have to paddle through the deep puddles to reach her son's side, on her recent journey from Fotheringhay? I swear that her elegant shoes are still damp from the experience.'

The Fool's jesting carried through the chamber to monstrous effect. I felt Earl Rivers stiffen behind me. The gathering held its horrified breath. All eyes were turned on the Queen. The Fool angled his head with a comic expression of despair, falsely shocked at his own outspokenness. Then there was a stifled laugh, an intake of breath, a mutter of excited comment.

How dare the Fool voice such an opinion in the face of the King? How dare he draw me into his jest, and what role did my son Clarence have in this? I held my breath lightly against the derision, resisting the urge to strike out with my hand to wipe the bright laughter from the Fool's face. All hung on Edward's reaction. Would he order the man to grovel in apology, to kiss the floor at the Queen's feet, or to get out of his sight? Anything to show this spiteful Court that the King's decisions were not to be the object of ridicule. Edward must stop this.

He simply laughed aloud in appreciation of the wit, aiming a light-hearted blow at the Fool who dodged and shook his staff in mock combat. The Fool might be fast and agile but Edward was faster. With a lunge and a swoop he had the man by the scruff of his tunic, lifting him so that his booted toes swung helplessly above the floor. The staff dropped with a clatter.

'Forgive me, Majesty. I meant no harm,' the Fool whined.

Edward shook him, a terrier with a rat. 'Best that you ask the pardon of my lady wife.'

'I will, sire. Or she assuredly will demand my head on a platter.' And as Edward dropped him to the floor in front of the Queen, the Fool flung himself to his knees.

'Grovel well, my friend. Or you'll find my boot against your backside. And at the same time extend your apology to the King's Mother.'

The laughter in Edward's face was still there but so was a warning. Oh, yes, I saw what Edward was about. To use humour, sharp and deadly, to draw the sting. The anger that had all but curled my fingers into fists drained away as reluctant admiration for my son crept under my skin. The fine art of compromise learnt at my knee had not been lost on him.

'Cry pardon, lady.' The Fool pressed his forehead to the floor at the Queen's feet, and then at mine. 'Spare me and I'll sing your praises for ever in poetry.' He risked a glance around, one bright eye gleaming through his mussed hair. 'Some *Rivers* are beautiful beyond the wit of man. I can compose verses to your fair skin and sparkling eyes.'

'Spare *me* your rhyming, Sir Fool.' To her due, the Queen found her voice and mimicked Edward's light buffoonery.

But all was not yet won.

I stepped in. Lifting the Fool to his feet, brushing down his clothes with a kindness at odds with my thoughts, I restored the staff to his hands. 'If your poetry is as dull as your wit, Sir Fool, mayhap *you*'ll be the one to be swept away by the *Rivers* in spate!'

The Fool kissed the hem of my gown, but his expression as he looked up, not at me but at the Queen, was as venomous as ever. I shook him, yet more gently than my son had.

'Take care with your footing in future, Master Woodhouse. It would be so easy to fall into the torrent.' I gave him a push in the direction of the door, and he stumbled away, brandishing the staff, whistling tunelessly.

It was the right thing to do. A crow of laughter sounded, a breathless chuckle, and the heavy insolence in the atmosphere dissolved into general, if uneasy mirth. I turned to engage Rivers in conversation again, as if the bite of the words had caused no wounds. But something made me glance over Rivers's shoulder toward the door. There was Woodhouse grimacing, still clutching the staff, his boots squeaking on the floor. Suddenly he was not alone and the anxiety was gone from his face, replaced by a cunning satisfaction. He bowed, a grin spreading over his lively features. And there it was. A heavy purse swiftly changed hands, from my son Clarence to the Fool, my son nodding briefly and clasping the creature's shoulder.

Clarence?

And then I saw Clarence's gaze shift from the Fool, across the room towards the Earl of Warwick. It was a momentary connection, eye to eye, before Warwick turned away, but I had not been mistaken. There was scheming here, of that I was certain. Warwick would use any means, high or low, to oust the Woodvilles from Edward's affections. My heart shuddered uncomfortably, reminding me of my age and the passing of years. Once it would have beat strongly, whatever the shock. There were unexpected dangers all around. Warwick would make use of my son George and the Fool. How far was he prepared to go to undermine the King?

Looking back as I departed, it was to see Warwick and Clarence in some exchange of words. I was right to be concerned about my son and my nephew.

Cecily, King's Mother, to Edward, King of England
Written from Baynard's Castle, February 1469

Edward,

It is my wish, as it has been for some time, that we reinter the earthly remains of your father and brother in the church at Fotheringhay. It is almost ten years now since the Duke of York died so tragically, and he should not lie forgotten in some meagre grave at Pontefract.

If you would put in motion the demands for the reinterment, I would be grateful.

My brother Salisbury was reinterred with suitable ceremony. Why not the Duke of York? It does not look good, Edward.

Your mother,

Cecily, King's Mother

Edward, King of England, to Cecily, King's Mother
Written from Eltham Palace

To my Lady Mother,

I will arrange for the reinterment of my father.

As long as you understand that at the ceremony my wife, as Queen, will take precedence over you.

Let me know if this is acceptable to you, and I will go ahead with arrangements.

Your dutiful son,

Edward

Cecily, King's Mother, to Edward, King of England
Written from Baynard's Castle

Edward,

It is not acceptable.

How could you possibly presume that it would be?

This is the reburial of my husband, in a church that I have refurbished, in a tomb that I will pay for. Fotheringhay is the keystone of the House of York. How can Elizabeth Woodville take precedence over the widow of the Duke of York and the mother of the Earl of Rutland?

Cecily, King's Mother

Edward, King of England, to Cecily, King's Mother
Written from Eltham, February 1469

To my Lady Mother,

I think you must give more consideration to this small issue.

Reply to me when you feel that you can comply with my desires in this matter.

Until then my father, sadly, remains at Pontefract. I will not have the tensions between you and my wife made more public than they are already. I am not willing to become a laughing-stock, hen-pecked between wife and mother.

I have an incipient uprising in the north to deal with, under the spurious name of Robin of Redesdale. No sooner is one spate of rioting put down, than another breaks out under the same leader.

If you have nothing to do with your time, you might com-municate with your Neville relatives in the north to discover the culprit. Taxes seem to be the main issue.

As for the reinterment of my father, I will have my way in this.

The ceremony must be after the birth of my third child. As you are aware, Elizabeth is in confinement until that date. I expect that it is too much to ask that you visit her and give her the benefit of your experience and skill in such matters as child-bearing.

The least that you might do is to pray for a son.

Edward

Cecily, King's Mother, to Edward, King of England
Written from Baynard's Castle

Edward,

I want the earthly remains of my husband and son to be returned to Fotheringhay.

And I will take precedence at the ceremony.

There is nothing else to be decided.

Of course I will pray for a son of York. It is essential for the stability of the kingdom.

I doubt that your wife will value a visit from me in her confinement.

Cecily, King's Mother

England's Chronicle, *February 1469*

Now here's an interesting development in the ongoing tale of the clash between our two royal ladies, one more royal than the other.

It is well known that the Dowager Duchess rarely presents herself at Court when the Queen is in residence. She shows the minimum respect required by a subject to a Queen. The nod of her head is equivalent to a nervous twitch from a cobweb brushing your hair in a dusty cellar.

But now, since neither royal lady can accept the precedence of the other in Court matters, even on the delicate occasion of a reburial, Richard Duke of York is destined to remain in his obscure grave in the north at Pontefract.

We hear a whisper that the King has put into operation measures that will drive the Duchess to her knees in fury and cause the shedding of many tears. We suspect the fell hand of the Queen who is in confinement at Westminster.

Not that there is a problem with an heir for the King. Until the happy day that the Queen bears a son, his brother George, Duke of Clarence, remains our King's heir. Much to that Prince's satisfaction, we imagine.

We hear that young Clarence is considering taking a wife. Since he has now reached the age of nineteen years, that would undoubtedly be good policy. Will he look abroad for a woman of valuable foreign connection? Or will he look closer to home?

There are few eligible women of rank and birth in England

after the winnowing of such at the hands of the Woodvilles. We hear rumours…

And if they prove to be true, expect more explosions in royal ranks.

Edward, King of England, to Cecily, King's Mother
Written from Eltham, late March 1469

To my Lady Mother,

It is my wish, Madam, to make changes in the occupancy of the royal residences.

My wife and I and our growing family will continue to enjoy the palaces at Greenwich and Sheen. Baynard's Castle is yours, for your use, for all time.

It is my will that Fotheringhay be available for the sojourn of Elizabeth when she wishes to remove from London for the good of her health. It is clear, from all you have said, that it is not possible if you are still in residence there. For that reason I wish that you restore all your rights and title to the manor of Fotheringhay to me.

I am aware that you need a replacement. It will please me if you remove to Berkhamsted. At your convenience, of course. Before the end of the year would suit me very well.

I regret it if you are reluctant to hand over Fotheringhay, but I know that you will soon make Berkhamsted comfortable for your needs. Do contact me if you need any help in the removal of your belongings and household.

Your dutiful son,

Edward

Cecily, King's Mother, to Katherine, Dowager Duchess of Norfolk

Written from Baynard's Castle

Dear Kat,

Berkhamsted!

He has ordered me to remove myself and my whole household from Fotheringhay to Berkhamsted! For the convenience of the Queen.

It takes my breath away.

I have made the journey to look it over. If it was intended as a humiliation, it was appallingly successful. Have you seen the state of it? It reeks of neglect and hopelessness, although I admit it was once a fine fortress, with much money spent on it by Edward of Woodstock. His wife Countess Joan of Kent spent her final years there. But that was a hundred years ago and since then it has fallen into sad desolation. I know my son Edward would tell me that our previous King Henry enjoyed a sojourn there, but Henry is no judge of the comfort of accommodations.

I detest it, Katherine. It will empty my coffers to make it habitable and fit for my household. My jaw aches because of my gritted teeth.

It does not win me over to any degree that he has called his third daughter Cecily. That I stood sponsor for the child, and without doubt a fair and healthy one, does not heal the deep wound that he has inflicted on me.

You know how attached I have always been to Fotheringhay, and so does my son. I lived there with Richard. A goodly number of my children were born there. Anne and Margaret and Richard. And William, who did not live. It was my final earthly desire that Richard and Edmund should be restored there with fine

329

funerary memorials, and that I would ultimately be laid to rest at Richard's side. I have already had new glazings to enhance the church against the day when Richard is returned here. Instead, Richard remains in Pontefract, and I am banished to Berkhamsted. All because I will not kiss the feet of this power-hungry Queen.

I am eaten up with fury. I can do nothing about it.

What do I do? Do I merely comply, a weakling subject to her daughter by law's scheming? I suspect it is the public humiliation that hurts most.

Cis

England's Chronicle, *March 1469*

When not in residence at Baynard's Castle, we hear that the Duchess of York is removing herself from Fotheringhay to Berkhamsted.

Was this her choice?

We doubt it. We are reliably informed that the new home of the King's Mother is little more than a crumbling and dilapidated ruin. The curtain wall is in a state of collapse and the gatehouse would keep no enemy at bay. The entrance towers lean at a dangerous angle. The keep is mostly unfit for human habitation. Better to keep pigs there.

What will Duchess Cecily do now?

We wager she will stay ensconced at Baynard's Castle, at the centre of affairs.

Cecily, King's Mother, to Edward, King of England
Written from Berkhamsted

My son,

Have you had recent conversation with your brother Clarence? If not, it is unfortunate. I suggest that you to do so immediately.

Are you aware that your brother is acquiring dangerous ambitions? You say that you have no fears for his loyalty, but you must have your suspicions. You see far more of him than I do.

It has concerned me, not least that he visited me. He has more important affairs to occupy him than visiting his mother in this isolated retreat. On this occasion he wished to gauge my opinion.

He has all the charm and wit and elegance, as well as the stature and handsome features, that you yourself have used so well to win the loyalty of the people. He has also acquired, through your generosity, a vast swathe of estates in the Midlands around the fortress of Tutbury. He is your heir apparent, and is like to remain so if the woman you chose to wed can produce nothing but females.

Clarence has acquired the idea of a marriage with Isabel Neville, Warwick's elder daughter. Warwick is in full agreement. How could he not be? I suspect the idea came from him. I did warn you. By sweeping up all the marriageable heirs for the Woodville girls, you have left Warwick with so little choice for his own daughters.

Can you not see the danger? Think of the consolidation of power in the Midlands. How powerful this will make Warwick, if connected so strongly to the heir to the throne. His daughter could be Queen of England in the fullness of time.

I suspect Warwick of making Clarence a weapon to use against you, and Clarence has come to believe that the crown could readily be his.

I have heard that Warwick has been calling his tenants to muster. Dangerous times, Edward. You might look into his interest in the northern rebellion.

What are you going to do about it?

Your father would already be closely involved to prevent any insurrection.

Cecily, King's Mother

Edward, King of England, to Cecily, King's Mother
Written from the Palace of Westminster, March 1469

To my Lady Mother,

The matter is dealt with. I have refused my permission for the marriage. Clarence must look elsewhere. I will personally take it in hand to discover for him a foreign bride. I do not deny that he has an eye to the throne.

There will be no marriage between Clarence and Warwick's daughter Isabel.

As for Warwick, who has indeed been summoning his tenants to arm themselves, under the pretext of marching against Robin of Redesdale and the northern uprising, I have issued the order that no man is allowed to assemble his retainers without my direct permission. I do not fear Warwick. I expect to see him take up his position of Captain of Calais before the month is out. I value his authority there, and think that he will not dare to defy me.

I myself am engaged in putting down the insurrection in the north. I will deal with Clarence's marriage when I return.

I hope that Berkhamsted becomes more agreeable during the summer months. Perhaps you could use some of your energies on improving the grounds. Could you grow flowers or fruit trees? It might be more satisfying than dabbling in my affairs.

Your dutiful son,

Edward.

England's Chronicle, *June 1469*

There is trouble brewing in the realm.

Rebellion in the north, breaking the peace that we had come to enjoy.

Our King has left London to put the rebellion down, in the company of his brother Richard, Duke of Gloucester, and a fair number of his Woodville relatives. There seems to be no urgency in the royal progress. He and the Queen are spending some days at Fotheringhay. There is even the idea of a pilgrimage to Walsingham and Bury St Edmunds. Why is our King not marching north with furious intent to restore our peace?

For those of our readers who enjoy the gossip, what are the rest of our pre-eminent families doing?

We imagine that the Duchess is still aggrieved. We might expect to see her returned to London and settle in at Baynard's Castle when she can stomach the tribulations and ruin of Berkhamsted no longer.

The Earl of Warwick and the Duke of Clarence have been summoned to come to the aid of the King in putting down the insurrections. We hear that Warwick is rousing his tenants to arm themselves, but the question is, how will he use them?

Do you recall our prediction? That the Duke of Clarence is looking for a wife. Would this not be the ideal match, to wed Warwick's elder daughter? We understand that the matter of a betrothal has already been broached between Clarence and the Earl of Warwick, but King Edward is unwilling. He has rejected it outright.

Will Warwick and Clarence obey the King's refusal? Will they go to the aid of the King with their soldiers?

God grant that the Queen bears a son. The daughter born in March is healthy and handsome enough but not a male heir, which gives much ammunition to Clarence's ambitions. And Warwick's, of course. It is not unforeseeable that we might have a Neville Queen of England. Except that our King has explicitly forbidden the marriage.

Marriages and family squabbles aside, we have the rebellion to put down.

Will family dispute take precedence over the rebellion?

You might ask, if there is an advantage to be gained from these circumstances in the north, how far is the mighty Earl of Warwick involved in Robin of Redesdale's uprising? We suggest that he is not entirely innocent in the plotting.

Chapter Twenty-Three

An Ill-Advised Marriage

**Richard Neville, Earl of Warwick,
to Cecily, King's Mother**
Written from Canterbury, June 1469

My esteemed aunt,

I trust that you are in good health.

I have reason to believe that you will be amenable to the plan that I have devised to further the future of your son the Duke of Clarence. I think it would be good for the country, for your family, and as you will doubtless say, it would be in my own interests too.

I hope that you will consider joining me in Canterbury. My courier will organise your travel arrangements and escort you in comfort and safety. I presume that your habitual inquisitiveness will be sufficiently awakened that you will not refuse my invitation.

I look forward to welcoming and entertaining you. I am most desirous of hearing your thoughts in a most sensitive matter appertaining to the present monarchy.

Your son Clarence will be here with us too.

We have much to discuss.

Warwick

Duchess Cecily confronts Warwick and Clarence in the lodgings of the Prior of Christ Church, Canterbury, June 1469

Did I not know exactly what it was that my powerful nephew was devising? I saw his stark aspirations; I saw the clever plotting. I determined that I might allow my nephew of Warwick to take the lead, but I would not be persuaded against my will to sign my name to his strategy.

Canterbury was ostentatiously welcoming, the journey made comfortable in every aspect by the people of Warwick's household, dispatched to escort me. After Edward's contentious treatment over the loss of Fotheringhay it was a sop to my dignity. Luxury and comfort were the order of the day, from a welter of damask cushions to restorative cups of ale, my small travelling household settled into the accommodations of the Prior of Christ Church. Warwick had a gift for charm and putting a much-desired visitor at ease. It would have been enough to rouse my suspicions, if they needed any rousing.

'Welcome, my most highly valued aunt. Enter and take your ease. I am gratified that you came at my request. I trust you journeyed well.'

He offered me a full Court obeisance, hand on heart, elegant and controlled. Yet his smile and the salutation on my cheek were quite genuine of his affection.

'I could not refuse,' I said. 'Such a subtle appeal to my curiosity. How could I not be here?'

Clarence was noticeably less effusive, wary even, but his bow was all I could ask from a dutiful son.

'We were not sure that you would come.'

While wine was dispensed, we sat at ease in one of the spacious chambers, discussing innocuous family affairs. The Countess and their daughters were in Calais, awaiting Warwick's arrival. Since there were still a good few hours of daylight remaining, I suggested a visit to the shrine of the Blessed St Thomas. Clarence accompanied me. We knelt and offered up prayers for the King, for the realm, for ourselves. For the repose of York and Rutland. While, within the grandeur of gold and jewels of the shrine, I prayed silently for some resolution to what, in the coming hours, could be a difficult exchange of views.

In the conflict of light and shadow as we walked from the shrine, when Clarence strode ahead of me, in brief conversation with one of the priests, his figure became blurred, the edges touched by an iridescence from the deeply hued glass. The years passing, how tall and strong he had become. And his resemblance to his brother Edward struck me. If he had worn a coronet on his fair hair the priests would be falling to their knees around him.

My thoughts slid into an uneasy channel, like the turbulence of oily water after a storm. Would Clarence make a King? A good King?

Blessed Virgin vouchsafe me the words to bring my son back into the royal fold.

I decided that Clarence was on Warwick's tight leash, like a young hunting dog, preventing him from speaking out the moment I had stepped over the Prior's highly polished threshold.

Returned to our lodging, I was the perfect guest, making no comment on the reason for my presence. Let Warwick broach this dangerous subject, waiting until we had eaten, I sparingly, the dishes removed, the servants dispatched. Then, as Warwick filled the cups once more, I braced myself for a disturbing exchange.

'Now, we talk.'

I allowed myself a benign smile. 'Why am I here? Is this the point when you tell me?'

Warwick raised his cup in acknowledgement of my previous silence.

'We would like your support.'

'For what purpose?'

I knew. Oh I knew. Every gossipmonger in the country knew.

'The marriage of your son Clarence to my daughter Isabel.'

I turned to my son, ingenuously innocent, desirous of making him squirm a little. 'You gave me no indication that you looked to Isabel as a wife.'

'I think it will be an excellent match.' Once he would have flushed under my regard. No longer. His face remained calm with a stern self-confidence, product of Warwick's tuition.

'Do you love her?' I asked.

'We enjoy each other's company.'

'Which is not at all the same thing. I presume that you have not been swept off your feet with earthly passions. But then I presume that love is not the purpose of this match.' I turned to Warwick, letting my son escape for a little while. 'I admit, I had heard talk of this plan. I am also under the strong impression that the King has forbidden it, citing the bounds of consanguinity since my son and Isabel are second cousins. Is that not so?'

'It is.' He bowed his head, again in acknowledgement. 'Yet I will pursue it.'

'How can you, if your King forbids it?'

My nephew produced a document that had been tucked

338

within the breast of his belted houppelande and laid it on the table between us. I did not touch it. I raised my brows in inquiry, even though the heavy seals told their own story. Let him explain the treachery of his recent actions. I could recognise the prints of Warwick's ambition all over that papal document.

'A papal dispensation, to allow the marriage,' he said as blandly as if it were a mere bill of lading for one of his commercial enterprises.

'You lost no time. How much did it cost?'

'Enough. It gives us every legal right to ignore the King's displeasure. The marriage between Clarence and my daughter will take place.'

I allowed the silence to hang a little. Then:

'If you have papal permission, why do you need my blessing?'

Did he think my humiliation over the Fotheringhay affair would provoke my plotting with Warwick and Clarence against my son the King?

And then, another thought. How far did Warwick's ambitions spread? Did he truly believe that I would prefer to see my son of Clarence steal the crown from Edward? To have Warwick as father to the Queen of England? Perhaps he did.

I said, lightly: 'Isabel is a fine girl and my own goddaughter, but how can I sanction this marriage, against Edward's express command?'

I knew, as clearly as if it were written in the papal script, that Warwick believed my agreement to join them in Canterbury would be enough to put pressure on Edward to retreat and give his consent. But my influence over Edward, since his marriage, was not as extensive as Warwick presumed.

Yet I smiled and answered with a light touch.

'I cannot in all honesty join with you in defying the King in this manner,' I said, crushing any further Neville ambitions.

'I will not be without much support in this,' Warwick said, unperturbed. 'I had hoped that you would join your voice to mine.'

Much support? Where was he looking?

'What of Diccon?' I asked, a sudden bolt of concern. 'Will he support you, or remain loyal to Edward?'

'Diccon will do as I say,' Warwick responded. 'Raising him in my household has built a strong relationship between us.'

Such assurance. And yet:

'Diccon is at this moment in the company of the King and will march north with him.'

'Diccon will come to heel when I call him.'

With that brutal assertion, I acknowledged the inevitability of this conspiracy, whether I supported it or not.

My final words were to Clarence: 'Do you not have enough power, as the King's brother and heir? Why would you set yourself up against him? You are his friend, his brother, his counsellor.' It seemed that the crown of England hovered between us.

Clarence's eyes flashed with visions of a bright future.

'My ambition is greater than being brother and counsellor to the King.'

'I forbid your marriage. Your brother the King forbids it.'

Useless words, as I realised. It seemed that all was descending into a spiral of danger, of implacable animosity between my sons.

And his reply: 'You cannot forbid it, madam.'

'If you value the peace of this realm, all that we have achieved, don't do this thing. Seek out a foreign bride who will bring wealth and a strong alliance with a European state.'

My son shook his head. 'But I must. I desire no foreign bride. I see my future unfolding here before me, and it is a splendid one.'

I saw the glance he cast towards Warwick.

'How can it be?' I persisted. 'If you defy your brother the King, what future can you have in England? Edward will surely cut you out of his sphere of influence. He can strip you of your estates. Or are you planning on outliving him? It is a chancy wager. It is my understanding that the King is to go on pilgrimage to Walsingham and Bury St Edmunds, with a Woodville entourage, of course, doubtless to pray for a son. If the Blessed Virgin grants him his desire, that is the end of your glorious future.'

A sly cast to his countenance flitted past, one that I recalled from his childhood when he had devised some secret ploy and been discovered. 'There are rumours...' he began.

But Warwick's hand gripping Clarence's arm brought the nascent confession to a stillbirth.

'I have a task for you,' Warwick said. And when my son would have argued the case, 'I wish to speak alone with the Duchess.'

Clarence left us in a cloud of sullen reluctance, so that we were alone and there was no point in my playing the innocent any longer.

'Do you seek the crown for yourself?' I asked.

'No.' Honesty crackled in the air between us. 'Edward is King. I am his cousin. When I am restored to his counsels, when I have his ear, I will be the most loyal of subjects.'

'But still you will pursue this marriage.'

'Edward has left me with no choice. His Woodville policy has been devastating.'

'I know how bitter you are.'

It was as if a flame had been applied to a smouldering log.

'How long must I tolerate this? I made Edward King, but I can no longer control him.'

'You are still powerful and handsomely rewarded. Edward still relies on you.'

'I see no reward. I see no reliance. My service to your son is no longer of any account. Nor will it ever be as long as the Woodvilles surround him.'

A judgement delivered in flat, emotionless accents at odds with the fire in his eyes. The room was full to the brim with his bitterness. It positively dripped from the tapestried walls, like blood from a huntsman's knife. I stretched my hand across the white cloth that still graced the table to touch his where it lay flat, fingers widespread. I was not without compassion.

'There is no moving you, is there?'

'No.'

'I am sorry for it. I see only bloodshed.'

'I think I am more sanguine. Edward and I can still come to terms, if he is willing to close his ears to the Woodville bellowing.'

I could not see it happening.

'Why do you need my support?' I asked, as I had at the beginning.

'Because you are the only one Edward will listen to, short of facing him on a battlefield and forcing him at the point of a sword.'

'Once that might have been true.' A little sadness trickled through my veins, as I admitted the truth. 'But now he has a wife whose pretty fingers have tightened on the royal reins, at the same time as they have dislodged mine.'

Which awoke a smile in my nephew. 'We might try together to dislodge her.'

And, then, because there was a softening between us and because I thought that he might be open with me, 'What was it that you stopped Clarence from telling me? What were the rumours?'

The vestige of humour promptly vanished.

'There are none. Just something Clarence has heard and mis-understood. Nothing that need disturb you.'

I angled my chin, my eyes cool on his.

'Will you object if I say that I do not believe you?'

He shrugged, smiled briefly.

'Will you be honest with me?' I asked.

'If I can.'

'Will this non-existent rumour that Clarence has misunder-stood hurt Ned?'

'Yes.'

'Will it hurt me?'

'I think it will.'

Honesty indeed. It hurt, but it was best to know the worst.

'Will you make use of this non-existent rumour?' I asked.

'If I have to,' the Earl of Warwick replied without hesitation. 'It is too good a weapon not to bring into my armoury.'

Cecily, King's Mother, to Katherine, Dowager Duchess of Norfolk

Written from Canterbury

My most erudite sister,

I have just spent some troubling days in Canterbury with Warwick and Clarence. More than troubling. This is written in the wake of a conversation over which I had no control, and one I did not like. I foresee absolute disaster. I am in severe need of advice. O, how I wish that Richard were alive. I know that he could be driven to reckless action, but he would never sanction what our son Clarence is doing. It is all such a mess of tangled skeins, I doubt they will ever be untangled.

What is clear is that Warwick is in careful alliance with King Louis who has promised him the principalities of Holland and Zeeland if he works for the overthrow of Edward. Warwick would not admit to this, but Clarence was voluble when I got him alone and pinned him down. With that now established, who is behind the rebellions in the north, led by the enigmatic and undiscoverable Robin of Redesdale? It takes no intelligence to guess.

With Edward fully occupied in dispatching the rebels, the plan is that Warwick and Clarence will sail for Calais with our clerical nephew, the Archbishop of York, in tow to see the deed done, the marriage of Clarence to Isabel. Edward's refusal stands for nothing. My family is falling apart, my sons in conflict, Diccon, I fear, strongly under Warwick's influence. All I can see is the crown being snatched from Edward's brow, even though Warwick denies that he has such ill will towards my son.

And who will wear it then? If it is Clarence, he will be very much the puppet of Warwick. I don't think he is strong enough to hold Warwick at bay. We did not speak of this, but it was clear in every unspoken nuance.

I tried. I advised caution and renegotiation. I talked myself hoarse, hoping that the constant dripping of water on a stone might wear away some of the intransigence. I will persist and do all I can in the name of my eldest son, yet I cannot change Warwick's mind over this marriage.

There is nothing I can do but disapprove and frown. For the first time in my life I feel alone and at the mercy of others. It is worse than standing before the drunken rabble in Ludlow.

At the end, I thought that Clarence was inclined to tell me more than Warwick wished. Some rumour that has begun to circulate. Warwick put a stop to it, and I had more dignity than to pursue what it might be. Something nasty appertaining to Edward, I suppose. Another mistress, another bastard child. Not that it matters. I fear that Warwick's plan will be carried out whatever objections I might raise. I see no hope of reconciliation.

That does not mean that I will not try.

Your anxious and irritated sister. And angry, of course, but that does not need saying.

Cecily

Cecily, King's Mother, to George Neville, Archbishop of York

Written from Canterbury

Nephew,

Can you not stop this?

I understand your resentment. I understand your fury at losing your post of Lord Chancellor at the same time as you are forced to watch the promotion of Earl Rivers. Of course you will blame Edward, as Warwick does for all his reversals. Nevertheless, to take revenge in this way, dividing the family, is foolhardy.

You owe me a debt. Without my influence I doubt that you would have become Archbishop of York.

I am calling in that debt.

Stop this marriage.

If it goes ahead the rift between Warwick and the King will be impossible to heal.

What will be the result for this country? I fear a return to civil war.

Set aside your mortification at your demotion. Get off your knees, or your episcopal backside, my lord Archbishop, and claim the ear of your brother. And Clarence's, while you are at it; I suspect you have more influence with either of them than I.

Cecily, King's Mother

If you thwart my son the King, in God's name you will pay for it!

George Neville, Archbishop of York, to Cecily, King's Mother

Written from Sandwich

My illustrious aunt,

There is no hope of dissuading either my brother or my nephew from this well-planned path. You failed at Canterbury in an impassioned plea, surprising in its eloquence, even for the Duchess of York. I can do no better.

Come to Sandwich where we will reside until sailing for Calais, if you think there is any hope.

I have to admit to you, dear lady, that I am in agreement with my brother. This marriage would be good policy. I will marry the two young people with a politically joyful heart.

I do not think I will ever recover from my resentment at being removed from office so ignominiously. Nor can I set myself to work amicably with Earl Rivers.

Dear lady, I cannot repay my debt to you. Or not at this instant.

George York

England's Chronicle, *the eleventh day of July 1469*

An announcement.

Who would have wagered a groat on such an occurrence?

The marriage of George, Duke of Clarence, brother of our present King Edward, to Isabel Neville, elder daughter of the Earl of Warwick, in Calais.

Solemnised by George Neville, Archbishop of York.

Does the King know?

Even more interestingly, does the Duchess of York, King's Mother, know? She was seen in the company of the two Neville brothers in Canterbury and Sandwich before Warwick's party sailed for Calais. Clearly she did not accompany them.

We hear that the Earl of Warwick had in his possession a papal dispensation.

If King Edward was unaware of the direction in which the wind was blowing, he will now be feeling the full force of the Neville gale.

Such blatant defiance!

What will our King do?

Cecily, King's Mother, to George, Duke of Clarence
                                        Written from Berkhamsted

My son,

I wish you and your new Duchess every happiness in your marriage. I only hope the repercussions do not come back to haunt you.

I cannot be sanguine about it, but have to make the best of a bad job.

If you were in any doubt as to my continuing care and affection for you, you will note that I sent my minstrels to play at your wedding. As well as arranging for a gift of trout for Isabel.

I enclose a recipe to do justice to the fish, not knowing the quality of your cooks in Calais. It makes a very bland fish more than edible.

Cecily, King's Mother

A Recipe for Chewettes on Fyssh Day

Take the trout with any other fish such as turbot, haddock, codling and hake.

Seep it and grind it small.

Add ground dates, raisins, pine nuts, good powder and salt.

Make a coffin, stuff with fish, close the lid.

Fry them in oil or stew them in ginger, sugar, and wine. Or bake them.

Serve them forth.

Cecily, King's Mother, to Katherine, Dowager Duchess of Norfolk

Written from Berkhamsted

Dear Katherine,

Warwick has sent Edward a letter in open support of Robin of Redesdale's uprising.

How do I know? I have my means of gleaning information. Ready coin can always buy it. If we were unsure of Warwick's motives, now all is as clear as the words on the document.

Oh, it is spectacularly deferential to the King. All the blame for the ills of this realm is placed at the door of others. Can you guess? The letter names those who must be brought to account for the use of our sacred laws for the promotion and enrichment of the few. Earl Rivers, his wife and their son Lord Scales. All the lords associated with the poisonous Woodvilles.

Jacquetta, to my regret for past friendships, has been singled out as a malign influence, for encouraging her daughter and bringing about the marriage in the first place. There is a viciousness here in the accusation. Will Warwick accuse her of witchcraft? Yes, I expect that he will if it serves his purposes. It may be too close to the bone to attack the Queen herself, but her mother is fair game.

You should be warned, my dear Kat. One of the list of malefactors is Sir John Woodville. I doubt he will need your warning but he should take care. I believe that Warwick is out for blood.

I fear the outcome. Edward is still engaged with the rebels in the north. I am not exactly certain where Warwick and Clarence are at the moment, but I anticipate their return to England's shores with their armies in readiness. I wish I could see their ultimate goal. To remove the Woodvilles and take their place as Edward's counsellors once more? Or do they have a more savage intent, to remove Edward, too, with King Louis' blessing.

I pray that it will not be.

Oh, Kat. Sometimes I can weep with frustrations at being unable to halt the malign spinning of the Wheel of Fortune.

But I will not weep. That will bring no remedy.

Your troubled sister,

Cecily

Do you have an effective method of ridding us of vermin? If we are not tripping over rats, we are overcome with a surfeit of cats and kittens to catch them. I suppose it is the only way, other than employing the local rat-catcher again with his traps and terriers and a constantly open palm. I will have to pay exorbitantly.

Chapter Twenty-Four

Rumour and Speculation

**Katherine, Dowager Duchess of Norfolk,
to Anne, Lady Mountjoy**
Written from Epworth, July 1469

Sister,

The rumours coming out of France!

Do you suppose that Cis has heard them? Even more apposite, do you suppose that they are true? I cannot believe them. But Cis was always a law unto herself. And she was a very handsome girl. Would she risk so much for a dangerous dalliance with a menial?

Someone needs to tell her. You are the closest and always have been. I will let you whisper these terrible rumours into her ear.

Good fortune.

Katherine

Anne, Lady Mountjoy, to Katherine,
Dowager Duchess of Norfolk

Written from the Palace of Westminster

My dear Katherine,

Yes, I have heard. It may not yet have reached Cis at Berkhamsted. In fact, I think she has been travelling, engaged in negotiating the sale and shipping of her wool with her pet Genoese merchant Pietro de Furno. I doubt she is listening to rumour.

I'll not tell her. We have been on opposite sides in the conflict for too long. We are now much reconciled, and I would not willingly risk shattering the domestic calm. She will not take any criticism kindly from me. Far better from you. You live too far away for an angry visit, and you have her advantage of age.

Do not be surprised if she explodes in fury.

Do you suppose that it actually is true? Who would have thought it!

Anne

Katherine, Dowager Duchess of Norfolk,
to Cecily, King's Mother

Written from Epworth

To my well-beloved sister,

Have you heard the rumours crossing the sea from France?

Anne and I are in agreement that you should be told of them. They are scurrilous.

Are they true?

I hesitate to write them down in case they are not, and this letter falls into hostile hands. My suggestion is that you go and talk to Anne. And try not to smite the messenger when she tells you what you will not wish to know.

Your non-judgemental sister, who is unsure what to believe,
Katherine

Cecily, King's Mother, to Katherine, Dowager Duchess of Norfolk

Written from Berkhamsted

Kat,

What rumours?

I have more to worry about than rumours from France. I haven't time to visit Anne.

Our family has suddenly become the most quarrelsome in Christendom, and rushing headlong towards open hostilities, unless something can be done about it.

A fistful of empty rumours, spread probably by King Louis to stir up the country on behalf of Queen Marguerite and restore Henry, are not high on my list of difficulties. At least we know where Henry is, shut up in the Tower with his books and his prayers. That's the only good news I can think of.

Is Louis saying that he has escaped and is at large? I swear he has not.

I do not understand why such rumours should concern you unduly? You were not wont to be nervous.

I am up to my ears in wool prices and the healthy state of my flocks in Suffolk.

Your busy sister,
Cecily

Well, well. Who would ever have believed this possible?

Our King Edward might not actually be a true child of our late lamented Duke of York and his wife Proud Cis. Our King might just be a bastard.

What does Dowager Duchess Cecily have to say about this? She may be King's Mother, but who is the King's Father?

We have heard it said that Proud Cis claimed it herself. Did she actually admit to so heinous a crime, a sin against her husband? Did she actually write the accusation in a letter to her royal son?

It seems that she did.

Although we have not seen such a letter, we are reliably informed.

If King Edward is illegitimate, then he has no claim to the crown.

If so, whose head should it grace? The smoothly handsome, charming, witty, ambitious George, Duke of Clarence. Is that what his mother would wish for? Has the Duchess been scheming with Warwick and her son of Clarence to remove King Edward?

This family is suddenly not short of scandal, despite the Duchess's name for magnificent piety!

Anne, Lady Mountjoy, to Cecily, King's Mother
                    Written from the Palace of Westminster

Cis,

Since you will not come to me, I will spell it out for you. It would be ridiculous if you remained in ignorance, and there is no longer any point in hiding it. I presume that you will deny it, but here is what's being said. You may not have heard it from the depths of Berkhamsted, but there is whispering in every corner at Court that Ned is not Richard's child.

Is it not shocking?

Ned, they are saying, is a bastard son of a man called Blaybourne whom you met, and with whom you had an illicit liaison, while in Rouen in the months before Ned's birth. Blaybourne was a handsome archer – well, of course he was! – in the Rouen garrison, a man who took your eye when Richard was away campaigning. Ned was born on the twenty-eighth day of April in the year 1442, I think. York was campaigning in Pontoise and did not return to Rouen until after the twentieth day of August in the previous year. Those who are interested in counting the months say that he was absent at the crucial time for the boy's conception. Whoever was Ned's father, it was not Richard.

It does not make for pleasant listening, or telling, unless you are of a mind to stir up trouble for the House of York.

The rest is hard to dispute. Ned was christened quietly in the small private chapel of the castle in Rouen. When Edmund was born – a legitimate child – he was christened with great ceremony in Rouen Cathedral. Why was Ned not given such a noteworthy baptism?

There can be no denying that Ned looks nothing like Richard.

It does not look good, does it, Cis?

You will argue your dignity and piety now, but once you were a beautiful young woman who might have enjoyed an intimate moment with a handsome archer.

If I have to hear it from one more empty-headed woman at Court, I will not answer for my reactions.

I have to say Cis, there is much evidence, even though of a shadowy kind, that you were at fault here. Perhaps you decided it would be best to cover it up. You were both always good at mumming.

The problem is that if there is even a half groat of truth in it, Ned should not be King. It should be Clarence, as the legitimate heir.

Are you going to ignore this? Or are you going to proclaim the truth and bury your critics with pearls of veracity?

I know you are not in good heart with Ned over his choice of wife. Would you use this to join with Warwick, undermine Ned and get Clarence as king? The Nevilles were always ambitious and chancy in their allegiances.

Your sister,
Anne

Sir Walter says that you never know what goes on beneath the sheets in any marriage.

Cecily, King's Mother, to Anne, Lady Mountjoy
Written from Berkhamsted

My dear sister,

So this is the gossip of the day, is it? And malicious at that. I cannot believe that you would think it of me, even as a young woman, but then I recall when you had me under your roof, my family scattered, when there was not one kind word from you. I should not be surprised.

Here's what needs to be said to deny all your accusations. Pearls of veracity, if you wish. I was always faithful to Richard. There was never any adultery.

Ned was born early. We had already lost Henry and so we feared for this child who was not as robust as he would later become. A fast christening in the castle was for the good of his immortal soul.

Richard never questioned the birth of the child, his heir. Edward was raised as Richard's heir, with negotiations to wed a French Princess. Would Richard have countenanced that if he had suspected him of bastardy and me of infidelity?

No, Edward does not look like Richard. Far more like the third King Edward and his sons, I would say, tall and fair. The strong Plantagenet blood is there.

For all his faults, Edward is mine and Richard's.

That is the end of it.

Of course I never announced it, either in an outburst of rage or of petulance. I am never petulant, even when roused to just ire. What mother does not say you are not your father's son, when the son commits some appalling sin. Like wedding a totally unacceptable woman. I expect I did. Which is not at all the same as pronouncing him a bastard. And even worse, myself as a harlot.

Really, Anne…

And I have absolutely no interest in what Sir Walter says!

If I write more, I will be entirely discourteous.

Cecily

Anne, Lady Mountjoy, to Cecily, King's Mother
Written from the Palace of Westminster

My apologies, Cis.

I wish I had not written.

I hesitate to question your veracity, but you have to admit there are grounds for speculation from those who wish to speculate and make mischief.

When Richard fled from Ludford Bridge, and when he marched north to deal with Marguerite's threat, it was Edmund he took with him. Ned went with Warwick to Calais, and then to the west to deal with Jasper Tudor.

Would Richard not have kept his heir close with him, under his eye? Ned had barely reached maturity. Did Richard care more for Edmund's safety than for Ned's?

Anne

Cecily, King's Mother, to Anne, Lady Mountjoy
Written from Berkhamsted

Anne,

Your premise is entirely wrong.

Did Richard care more for Edmund's safety than for Ned's?

Not if it ever crossed Richard's mind that if he came under fatal attack, then his heir would die as well. Far better to send Edward away with my brother Salisbury to Calais. When Richard marched to Sandal, Edward was of an age to lead his own army, so to send him west against Pembroke was good planning.

Richard never showed less concern for Edward than for any of our other children.

This is all empty posturing, Anne.

Any birth abroad can be raked over for political purposes. Was not the birth of John of Gaunt declared to be questionable, yet a more honest woman than Philippa of Hainault would be difficult to find.

It is so easy to slur a woman with claims of sexual immorality. Since it has become a project of value to brand the King a bastard, it is my name that has been dragged through the mud of sin and shame.

And I have suspicions of where all of this originates. I know who will have the most to gain from it. I am coming to London and will stay at Baynard's Castle. I detest Berkhamsted anyway. Come to me there, if you wish.

If you dare chance my wrath.

Cecily

Chapter Twenty-Five

The Great Rebel Calls the Tune

England's Chronicle, *July 1469*

We have, my erudite readers, a Manifesto.

What is this? we hear you ask. Do we need a Manifesto? What we really need is an end to the troublesome rebels in the north. That's what needs to be sorted out, by a vigilant King!

Here is a little apposite history lesson for your appreciation.

In the bad old days, mistakes and poor judgement in this land resulted in the forcible removal of three of our kings: King Edward II; King Richard II; King Henry VI. Thus Kings, despite all the sacred anointing, have been tipped from their thrones by their disgruntled subjects.

Our King Edward should read his chroniclers. Here is a threat. A challenge to his power. His position is not sacrosanct if he estranges the great lords of the land from his counsels, driving them into insurrection.

It should be said that by the term 'great lords' we do not

suggest the Woodvilles who are mere upstarts and interlopers. Furthermore their advice is never rejected.

Where, then, does this incipient treachery originate? Not with the northern rebels, I wager. Not from Robin of Redesdale who can barely put pen to parchment, much less a reasoned argument.

The hand holding the pen that wrote the Manifesto has a subtle way with words and argument. The hand of the Earl of Warwick is here. We suggest that Warwick, now father by law of the heir apparent, will cure the ills of this kingdom. Will Warwick not rid us of the plague of Woodvilles?

Where is he? Some say that he has already put to sea from Calais, to return and bring this country to heel. If King Edward will not do it, then the Earl of Warwick will.

Prepare yourselves, citizens of London, for battle and bloodshed.

We imagine there will also be bloody battle within the House of York.

Will Duchess Cecily be forced to answer to her royal son for his bastardy? Will she kneel in penitence, or deny it as a total calumny?

Cecily, King's Mother, to Edward, King of England
Written from Baynard's Castle

Edward,

I trust that my courier finds you at Walsingham.

Have you read the Manifesto? It is a dangerous document.

Warwick and Clarence are back in England. By the time this reaches you, it could be too late for you to pre-empt their plans.

Where are you? This is no time for pilgrimages to petition for a son. If you do not take care you will lose all.

I think your crown is in danger.

Now is the time to take action against the traitors who seek to depose you.

What a terrible indictment of our family.

Cecily, King's Mother

I think that Diccon is with you. You must ensure that his loyalties remain with you. Do not let him go to Warwick, under any circumstances.

England's Chronicle, *late July 1469*

We have had our battle. We have suffered our bloodshed.

We warned you, did we not?

The conflict was fought far in the north on Edgecote Moor on the twenty-sixth day of this month.

What should we tell you, that you do not already know? The northern rebels who were victorious were aided and abetted by the Nevilles. Soldiers from Warwick's garrison at Calais were clearly visible in the rebel ranks. The Yorkist Herbert Earl of Pembroke and his brother Sir Richard Herbert fought with great heroism, but their Welsh forces were no match for Warwick's army.

What a devastating blow for the King.

Even worse! Pembroke and his brother were brought before the Earl of Warwick and the royal brother, Clarence. The King's two loyal lords were condemned as traitors and put to death.

How could this be so?

The Woodville Earl Rivers and his son Sir John Woodville are fled, gone into hiding. They know that Warwick will hunt them down.

Thus we can announce: Warwick is triumphant.

But where is our King? He was not on the battlefield.

Where is the peace in our realm now?

We commiserate with Duchess Cecily who will be in some torment with one son in bloody confrontation against the other. We imagine that she does not sleep well.

Cecily, King's Mother, to Katherine, Dowager Duchess of Norfolk
Written from Baynard's Castle, late August 1469

My most dear and well-beloved sister,

What do I say to you?

This is written in a spirit of true despair, my nights spent in sleepless anxiety. My knees are worn with prayer, my tongue with petitions to the Blessed Virgin. But for whom do I pray? For Edward, of course. It must be. Here are Warwick and Clarence returned to wreak havoc on this country that Edward tried so hard to mould and settle.

I fear the Battle of Edgecote Moor has been a disaster from which we will never recover. Where is trust when it is cut off at the knees on the battlefield? Can it ever be repaired? Not when it is stained in blood, both on and off the field. Such crude justice. So much death at the hands of a man whom we loved and admired as a nephew of renown. The executions of Earl Rivers and John Woodville after summary justice at Kenilworth are on Warwick's head. An outrageous Neville revenge against the Woodvilles.

I weep for you, dear Kat, even though the marriage was a travesty of an alliance. I know you had an affection for Sir John. Now you are once more widowed and must bear the burden of loneliness into old age. Will you laugh again? I find there is little laughter in my life. I am no longer the woman who could command the gift of happiness.

It all brings back the bitter memories of Richard and Edmund, and my brother of Salisbury, their bodies demeaned after Wakefield, heads displayed on gateways. How many widows must be haunted by such images? Memories do not fade as the years pass. I still wake in horror with such visions.

To whom do I turn? It must be to Edward, for he is the only power in this country who can stop Warwick. I must perforce heal my relations with the Queen. I find it impossible to even consider Clarence with any charity, a son prepared to destroy the reputation of his mother for the cause of his ambition.

Gone are the days when we sisters had nothing better to do than exchange recipes and comment on the deficiencies of Burgundian fashions in head-coverings, all rolls and padding and wire lappets, neither flattering nor comfortable.

I am anxiety-ridden. I don't know where Edward is! It may even be that he is executed, too, although I think that not even a victorious Warwick would go so far.

Your sister in extremity,
Cecily

George, Duke of Clarence, to Cecily, King's Mother
Written from Warwick Castle, August 1469

To my noble mother,

Warwick says that I should write to you, and so I will. I confess to some reluctance since you were less than lukewarm in your promises of support at Canterbury. In fact you denied me. The presence of your minstrels at my marriage ceremony and the dish of fish chewettes did nothing to plaster over the bitter wound you created.

But now affairs have changed. I, as the true, legitimate-born heir, should be King.

If you would still support your bastard son, then you should know this.

Edward is our prisoner.

He was discovered, deserted by his men, in the village of Olney outside Coventry. Our useful Neville Archbishop came across him there and took him into custody. Warwick has him now under guard here in Warwick Castle. It will please you to know that he is unharmed. The Archbishop was persuasive and Ned was as meek as an old ewe. Diccon was with him, although he is not under restraint. He is still at liberty with my Lord Hastings. My cousin of Warwick believes he can readily call on the loyalties of both when the time comes.

So who is King now?

Not Ned, son of a common archer.

Warwick says that he regrets the use of the knowledge of Ned's bastardy if it hurts your pride, but I think it needed to be broadcast far and wide. I am the rightful King, and my cousin Warwick will support me in my bid to take the crown.

I look forward to receiving your good wishes.

Your dutiful son,

Clarence

Cecily, King's Mother, to Richard Neville, Earl of Warwick

Written from Baynard's Castle

My nephew of Warwick,

How could you even consider so outrageous an act against me!

How dare you play ducks and drakes so blatantly with my reputation? How dare you broadcast my supposed infidelities? How dare you use my sons to further your own ambitions? I see no honour in you.

You take one son prisoner and use the other as a pawn to tell me of the bad news. Do you intend to rule England through Clarence, a malleable puppet? You denied it to my face at Canterbury, but all I see in you is lies and deceit.

I know where the rumours of my infidelity began, not to destroy me, but to undermine the legality of the King. I was not your target but you had no care that I too would be damaged. At Canterbury, you stopped Clarence telling me. Were you ashamed of your use of my own honour to destroy my son? I doubt you know the meaning of shame.

There is no truth in the rumours of my past indiscretions. Of my *adultery*. How vicious a word. You know that as well as I, but I remember your claiming that you had a useful weapon to hand. I cannot stop you from using it, nor can I prove you wrong except to say – look at Edward. His height and colouring may not be those of his father, but he has the physical beauty of the third King Edward. Nor can Clarence proclaim his father's height and colouring – he is much like Edward – but you make no claim that he too is a bastard.

How despicable you are. You pick and choose to your own advantage.

Would I consort with a common archer? I would no more join flesh with such a man than I would walk naked through the streets of London. Not even in the days of my youth when some might say I was a mere foolish girl. I was never so deficient in knowledge of what was owed to my birth.

That aside, my concern for Edward is paramount. Do you intend to murder him, to have him quietly removed in one of your northern fortresses? I have read the Manifesto. It is your plan, as you say, to save the King from the covetous rule and wilful guiding of certain seditious persons. And if Edward will not be saved then he deserves the fate of those previous kings who were deposed. Deposition will answer nothing in such a case, for Edward will never agree. Only his death will solve it for you and for Clarence. Whether it be by starvation or smothering or cold steel, I am sure that you can accomplish it.

Is it even possible that you want the crown for yourself? Do you see it gleaming on your own brow? Far more efficient for you to wield the power than Clarence on a leash as your lapdog. Can you persuade misguided Clarence to hand it over to you in the manner of a New Year's gift?

Sometimes I forget that you are my nephew, that your blood is my blood. You have done great damage to me and to my family.

I curse you for it.

I will pray for you.

Cecily, King's Mother

Richard Neville, Earl of Warwick,
to Cecily, King's Mother

Written from Warwick Castle

To my most revered aunt,

I regret your disfavour but in government there is no room for mawkishness. I wish my cousin Edward no physical harm. You do not need to fear for his life, for I will have no murder on my soul. And with that in mind it is my plan to move him from Warwick to my northern fortress of Middleham where I can guarantee his safety.

There is insurrection, which must be put down. Once it is laid to rest and the rebels destroyed, then we will plan the crowning of Clarence. Until that time, I will hold the reins of government and bring the realm back to a state of peace. I will use the Great Seal and have writs issued to summon a parliament to meet in York on the twenty-second day of September. This should reassure you that I have no intention of taking the crown for myself. Parliament will be convened and consulted.

I was reluctant to use the accusation of bastardy, but as a woman well versed in the political world, you will see the need. It was unfortunate that your chastity, or lack thereof, was the most potent weapon to further Clarence's cause and my own.

Will you not enjoy being relieved of the surfeit of Woodville influence? And you will of course still be acknowledged as the King's Mother. There is much to be gained here for you, too.

Warwick

Cecily, King's Mother, to Richard Neville, Earl of Warwick

Written from Baynard's Castle

Treacherous nephew,

Much to be gained?

Your carefully disseminated 'knowledge' of my most private affairs has just branded me a whore!

Your reply does not convince me of your good intentions towards my eldest son. I see no weaknesses in Warwick Castle as a place for Edward's incarceration. I dread that you plan to send him to Middleham. I expect that you will dispatch him at dead of night. Out of sight, out of mind.

You talk of crushing the insurrections. How will you accomplish that when the King is a prisoner? Do you expect the great lords to rush to your aid? I am not so sanguine. Nor, I think, will a parliament in York be a body over which you can ride roughshod. I presume that you think that you can win them over with your accusations of lack of government and corruption of justice. I warn you. My son has more personal following in the country than you might believe.

Edward will never give in to your demands.

Beware of hubris and conceit. They can bring a man down.

I will never forgive you. I will have much difficulty in forgiving my own son Clarence also. I think that we all need heavenly intercession in what has become a deplorably sordid tale of treachery and betrayal.

Cecily, King's Mother

Katherine, Dowager Duchess of Norfolk, to Cecily, King's Mother

Dearest Cecily,

You must remain strong, stronger than you have ever been in your life. You are the only firm footing in the foundation of our family when all is awry. What a conflagration of conflict this has become. Edward imprisoned, Warwick, the Archbishop and Clarence seeking the ultimate power in the country, and Gloucester still too young to make much of an impression.

You must hold fast, Cecily.

Pray that Edward will find some means of ensuring his release. It is the only hope if the country is not to fall foul of further bloodletting. Our nephew Warwick's arrogance has become menacing. If Clarence becomes King, it will be Warwick who pipes the tune for us all to dance at his bidding. Clarence will certainly caper appropriately.

My spirits are low on my own account. Of course I knew the dangers for John and all the Woodvilles if Warwick had his way, but such manipulation of justice at Kenilworth was a disgrace to the Neville name. I know not as yet where he is buried. His head was placed beside that of his father, Earl Rivers, on the gates of Coventry. Such a terrible end to so short a life.

No, I did not love him, nor was it a marriage I sought, but this is monstrous. And at Warwick's hand too. I always knew it would come to an inglorious end for the Woodvilles. They had just too many enemies.

Can you do nothing to gain Edward's release? No, of course it is impossible. There is a limit to a woman's persuasive abilities when a man of Warwick's calibre has the bit between his teeth.

What is the Queen doing? I have no news of her. Not that she will have any power over Warwick. It behoves her to keep her head down if she values her life and those of her children.

Katherine

Queen Elizabeth to Cecily, King's Mother
Written from the Tower of London

Madam,

I have no choice but to beg your intervention.

I was in Norwich when news arrived of the death of my father and brother. There was no justice in that execution. I have no hesitation in naming it an act of murder by Warwick.

What of me? What of the children? I know Edward is Warwick's prisoner at Middleham Castle, while I am in the royal apartments in the Tower with my children. I am free to order my household as I choose but I am ordered by Warwick to keep scant state as if I were not Queen. I am not free to travel.

My mother has been accused of witchcraft, to achieve my marriage to Edward. It is said that she used a lead image, to bind me to the King.

I am sunk in fear and distress. Until now, no one has attacked me, but how long can my immunity last?

My fears are for Edward's safety as much as for my own and for my daughters. For the sake of your son, can we not repair our differences? You are the only influence strong enough to weigh with Warwick or Clarence. Once you had a warm relationship with Jacquetta. Can you not resurrect memories of the good times when you were together in Rouen? I beg that you come to our aid, for the sake of your son and your granddaughters, even if you have no compassion for me.

The rumbling storm cloud over Edward's legitimacy has reached me in my isolation. Is it true? If so, it is a disaster for all of us. It must be a burden on your soul.

Elizabeth, Queen of England

Cecily, King's Mother, to Queen Elizabeth
Written from Baynard's Castle

Madam,

I can do nothing. Warwick has his plans and will not be moved by me. Clarence does what Warwick tells him to do. I cannot be hopeful.

To speak plainly – for what value in dissembling? – I fear for Edward's life.

As for the witchcraft – be afraid. There need be no truth in the accusations, merely the suspicion. How easy it is to pay men and women to bear false witness against a well-born woman, to taint her soul with witchery.

My only advice, for what it is worth, is to remain where you are. We must wait to see how this develops. If there is anything to be done in the future, then rest assured that I will do it.

I must offer my condolences on the death of your father and brother. Our past enmity does not make me cold to your loss and I have compassion for your mother's situation.

Be assured, I will not allow Edward to go easily to a death at Warwick's hands. Nor will I allow you and your children to suffer. I may not have rejoiced at your marriage, but I acknowledge your loyalty to my son. I will support you.

I will not discuss the state of my soul or my relationship with the Duke of York.

Cecily, King's Mother

Duchess Cecily's intercession to the Blessed Virgin Mary

Hail Mary, full of Grace, Our Lord is with thee.

I bring before you the fate of my son. I am full of apprehension. What can I do but sit here in Baynard's Castle and hope for the smallest spark of conscience in Warwick's breast? I am powerless. Only you can intervene in this impasse.

Or if not, send me a sign that all is not lost. In God's name, send me a sign.

I cannot bear to bury another son.

Only you know the truth of my loyalty to Richard, my lord and husband.

Amen

England's Chronicle, *September 1469*

Be concerned! What terror we are facing, when we need a King to be a source of strength. We have no King.

This will be no news to you if you have suffered at the hands of the violent mobs that roam the streets of London, both in daylight and after dark. If you have been robbed and beaten, you will already be barricading your doors and sending your womenfolk to stay with family in the country.

How has this come to pass?

Lancastrian forces have invaded our realm from the north under Sir Humphrey Neville of Brancepath, a Neville who has remained loyal to the old regime. How well he has timed it, to raise once more the dusty banner of our previous King Henry the Sixth.

The country is in turmoil. Magnates are settling old feuds under the pretext of renewing the fight of York against Lancaster. No one is safe. The Duke of Clarence and the Archbishop of York are powerless to stop the collapse of law and order in London. We hear that the parliament, called so hopefully to meet in York, has been cancelled by the Earl of Warwick.

Who is King now? Edward or Henry?

Not Warwick, nothing is more certain since the lords will not obey him.

Will we see this invading force at the gates of London? Panic is building in the streets. We have had no news of our King Edward for some weeks.

Do we lose hope, and invite King Henry and Queen Marguerite to return?

What would Duchess Cecily advise?

Duchess Cecily's intercession to the Blessed Virgin Mary

Blessed Virgin.

Warwick and Clarence have lost control. There have been seen shooting stars in the heavens. On my knees I give grateful thanks for this sign. I know what I must do.

Guide my hand, Holy Mother, as I try to rescue my son. Guide the words I write. Give them power to drive Warwick to compromise.

Amen

Cecily, King's Mother, to Richard Neville, Earl of Warwick

Written from Baynard's Castle

Nephew,

I understand that things are not going to plan.

Who is King in this realm? The question I hear on every tongue, spurred by the mischievous writings of *England's Chronicle*. Not you. You are neither crowned nor anointed. You cannot command the loyalty of the English people to face this Lancastrian invasion from the north. All is collapsing around you.

You must see it and accept it.

Here, after many years of experiencing war and dissention and death, is the best guidance I can give.

Release my son. Restore him to his rightful power and the people will flock to him. It is your only hope, and a man of your wit must realise it. You know Edward's abilities. Even though he may be locked away in Middleham Castle, he will not sit by forever and allow you to take his inheritance. Unless you are prepared to kill him, which I pray fervently that you never will, you will always live in fear of his retaliation. You will spend your life looking over your shoulder.

Negotiate, nephew. Play the great statesman and return to London at Edward's side. Before God, you have removed enough Woodvilles and their supporters to sate your bloodlust. The way open for you to redeem yourself is to appear at the King's right hand as his friend. Your authority has crumbled. Your reputation is as dust.

Set the King free and come to terms.

And drag Clarence with you, to make amends to his brother.

One final word. However much you dislike the Woodvilles,

leave the Queen alone. Allow her and the children to live in peace in the Tower. Through Edward, they have Neville blood, too.

Cecily, King's Mother

Cecily, King's Mother, to Richard, Duke of Gloucester
Written from Baynard's Castle

I commend you, Diccon, on your loyalty to the King. Cleave strongly to your brother Edward. Under no circumstances must you give your allegiance to Clarence. I have no time to write more.

Where are you? What are you doing?

Cecily

Richard, Duke of Gloucester, to Cecily, King's Mother

I have no intention of joining my star to that of Warwick and Clarence. I am in Lancashire with my Lord Hastings, stirring disaffection against Warwick. Hastings is proving, in words and deeds, to be a fervent friend of the House of York.

I will write more soon. All wobbles here on a knife-edge. All I can say is that the days of amity with my brother Clarence, when we squabbled over my father's gift to me of a dagger, to mark the day of my birth, are long gone. The power that we now play for is far more deadly than a pretty knife, however costly the jewelled hilt.

Diccon

It will please you to know that I still keep my father's dagger by me. It reminds me of his strong principles and his ambitions for the House of York. I will not fail him.

Cecily, King's Mother, to Katherine, Dowager Duchess of Norfolk

Written from Baynard's Castle

Thank you, dearest Kat, from the depths of my heart. Your letter, that Ned had been seen at liberty in York, ignited my hopes, and now I can tell you that I am reunited with him.

You will note that he is once again Ned. I am feeling kindly towards him. My antagonism over the possession of Fotheringhay is a thing of the past. In the face of war and treachery, the fate of one castle tends to fade into insignificance.

What a magnificent entry into London there was, and a full public reconciliation between King and traitors, Ned hemmed in by royal banners and much ceremony. Clearly at ease, clad in costly fabrics, his cap adorned with a jewelled clasp that rivalled the sun, there was no hint of his being captive. Lords pressed forward on all sides, intent on renewing their vows of homage.

And where was our treacherous Neville nephew during all this?

Warwick was riding at Ned's side, as if they were the best of friends. They were both smiling in greeting to those who came forward. Even so, I could feel the rancour shivering in the air as they exchanged hand clasps. It cannot all be wiped away as the dairy maid cleans the debris from within the churn when the cheese is made. The taint of treachery will always be there between them.

There was strain in Warwick's eyes and more lines on his brow than I recalled. He looked as if he expected a charge of treason to be levelled against him at any moment. Clarence, too, I expect, and our needy Archbishop. And so they should be afraid. Humphrey Neville, our distant and unfortunate cousin who led the Lancastrian forces, has had his head separated from his body here in York, in Ned's presence. Thus a traitor is punished.

Attempts have been made to bind up the wounds. It is suggested that little Elizabeth of York, Ned's eldest daughter, should wed Warwick's nephew, so in the event of Edward not having a son of his own, the crown would pass to the Neville nephew through the royal blood of the little Princess. Rather than to Clarence, of course. Clarence said nothing but the cloud on his brow was of torrential proportions. He will never accept such an eventuality, but for now, Ned, Warwick and Clarence are reunited. It is Ned's intention to call a Great Council to thrash out pertinent matters.

I need not tell you that Ned will never forget the rough handling of his sacred person. One day he will have his revenge.

At least for the moment the ship is on an even keel.

I pray that the Queen will still surprise us all and produce a male heir now that she and Edward are restored to marital bliss.

By the by, Queen Marguerite, as she continues to style herself, has been invited to the French Court. What will be the outcome of that? I wonder. It worries me. It should worry Ned and Warwick too.

It is my intention to arrange a family gathering, to bring about a rapprochement if that is at all possible. If you will not come, I will write and tell you of my success. Or failure. These days it is impossible to take anything for granted. I am merely reassured that throughout all that has happened, Diccon has remained steadfastly loyal to Edward. It gives me some hope for the future.

I should tell you that Earl Rivers has been buried in the Church of All Saints in Maidstone. I think John Woodville has been taken there with him, which I suppose is some consolation for you.

Cecily

Chapter Twenty-Six

The House of York Is Wrenched Apart

England's Chronicle, *March 1470*

A celebration is mooted at Baynard's Castle at the behest of Duchess Cecily.

A magnificent banquet to soften the antagonisms of the Duchess's sons. We do not need to allude to the fact that it is still Lent and feasting much frowned upon. We anticipate much confessing of sins after the event. Gluttony will be one of the foremost. And perhaps Pride.

Do we presume that there will be reconciliation, sweetened by the tasting of such extravagant morsels as the Duchess is preparing? Will binding promises be made?

We cannot possibly predict.

Banquet at Baynard's Castle

Held at the Invitation of Cecily, King's Mother.

In the presence of the King, his brothers the Dukes of Clarence and Gloucester.

Also present her two daughters, Anne, Duchess of Exeter, and Elizabeth, Duchess of Suffolk.

To celebrate the Feast day of St Matilda.

A Saxon lady who had many disputes with her sons but was noted for her works of piety and charity.

First Course

    Fylettys in Galentyne
    Capon in High Grease
    Cygnets
    Chawettys Fryidde

Second Course

    Venison with Frumenty
    Jelly
    Rabbits
    Stuffed Pullets
    Braun

Third Course

    Crème of Almonds
    Pears in Syrup
    Roasted Venison
    Woodcock
    Sturgeoun
    Quail
    Pig in Sage

A Subtlety

A fantasy of gilded sugar, sculpted and decorated with the Falcon and Fetterlock, Symbol of the House of York

Duchess Cecily attempts a family reconciliation at Baynard's Castle, early March 1470

'Welcome, my son. It pleases me to see you here with your brothers and sisters.'

I placed my hands on his shoulders, reaching up to formally salute his cheeks. Trying hard not to dwell on the pain he had caused me, the blow he had dealt to my pride. George was as comely and genial as ever, marvellously garbed in a short doublet of figured silk, thighs smoothly encased in fine hose, shoes extravagantly pointed. Was this handsome, fashionable, young man George of Clarence, the two-faced monster I had created?

'Greetings, madam. I could not refuse the invitation, could I?' He allowed his gaze to drift around those present in my hall. 'How could I resist becoming part of this happy reunion? Although I am unsure why we are holding a celebration...'

With a smile that appeared genuine, he handed me a packet wrapped in leather.

'My thanks, George. I needed no gift. Just to see you here.'

There he was, surrounded by the family I had summoned for this purpose. To lure him back into the fold with the promise of fair words and rich food and memories of past loyalties. Now the banquet was over, the remnants removed, my daughters sent to hover outside the doors. On the whole it had been a more amicable occasion than I could have hoped for, my daughters carrying the flow of conversation. Thus my attempt to heal a quarrel as if my children were still young and innocent of the meaning of power. But they were no longer young, and this was no childish quarrel. As if released from the formality of good manners, Ned and George eyed each other like a pair of fighting cocks.

At least I had succeeded in getting them through the door at Baynard's Castle at one and the same time without coming to blows. If they had been younger I would have had them both beaten for wilful intransigence.

Here was an opportunity to see how strong was the old bond between Ned and Clarence. Had it survived at all? Could it be re-formed, like a once-firm rope re-spliced by a master rope-maker? For the first time in their presence I felt the insecurity of failure set its hand on my shoulder. The gaze they levelled at me was just as hostile, as if I were the instigator of their ills, before they turned on each other.

'I am surprised that you agreed to come,' Ned said. 'I thought Warwick would have a far stronger claim on your loyalty than I.'

'Was I not under royal command to be here?' George snarled.

Ned was not smiling. Could I blame him? It would be difficult to forgive being branded a bastard, as I found it wretched being labelled harlot. It would be impossible to forgive being taken prisoner and held in captivity, however soft, by a brother and a subject.

'Your accusations against my birth are unforgivable.' There was Ned's ire, as I had known it would be.

'I only repeat what is on every tongue.' George scowled mightily. 'Is it not true, then?'

When his gaze slid to mine in rank discourtesy, I achieved the well-nigh impossible and feigned amusement.

'You would smear mud over my reputation, under my own

roof, George? You would call into question my chastity in my presence? For shame, my son. Are you then also illegitimate?'

'You should fall on your knees and ask forgiveness.' Ned took up the cudgel on my behalf. 'From both of us.'

'I will not.'

I changed my role, to that of the commanding King's Mother. 'Would you listen to every desperate rumour that is spread around?' I demanded. 'Rumours that are concocted to spread disharmony. You are both politically astute. Will you snipe and growl at each other for ever? Will you tear apart the kingdom?'

When that was met with a blistering silence, I turned to heap my censure on George's treacherous shoulders. 'Ned is crowned and anointed. You have paid homage to him, you have given your oath of featly to him. Such holy bonds demand that you owe him your unequivocal loyalty.'

Seeing the mulish arrogance still engraving hard lines on George's face, I directed my next advice to Ned: 'You must forgive him. You must accept that loyalty and offer your brother a high position at your side, for all to see. If you had spent less time in devising elaborate rituals for taking to your bed and rising from it, more concerned with the quality of the bleached linen sheets and an ermine counterpane, sprinkled with holy water, you would have seen this rift developing between you long ago. You should have stopped it before it became so lethal.'

The King blinked as if surprised by my attack.

'Must I also accept the loyalty of my devious cousin, Warwick?' Ned was not persuaded.

'If necessary, yes.'

'I will not unless I see that he is willing to do more than make empty gestures.'

George promptly waded into the developing melee to grasp another bone of contention. 'You have arranged that your daughter will wed Warwick's nephew. Will he get the throne, then, after your death, if your lady wife fails to produce a son? Anyone rather than your brother. I think you would choose Diccon rather than me.'

Both Ned and George turned to stare at a silent Diccon who sat, elbows planted on the table, chin resting on his clasped hands.

'At this moment I probably would,' Ned replied. 'At least he has not shown such overt hostility. He remained loyal to me when you took me prisoner. He and Hastings rode north to try to raise support for me. But that is by the way. You presume that I will have no son of my own.'

'There's no evidence of it.'

'I swear I will have my heir to step into my shoes.'

'And will he be legitimate? Or the product of an hour's pleasure with a kitchen wench?'

Clarence's sneer was unfortunate. I saw Edward's spread hands clench into fists.

'The future is not ours to determine,' I said, to stop worse things being said. 'All I can do is advise a rapprochement. The alternative is too terrible to contemplate. Your lives are not your own, to be determined by your own pleasure. You are at the vanguard of the House of York. If you are daggers-drawn, the Lancastrians are waiting to pounce and take over. Marguerite will be offering up prayers of deep gratitude if you cannot seal an agreement between you. Louis will be quick to take advantage of any weakness. Is that what you want? If Marguerite returns with a French army, you could both end up with no power or lands to fight over.'

'I don't believe Louis will risk supporting Marguerite,' George said. 'He'll never see victory in her hands. The rumour that she was at Harfleur with an invading force was all falsehood.'

'Then you are not well informed,' I stated, making the most of my information. 'She is at Tours, discussing strategies with Louis and her French relatives. Louis invited her to plan a possible invasion.'

'I have not heard it.'

'I have,' said Diccon, entering for the first time in my support, surprising me, when indeed I should not have been surprised. Here he was, with all the dark authority and level gaze of his father. I realised that with eighteen years of experience of a multitude of loyalties and treacheries on his shoulders, I must not underestimate my youngest son's grasp of what was required in this dispute. He added, with a courteous bow in my direction: 'They are indeed planning war against us.'

It pleased me to see the crease grow between Clarence's brows. Seeds of doubt had been sown in his self-interested mind, but would these tiny seedlings sway his fealty?

'Marguerite is writing to her supporters here in England, to be ready when the invasion comes,' I said. 'Her clarion call is that King Henry will once more be King of England. And you would risk all of that by refusing to stand by your brother? You are a fool if you do.'

'Is this true?'

'Yes. Would I lie on so critical a juncture?'

George's glance slid away again. 'I will agree. I will not break the oath I have taken. As you say, it would not be in my interests to do so.'

Here was neither grace nor elegance, but it was the best I could hope for. I fixed my gaze on Ned, willing him to step forward and draw his brother in. Which he did. A reluctant conciliation, with a thin smile and a hand clasp.

'I will accept your renewed fealty, brother. I welcome it.'

His tone was not exactly warm but Ned was nothing if not pragmatic. I began to breathe more easily. Until:

'You will stay here in London, of course, until we know more of Marguerite's invasion,' Ned said. Unwisely perhaps.

Clarence's brows flattened. 'That is not my plan.'

'And your plan is what?'

'I go north again.'

'Into Warwick's territory.'

'And my own. My wife is there.'

'Bring her to London,' Diccon suggested softly.

'No. She is expecting a child and must not travel.'

'Is that all our rapprochement means to you?' Ned's anger was relit, his voice echoing in fury from the stonework. 'That you disobey your King at the first request? You will be able to report all to Warwick. Will you laugh over a cup of wine with him when you tell him that you have fooled me into thinking that you will be my man? Can I believe any word you say?'

'You can believe anything you wish. There is no reconciliation,' Clarence shouted back, then stormed from the room, leaving me knee-deep in the dregs of my plans. His sisters, waiting in the antechamber, watched him go.

Until I, with a few swift strides in his wake, raised my voice to bring him to a halt.

'You will hear me, Clarence.'

He turned, with some remnants of childhood obedience.

Slowly I walked and stood before him, looking up into that ravaged, wilful face.

'You will not leave this house until I permit it. You are my son; your present ambition has no influence over me and my desires. You will hear me and obey.'

My children faded away into the background. Even Diccon, who offered me his quiet support, departed after a sharp lift of my chin. The ensuing conversation was conducted in privacy, essential for George's dignity. I reminded him of his duty, his loyalty, his inheritance of honour from his father; the sins of betrayal if he left my house in this mood. It was lengthy and one-sided, my son answering in monosyllables.

The result was an acquiescence; reluctant, sullen, but still given.

When he had gone, when I was alone, I unwrapped the package. From the protection of the leather pouch, the beads of a paternoster fell into my palm. They were heavy, gilded and enamelled, and I could pick out the tiny letters to read 'Ave' on each bead. It was a costly thing, quite rare, and to my mind Venetian. I would use it when I prayed for George's immortal soul. Sadly, for once close to tears, I let the paternoster slide back into its safekeeping.

And then there was my son the King to face. The manner of his birth to discuss.

What I said to him, and he to me, would remain close hidden between us. It was a matter of interest to no one else.

Cecily, King's Mother, to Margaret, Duchess of Burgundy
Written from Baynard's Castle

To my well-beloved daughter,

Did I salvage anything from our reuniting? Some might say

it was little indeed. At least Edward and George left London together, ostensibly in amity, rather than glaring at each other and with weapons in their hands.

Will it last? Impossible to foresee the future.

I wished you could have been here with your calm good sense, but nothing would cleanse all the past bitterness. Your sisters Anne and Elizabeth did their best but there was no softening the underlying distrust.

One note of hope emerged out of all this: news that Isabel is pregnant. Seven months so not long for her to reach full term. I would like to wish them both well in their new family. Warwick will be pleased if she carries a son.

It is all too desperate. I am in fear for the future days.

I hear your words, 'But what is Warwick doing?'

I do not know, and I have asked nothing of the situation in Burgundy. You will consider me selfish. And it is true. All my thoughts are taken up with this impasse.

Your wretched mother,

Cecily

My cook's efforts with gilded sugar to create a falcon and fetterlock went disastrously awry.

England's Chronicle, *March 1470*

Don't look to see the King in London this month.

We have an outbreak of hostilities again, this time in Lincolnshire. Yet another local dispute between two power-hungry magnates, but our King has had enough. He has ridden out to deal with them.

We do not expect that it will take long. Since the Queen is

once more carrying a child, he will wish to be here if he is to celebrate the birth of a son.

Are we not all hoping to celebrate such an event?

All except the Duke of Clarence, who would not be so pleased. He will be praying for another daughter, although we know that he has recently assured the King of his allegiance.

Quite what the Earl of Warwick will do is outside our present comprehension. It all depends on the direction of his ambitions. We hope that he will return to the royal fold. All is quiet on that front, which makes us think that the puissant Earl is up to no good.

**Katherine, Dowager Duchess of Norfolk,
to Cecily, King's Mother**
Written from Epworth, April 1470

Cis,

Some spectacularly depressing news to cloud the start of your day and give your everlasting prayers at Mass an urgency. If, dear sister, you thought that you had brought your sons together in lasting brotherly affection, you were completely misguided. I'd say it was a waste of your valuable breath and your cook's gilded sugar, although I cannot fault you for trying. I regret that your majestic efforts with a celebratory banquet were wasted on them.

What started out as a local dispute here in Lincolnshire – a bitter but private one between Welles and Burgh over land and cattle – has been blown out of all proportion into a major rebellion against Edward. It will take no wit on your part to guess the stirrer of trouble.

Warwick has raised an army of his northern tenants and joined the rebels led by Welles. Clarence is with him. Edward's marching north in full royal panoply has forced Warwick, who saw it as a threat to his own northern power-base, to take such a risk and declare openly against the King. We await the outcome with some trepidation. You may know before I do if Edward sends you news.

I do not like it.

Katherine

Cecily, King's Mother, to Katherine, Dowager Duchess of Norfolk
Written from Baynard's Castle, April 1470

Kat,

Neither do I like it. Will I ever sleep quietly in my bed again?

As you say, I should have known better. I think the damage has been done and is way past mending.

I would never have believed George guilty of such bitterness, of such self-interest. Did I instil no element of trustworthiness in him? No sense of morality? I have failed him, it seems. I will have to answer to God on my deathbed.

Since I am still fully alive, I will do all in my power to keep Edward's crown safe.

I have heard from him. A courier arrived today. There was a battle which has been quaintly named Lose-cote Field since the rebels ran so fast they discarded their garments as they went. Near Stamford, so you will know the outcome before it reached London. Edward is victorious, thank the Blessed Virgin. What will happen to Warwick and Clarence, I have no notion. Nothing quaint about this battle and its aftermath. Warwick and Clarence may not have been evident in the thick of it, but when the rebels charged the King's forces, some of them were bellowing, *A Clarence!* Others,

A Warwick! Some were even wearing Clarence's livery. Even worse, there are tracts calling on the rebels to destroy Ned and make Clarence King. There is no need to express surprise at where they originated.

Which lowers my spirits even further. Pray with me that the Queen carries a son at last. It is our only hope of a secure succession, although it will not heal the breach between Ned and Clarence.

Cecily

England's Chronicle, *April 1470*

Citizens of London. Our King, hot from his victory at Lose-cote Field, has summoned the recalcitrant Earl and Duke to appear before him to answer for their sins.

They have refused. They could expect no leniency this time.

We hear that they and their families are in flight. Probably to Calais where they will take refuge from the royal wrath.

We presume it will be a long stay if King Edward is breathing hard on their heels.

Will this solve the question of who owns the crown, once and for all?

Duchess Cecily must be at her wits' end. The reconciliation she wove together from such broken threads at Baynard's Castle is in tatters and can never be mended. Even she must find it difficult to believe any word that comes from Clarence's treacherous mouth.

Cecily, King's Mother, to George, Duke of Clarence
Written from Baynard's Castle

Clarence,

They tell me that you are headed to Dartmouth to take ship for Calais.

Do not do this. I command you not to go.

If you choose to disobey me, risking a permanent exile, do not under any circumstances take Isabel with you. She is too near her time. It would be hazardous for her, and you do not yet know that Calais will receive you. I fear that you will be refused by the Captain of the garrison there. If you value the health of your wife and your unborn child, send her to me at Baynard's Castle where Isabel can carry her child in ease and comfort. I give you my word that Ned will not use them as a pawn in this vicious game you are playing.

It will be no surprise to you that I am appalled at your dis-honesty and the length to which you will go to oust your brother from the throne, but I will stand sponsor for the child.

I might understand your reluctance, but Ned will never be vengeful against a woman and baby, a woman who is of his own blood, and my godchild.

In God's name, George, do not be swayed by petty antagonisms. On this occasion, Warwick's advice might not be appropriate. At least I have your family's interests at heart.

Cecily, King's Mother

Cecily, King's Mother, to Edward, King of England
Written from Baynard's Castle, April 1470

Edward,

By now you will know of the consequences of your failure to

achieve a lasting alliance with your cousin and brother. They fled to Calais from where they would renew their assault.

I wring my hands with unnumbered forebodings. All my hopes have become atrophied and stale.

It is so perilous a situation. I understand why you would order Lord Wenlock to deny their entry into Calais, but by so doing you have driven them to make landing at Honfleur, thus into the hands of King Louis and Marguerite.

You will tell me that such an alliance is beyond belief, but desperate situations can create desperate bedfellows. I can't envisage the perilousness of such an outcome if King Louis decides to wade into our troubled waters. Can you repulse an invasion of such calibre if Louis lends his French armies to Warwick? It's one thing to destroy the rebels at Lose-cote Field, another to stop Marguerite with Warwick and Louis from establishing a base somewhere on England's south coast. Louis will be delighted at the prospect. I doubt he has ever forgiven the Burgundian alliance.

What will the English magnates do, offered such a choice? How many of them are uncomfortable with your rule and the Woodville hegemony? It has not brought peace and prosperity, rather disharmony.

I do not blame you entirely for this. I know that Warwick and Clarence are as much to blame, if not more. But I despair of the outcome.

Isabel lost her child when she began labour in the sea off Calais, with no one for her solace but her sister and mother. The Calais commander sent her two flagons of wine. Of what use was that? I am not told whether it was male or female but the child was stillborn.

I could weep for Isabel. Who knows better than I what it is to lose a child soon after birth?

Don't forget that they are our blood, our family, not just to be dispatched as enemies, and yet I cannot contemplate the idea of my son and nephew being in league with Louis and Marguerite against you. It is a shocking betrayal. I can do nothing to offset it, and neither, I fear, can you.

It is my intent to retire to Berkhamsted since to be here in London is of no value to me or to you.

Cecily, King's Mother

Edward, King of England, to Cecily, King's Mother
Written when heading south to London, September 1470

My most revered mother,

The diabolical alliance is made, despite all our efforts.

Warwick and my brother Clarence have returned to England, landing in Devon where they are collecting troops to use against me. Even worse, since it brings Marguerite back into the fray, Warwick's daughter Anne is betrothed to Marguerite's son Edward, once Prince of Wales.

Warwick and Marguerite will remove me and place Henry back on the throne.

All that we have fought for. All the deaths. We face defeat and ignominy at the hands of the Lancastrians and the French. If I had time I would find it in my heart to have compassion for the Neville girl, for she is nothing but a pawn.

It was my plan to march to London, to safeguard the City from Warwick's troops, but his strength is clear. There are enough magnates bearing a grudge who have joined him and will support a restoration of Henry, whatever the state of his mind. I am not strong enough to face them.

And yet I cannot abandon the oaths I made at my coronation. I will come to London and fulfil my duty to this realm that anointed and crowned me King. Nor can I leave my wife to Marguerite's tender mercies.

I will meet with you at Baynard's Castle and plan what might become a last-ditch stand against Warwick's forces. The future of the House of York may well depend on it.

Edward, still King of England, by God's Grace

Duchess Cecily's intercession to the Blessed Virgin Mary

Hail Mary, full of Grace, Our Lord is with thee.

My despair grows daily.

Warwick has sunk his fortunes with the woman responsible for Richard's death. For his own father's death. Where will it end? How did Warwick bend his proud head to do this? How could he agree to join his daughter's hand to that of Marguerite's son?

I cannot be charitable, despite the example of the Blessed Saint Matilda.

Clarence sees nothing despicable in Warwick's change of allegiance. He remains a firm friend of Warwick, continuing to denounce Edward as a usurper and an oppressor. It is a blade buried deep in my heart.

What counsel do I bring to Edward when we meet? Never have I felt so adrift in a sea of moribund desires.

Have mercy, Holy Mother.

Cecily, King's Mother, to Edward, King of England
Written from Berkhamsted

To my dearly beloved son,

Get yourself out of England!

Forget duty. Forget loyalty.

Flight is your only choice. Your Queen can go into sanctuary. I'll talk to the Abbot at Westminster Abbey who will open the doors of his apartments to Elizabeth and your daughters. Warwick and Marguerite will not touch them there, I give you my word.

Do not come to London. Go to your sister Margaret in Burgundy. To put yourself into Warwick's hands again would be a fatal strategy. Even if he might be won over to preserve your life, I would not wager on any compassion from Marguerite. She and her son have spent almost ten years in exile, during which her hatred of our family has festered into a running sore. I do not wish to see your head on a spike on London Bridge.

When you can see a way forward, return with a force. If Henry is brought out of captivity, then so be it. Accept that it is beyond your power at this moment to prevent such a fateful spinning of the Wheel of Fortune.

Warwick's brother, the Marquess of Montagu, has withdrawn his loyalty to you, to join his brother. Such fickle cousins. He claims that you bought him with a marquisate, but with no more than a magpie's nest of income to uphold it. Which is a lesson you can well learn, if you have not already done so, that greed can make enemies of the closest of blood.

Go to Burgundy. Charles the Bold will support you and give you the means to return.

Where is Diccon? Where do his loyalties now lie? Take him with you if you can.

Any step that Burgundy can take to undermine French policy will be happily taken.

Get out of the country, Ned! Remaining here, while Warwick's blood is up, with an army at his back, is of no value.

Cecily, King's Mother

Cecily, King's Mother, to Richard, Duke of Gloucester
Written from Baynard's Castle

To Diccon, my well-beloved son,

This is a rare apology from your mother.

It may be that I made one of the most severe mistakes of my life when I gave you into the hands of my nephew of Warwick for your raising as a man of honour and chivalry. In my own defence, how could I have ever foreseen that my nephew would sell his soul to the House of Lancaster?

Where does your loyalty stand today, Diccon? Do you remember the lessons taught by Warwick? Or do you step across the divide to your brother the King, despite the perilous situation that stalks him?

I already have one son who is doing all he can to destroy the King. I cannot bear to lose another. If you are indeed a man of honour, stand with your brother the King.

I regret if I have in any way conflicted your loyalties to your closest family. It is a matter of deep remorse, when a mother must bow her head in penitence before her youngest son.

Cecily, King's Mother

Richard, Duke of Gloucester, to Cecily, King's Mother
Written from York

To my inestimable mother,

Do you need to ask? There is no cause for concern. My loyalties are not conflicted to any degree. My loyalty is, and always will be, to my brother the King. I go with him into exile. Nor am I alone. It will reassure you to know that Ned has good friends. Lord Hastings is with me and Lord Scales, now Earl Rivers, of course. We sail from King's Lynn.

I am no turncoat, following in the treacherous steps of my uncle Montagu who put earthly promotion before the power of a God-given oath of fealty.

Flight is not what I wish for, but I look forward to renewing old acquaintances at the Burgundian Court.

One day we will return and restore glory to the House of York. I swear it.

Diccon

Cecily, King's Mother, to Queen Elizabeth
Written from Baynard's Castle, September 1470

Madam,

My son Edward the King is fled to Flanders.

Now you must take your future into your own hands. Do not hesitate.

Take your children and seek sanctuary with the Abbot at Westminster Abbey. He has been warned. He will care for you and see that you do not starve or come to harm. Take all your possessions, your clothing and your jewels. Do not loiter.

Sanctuary can be a form of imprisonment, but better that than a helpless pawn in Warwick's schemes. In your fragile position with the child due, you really have no choice.

All is arranged for your arrival.

Cecily, King's Mother

Queen Elizabeth to Cecily, King's Mother
Written from the Palace of Westminster, sent by return of courier

Madam,

We are already on the move.

My thanks for your concern for me and my children.

Do you flee with your sons? It might be safer for you. Or do you join us in sanctuary?

Elizabeth

Cecily, King's Mother, to Queen Elizabeth
Written from Baynard's Castle

Neither. I do not flee.

I stayed in England when the Duke of York fled to Ireland. I remained here when I sent my sons to Burgundy, away from Marguerite's revenge. I do not flee now.

I will face Warwick and Clarence on English soil.

Cecily, King's Mother

Chapter Twenty-Seven

A Collision of Hope and Fear

England's Chronicle, *the sixth day of October, 1470*

And what is the question on everyone's lips this morning?

Do we have a King after all?

One is fled to Burgundy. One until today has been resident under restraint in the Tower of London.

It seems that we have, courtesy of the hand of the mighty Earl of Warwick.

Henry of Lancaster has been brought out of the Tower, stumbling and blinking in the light, looking older than his forty-eight years. The time shut away from public view has not been kind to him, and those who witnessed his release and his procession through the streets claim that he was none too clean. Bemused, bedraggled, his mind struggled to make sense of what was occurring. Let us hope that Warwick can work a miracle before the approaching feast day of the Translation of St Edward the Confessor, the day on which Henry will once more be crowned King of England.

There are few Kings who can claim to have been crowned twice in their lifetime.

Do we rejoice?

Henry of Lancaster was not responsible for all the ills of his reign.

We had such hopes for Edward of York, but what did he bring? The plague of Woodvilles, little peace, and battle after battle to cut down the flower of our nobility.

Ah, but do we want the return of Queen Marguerite and her warlike son?

Poor Henry. Even with the crown restored to his head, and a marked improvement to his royal garments, there is nothing surer than that the power in this land will never rest in his hands. He is destined to be a puppet, manipulated by Warwick and Queen Marguerite.

At least Warwick's pride will be assuaged, at being forced to make the alliance with Queen Marguerite. The hours spent on his knees before her at the French Court might just seem worthwhile.

Royal Proclamation

On this day, the second day of November in the year 1470
    Born to King Edward the Fourth and his wife Queen Elizabeth
    In Sanctuary in Westminster Abbey
    A son
    Edward
    King Edward is in exile in The Hague

Recorded by the private hand of Cecily, Duchess of York

At last the Queen is deserving of my approval.

The birth of a son and heir to the King.

The boy is healthy and will be called Edward.

All remain safe in sanctuary.

The inheritance of the House of York is secure for the future.

I should be full of joy. Instead I am weighed down with a dark urgency. Yet I cannot see how this game of chess will end. Which King will emerge triumphant? Which Queen will rule the chessboard? I fear that I have no part to play in the game, however encouraging my advice to others. Sometimes I would wish to draw around me the curtains of my bed and sit in the dark.

I know that I must not give up. I must not retreat from this battle.

England's Chronicle, *November 1470*

All our good wishes to the Queen in sanctuary.

At last we have our heir.

We hear that there has been a rapprochement between the Woodville Queen and Duchess Cecily, with much communication between them. Do we believe it? There is nothing like the birth of a royal child to heal old wounds.

Despite this good news, nothing is comfortable in our fair land. Queen Elizabeth and Duchess Cecily will still suffer sleepless nights.

Parliament, under Warwick's aegis, has denied the legitimacy of Edward's kingship, freeing the Lancastrian lords from the attainders passed against them. We look to see a good handful of them, Somerset and Exeter amongst them, returning to England to pursue the Lancastrian cause.

What of Clarence, faithless rebel, who has caused this realm so much trouble? He is even further from the throne. Will he accept this volte-face in kingship, accepting that the crown will never be his?

And what of Edward of York in exile?

Henry's Readeption has a grand ring to it, but can it be a lasting achievement?

Polish up your weapons, citizens of London. Prepare for battle once more.

Cecily, King's Mother, to Queen Elizabeth
Written from Baynard's Castle

Madam,

I send you my good wishes for your health and that of your son.

It is a matter for rejoicing that Edward now has his heir.

I will pray for you, and for Edward's return. I advise you to do likewise. We can do no more. We must accept that for now King Henry is restored to the throne. I do not accept that Edward will remain abroad and allow this situation to continue.

Remain in sanctuary. To do otherwise would be too dangerous.

Cecily, King's Mother

Queen Elizabeth to Cecily, King's Mother
Written from Sanctuary in Westminster Abbey

Madam,

My heart is touched with joy. I have spent so long a prey to trouble, sorrow and heaviness of spirits. Now I have hope. The child is strong. I will pray. I will pray that Edward can get a letter to me.

My one regret. My son was born as a commoner's child, without state. His godparents are my mother and the Abbot. Is this fitting for the heir to the throne?

I must not resent it. We are safe and will remain so, God willing.

But what of Edward?

Elizabeth, one-time Queen of England

Cecily, King's Mother, to Queen Elizabeth
Written from Baynard's Castle

Madam,

Give thanks that you have a living son. Edward's fate is in the hands of God.

Get on your knees and pray.

The lack of a cradle embellished with gold and ermine is the least of your troubles.

I have sent a gift of two altar cloths of embroidered blue damask, as well as clerical vestments of crimson satin. They are favourite possessions of mine. I pray they may help to keep your spirits in good order when you hear Mass daily, as I presume that you will.

On no account must you leave sanctuary!

Cecily, King's Mother

Margaret, Duchess of Burgundy, to
Cecily, Duchess of York

Written from Brussels, November 1470

To my much-revered mother,

How have we come to this, our family rent apart, with no chance of healing?

We are doing what we can to aid Ned and the Yorkist cause. My husband the Duke sends funds to them, and I write frequently. Both Ned and Diccon are in good heart in The Hague, but to say that Ned is not restless is to say that the sun never rises.

I think you will understand the difficulty here. We are constrained by a need to keep friendly relations with France. To receive my exiled brothers formally at Court would exacerbate French hostility. I have to admit to you that Charles was not slow in supporting Exeter and Somerset when they too were in exile. Charles does not always listen to my advice.

Nevertheless I will persuade my husband, who is in Hesdin, to invite my brothers to spend Christmas there with us. It grieves me to say that Ned's return to England is a matter of grave uncertainty.

I pray for your health and strength in this trying time. You will always be welcome here.

Your loving daughter,

Meg

**Katherine, Dowager Duchess of Norfolk,
to Anne, Duchess of Exeter**

My dear niece,

Visit your mother, the Duchess. Visit her immediately on receipt of this.

Her letters are as forceful as ever, full of information and character, and not least a determination to put all to rights. But I fear for her. Clarence's betrayal has hit her hard, while Warwick's treachery is too duplicitous to be spoken of.

She is alone now, with both Diccon and Ned in Flanders. I know that Margaret would wish to do more but Burgundian politics are delicate, the Duke's hands tied firmly with France. Your sister Elizabeth does not have your dedication or strength of will. So it is to you that I appeal.

Your mother will never admit it but she might need your company. If you should think of asking why do I not visit her: if I did we would end up discussing the fate of Sir John and the rest of the Woodvilles, and little else.

It is a grave pity that she has so little compassion for Queen Elizabeth. (What do we call her now that Ned has been disinherited?) Cecily ought to go and observe the perfection of the new heir, which she might in fact enjoy.

Your mother will deny any need for your visit, but still I think it would be a daughter's duty to give succour at this time.

You have my consolation that the treacherous Exeter may once more set foot on our shores. I can offer you nothing but my hearty good wishes for your patience. I have become an expert of such tolerance through my marriages.

Your concerned aunt,

Katherine

Anne, Duchess of Exeter, to Katherine,
Dowager Duchess of Norfolk
Written from Coldharbour, London

My dear aunt,

I have done as you requested. I should have taken it on my own shoulders without your prompting. We presume that the Duchess will exhibit the same strength and fortitude, even when the years encroach. My report is a good one. She is in fine health and still inclined to dress as if for a Court reception, whatever the hour of the day. When she locks away her jewels and takes to sackcloth and ashes, then I will be concerned. Today she managed a marvellous wiring of veils with aplomb, her gown was deep-blue velvet and the sapphire collar at her throat worth a ransom for Ned if ever he needs one.

I took my children along to lighten the atmosphere. It was difficult, because her interest is primarily in the events of the day rather than the exploits of my offspring. But then that was always the case, even when I was growing up.

Yes, she is anxious, that Ned will not be able to return. Her anger is of an incandescence when she begins to talk of Warwick's treachery. And Clarence's double-dealing has undermined her confidence. I doubt she can forgive either of them for the slur on her good name. I think that hurts the most.

The Duchess has a new project in mind. To persuade our brother Clarence to abandon Warwick and return to Ned. Is it possible? I have promised to lend my support, although I think we are grasping at straws in a high wind.

We refrained from discussing my husband who has indeed returned from exile but managed not to visit me, for which I offer up prayers of thanks to the Blessed Virgin.

My mother, by the by, regrets the official loss of her title. I think that she envisaged being King's Mother until the day of her death. If she could not be Queen, it was the next best thing.

You will notice that she continues to make use of it when writing letters.

Anne

My mother gave me a most costly paternoster. It is a magnificent piece, the beads all gilded and enamelled with Venetian craftsmanship. I think it was a gift from Clarence. I think that, in her heart, she has given up on him, and cannot bear to use it.

England's Chronicle, *March 1471*

The House of York is back!

Some news that will disturb all the troublesome fish dominating the pond at the English Court. Our erstwhile King, Edward of York, is no longer hiding with the Burgundian merchants. His feet are once more firmly planted on English soil. Supplied with ships and money by Charles the Bold and the Flemish merchants who are hoping for trade, and with the support of Earl Rivers, Lord Hastings and the Duke of Gloucester, Edward has landed at Ravenspur.

Many of you might recall the last invader to land at Ravenspur. Henry Bolingbroke. Who went on to reclaim his inheritance and snatch the crown from the second King Richard.

The supporters of King Henry might be quaking at this news. So might King Henry if he has the wits to know what's going on around him.

We have just witnessed an example of Edward's cunning, far more highly developed than that of his father, the late Duke of York. (If, that is, he is not the son of Archer Blaybourne.) Stating that he had returned only to reclaim the title Duke of York, he made no display of flying the royal standard. He was, he acclaimed, a loyal subject. The city of York welcomed him with great rejoicing.

We wait to be persuaded of this.

We hear that the three sisters, the esteemed Margaret, Duchess of Burgundy, Anne, Duchess of Exeter, and Elizabeth, Duchess of Suffolk, are being drawn into the battle by Duchess Cecily who is once more emerging to don her armour and take up her weapons. A combined and powerful force of Yorkist women to bring the King and his estranged brother back into an alliance. Can it be done?

Will Edward take back the crown in conquest, after abandoning it in flight?

'It is a difficult matter to go out by the door and then want to enter by the window,' the Milanese ambassador to the French King has written.

It is difficult indeed, when the window is bolted shut by the Earl of Warwick.

Duchess Cecily sacrifices her dignity in the Palace of Westminster, March 1471

We regarded each other across the room.

I had had no difficulty in discovering where he might be, or in getting access to my nephew who had suddenly, to my chagrin, become the most powerful man in the realm. He did not seem surprised to see me. Once at this time of the late morning he would have been returning from the hunt or conversation with courtiers. Now his time was taken up with affairs of state. King of England in all but name, and I could not deny that he looked the part. His sleeves hung impressively from shoulder to knee; his low-crowned hat was graced with a cabochon ruby as large as a pigeon's egg.

'Well, my bold nephew?'

'Well, my esteemed aunt.'

His face was expressionless. He stood, walked around the table where he had been seated, but halted next to it, one hand splayed on the surface, the other still holding the quill he had been making use of to order my son's realm.

I folded my hands lightly together at the high waist of my gown. This was no occasion for emotion. I felt the weight of my paternoster beads slide against my thigh. This was no occasion for praying either. This was the time for hard-bargaining, and I feared that I would lose.

'My son the King is returned to England,' I said.

'The King is now Henry, of the House of Lancaster,' he replied lightly enough.

'I would argue differently. So should you. You made Edward King.'

'As I unmade him. As I remade Henry.'

Casting aside the pen, Warwick walked towards me and sank to one knee, taking my hand and pressing his lips to my knuckles. It surprised me, so that I almost snatched my hands away at such hypocrisy. But I did not, acknowledging all his political skill in achieving what he wanted.

'You are most dutiful,' I remarked to his bent head. Inconsequentially I noted that his hair was the same richly brown tones of Salisbury, my brother. 'But I see little duty in your life.'

'You will always have my respect, madam.'

I raised my chin. 'Even when you branded me harlot?'

'It was necessary. You were not my enemy.'

'Neither was my son Edward your enemy.'

'He became so when he swam into the Woodville shoal.' Warwick's voice had grown less than soft. 'He became my enemy when he thrust me to the edge of my rightful place in government.'

I drew him to his feet, so that once more I was forced to look up into his face. We had come so far since the day when he and the rest of my adult family had fled from Ludlow. Age had touched both of us. Here was a battle-hardened man, bent on a policy I could not envisage. Perhaps I was chasing wild geese, but it must be done.

'I have come to beg for your indulgence. I should be the one kneeling before you.'

'I'll not ask it of your knees, aunt.'

'If I can kneel before the Blessed Virgin, I can kneel before you.'

I watched as his brows rose, as if in disbelief. He thought I had too much pride, too much dignity, to kneel before any man.

Yet I did so. Abandoning all my dignity, and my pride, I knelt before my nephew. There was a sudden tension in the room, empty as it was apart from the two of us, almost as if I had blasphemed. Or struck him.

'Indeed you must not, my aunt.'

He looked as shocked as I felt, that I had done what I had sworn I would not, when I set forth on this mission.

'Why must I not? Do you fear for my honour,' I asked bitterly, 'that I should kneel before my nephew? A mother must fight for her son in any manner presented to her, like a vixen for her cubs when an eagle swoops. So I will lay my dignity at your feet, Warwick. Stop this. Don't let it come to a final decision through metal and blood and death on a battlefield. You are my own blood, my brother's son.'

I raised my hands in an open gesture of appeal.

'What would you have me do?' he asked. 'Withdraw? Hand victory to a man who had no place for me in his government?'

'Yes, I would, if it is necessary. Is your pride too great?'

'Yes. As is yours. Would your son withdraw his challenge to me? Would he return to exile rather than risk battle?'

'No. But he is King.'

'He is not, Henry is King.'

'A myth. A ruse to buy time. Henry is incapable of ruling. Is that all you desire, to rule England with a Lancaster puppet in your hand? Or Clarence? Edward would never become your creature, but my son of Clarence might. As for pride... How much pride did you abandon when you had to kneel before Marguerite and sign away your loyalty to her? I know all about the power of pride, yet I am here on my knees before you, to beg your indulgence.'

I watched as he inhaled slowly, as if to shackle the rags of temper. I waited for his excuse, his flawed reasoning, but he made none. Instead he helped me to my feet, but I drew away.

'There was no need for such mummery. You knew I would not be moved,' he remarked mildly.

'How could I not know it? But I need to hear why you would change camps so irrevocably. I need to hear it from your own mouth.'

'You know the reason. My life is nothing without the ability to wield power over my own possessions. It is my destiny to be a royal counsellor, to see the policies of the realm open out beneath my hand. Your son wilfully destroyed that possibility. In the end, unless I was to live in permanent exile, I must make any alliance which would enable me to return and take up what is mine.' He lifted his shoulders in a shrug of acceptance. 'It was Marguerite.'

'And I despise you for it.'

'I know. You should not have come here, my aunt.'

'I had to. Neville and Plantagenet. They should not be divided. They should not meet in a clash of arms.'

'But they are divided.' His expression was not unkind but his eyes were dark with resolve, his words relentless. 'There have always been some Nevilles who raised their arms for Lancaster. I have merely joined them.'

'Is there nothing I can say?'

I knew that we had come to the end of words.

'No.' Stepping forward, he kissed my cheek, and I did nothing to prevent it.

'All is not lost,' I persisted. 'I can still work on my son the King. And on Clarence.'

'I think it is all lost, Duchess Cecily. It may be that we will not meet again on this earth.' His fingers tightened around mine, then released me. 'If I die on some battlefield, pray for me.'

'If you do not die,' I replied, 'Edward will.'

'And where will your family loyalty be then, my dearest, most astute of aunts?'

I felt tears damp on my cheeks as I turned and walked to the door, only to look back. Loyalty was so strong, and yet so fragile. For a moment I studied the Earl of Warwick in the full panoply of his power. It might be the last time that I would see him. Or it might be that he would govern my future until the day of my death.

Cecily, King's Mother, to Anne, Duchess
of Exeter; Elizabeth, Duchess of Suffolk;
Margaret, Duchess of Burgundy
Written from Baynard's Castle, March 1471

To my three daughters, written at my dictation, by my clerk.

Pick up your pens and start writing. Send out your couriers.

I have failed to move Warwick. Now we must focus all our
efforts on the King and Clarence. It may be that they will listen
to their opinionated sisters, when their mother's advice falls on
stony ground.

Use every means at your disposal to bring them together before
they kill each other. Anne, write to Ned, who says that he can
never again forgive or trust Clarence. Margaret, stir Clarence
into a spirit of reparation. He can never be King of England,
whether the throne is warmed by a Yorkist or a Lancastrian rump.
Elizabeth, write to both. You are the calmest of us all. The fact
that you are not involved in the cut and thrust of politics might
just tip the balance with one of them.

Offer them prayers, stern advice and gifts of bribery if necessary. Call on all your memories of childhood. Shame them into
listening to the wise words of mere women.

By the Virgin, it will take a battering of cold fact and hot
emotion to extract us from this entanglement.

Send out streams of messengers until they can only comply
to shut us up. In my experience, no man can stand a constant
abrasion on his ear of female complaint.

Once your two brothers have come to terms, then it is in their
own hands, but we have to get them to see sense before they meet
on a battlefield.

If we fail, English blood will once more be shed, and it may well be Edward's.

Your desperate mother,

Cecily, King's Mother

England's Chronicle, *April 1471*

Surely a battle was inevitable.

Two armies facing each other on the flat lands without the mighty castle of Warwick.

One army led by the returned Edward of York, his brother the Duke of Gloucester and his brother by law Anthony, Lord Scales, now Earl Rivers. The other under the command of George, Duke of Clarence.

Yet what an astonishing outcome. Imagine this dramatic scene, if you will.

Clarence, with a small escort, abandoned his forces and approached his brother who was once King. Clarence walked on foot, fully accoutred in armour and weapons. Edward saw him coming. He waited before his own troops, without moving, not even to draw his sword, not even when Clarence did so.

What then?

Clarence fell to his knees, head bent, his sword cast aside, speaking words of repentance, we presume, sadly lost when Edward waved away those who might have furnished us with the pertinent exchange. Edward's face broke into a smile. He lifted his brother to his feet and embraced him, leading him into a knot of Yorkist supporters to accept a cup of wine.

Edward's army cheered.

Clarence's army looked understandably nonplussed.

An unprecedented outcome in these troubled times.

The Yorkist sisters have been delivering effective admonitions of fire to their warlike brothers. Thus the Earl of Warwick has lost one of his main weapons. He will be praying for the fast arrival of Queen Marguerite with the promised French troops.

Duchess Cecily has wisely won a few days' grace before the next conflict.

**Cecily, King's Mother, to Katherine,
Dowager Duchess of Norfolk**

Written from Baynard's Castle, Easter 1471

Dear Katherine,

What miracle was achieved on that abortive battlefield?

I owe so much to my daughters who wrote, and wrote, and wrote again, until my sons could not withstand the force of their exhortations.

We have spent a day of joyful reuniting here at Baynard's Castle. Ned is returned, Elizabeth and the children collected from the Abbot's lodging at Westminster. Diccon is here. George is here and his wife Isabel, too. The Blessed Virgin be praised. All are under my roof, the new generations of the House of York. It makes me feel my years and a deep weariness.

Yet my heart is overflowing with thanks. The Wheel of Fortune has once more turned to the glory of the House of York. Perhaps we shall see the end to hostilities, even though I tell myself that the cloud of fear can never be entirely dissipated.

But for now, Henry is sent back to the Tower, while our clever Neville nephew has managed to cling onto his York archbishopric by coming to terms with Edward. But only when he was ridiculed for parading sad Henry through the streets of London as a man worthy to be King. Rather a man not capable of putting on his own shoes. Such a sad occasion. I think Henry is not aware of his residence or his future. When Edward visited him, he beamed with pleasure, unaware that his life will always be in danger.

Today, as I write, it is Good Friday. We are all black-clad like a parcel of rooks. We have all knelt together to give thanks in solemn Mass, but then came the necessity of looking to the future. On the surface as we partook of a simple abstemious meal, all are united, but Warwick is out there with an army and Marguerite is preparing to sail to make contact with him. With Anne Neville's marriage to Edward of Lancaster now complete, it remains a formidable alliance.

As King's Mother, and in my own home, I claimed the right to speak, urging them to bury all old disputes and take up the burden of fulfilling their father's wishes, as Christ took up the burden of the Cross on that first Good Friday. How difficult to advise Ned and George to grasp forgiveness and acceptance. But they concurred. Or at least on the face of it.

With Warwick at large, Ned has taken his wife and family to the Tower for safekeeping, and I will go with them. Who would have believed that I would willingly inhabit the same space as the Woodville Queen?

Ned has now ridden out to face Warwick.

My consternation is beyond imagining, but I have learned to live with alarms and excursions.

Cecily

Duchess Cecily visits a forlorn King, April 1471

Out of duty, out of compassion, I visited Henry of Lancaster where he was kept safe in the Tower of London. Perhaps I had a strange presentiment that the future of this man, born to rule, lay in the gutter, to be tossed and turned like foul debris by whoever emerged as the victor in the coming battles.

I immediately wished I had not sought this interview. Nothing could have convinced me more of his unfitness for the crown that still graced his brow. Dishevelled, unkempt, with only one candle for lighting in the dim room, he rose slowly to his feet as if it were almost beyond his strength. His cuffs were frayed, his hem cobwebbed. How many weeks since he had been provided with clean robes, or even combed his hair? Henry blinked as I walked forward and curtsied, through habit. The room had a rank, musty smell that caught in the throat.

'You must not curtsey to me. It is not fitting,' Henry said, his voice that should have moved men on the battlefield little more than a croak.

He appalled me by falling to his knees before me, hands clasped against his breast.

'No! Henry…'

'Are you not the Blessed Virgin Mary?' He looked up, fear darkening his eyes.

'No. Of course I am not.'

'But you wear a blue robe.'

Taking his arm, I lifted him and pushed him towards a chair, where he slumped in a sad heap of neglected humanity. I realised that the rancid aroma came from his body and clothing.

'I have visions of the Holy Mother,' he told me, quite confidentially. 'She sits in the room with me.'

'I am Cecily. Duchess of York.'

Henry drew his sleeve across his face as if he might wipe the vision away.

'Yes. Yes, of course. I see that you are.'

I was not sure that he recognised me at all. His eyes glazed, staring into the distant corner. I could rouse him to no further conversation, not even when I bade him farewell. I left him, aware of nothing more than a deep sense of helplessness. Even of sadness. Henry would be used by Warwick, until he was of no further value to anyone, even to himself. I prayed that the Blessed Virgin would continue to come to him and give him comfort.

A few sharp words were delivered to Henry's body-servants. A man of royal birth should receive better care. His dignity should not be squandered in filth and degradation.

Chapter Twenty-Eight

The High Price of Victory

Duchess Cecily's intercession to the Blessed Virgin Mary

Hail Mary, full of Grace, Our Lord is with thee.

For whom do I pray?

For the King and his brothers. Yet my own brother's son will face them on the battlefield. Give me courage and strength to withstand what is to come. The years weigh heavily on me this day. Watch over my sons, as I keep vigil on my knees.

Whoever dies, it will be my blood. We are all so culpable.

Did we start all of this? When Richard stood against the powerful magnates and Queen Marguerite, when we rode in triumph from Hereford and he made his claim to the throne?

Watch over the Queen. Watch over her children, Blessed Virgin, all so innocent.

I prostrate myself before you, Holy Mother, in abject and anguished penitence. Have mercy on us sinners. We do not always see the consequences of our actions.

Amen

Cecily, King's Mother, to Anne, Duchess of Exeter
Written from Baynard's Castle

My daughter,

I need you to meet with me outside St Paul's Cathedral tomorrow at dawn before the crowds. Control your grief, dress for mourning but inconspicuously.

Your mother,

Cecily, King's Mother

Duchess Cecily stands witness to the death of traitors in St Paul's Cathedral, April 1471

The deed had already been done by the time Anne and I reached the environs of St Paul's Cathedral. The common farm cart was pulling away, lumbering through the streets, the two horses making good time with their lighter load.

'Deliberate!' Anne observed. 'All done before the crowds could gather.'

'Except that Edward would wish the crowds to see what he had accomplished,' I reminded her sharply. 'There is to be no secrecy here.'

We would not be recognised, clad in dark wool, hair hidden in simple coifs, nothing to draw attention to our rank. Not that I thought we would come to any harm from those who crowded with us to witness the tragic outcome of the Battle of Barnet. I felt Anne take my arm, but whether for her comfort or mine I was unsure.

We followed the push and jostle of curious Londoners to the space before the altar, aware of the reek of ale and unwashed bodies, soon overlaid by the pungent clouds of incense. I pushed my way through, and we were allowed, two harmless women, until we could stand at the front.

A heavy canvas covering had been stripped off to lie in a heap beside a single coffin, its lid removed to reveal what had been brought here into this holy place with so little formality.

Two bodies. Two brothers. United in death.

Richard Neville, Earl of Warwick.

John Neville, Marquess of Montagu.

Naked, exposed without dignity, there they lay revealed for the crowd, now increasing in number, to gawp and point. Bruised, bloody, carrying the sword-cuts and grazes of battle, yet still they were recognisable with their Neville features and dark hair. There had been no maltreatment before or after death, except for the blade of a dagger that had been driven into Warwick's head, through the open helm. His brother bore a sword wound to belly and neck.

'This should not be done in this manner,' Anne whispered.

'It is for a purpose. There will never be any rumour that they survived to fight again,' I replied.

'Is this Edward's doing?'

'Yes. And before you damn him for it, your brother could have justifiably had them quartered and beheaded, to be displayed on every bridge and gateway from here to York.'

And I meant it. Warwick had done much damage to my son's kingship. It was beyond forgiveness, but Ned had in the end shown some respect for my brother's son. Regret blocked my throat. All that promise and authority, lying naked in the cathedral. Forty-three years old with still so much to offer.

A brief memory lodged itself in my mind, of Warwick when I had last seen him at Westminster: vital, imposing, when he had asked for my prayers. Yes, I would pray for him.

A slight lifting of his hair in a draught caught my attention, as if it were alive.

Oh, I wished that he could be resurrected, that the fateful hours could be returned to the day when Warwick brought my son to London to be crowned King.

I was aware of moisture on my cheek. I had had no thought of weeping but this was a sight to attack the strongest of emotions. I wiped them away with my sleeve.

'Exeter survived the battle,' Anne observed with commendable calm.

'I know.'

'He was thought to be dead. Stripped of his armour and left all day on the field. But he was not. He was rescued although badly injured.'

I slid her a glance. 'And you, as a good wife should, will nurse him back to health.'

'Yes. Am I not his wife?' Then she smiled, dry as dust. 'Of course I will not. I doubt he would trust himself to me. He is in sanctuary in Westminster where the Yorkists cannot get their hands on him. Nor can I.'

I linked my fingers with hers, reading her pain as well as her disgust. Neither of us was prepared to speak the words in our hearts.

'Do you think that Edward will support me in achieving a divorce from him?' Anne asked.

'Ask him,' I said, feeling her fingers grip mine more tightly. 'If there is a way to achieve it, then he will.'

'Shall we go?' I asked when my daughter made no reply. 'We have borne witness to a terrible deed. We can do no more.' How quickly the citizens of London could change allegiance when it suited them. I spoke to the cleric who wafted incense over the growing crowd. 'When will they be removed?'

'What's it to you, mistress? In three days.' He did not recognise me.

'Can it not be done today?'

'No. The death must be seen.'

But the humiliation was a terrible thing. 'Could I pay for it to be done now?'

'You don't have enough money to deny the wishes of the King.'

'What will happen after three days?'

'We have orders to take them to Bisham Abbey, in Berkshire.'

'Of course.'

Anne and I turned away. They would be buried beside their parents, Salisbury and Lady Alice. There was some humanity in Edward even towards his enemies.

'It is fitting,' I said.

'So the great Warwick is dead,' a well-to-do citizen at my side growled. 'If he'd died sooner, we'd have saved ourselves a lot of blood and heartache. The Nevilles have always aspired to more power than was their right.'

I turned on him. 'He is dead. He deserves your respect.'

'What do you know about it? Keep to your hearth, mistress.'

Anne was already leading me away.

'It is not over, is it?' she said.

'No. It is not over.'

Marguerite and her son were still out there with their army.

'What now?' Anne asked in utter desolation.

I did not know. Her desolation was a mere echo of mine.

Recorded by the private hand of Cecily, Duchess of York

In memoriam of those who fell in battle or met death by other means in this apocalyptic year of 1471

On this day, Easter Day, the fourteenth day of April in the year 1471, when my heart was broken and remade again.

Dead on the battlefield at Barnet on this day with many others known to me:

Richard Neville, Earl of Warwick

John Neville, Marquess of Montagu, his brother

Henry Holland, Duke of Exeter, husband of my daughter, Anne. Wounded and left for dead but alive.

★

On this day, the fourth day of May in the year 1471.

Dead on the battlefield at Tewkesbury on this day with many others known to me:

Edward, Prince of Wales

Edmund Beaufort, Duke of Somerset

John Beaufort, Marquess of Dorset

Taken prisoner: Marguerite of Anjou, once Queen of England

★

On this day, the twenty-first day of May in this fateful year of 1471.

Dead in the Tower of London between the eleventh hour and midnight:

Henry of Lancaster, once King Henry the Sixth of England

By some foul means

Friend or Enemy. Rest In Peace.

Survived the battlefields and other malign opportunities for death, to my heartfelt gratitude:

Edward, King of England

George, Duke of Clarence

Richard, Duke of Gloucester

★

So many noble families riven by death.

May this be the end of the carnage.

May this be the beginning of the glorious reign of King Edward the Fourth.

The Wheel of Fortune smiles on the House of York, and on me, Cecily, King's Mother.

Cecily, King's Mother, to Marguerite of Anjou, one-time Queen of England
                              Written from Baynard's Castle, May 1471

Madam,

I am persuaded that it is my duty to write to you in your loss and grief, emotions of which I have considerable experience. I trust that the Blessed Virgin will bring you comfort and I offer prayers, as any pious woman must, that you will sustain the courage that has been one of your greatest assets throughout the vicissitudes of your life with Henry of Lancaster.

I know that my son the King will treat you with respect. I will petition him to allow you more comfortable accommodation than your present sojourn in the Tower. It will have raw memories for you, as the place where Henry of Lancaster died. The King is considering an easier confinement with Alice Chaucer, Dowager Duchess of Suffolk, at Wallingford Castle.

I will not visit you, either at the Tower or at Wallingford.

You were the cause of much heartache for me. My husband's death at Wakefield, your callous treatment of him, the degrading of his body and that of my son Edmund. That is not how a Queen should act. How could I sit with you and bemoan your own losses? If you had given better advice to Henry, neither you nor I would have been burdened with such terrible sorrow. If you had been willing to accept the Duke of York's advice rather than that of the Beaufort Duke of Somerset, we should not be here now surrounded by such misery.

I pray that God will forgive you. Although my conscience might trouble me, I find it impossible to do so.

Cecily, King's Mother

Marguerite of Anjou, Queen of England, to Cecily Neville, Dowager Duchess of York
Written from the Tower of London, May 1471

Madam,

Your prayers and commiserations are nought but a stone rattling in an empty vessel. They mean nothing to me. I have lost everything: my husband, my son, my crown, through the treachery of you and your family. The death of my son at Tewkesbury is a sin beyond my encompassing. I denounce the sons of York for so foul a deed.

Keep your prayers for yourself and your own family. I suspect that you may need them. I think that you are not destined to live a quiet life.

If you visit me, I will deny you.

Marguerite, Queen of England

Chapter Twenty-Nine

Trouble Stirs Once More in the House of York

England's Chronicle, *summer 1471*

What do we have in England in these balmy days of 1471?

A King who is without question the undisputed ruling lord of his kingdom.

Ruthless Edward! Clever Edward! Busy Edward!

Only eleven weeks since our King, when he could barely lay claim to that title, returned to England with his brother of Gloucester against desperate odds. Since then we have seen him raise an army, rescue his son and heir from sanctuary, and the Queen, of course. Nor was this the only reuniting within his family. Under the auspices of Duchess Cecily, King Edward has made amends with his brother Clarence. Since then he has fought two major battles and put down any number of northern rebellions, removing his most vicious enemy of Warwick from the scene. Edward of Lancaster is dead, and so is our previous King Henry. What King Edward's involvement might be in the death of Henry in captivity, we can only conjecture, but without doubt he has, through diplomacy and force of arms, won back his crown.

Has he not wiped the board of all the chess players that would threaten his position? It may astonish you, although nothing astonishes us in these difficult days.

So what of the rest of the Lancastrian remnant, I hear you asking, where are they? Margaret of Anjou is his prisoner in the Tower of London. Henry Tudor, the final male link with the Beauforts, has fled into Europe for refuge with his uncle Jasper Tudor, Earl of Pembroke.

Through death and imprisonment and flight, our King Edward faces no threats. With only twenty-nine years to his name, with much of his life before him and a thriving family, can we now expect to live our lives in peace?

We are happy to make the prediction that we can.

Duchess Cecily must be relieved that her sons are once more hand in glove. Family disputes can be exhausting and she is no longer a young woman. We wish her well. Maybe she will retire into a quiet life, leaving her sons to handle the reins between them. The Queen will be thankful if she does. Berkhamsted is far enough from Westminster that the sound of Duchess Cecily's voice will be much muted.

Cecily, King's Mother, to Edward, King of England
Written from Berkhamsted

My well-beloved son,

It may be that we have a problem, once again, with your brother of Clarence.

You have treated Clarence with astonishing generosity after his disloyal conduct in the past, yet it would be unwise to adopt complacency. I advise you to keep an eye on any conflict of interest that develops between your brothers. You have made Diccon a lord of power with land from the Duchy of Lancaster, as well as estates in Wales and East Anglia. He is Constable and Admiral of England. Have you made a rod for your own back here? At the moment he and Clarence are enjoying the heady gloss of reuniting. It may not always be so. Clarence can be combative and has a jealous streak as wide as the Thames at Gravesend.

Regretfully, I find that I have to take you to task, which you will not like. I hear too much of your reprehensible behaviour. It is unseemly and immoral in a King. Gone are the days when you could give yourself over to dancing, hunting, hawking and banqueting. You have a wife whom you claimed to wed in a surfeit of love. You have a family. Your own loyalty to them should not be a source of gossip, innuendo and coarse comment from tavern to Council chamber.

I would like not to hear the name Elizabeth Shore in connection with yours ever again. A mercer's daughter forsooth. Could you do no better, if you must take a mistress?

One further suggestion which I hope you will not ignore. Diccon lacks a wife. Anne Neville, now widowed after her unfortunate alliance with Edward of Lancaster, would be a most useful bride. The vast estates of Warwick and Montagu, which must be disposed of sensitively, can then be divided between your two brothers. It would be unwise to allow Anne to fall into other less friendly hands. Clarence won't like it, but he must learn to tolerate what he does not like.

Cecily, King's Mother

You might also consider your attire, my son. The close fitting of your short doublet and hose is becoming a source of scandal amongst the monastic chroniclers. It may not be best policy to flaunt your undoubted masculinity too obviously. You might also consider discussing with your wife that so much bare flesh exhibited around the throat and shoulders is not fitting for a Queen of England.

Edward, King of England, to Cecily, King's Mother
Written from the Palace of Westminster

Grateful thanks to my Lady Mother for the maternal lecture.

I will try not to let the rumours reach your tender ears. If I fail, you must practise political deafness, which should not be difficult if you remain in Berkhamsted.

Gloucester is an able administrator, thus I will continue to promote him. As for Clarence, I will do what I can to treat him fairly. All I can do is hope that my leniency will keep him loyal.

Sometimes I could wish to deliver a punch to his jaw to lay him out at my feet. But I won't, having a more thorough grasp of statesmanship than he does. Or not unless he commits more crimes against me and the realm.

Do not let it be an anxiety for you. I will not let him disturb the peace of the realm.

Now, rejoice with us, madam. Elizabeth carries a child. We hope for another son at the turn of the year.

My sister Anne has petitioned me for a divorce from Exeter. I am of a mind to consent. Do you have any opinions on this? I can only think that you will be in agreement to release her from a man who has been a permanent Lancastrian blot on our Yorkist landscape. It was inconsiderate of him not to die at Barnet or Tewkesbury. I will relieve my sister of his presence in her life and guarantee her financial security.

Your dutiful son,

Edward

Anne Neville would be an exceptional bride if Gloucester wants her.

England's Chronicle, 1472

Signs and Wonders.

Blazing comets, red with blood.

Are these ill omens? All our readers must be aware of the comet that has blazed its way across our heavens for the last two months. All must have stood and gazed in wonder, or fallen to their knees in fear. Is it a portent of grave evil?

We hear that there has been an outbreak of fever and the bloody flux.

There have been deaths too. The royal daughter, Margaret, so recently born, has swiftly gone to her grave. The Queen's mother Jacquetta, dowager Countess Rivers, too has gone from this earthly torment.

Fortunately, the heir to the throne, Prince Edward, now approaching the second anniversary of his birth, is in rude health. If you have wondered why you have not seen him in London, riding through the streets in the arms of his Governor. If you have wondered why he should not be present with the royal household, quite simply it is because he has been sent to the great Yorkist base at Ludlow to his own household with Earl Rivers as Governor. Our King spent some of his childhood years in that castle and will have fond memories of the good hunting. The Prince will be raised there as a future King.

Many of you will enjoy this final piece of news.

Our Neville Archbishop of York has at last paid for his sins against the House of York.

Cecily, King's Mother, to Anne, Duchess of Exeter
Written from Berkhamsted, 1472

To my much-loved daughter,

It is difficult for me to accept the necessity for a divorce, but how can I not? It was a very painful union for you with a man who, like a worm, lacked backbone. You have attained your legal separation from your estranged husband through a most legitimate argument. I commend you in taking my advice when petitioning your brother. It could be argued that the original papal dispensations for your marriage, to release you from the bounds of consanguinity, were inadequate since it never revealed that you and Holland are both descended from my grandfather John of Gaunt. Thus your marriage was never valid.

I regret that it has taken so many years of your unhappiness to prove it.

Perhaps you can wed Thomas St Leger and legitimise the relationship you have had with him. At least it will put a halt to that scandal.

I do not wish to sound lacking in compassion. You deserve some marital happiness.

The marriage of Diccon to Anne Neville will give the gossips something to talk about. I understand Clarence is once more in a state of common disgruntlement over this alliance and the apportioning of the Neville estates. As Isabel Neville's husband, he wants them all.

No surprise there!
Your loving mother,
Cecily, King's Mother

Cecily, King's Mother, to George Neville, once Archbishop of York

Written from Berkhamsted

You can never claim that you were not warned for taking issue with my son. The King can be a good friend, but a ruthless enemy. Did you truly believe that he would forgive you? To take it upon your authority to solemnise the marriage of George, Duke of Clarence, with Isabel Neville, in Calais, when King Edward had strictly forbidden it, was a calamitous decision.

You have now paid the penalty. And I can honestly say that I am not sorry.

Arrested and charged with treason.

Banished to Calais.

All your property and treasure confiscated.

Your mitre broken.

All lost within the space of one day.

You should give heartfelt thanks that you have not paid with your head.

It will please you to know that your land will be given to the young Prince Edward. Your jewels are to be set into a new crown to grace King Edward's brow. There is a lesson here which an ambitious churchman might preach to the sinners in his care.

Your aunt, who finds it difficult to be compassionate,
Cecily, King's Mother

Royal Proclamation

On this day, the seventeenth day of August in the year 1473
   Born to King Edward the Fourth and his wife Queen Elizabeth
   In the Dominican Friary in the fair town of Shrewsbury
   A son
   Richard

Duchess Cecily's intercession to the Blessed Virgin Mary

Hail Mary, full of Grace, Our Lord is with thee.

How much grief and loss must I bear?

I lift before you the daughter I have lost. Blessed Virgin, I pray for the soul of my daughter Anne. Released from the Exeter marriage, she had hopes of such happiness with Thomas St Leger. Death claimed her in childbed.

Forgive me my impertinence. You know all that, Holy Mother. You know the depth of the afflictions heaped on me. I weep for such cruelty. I rage at fate that has taken her from me. I ask forgiveness for the marriage we forced on our daughter.

I must give thanks that the infant daughter lives.

Grant me some ingenuity to draw my son Clarence back into the royal fold. I fear that treachery is once more engraved on his brow. He is become as dangerous as a pike in a carp pond.

I will not bow down before such outrageous burdens. I will fight on.

Amen

Cecily, King's Mother, to Margaret, Duchess of Burgundy
Written from Berkhamsted

My very dearest Meg,

Your brother Clarence is prowling around the royal sheepfold like a hungry wolf.

How is it that he has learned no lessons from the past? Why did I ever lull myself into believing that Clarence's reconciliation with Edward was a genuine meeting of minds? I should have known better after all these years.

Now his restlessness is all centred on brotherly jealousy. Clarence is dissatisfied with the portion of land given to him by Edward, and feels that Diccon has been treated with a more generous hand. Clarence refuses to come to Court unless Edward summons him. When he does, he sulks, lounges in silence through meetings of the Royal Council and refuses to eat or drink in Edward's company. Edward remains remarkably tolerant, but his brother will not bend.

I expect that Clarence feels humiliated. Edward has taken Clarence's favourite manor of Tutbury from him, as well as stripping him of his authority as Lieutenant of Ireland. But that does not excuse Clarence's behaviour. Being Edward's heir for ten years has given him such overweening pride. But now Edward has two sons. Clarence must accept that the crown is lost to him.

I fear it will only get worse. Could you exert any influence over him? Where is the brave, laughing child I recall, the one who enjoyed the tricks and ploys of Hesdin? I seem to have bred a dissatisfied lout.

I fear what will happen when Edward's patience runs out, as it must. We know that he has a temper when roused.

Do you suppose that Isabel could make him see sense? She has not had spectacular success so far. She is a kind, well-mannered girl but I have not seen real strength of character there. I think that she may be very much within Clarence's dominion. She is carrying a child so will have enough to concern her.

I cannot get close to him. He has shuttered his mind to every one of his family.

I think you are the only one who can demand his attention now that your sister Anne is dead. A word of warning from a displeased sister might be more acceptable than one from his mother. He will assuredly not listen to Gloucester. More like to bury a sharp blade between his ribs.

Do what you can.

Your affectionate mother,

Cecily, King's Mother

Margaret, Duchess of Burgundy, to Cecily, King's Mother

Written from Hesdin

My most well-beloved mother,

I tried; in all good faith, I tried.

I sent an official herald to Clarence, resplendent in all the red, gold and blue of Burgundian panoply, lions rampant on his chest. I thought it would make a suitable impression. Sadly, he was received no further than the entrance hall at Warwick, kept waiting in the draughts without even a cup of ale, until Clarence strode in and demanded what he might want.

My herald was most precise in recording the exchange. My brother was rude, discourteous and crude in his response, using words and expressions I will not write. He mocked the Burgundian magnificence. He will remain where he is, a wounded boar in his lair, to defend his estates against his brother Gloucester.

The warning will have to come from his mother, although I hold out no hope.

You might try Isabel as a last resort. Clarence might at least listen to his wife if she is carrying his child.

Your faithful daughter,

Meg

Chapter Thirty

Clarence Places Himself beyond Redemption

Cecily, King's Mother, to George, Duke of Clarence
Written from Berkhamsted, March 1476

My son,

It is my wish that you come and visit me.

Do I have to spend my life summoning my sons to my presence? It seems that I do.

It is inordinately bad policy that you should be estranged from your two brothers, and particularly from your King. Any man of sense would know that. I regret that you could not be receptive to your sister's request. It is discourteous in the extreme to keep a Burgundian herald with crown and staff of office loitering in the entrance.

I request that you come to Berkhamsted on receipt of this letter.

Give my kind thoughts to Isabel as she awaits a new child. I send her an excellent nostrum to guard against another unhappy outcome to her pregnancy. I am aware that she has carried two sturdy children but your wife, from past experience, is vulnerable in childbirth. I would not wish her to lose another child.

The tragic loss of your sister Anne in childbed at the beginning of this year has left me with an acute anxiety for Isabel.

Cecily, King's Mother

A Recipe to Guard Against the Sad Event of the Death of a New-Born Child

Take the following:

Oil

Wax

Powder of Frankincense

Mastic

Mix well and anoint in front and in back two or three times every week in the final weeks before the babe is due. May the Holy Mother have mercy on you and the child.

George, Duke of Clarence, to Cecily, King's Mother
Written from Warwick Castle

Madam,

I see no purpose in journeying to Berkhamsted.

I will not speak with the King. I will not speak with you. I will not speak with Gloucester. Nor with my sister Meg, so do not set her onto my heels again. I can do without sisterly lectures on what is expected of me.

Clarence

Cecily, King's Mother, to Isabel, Duchess of Clarence
Written from Berkhamsted

To my beloved godchild and daughter by law,

I trust you are in good health, and your children.

Did you find the nostrum to strengthen the womb comforting? I pray that you will, for there is no greater loss than an unborn child. As we have both experienced.

But here is an urgency that I must broach. If you have any influence on your husband, now is the time to use it. I foresee no good from the present surly behaviour, most of it at your husband's door. Edward's patience is not without limit.

Clarence must find a way to return to Court with some degree of dignity. Even the youngest of your children would know better than to sulk through a Council meeting, his back turned to the King of England. Which is what Clarence managed to do.

Your affectionate mother by law

Cecily, King's Mother

I was wrong, Isabel. There is a greater loss than an unborn child. To lose a much-loved husband is an everlasting wound to the heart. The bleeding never stops.

Isabel, Duchess of Clarence, to Cecily, King's Mother
Written from Warwick Castle

Madam,

I am grateful for your kind wishes.

I have no influence. My husband is beyond reasoning. I might have some compassion with him, but he is constantly on the move to oversee the security of his estates from attack, whether real or imaginary.

I am suffering from a lowering darkness that assails my spirits. I cannot shake it off, but I have hopes to find use for the gift you sent. I pray for the blessing of another child.

I can only hope that time will heal all wounds between my husband and his brothers. I will do what I can.

Your affectionate daughter and godchild,

Isabel

Edward, King of England, to Cecily, King's Mother
Written from the Palace of Westminster

Madam,

It is my proposal to have my new son Richard proclaimed Duke of York, and as such it is my wish that he will hold the lands of his namesake, my father. Currently many of these are in your possession and, for the present, there they will remain. My son will not come into his lands until he reaches the age of sixteen, but I thought you should know my intent; I have written it into my will. I foresee no difficulty and do not think that you will be unwilling.

It is my plan to now organise the reburial of my father at Fotheringhay which you have long desired.

If it should come to your ears that I was responsible for the sad demise of Henry Holland, Duke of Exeter, falling from a ship on his return to England when in my employ, there is no truth in it. Although I find it difficult to do anything but give thanks.

Your dutiful son,

Edward

Cecily, King's Mother, to Anne, Lady Mountjoy
Written from Berkhamsted

My dearest sister,

Edward has perfected great skill in the use of sleight of hand when dealing with me, although without subtlety. My lands for his son Richard in exchange for the reinterment of my husband.

How can I refuse?

If I do not give my consent, Richard's remains may well remain in Pontefract for ever. As the day of my own death must draw closer, it is imperative that I see his removal to Fotheringhay. Thus I will give up my lands for him to return home. Even though it is no longer my home.

It pleased me that the child will be known as Richard, Duke of York. A fitting memorial in flesh and blood to my own lord. It gives me some solace, to relieve my mind of the perpetual problem of Clarence. At least my Richard was spared that! Nor do I repine over Exeter's death. His deviousness knew no bounds.

Cecily

England's Chronicle, *July 1476*

A magnificent ceremony, long overdue some would say.

The earthly remains of Richard, Duke of York, are finally laid to rest in the church at Fotheringhay.

We have the words and impressions of an onlooker. Enjoy it, as if you too were there to witness this spectacle.

The travelling carriage approaches, all clothed in black, black velvet in deep folds sweeping down over the bier. On top an effigy, life-sized, clad in the darkest of blue.

Richard, Duke of Gloucester, rides as chief mourner behind

the coffin of his father. At every church where they have rested on this long, slow journey from the north, the Choir Royal sang. Such honour and dignity has been shown to the Duke who should have been King.

Or so he claimed.

This is no day for old divisions. This is the day when he is returned home to Fotheringhay where the stained-glass windows that Duchess Cecily had first commissioned are now complete. At the entrance to the churchyard the cortege is met by King Edward himself, to show all honour to his father. By his side stands the Queen. Cloth of gold is offered by the King and Queen and the attendant nobility, to be laid in the shape of a cross on the effigy.

It is noted that the King bows, kisses the effigy, and weeps.

A horse is led to the church door, and with it is brought the Duke's knightly trappings: his coat of arms, his shield, his sword and his helmet, all offered up in his name. Lord Ferrers rides the horse into the church, through the nave to the choir, carrying an axe, point lowered towards the floor. The harness is removed and offered at the altar.

The Duke of York is laid to rest in the choir.

His son Edmund, Duke of Rutland, is buried in the Lady Chapel.

Thus it is done, recorded in this *Chronicle*.

Who is present at this stern interment? The Queen, soberly clothed, is accompanied by her two elder daughters, Elizabeth, recently betrothed to the Dauphin, and Mary.

Who is not one of the mourners?

The Duchess of Gloucester, despite the prominent role of her lord. Is it perhaps that she is carrying a child? They have only one son, Edward of Middleham, now two years old. Nor is the Duke of Clarence and his wife here. Is there still a lingering element of mistrust?

Most pertinent, Duchess Cecily, King's Mother, is not one of the royal crowd.

But then it is not customary for widows to attend their husband's public interment.

We imagine that she was there in spirit. And some disgust at the Woodville Queen's lauding it over the proceedings.

We applaud King Edward's sense of what is due to his family, even though it is now more than fifteen years since the tragic death of his father and brother on the field at Wakefield.

May he finally rest in peace, Richard Plantagenet, Duke of York, the King who never was.

Cecily, Duchess of York, to Richard, Duke of York
Written at Berkhamsted, August 1476

The final letter, my love.

All is now complete. I shall not write again.

At last Edward has fulfilled my deepest desires, for which I must not neglect to give him my heartfelt thanks. At last your body was brought from Pontefract to lie as I had always intended at Fotheringhay. At last you were finally brought home, after a mournful procession for ten days from Pontefract to Fotheringhay.

I was not there to bear witness, but I know what was arranged.

Above your head an angel held the crown that you should have worn in life.

I weep for it. I weep for such a loss to this kingdom. I weep for such a loss for me.

I should have been there to welcome the coffin at the graveyard. To kneel and kiss the effigy.

I was not there, and it was my choice to be absent.

They say that I would not share the space with Elizabeth Woodville. It was true. This should have been my day, but Edward was immovable. Rather than inflict my sour mood, I remained on my knees in the chapel here at Berkhamsted. But my thoughts were at Fotheringhay, the sun shining down through the windows I had completed in your honour.

I must acknowledge that the Queen was not lacking in respect, wearing neither hennin nor wired veils, but garments of seemly mourning. I am told that it was a simple affair, befitting the occasion.

The Queen conducted herself as I would have wished. She has at last overcome her Woodville beginnings.

One day I will visit the tomb for myself.

Lie in peace, my dear love, my heart.

As I pray that England will now lie in peace under our son's care.

Yet I feel the weight of some presentiment.

Your loving wife,

Cecily

To be kept safe with all the other legal documents appertaining to the life of Cecily, King's Mother, Duchess of York.

England's Chronicle, *December 1476*

An untimely death!

After our pleasure to report such a regal ceremonial to bring Richard Duke of York home, it is our sad task to announce the death of Isabel, Duchess of Clarence, elder daughter of the late Earl of Warwick, on the twenty-second day of December in this year of 1476 at Warwick Castle. It is less than three months since the birth of a son, Richard, who is thought to be ailing and not long for this world.

The Lady is buried in Tewkesbury Abbey.

The Duke of Clarence is said to be distraught with grief.

Some say he is out of his head with madness, with wild accusations over the cause of her death.

We offer our condolences. May the Lady rest in peace.

Cecily, King's Mother, to George, Duke of Clarence
Written from Berkhamsted, January 1477

My son,

I am deeply concerned by the rumours that reach me.

Without doubt, you have all my prayers. I have instructed my priest to offer Masses for the soul of Isabel, and for the child, a son, who has since died.

I understand your grief. What I fail to comprehend is why you are declaiming with such force that Isabel died of poisoning at the hands of one of her women. Mistress Twynyho was well loved by Isabel and most certainly trustworthy. What possible evidence do you have for such an accusation?

I advise you to refrain from spreading such calumnies. The death of my goddaughter was more akin to a weakening of the body and spirits after the birth of the child, as the midwife will probably tell you.

To spread such wanton misjudgements hampers the healing

of your own grief. Look to your children for consolation. I can heartily recommend it.

Cecily, King's Mother

George, Duke of Clarence, to Cecily, King's Mother
Written from Warwick Castle

You know nothing of my wife's illness. You did not see her in those final weeks. You did not bear witness to her distress as she was forced to live with the pain for more than two whole months.

My household says that it is poison. I do not need evidence.

It is my intention to seek justice on the woman involved.

It is also my intention to seek a new wife.

I do not need to be taken to task by my mother in this time of mourning.

Clarence

England's Chronicle, *spring 1477*

What's this?

The Duke of Clarence, who so recently lost his wife, is seeking a new bride. Who does he have in mind? He has not been short of offers, since he is the brother of our King.

His sister Margaret, now Dowager Duchess of Burgundy after the tragic death of her husband in battle in January of this year, has put forward the name of her step-daughter Mary, the new youthful Duchess of Burgundy. It would be a strong alliance, and one which France would not regard with favour. An excellent reason for it to take place.

The King of Scotland, King James the Third, has offered his sister Margaret Stewart.

Both prestigious matches.

Which bride will Clarence prefer?

Which bride will our King allow him to take?

Will Duchess Cecily have any commanding voice in the matter?

Cecily, King's Mother, to Margaret, Dowager Duchess of Burgundy
Written from Berkhamsted, April 1477

To my well-beloved daughter,

There will be no Burgundian marriage celebration. Edward has put his foot down, hard enough to raise a cloud of royal dust.

Clarence is understandably aggrieved at Edward's high-hand-edness in refusing your offer of the Burgundian heiress Mary. He has also refused Clarence's marriage to Margaret Stewart. You can imagine Clarence's reaction. Edward says that he has no intention of allowing Clarence to remarry.

The atmosphere at Court is redolent of an impending battle.

Clarence claims to suspect that Isabel was poisoned, as I told you. Even without evidence that the poor girl was given some noxious substance, he is determined to take his revenge. He will not listen to sense. He has taken action which I fear will only have terrible consequences.

What has he done? He dispatched a body of men to arrest Mistress Twynyho, the waiting-woman he suspects, at her manor in Somerset, from where he dragged her across England to Warwick Castle, and shut her in a prison cell. On the next morning she was brought out before Clarence and a jury. Clarence accused her of murdering his wife, and the jury promptly found her guilty. In no time at all she was taken through the streets of Warwick to the gallows where she was hanged.

That is not right! Some of the jurors are already claiming they were intimidated by Clarence. This is an ugly and dangerous step my son has taken.

I await the repercussions.

Edward cannot keep forgiving and making excuses for Clarence's wayward behaviour, I fear. It is my intent to keep out of this until I see which way the wind is blowing.

My heart is still with you in your mourning, my dearest Meg. You have a stalwart spirit and I know that you will prevail over all lowering thoughts.

Your affectionate mother,

Cecily, King's Mother

Edward, King of England, to George, Duke of Clarence
Written from the Palace of Westminster, April 1477

I desire that you present yourself at Court.

Edward

Edward, King of England, to George, Duke of Clarence
Written from the Palace of Westminster, April 1477

I received no reply from you. I request that you come to Westminster immediately.

Edward

Edward, King of England, to George, Duke of Clarence
Written from the Palace of Westminster, April 1477

As your King I command, on the receipt of this, that you appear before me and the Royal Council at Westminster.

Edward

England's Chronicle, May 1477

Witchcraft! Sorcery!

Involving the royal brother, the Duke of Clarence, himself.

You will all know about this and have relished the colourful scandal.

A certain John Stacy, known to us as the great sorcerer, along with two compatriots, have all three been arrested and charged with having attempted to predict the day of death of our King and his eldest son, Prince Edward. Brought to trial, two were hanged at Tyburn and one pardoned.

Which would have been the end of it, except that the man Burdet, one of those hanged, was a servant of the Duke of Clarence, and so became the object of the Duke's compassion.

We hear that the Duke is coming to London to make his point in the case.

But what will the King say to his brother? Has the royal well of patience run dry?

Duchess Cecily's intercession to the Blessed Virgin Mary

Hail Mary, full of Grace, Our Lord is with thee.

Hail Mary...

I have no words.

I can bear no more loss. My shoulders can carry no more weight. My world is breaking apart around me.

England's Chronicle, *the tenth day of June 1477*

Sensational event!

The Duke of Clarence is at last here in London. How many royal commands has it taken for Clarence to fall into obedience? But, once here, Clarence did not seek to meet with the King, his brother.

What has he done?

Only marched into a meeting of the Royal Council, in the King's absence, it has to be said, and once there our royal Duke issued a declaration of innocence on behalf of those condemned to death for predicting the day of death of the King and his son, and instructed a friar to read it aloud to the assembled Lords. Having challenged the King's judgement, the Duke promptly marched out. Why would our royal Duke defend a convicted traitor? How dangerous is it, calling into question the King's justice? How hazardous is it to defend a man engaged in sorcery against the King?

Our King and Council will not enjoy their powers over England's justice being called into question by an apparently deranged royal brother.

We understand from many parties there present that the exchange of words between the Duke and the Council was harsh and unforgiving.

Surely the King's inimitable patience is at an end.

Oh, Duchess Cecily, our thoughts are with you on this tumultuous day.

Edward, King of England, to George, Duke of Clarence
Written from Windsor

You will meet with me in Windsor. I command it. If you refuse to come, I will send an armed guard to fetch you. Do not mistake me.

Edward

England's Chronicle, *June 1477*

Royal arrest and imprisonment!

Faced with continued defiance, the King has dispatched his brother of Clarence to the Tower of London, to be imprisoned at royal pleasure. As we predicted, it was a risky affair for the Duke to become involved in the use of sorcery to predict the King's death.

We further predict some harsh words between the King and his recalcitrant brother of Clarence. We anticipate hearing the raised voices all the way to Berkhamsted where the Duchess will be waiting to be informed of the outcome.

We look for a trial before parliament before the year is out.

We commiserate with Duchess Cecily in this family dispute.

Will Clarence's defiance continue?

Edward, King of England, to Cecily, King's Mother
Written from Windsor

To my Lady Mother,

By now you will know the depths of the treason committed by your son of Clarence. His guilt is beyond question. I cannot have my brother denying the justice dispensed through my courts. For the good of the country, an attainder against him is essential.

I regret the pain this will cause you. You and I can make no more excuses for him.

Your dutiful son,

Edward

Cecily, King's Mother, to Edward, King of England
Written from Berkhamsted, by return

Pain?

I cannot quantify it, and nor can you.

Treason?

On what grounds do you accuse your brother of treason?

I understand your wrath that he should dare to question your justice, but are you certain that he sought your death? Is it more perilous for you to condemn him to death than to let him live?

I advise you to have a caution.

Cecily, King's Mother

Edward, King of England, to Cecily, King's Mother
Written from Windsor, January 1478

I am always cautious, Madam.

It would be good policy for you to travel to Baynard's Castle. We need to discuss this matter. There is also a family wedding for you to attend. It is my intent to show this realm the strength and unity of the House of York, despite the blatant disloyalty of the Duke of Clarence. As King's Mother I expect you to be here at the centre of the festivities that will give the citizens of London something to talk about, for ten whole days, which is not riddled with treachery and scandal.

Edward

Duchess Cecily attends a family wedding in St Stephen's Chapel, on the fifteenth day of January 1478

'I thought I should be here. To show a united front. Although I suspect it will be like trying to unite a bag full of feral cats.'

She might be more than a little gaunt, her shoulders bowed with age, but my sister Katherine's tongue continued to be as acerbic as her pen. I could do nothing but laugh aloud. So many years since we had last stood in the same chamber – all of sixteen long years since she had come to strengthen me at Richard's Year's Mind – but here was Katherine, once again abandoning her isolation in the north to keep me company when I most had need of it. We hugged each other, veils entwining. She was worryingly thin but her spirit was as strong as ever. What signs of age did she see in me? I would not ask. I knew that beneath her flamboyant butterfly head-dress, incongruous with the age of the wearer, her hair would be as grey as mine. Her knuckles were as gnarled as the burrs on an old oak, but I clutched them with true gratitude.

'You cannot imagine how grateful I am to have you with me.' I fought against any suspicion of moisture on my cheeks.

Katherine sniffed her derision. 'I thought that these macabre festivities demanded my authority and dignity in the face of the Woodville victory. We will stand shoulder to shoulder for this graceless marriage.'

I turned to look over towards the bride, all of six years old, nobly clad in silk and velvet, her hair neat beneath a fine linen coif. Clutching the hand of her nurse, she was unaware of the path that was to unfold for the future. I pitied her. The little bride was Katherine's great-granddaughter, the Norfolk heiress. She and her wealth would now be absorbed into the Woodville ranks with her marriage to my royal grandson Richard of Shrewsbury, Duke of York.

'Then come and we will make our presence felt,' I said. 'And we will pretend that we do not see Clarence's life hanging, thick and noxious as a plague cloud, as these children take their vows.'

We tried. Oh, we tried.

We stood beside Edward and the Queen and the two children, beneath the golden canopy. No one would say that there was any rift between us on this auspicious occasion, even though our smiles were as rigid as a lizard's grin. St Stephen's Chapel at Westminster was the appropriate setting for the glittering ranks of guests, most of them Woodvilles and their connections. Our own family has become sadly short of numbers of late. It was only at events like this that we realised the effect of Death. It was a relief to know that Diccon was here, to remind me how he had grown into a great magnate and the King's staunchest supporter.

And there, hovering in the shadows, throughout all Edward's majestic organising, the splendour and celebration, feasts and pageants, was the malign presence of the one absent brother.

'How is Clarence?' Katherine asked when the clerics had done their work and we regrouped to drink wine as if there was nought amiss.

'I know not,' I admitted. 'He is imprisoned.'

We pretended, as we toasted the children, wishing them long and happy lives, not to notice that the assembled nobles were there for quite another purpose: to sit in judgement on my son of Clarence.

'What an unsettling day,' Katherine said, expressing the thoughts that dominated my mind. 'A child marriage, Clarence in the Tower since June, and the fatal session of parliament looming over all.'

'I cannot bear to think of it.'

'Well, you must. Do smile at Edward, Cis, even if it is like a crack in thin ice. What will be the charge against your son?'

With that question, I must face the truth behind what Edward was planning.

'High treason.' An accusation to whisper, in secret, in corners. I never thought to hear it used against Clarence in parliament, even when he raised his standard with Warwick against the King. I swallowed, my throat dry despite the wine poured by the King's servants. 'If an attainder is passed, my son Clarence will die.'

'Will Edward go that far?'

'He can see no other means of controlling a brother he cannot trust. How have we come to this? Death on a battlefield is one thing, by execution at the wish of his brother is worse.' Desolation washed over me. 'I will not merely accept it, Kat. I will face the wolf at the door. All I need is the courage to resist its teeth.'

'But if an attainder is passed, what can you do?'

'I will do what I have always done.'

There was no need for me to explain. Katherine knew me well and the years had not sullied her mind.

'Do I come with you?' she asked, tucking her hand within my arm.

'No. It is not necessary. But for the first time in my life, Kat, I think that I fear my son the King.'

England's Chronicle, *the sixteenth day of January 1478*

Do we have an attainder?

Today we must report the happenings in the Painted Chamber at Westminster where the King has called his parliament to meet.

After all the junketings of the royal marriage between two innocent children, parliament turns its mind to the crimes of the less
than innocent Duke of Clarence.

And what a piece of drama has been carried out by the King
himself as he faced his errant brother.

Only one voice was raised to deliver an accusation against the
Duke. Only one voice. That of the King himself. No one made
a reply to the King except the Duke. It was a moment of the
highest tension between the royal pair, as if they were alone in
the room, one desiring the destruction of the other.

And the cause? An accusation of high treason, presented by
King Edward himself.

Here for your information are the crimes listed against the
Duke. What an all-encompassing litany of political sins they
are.

He conspired against the King, the Queen, their son and heir,
and the nobility of England.

He forced the King into exile, persuading parliament to exclude
him and his heirs from the throne, so that Clarence might take
it for himself.

He continued to conspire, attacking royal justice in the sorcery
case of Thomas Burdet.

He accused the King of attempting his destruction.

He conspired to raise war against the King within England.

Worst of all, the Duke of Clarence accused King Edward of
being a bastard and not fit to reign. We will say no more on this
count, in honour of the Duchess, but we doubt it will be the last
time that this accusation raises its ugly head.

All of which amounts to high treason.

Can our King pardon such an array of crimes? Surely to release the errant Duke of Clarence would be a threat to the peace of the realm and undermine his own sacred position.

We see a Bill of Attainder fast approaching for the Duke of Clarence.

There are few who will argue for the Duke's innocence. Not even the Duchess whose honour – or lack thereof – has once more been brought into the open by this unsavoury case. The Duke has much to answer for.

Chapter Thirty-One

A Desperate Loss

Duchess Cecily petitions for the life of her son in a chamber in the Palace of Westminster, January 1478

'My son will die. You will condemn your brother to death.'

It was a statement of what I knew, not a question. I could read it in Edward's face, in the flat depth of his eyes that could so often shine in merriment or mischief. Today they were as lethal as a new-honed blade, while spread on the table was the death warrant. The pen. The pot of ink. All it lacked was the damning signature.

'Yes, I will condemn him. He will be hanged, drawn and quartered, the punishment for any traitor to the King.'

There it was. The cruel consequence. I found difficulty in drawing in a breath.

'Are you so intransigent?' I asked, knowing what Edward's reply would be. And how could I blame him for it?

'I have given him chance after chance, to work with me, to prove the loyalty inherent in the oath he took at my coronation. I rewarded him, ennobled him, enhanced his status. There is no gratitude in him. No sense of what he owes to me. He is the one who is beyond reason. He has proved himself to be a traitor, again and again. How often do you wish me to forgive him?'

Edward, his face marked by lines of dissipation, his body thickening with decadent living, was immovable now that he had made his judgement.

'Again and again, if it is necessary. Tell me why you cannot.'

'Have you time for all the reasons? It will take a lifetime to list them.'

'If you have the energy to kill your brother, then I have the energy to listen.'

'Listen as you travel home and you will hear them dissected and discussed at every street corner. Or ask your servants. They will tell you. But this one will persuade you, if nothing else will.'

I knew what he would say. The old rumours, of course.

'The unsavoury details of Archer Blaybourne and my bastardy. Whether he believes it I know not, but it is a useful whip to use against me and my family. If I am a bastard, then he, my vicious brother, has every right to be King. *If* he is a true son of you and your husband.'

How his cold words struck home.

'Are you questioning my fidelity again?' I forced myself to ask.

'Would you tell me the truth?'

I kept my eyes resting lightly on his. 'I am not known for dishonesty.'

Would he force me to declare my honour? But he did not, because he wished to spare me. Or because he could not accept my veracity. It was a harsh wounding, twisting the knife in my heart.

'But you are known for your pride,' he said, 'which might colour your response. Wherever the truth lies, it is an unpardonable attack on me and mine. Do I forgive Clarence for that?'

'I still think you would not want your brother dead.'

'Yet I will do it.'

He was, it seemed, beyond moving, but I could not merely step back and allow Clarence's death. I would not be so weak. 'Does the Queen persuade you?'

For the first time, the slightest hesitation. 'I am of the same mind as the Queen.'

I watched him, wondering how far he would go to allow Woodville ambitions.

'I think the Queen would rejoice to see the end of a royal brother who was once heir to the kingdom.'

The hesitation was gone. 'The royal brother who was involved in predicting the date of my death. Do you think he has no personal interest in it? What does Elizabeth think? you ask. She thinks he is too unpredictable, too driven with selfish desires. So do you, madam, if you will be honest, but after so long, I doubt if you will allow yourself to be in agreement with my wife. You have never liked her.'

'Liked. So trivial a response. She is not important in this matter. Clarence is.'

Edward was turning away, his mind closed.

'You can do no more. I have listened, but even you, his mother, know that he is beyond my control.'

He was gentler now, the decision made.

'Send him into exile,' I urged.

'To return with a French army against me? No.'

I could see the exasperation building at my persistence, but I could not let it go until every stone, every pebble of our family relationships had been turned and re-turned.

'Would you not fight for the life of your own son?' I asked.

He walked away to where the dread document still lay. He would not answer.

'I acknowledge that there is nothing I can do.' I pursued him. Had I not known this even before I sought him out?

'As I acknowledge your pride and your care for all of us,' he said. 'But you care for this realm too. You know what the end must be.'

'Yes. Except I would petition you, Edward. To show mercy.'

'There is no mercy.'

I remembered falling to my knees before Warwick, in desperation that the battle at Barnet would never happen. Should I do the same now, before my son? I saw the hard-etched lines that bracketed his mouth. Kneeling would have as little impact here as it had on Warwick. Sometimes a woman's powers were not enough.

'And yet I would petition you,' I said, with one thought.

Irritation gave an edge to his voice. 'Enough! Have I not already said—'

'Not in granting him life. I see his death written in your face. Not that, but in the manner of his death. I would beg you, Edward. Would you condemn your brother to the punishment deemed suitable for a traitor? The public humiliation of hanging, drawing and quartering. Of beheading, his severed head exposed on London Bridge. It is not worthy of you.'

'He would have rejoiced at my death.'

'You are a more worthy man. I plead with you. Let him die in a more equable fashion. For the sake of the woman who bore you both, if not for his.'

Silence filled the room as I waited. A shiver of a cold draught that flirted with the furred edge of my sleeves. The faint sound

463

of some small bird singing lustily beyond the window. It would be so easy for Edward to comply, but I knew that he had every right to refuse.

'You astonish me,' he said.

'Why?'

'Even though he cast doubt on the sanctity of your marriage. Yet you would still beg for mercy.'

'Even then. You are my dear son. I would not want this on your conscience. Nor on mine if I failed to at least entreat.'

He picked up the document, reading it as if he did not already know its content.

'You do not kneel.' He threw down the sheet of attainder. 'I heard that you knelt before Warwick to plead for my life.'

'I did.' And who had told him that? I wondered. 'I hoped to impress him. I can no longer impress you. But I think that you are not without honour. History will not think well of you if you send your brother to the executioner's blade.'

His features relaxed infinitesimally. 'I think history would not care greatly. But I see that you do. As King's Mother, what is your advice to me, after so many pieces of advice?'

'Use some other means.'

He tilted his chin, thinking. 'Very well. I will allow him to choose his own death, if that pleases you.'

'It is as much as I can ask.'

I curtsied low and deep. I had achieved all I could and must be grateful. I left the King putting his signature to the document that would bring his brother, my son, to his death.

England's Chronicle, *January 1478*

As we predicted.

A Bill of Attainder is passed, signed by King Edward's own hand. The total destruction of the Duke of Clarence is complete.

He is convicted of treason, and so is condemned to death.

Many will say that the unfortunate Duke has paved his own path to this terrible outcome. Treachery had become a way of life for him.

It is a moment of great sadness, and we will all mourn with Duchess Cecily, that the House of York has come to this terrible pass.

Duchess Cecily visits the Duke of Clarence in the Tower of London, February 1478

I was allowed to see him once more, in his confinement in the Tower. Around him was spread all the comfort that might be expected of a royal Prince: the tapestries, the cushioned chairs, the enamelled hanap and cups. He was well groomed, with servants to attend to his needs, his hair neatly trimmed around his ears. The velvet and satin doublet, patterned in black and green, glorious with its extravagant sleeves that draped to the floor as he sat, proclaimed his wealth and importance. Only his face told me of his unquiet mind. Still so young and defiant, but he was worn, weary.

The door was locked behind me. Slowly he rose to his feet. He had been sitting immobile, looking out at freedom beyond the walls. The books he had been given were unopened. I could not even guess the measure of his thoughts. Was he repentant? Or merely intransigent?

He bowed, through years of long practice. He might be full of hatred but still he showed me respect, while I struggled to quench the anger that rose like bile in my throat. I had done all I could, as had his sisters. Nothing had destroyed that worm of malice and deceit and raw ambition that thrived and grew within him.

It was the defiance that spoke out.

'I know what you have come to say, my Lady Mother. It makes no difference now. My brother will have my life. You should be grateful to him, for removing a burr that has long irritated your own flesh. Soon you will be able to forget the son who questioned the very foundations of your marriage.'

His voice croaked through lack of use in recent hours. I spoke, moved by grief and imminent loss. There was no pity for him. Pity had expired long ago.

'I did all I could to bring about your restitution. You were given every chance by the King. You repay me by resurrecting the dishonour of my infidelity. You attacked the justice dispensed by your brother. There is nothing I can say to commend you, except that you should make your peace with God. Any pity I felt for you has been destroyed by your wilfulness.'

Clarence blinked. I had never spoken to him in such a manner, not even when I had brought him to heel at Baynard's Castle.

'All true,' he said. 'Why are you here at all?'

He would have moved away, except that I stepped before him so that he must look at me, take note of my words.

'I am here because I cannot let you go to your death without a final meeting. I gave you life. I will be here in the moments before your death.'

'I do not want your sanctimonious maternal offerings. I do not want your prayers.'

'You cannot prevent me from offering them. It is my duty. You are my son. You will always be my son, however much you wound me.'

His mouth curved in a smile that was not pleasant.

'And am I legitimate? Perhaps I am the only one of us all?'

I felt like striking him. Even now, with death at his side, he would hold to the old well-used political lies.

'You will believe as you wish.'

He stepped away, picking up a book, immediately flinging it onto his bed. 'He will not execute me.'

'No.'

'He has given me a choice in the manner of my death.' His smile was a death's grimace. 'Is he not generous in his victory over me?'

I would not ask what my son had chosen. Instead: 'Why? Why could you not accept the power and status that he gave you?'

'Because I think I have the right to be King.'

'Edward is the legitimate King.'

'How would you say other, without branding yourself as unchaste within your marriage to my glorified father? You will never brand him cuckold. You could think no wrong of him.'

'Oh, but I did. Your father could be impetuous and misguided. He could make the wrong choices, and did so. I loved him no less.'

'But you were unfaithful to him. What was it? A momentary whorish itch when he was away on campaign? Was there more than one archer? A servant? An ostler? Who's to know the status of my father...'

Rising within me like a spring tide, I felt the uncontrollable urge to strike him, flat-handed against his cheek. And yet I could not.

467

'Be silent!'

My voice, in my hurt, was as harsh as a magpie's cry.

'Your father would be ashamed to hear you speak in this manner. You will believe what you wish, but you will not so accuse me. Since there is no hope of the King's leniency, all I ask is that you make confession and go to your end with a quiet heart.'

'I cannot,' Clarence hissed. 'I will curse my brother with my final breath.'

The terrible anger in his face defeated me.

'Farewell, my son.'

Suddenly he fell to his knees before me, lifting my hands to his brow, pressing them there against his disordered hair. I could feel him tremble, in spite of all his bold defiance. I recognised the fear that he had been determined to hide. I stooped and pressed my lips to his hair. Memories of him as the child I had loved softened my heart.

Yet as I left him I realised that not once had I called him by his given name. I should have given him that final recognition.

Recorded by the private hand of Cecily, King's Mother

On this eighteenth day of February of the year 1478, in the Tower of London, was done to death George Plantagenet, Duke of Clarence.

My son.

For treason.

He will be interred with his wife, Isabel Neville, in Tewkesbury Abbey. The funeral, the monument, and the chantry foundation at Tewkesbury Abbey, all in the generous hands of King Edward. I hope that it is a sign of his repentance. Or perhaps it is guilt. It is said that the King bewailed his brother's death. I do not know the truth of it.

May this be the end of the treason and turbulence that has so bedevilled my son's reign.

I must make my own amends in the manner in which I conduct my life, for my sins of omission and commission.

There is no further role for me in this reign.

My emotions are frozen, my grief a hard knot beneath my heart.

I dedicate my life to God.

**Cecily, King's Mother, to Katherine,
Dowager Duchess of Norfolk**

Written from Baynard's Castle

With many tears and lamentations.

I failed. A final plea to the King was brushed aside and my son was put to death in the Tower of London. My only achievement? That Clarence could determine his own manner of death.

It is a matter for drunken gossip, so I am told, in the inns and gutters of London. He was neither hanged nor beheaded. He was not drawn and quartered. His head was not placed on London Bridge. It is said that he was drowned in a butt of malmsey wine, through his own choice.

Do I know the truth? I do not. Nor do I wish to discover.

They say that Edward was reluctant, that he regretted signing the document. In the end it was the Speaker of the Commons who pushed for the death penalty to be applied, and he was a Woodville supporter. Edward did not resist. As ever, pragmatism overcame reluctance.

Is there any compassion for my son Clarence at Court? I detect none. The Woodvilles were determined to see the end of him. My own son's death is nought but a judicial murder organised by the family of the Queen, who pushed Edward to participate against his better judgement.

Now it is done and I have an inconsolable loss. It is a pain beneath my heart, even though, for the sake of the realm, I acknowledge that there was really no choice. This does not take away the anguish for a mother to lose a son in such circumstances.

I will retire to Berkhamsted, clad in black and heavy veils, and make my peace with God.

Life weighs heavily on me at this time. My thoughts are full of those close to me who have died. I feel the presence of my own death. First I have some travelling to do and business to attend.

Cecily

Cecily, Dowager Duchess of York, for the attention of my Steward, Master Richard Lessy

Written from Berkhamsted

As a consequence of my recent journeying around my estates in East Anglia, I desire your attention to these issues.

One of my tenants, a widowed lady near my castle at Clare, is receiving unwelcome marital advances and threats to her property from a man called Benet. He must be stopped.

I am granted by my son the King six hundred acres of pasture, woodland, and meadows, including a watermill, all of which were once held by my lord the Duke of York. My authority must be imposed here. Appoint suitable Stewards.

The shipping of my wool into Europe I have placed in the

hands of Pietro de Furno, a merchant from Genoa. An able man, but he should be watched. Make sure that he does not make his own fortune.

There is a dispute over the land of my servant John Prince in Essex. He is harassed by men belonging to the household of my son the Duke of Gloucester. Send a man of merit to Gloucester's London residence to discuss this matter. Keep me informed of the outcome.

I look forward to your prompt and appropriate action.

I know that you will uphold my authority in all things.

Cecily, King's Mother

Chapter Thirty-Two

A Time of Terrible Loss

Elizabeth, Queen of England, to Cecily, King's Mother
Written from the Palace of Westminster, April 1483

Madam,

I am concerned for the health of the King, your son. After a day spent fishing on the River Thames last week, he has fallen ill. He denies the severity of it, but I am uncertain. He cannot shake off the symptoms of nausea and aching limbs, despite the good offices of our household.

Perhaps you would consider a visit to Westminster. Your presence would give him comfort. You were always close in spite of your disagreements.

My invitation to you, unusual, I agree, will indicate the depth of my concerns,

Elizabeth

Cecily, King's Mother, to Elizabeth, Queen of England
Written from Berkhamsted

Madam,

This is probably little more than an ague, and not worthy of such anxiety. Can your household not bring him ease? He was always as strong as a draught-ox. Dose him on a decoction of powdered agrimony in warm wine. It guards against all manner of ailments, as well as the biting and stinging of serpents.

I am not well enough to travel. My spirits are still low from the death of my sister Anne, Lady Mountjoy, such that I cannot contemplate Court extravagances and levity.

Age afflicts us all.

Furthermore I continue to be engaged in the foundation of the guild at St Mary's Church in Luton, at the King's behest. It demands much of my time.

I hope to hear better news.

I expect that my son will be hunting in Eltham Forest when this reaches you.

Cecily

Elizabeth, Queen of England, to Cecily, King's Mother
Written from the Palace of Westminster, sent by fast courier
Written by a clerk on the command of Lord Hastings, the
Chamberlain of the Royal Household

I am instructed by Elizabeth the Queen to inform you that on this day, the ninth day of April in the year 1483, our Lord King Edward, the Fourth of that name, died in the early hours of the morning in his chamber in the Palace of Westminster.

His death was unexpected.

Any suggestions that it was poison or malpractice are false.

The Queen is in mourning.

I have informed the King's brother, the Duke of Gloucester, as well as the household of the heir, Prince Edward, at Ludlow.

All my condolences to you, my lady, on this tragic occurrence.

Hastings

Duchess Cecily's intercession to the Blessed Virgin Mary

Hail Mary, full of Grace, Our Lord is with thee.

I am stricken. I am disbelieving. I am struck with the utter desolation of loss. I cannot weep but there is a vast emptiness within me.

How can death stalk us so silently? Who had presentiment of this, a healthy man in his fortieth year, to be struck down so wilfully?

Will God continue to punish me for my sins? I recall the thoughtlessly cruel words I wrote to Edward, in the aftermath of union with Elizabeth Woodville. I see them in my mind's eye as if I wrote them yesterday.

Are you so lacking in political sense? This marriage is a travesty of your birth and your inheritance. You are not your father's son.

I should never have penned those words. Guilt has tracked me through the years and I never made my peace with Edward. I have sought God's infinite mercy, felt his hand of kindness and blessing in my days here in retreat from the world, yet I have lost my eldest most well-beloved son.

My heart is broken. My own sixty-seven years bear down on me. I regret when Edward and I were estranged, driven by jealousy and family division. I ask for your ineffable grace, as I pray that

God will receive his soul and take Edward to his bosom. I regret that I did not see him before he died, to say farewell. That we could not have mended all our past hurts.

Holy Virgin, you know full well the agony of losing a son. Have mercy on me and give me comfort.

What do I do now? I am afraid. A realm with a child King is a realm with a weakness at its heart.

Grant your servant Cecily the strength to return to Court.

Grant me the will to show honest compassion to the Queen. It would not be appropriate to resurrect past hostilities, no matter how deep my suspicion of her lust for power.

Amen

Cecily, Dowager Duchess of York, no longer King's Mother, to Katherine, Dowager Duchess of Norfolk
Written from Berkhamsted

I am sitting here in my Great Hall at Berkhamsted, my baggage and coffers stacked around me, determined to return to Westminster after being in receipt of the news of Ned's death. They say he had suffered from a severe chill after a day of leisure, fishing on the Thames. Such an ignoble end for a King. Or perhaps it was a fever from his campaigning days.

I feel a presentiment of danger, strong enough to bring me out of my self-imposed isolation. I cannot remain in daily prayer and contemplation of God's holy word when the House of York might be under threat.

The Prince is still so young. A child King is an invitation for overweening magnates to scuttle out from the tapestries, to seize what they can. I know full well that the Council will guide him.

Does he not have an uncle perfectly capable of standing as Regent, to advise and counsel him? I must have faith in the work my son did to make England and the Yorkist monarchy strong.

Besides, the Prince is twelve years old, and will soon be considered of an age to begin to take command for himself. I can think of no man better to guide his feet and his hands in the burden of ruling than his uncle of Gloucester, who I expect is travelling fast from the north to pick up the reins. Gloucester will collect him from Ludlow, escort him to London and arrange for his coronation, if the Council has not already done so. What is amiss?

The only true fear that I cannot shake off is that the Queen will object to any power that Gloucester claims. She may wish the Regency for herself. Will any man stand against her? I have lost touch with the competing factions at Court. Once I would have known. My only certainty is that I must be there. I expect that I will soon pick up the threads, when I have been at Court for even a single day. I doubt that I have lost my skill in weaving those threads into a pattern of my own liking.

First, I must mourn my son. Oh, Katherine, I grieve. It is unnatural that a mother should outlive so many of her children.

Do come and we will overlook this transition of power together. I had thought to live a retired life until the day of my death, but it cannot be. With good planning we should be able to settle the new kingdom on the Prince's slight shoulders. It worries me that all Edward achieved rests on the authority of a boy of twelve years. Or, more truthfully, on the ambitions of the adults who surround him. Most notably Anthony Woodville, Earl Rivers. Governor, tutor and uncle, a man of vast influence on the mind of a young boy.

I suspect that my son Diccon will have much to contend with, fighting off the Woodvilles who will range themselves next to the inexperienced King. We must not allow them to bury the Plantagenet counsel in an onslaught of Woodville clamour. At least Diccon will have a loyal ally in Lord Hastings.

I know that I must exert myself once more.

Your sister,

Cecily

I cannot sleep. Our lost sister would urge me to dose myself with tincture of valerian, but she is not here to do it. Such little things remind me of her.

England's Chronicle, *April 1483*

Disturbances in the dovecote.

The Woodvilles are emerging, in warlike mode.

The late King's wishes, expressed in his will, are ignored by the Council which leans dangerously towards the Queen's family. Lord Hastings's vehemently loyal arguments are cast aside. So is he. No longer Chamberlain, we hear, and will probably lose the Captaincy of Calais.

It has been decided. There will be no Protectorate with the Duke of Gloucester at the helm of the new ship. The King will reign in his own right on the day he is crowned on the fourth day of May. With a Council to advise him, of course. A Council with a surfeit of Woodvilles.

Where will this leave the Duke of Gloucester, the last remaining son of Richard Duke of York and Duchess Cecily? As a mere member of the Council, outnumbered by the Queen's family.

And what will Gloucester have to say about that?

Even as we bear witness to the obsequies of the late King, as he is laid to rest in St George's Chapel in Windsor on the twentieth day of April, we watch in interest and some trepidation.

**Cecily, Dowager Duchess of York,
to Edward, Prince of Wales**
Written from Baynard's Castle, in the first week of April 1483

To my grandson,

There will be difficult days ahead for you.

Here is the advice of your grandmother. Come to London as quickly as may be, where you will be received as King. Put your trust in those around you, but keep your own counsel until your uncle of Gloucester meets with you. There are many who will see a youth as fair game, to be hunted down to be used for their own ends.

No matter who tells you otherwise, beware how many you gather around you in your entourage when you make your journey. I speak from experience when your grandfather marched into London, long before you were born. Too great a retinue smacks of an army. The crown is yours, without question. There is no need to enforce your claim with a vast force.

I will be in London to greet you.

Take advice from your uncle of Gloucester who will always be loyal to you, as he was to your father.

I have sent with this letter a ring which once belonged to your grandfather, Richard, Duke of York. It is engraved with the falcon and fetterlock, a most mystical symbol of the strength and duty of the House of York. It was the livery badge of your grandfather and your father. It should be yours also.

With prayers that the Blessed Virgin holds you in her safekeeping,

Cecily

**Prince Edward, Prince of Wales, to
Cecily, Dowager Duchess of York**

Written from Ludlow Castle

My thanks to you, my grandmother. Your concern for me is heartwarming at this sad time.

Thank you for the advice. I am receiving much in recent days. I have had discussions over the size of my escort. My Lady Mother commands me to take no more than two thousand men with me on the road, and I will do as she bids. I will be escorted by my half-brother Richard Grey and my uncle Earl Rivers. I know they will have my best interests at heart.

I look forward to meeting with my uncle of Gloucester. And with you, too.

The Council has arranged for my coronation on the fourth day of May. I will be twelve years old and so well able to take the reins into my own hands. So my uncle Rivers tells me. He has always been a strong friend and support, as has my elder half-brother Thomas Grey, Marquess of Dorset. I will of course appoint my own Council, with advice from my Woodville uncle and brother.

My thanks for the ring belonging to my grandfather. It is yet too big for my fingers, even for my thumb. I am wearing it around my neck on a chain so that I will never forget my allegiance to the House of York.

Your grandson,

Edward, Prince of Wales

**Cecily, Dowager Duchess of York, to
Richard, Duke of Gloucester**

Written from Baynard's Castle

My son,

I trust this meets you on the road.

A warning, although you are probably aware without my courier.

I fear for the independence of the young Prince. I doubt that the Dowager Queen will be allowed the powers of a Regent, which she covets above all, but the boy is surrounded by Woodvilles on his journey into London. Even the present Council is strongly Woodville in nature.

Rivers and Sir Richard Grey have a considerable body of troops in the Prince's retinue. I esteem Earl Rivers as the best of the Woodvilles, but he is not without ambition. Ned gave him true power over his son's life and education. It may be that he sees himself as the most powerful man in England with Ned's death. He is at the boy's side, every hour, every day. I know that the Prince sees him as a friend, a man to look up to. And why would he not? Rivers has been at his side for the whole of his young life.

Tell me what you plan to do.

I hear that you attended a funeral ceremony for your brother in York, where you wept for his passing. I commend you on it. Your loyalty was well received by all who support the House of York. I was not at Ned's interment in St George's Chapel at Windsor since it would have been awash with Woodvilles.

Your affectionate mother,

Cecily

Richard, Duke of Gloucester, to Cecily, Dowager Duchess of York

Written from the road to London

Madam,

Your courier met up with me and your warning is well timed and most apposite.

I think we have little to fear.

I am informed by my legal people that my brother Edward had the political acumen to add a final codicil to his will, appointing me as Protector of the Realm during my nephew's minority. Which should put a spoke in the ever-turning wheels of the Woodville ambitions. Were you aware? It seems that Ned was never without his suspicions of his Woodville relatives by marriage.

I will be Lord Protector. I will ensure the safety of my nephew as King of England.

I know what you will say: that royal uncles who have taken on the mantle of Regent in the past have died in imprisonment, under attack from those who resented their power. I could even find it amusing that they both bore my title of Gloucester. I swear it will not be my end. I also know the dangers of royal wives taking control. Marguerite did no good for King Henry when demanding authority in her own name. Elizabeth, I suspect, is certainly moving in that direction. I am by blood the natural Regent for the boy, and I have allies at Court. Lord Hastings will prove a strong right hand.

I must move fast. Hastings encourages it.

I will be in London soon and will visit you at Baynard's Castle; I would be grateful if you would keep your most regal ear to the ground.

Your dutiful son,

Richard

Cecily, Dowager Duchess of York, to Richard, Duke of Gloucester
Written from Baynard's Castle, April 1483

My well-beloved son,

Events here move on apace.

You might feel secure in being appointed Lord Protector but there are moves afoot to end your Regency before it has even begun. The plan is to deny Edward's will. Dorset and his mother the Queen have the ear of the Council. It is promoted that the Prince be declared adult on the occasion of his coronation, with the Council ruling in his name under his nominal control.

And who will rule the Council? The Woodvilles, of course.

The Prince is summoned, and certainly expected to leave when he last wrote to me, but is to my knowledge still at Ludlow and will remain there to celebrate St George's Day. After that he will travel to London to be crowned on the fourth day of May.

Might I make a suggestion?

Bring your cousin the Duke of Buckingham into your sphere of influence. He might prove to be another strong ally when you face the Council in London. You will need all the friends you can get.

I have no power in such dealings. You must take control yourself.

Can you trust Hastings? I suppose that after all the years of friendship he will be your man, as he was the most fervent friend to Edward. You will need to be sure of your friends, or you will indeed be swept away by the spate of Rivers. All is in flux although the atmosphere in London is calm enough.

Your affectionate mother,

Cecily

Richard, Duke of Gloucester, to Cecily,
Dowager Duchess of York

Written from the road to London

Madam, in grateful thanks.

Written in haste.

Hastings has proved to be a good friend, and my cousin of Buckingham is worth luring from his habitual position on the edge of affairs. I am in touch with Rivers. We have agreed to meet at Northampton, from where we will travel together, a combined force, to present the Prince with much celebration in his capital. If any man should question my position, I have, in York, taken an oath of loyalty to my nephew.

I will not allow Edward's will and final desires on his deathbed to be rejected.

Be strong and pray for me.

Your dutiful son,

Richard

England's Chronicle, *the first day of May, 1483*

Royal coup at Stony Stratford?

Can this be true?

We are hearing of chilling events. Arriving every hour as our couriers ride in, from near the old Woodville manor of Stony Stratford near Northampton. A meeting had been arranged there on the twenty-ninth day of April so that the Duke of Gloucester, riding fast from the north, could accompany his nephew and Earl Rivers on the Prince's triumphant and ceremonial entry into London.

We would commend this decision by the Duke of Gloucester.

So what has happened?

Following a genial evening spent between Gloucester and Buckingham, with Rivers and Sir Richard Grey, with much ale and laughter and exchange of news, Gloucester and Buckingham rode together to Stony Stratford to meet with the Prince and his vast retinue of two thousand men. All would ride together to London on the next morning.

Not so.

Do we truly believe what we are hearing? Gloucester has ordered the arrest of Rivers, Grey and the Prince's Chamberlain Sir Thomas Vaughan, accusing all three of them of causing dissention in the realm. They have been sent north to Gloucester's lands. We do not know of their ultimate destination or what is to become of them.

Nor do we know what evidence Gloucester had procured against them.

Meanwhile, we hear that it is now Gloucester who is escorting his nephew to London. It is expected that they will arrive on the fourth day of May, which should have been the coronation day. Obviously this event must be postponed. We see nothing contentious about this development.

What will happen next? You may well ask.

Prince Edward is under the control of his uncle but there seems to be no duress. They ride side by side in what appears to be perfect amity. We claim all ignorance of what is in Gloucester's mind until we receive further news. Rumour is always rife and cannot be trusted. Is the Prince helpless in Gloucester's hands?

Duchess Cecily is in residence at Baynard's Castle. Perhaps she knows what her son has in mind for her grandson.

Is any man brave enough to ask her?

What is it that has brought her out of her self-imposed isolation at Berkhamsted?

Elizabeth, Queen of England, to Cecily, Dowager Duchess of York

Written from Westminster Abbey

Madam,

Despite all the ill-will that has existed between us in the past, I find a need to send this. It is not the first time that I have turned to you when I have foreseen danger to myself and my children. I cannot peer past these clouds into the future. I have not the gift of prediction, nor did my mother, whatever might have been said of her connection with sorcery, but I am shaken with terror.

Once again I have fled to the sanctuary of Westminster Abbey, taking my children with me.

What does Gloucester intend?

Since you are here in London, I presume that you know what his strategy will be.

I beg you to intercede for me. For my son and brother, who are imprisoned in the north, awaiting a judgement which I fear will have no justice in it. Do I have to beg on my knees for the safety of my daughters?

In your mercy, my lady, plead for me and your son's children. They are your blood, too. It was your son's wish that Prince Edward would rule after him.

If you have any influence, use it for the good of the realm. All I see is my husband's inheritance drenched in blood. I know that you will have no desire for a return to battle and bloodshed.

I demand that my son, Prince Edward, now King, be restored to me here at Westminster Abbey.

Elizabeth

Duchess Cecily makes her feelings known to the Dowager Queen in Westminster Abbey, on the fourth day of May, 1483

If I knew anything of Elizabeth Woodville, this would be a confrontation, and I knew not who would emerge the victor.

At my request, and most promptly, I was escorted into the apartments put aside for sanctuary at Westminster Abbey where the Dowager Queen had fled for safety from my son Gloucester. I considered this flight entirely unnecessary. She was in no danger, other than from the consequences of her own unfortunate actions. Indeed I felt the strong grip of anger. It might well be that she had made this decision deliberately, to put my son in the wrong, and build support for her own family; it would be a simple matter to stir up fury against the Prince's uncle who wished her ill.

My first impression as I entered was one of chaos within the stark setting, servants staggering under her chests and coffers, setting them down without plan or direction. Crowded into the room were Edward's daughters and Richard, his younger son. Elizabeth was there, her son Dorset and her brother Bishop Lionel. And, surprisingly, the Archbishop of York, Thomas Rotherham, Edward's Keeper of the Privy Seal, looking to my eye uneasy, trying to manoeuvre around the small children under his feet.

I exchanged cool acknowledgements with brief courtesy. I could not abide disorder.

Motionless, her hands clasped in her lap, Elizabeth was sitting on a low stool, her face a reflection of utter despair, her mourning robes spread in luxurious folds around her.

'You wrote to me, asking for my support for the Prince,' I said, ensuring that my voice engendered command. 'I have come in person to assure you of it.'

Elizabeth rose to her feet, moved by a nervous energy. The shadows imprinted beneath her eyes were as dark and deep as the veils that shivered with her movements. Her knuckles were white as she clasped her hands against her bosom in a dramatic gesture. I might have discovered some pity for any other woman.

'I did not expect to see you here, madam.' Her eyes were distraught.

'It is my duty to come, to right an obvious wrong. Do you fear for your life?' I asked with a faint lift of my brows. 'I see no threat against you. Was this flight to sanctuary necessary? It gives the wrong impression to the people of London. Was that what you intended? To smear the Duke of Gloucester's reputation with foul implications?'

I had thought that she was weary. Instead her face blazed with emotion. 'You are blind, madam. Your son would have me removed, so that he might have power over the young King.'

'My Lady Mother is distressed...' Dorset came forward to take his mother's arm but was shaken off, the Dowager Queen's response bitter.

'The Duke of Gloucester will destroy the peace of this realm for his own advantage.'

'How could casting England once more into war be to anyone's advantage?' I allowed my gaze to slide briefly over the Marquess of Dorset, disliking what I saw. 'If my information is accurate, your son Dorset, with your blessing, attempted to do exactly that. Did you not collect an army, under pretence of defending yourselves and releasing the young King from what you described as malign influences?' I kept my voice cool and low. No room for heated arguments here. 'Would such a wayward stratagem not have brought the threat of renewed war? It was only when you were forced to accept that the name Woodville was anathema to so many of our magnates that you abandoned the scheme and fled here to take refuge. There was no threat against you from my son.'

'The lady is in sanctuary and in fear for her life, madam.' Bishop Lionel came to his sister's defence. 'She has not been allowed to see Prince Edward and so is understandably anxious. She deserves our compassion.'

'I might have compassion,' I agreed with the thinnest of smiles. 'But the Duke of Gloucester has done nothing to break his oath of loyalty to his nephew. It is malice in you to suggest otherwise, sir.' My attention returned to Elizabeth. 'Why is all this excess emotion necessary?'

'Whatever you say, I fear the Duke of Gloucester's power. He has the Prince under his control.' She gestured towards her youngest son who, in the midst of his sisters, stood silently watching the domestic drama unfold. 'He has asked that Richard join his brother, to be with him at the coronation.'

'And why will you not allow it?'

'Would I give him control of both my royal sons? I will not.'

Accepting that this might be a lost cause, still I pursued what I believed.

'The Duke of Gloucester is faithful to your husband's wishes. Which you were not. Edward named him Protector of the Realm until the young King comes of age, but you brought to bear all your influence to prevent it. Nothing has been done to threaten your son, either of your sons. All that has been done is to rebalance the power in this land.'

Dorset cleared his throat. 'Perhaps it would be possible to allow the young King to sojourn with his mother when he has arrived in London. There can be no fault found with that.'

I swung round, the jewelled reliquary on my breast moving heavily, my words a challenge. 'Why would he not be in the company of his paternal uncle, his Protector? You found no difficulty in allowing him to be in the control of his Woodville uncle, Earl Rivers. I suggest that Gloucester deserves an apology from you for impugning his reputation.'

Elizabeth was not moved. 'This should have been my son's coronation day.'

'And a new one has been designated by the Council. It was not Gloucester's fault that the journey from Ludlow was so tardy. Look to your own family, Elizabeth.'

'I do.' Her face was near-white, her lips hard-pressed together. 'Oh, I do. I fear for Rivers's life. And that of my son, Richard Grey.'

'They will be dealt with justly, when they have answered for their crimes.'

'And what are their crimes?'

I did not know, but I would not admit to it. 'We will know soon enough.'

'I see no pity in you.'

'I see no need for it. You and your children are safe enough here.'

'And you can give me no hope?'

'Hope for what?' My patience was wearing thin. 'The new day of the coronation is fixed. Your son will wear the crown and will be given royal powers. I can pray with you, if you will, that the Virgin will bring you peace of mind.'

Elizabeth turned away with much hand-wringing. 'It is all so ephemeral. What proof have I that the Duke of Gloucester might not wield the power behind the throne, even if my son is crowned?'

Which was the final nail in the coffin of my long-tried patience.

'You must trust in his good offices to his nephew.'

There was nothing to be achieved. I turned to go, except that the Archbishop of York, who had thus far taken no part in the proceedings, intervened, addressing the Queen. I thought that he appeared less than trustworthy when he refused to look in my direction.

'I am Keeper of the Privy Seal, my lady,' he addressed the Dowager Queen. 'If it is something tangible that you desire, that your son will indeed keep a firm grip on his inheritance, I can leave the Great Seal in your hands, as a sign of good intent.'

'Not so!' I could not believe what I had heard. And spoken so openly in my presence when the cleric must know that I would oppose any such action. Had Rotherham lost what few wits he had, in a moment of panic? He would never have been my choice for Archbishop of York. George Neville might have been as poisonous as a toad but at least he did not lack for keen perception. 'Not so!' I repeated. 'First and foremost you must answer to the Duke of Gloucester. The Seal must remain in your possession until Gloucester decides otherwise.'

The Archbishop's eyes caught, then slid from mine. 'Why would I not give it into the keeping of the King's own mother? It will be of comfort to the lady. To prove that there is no malice intended towards her or her children.'

Reaching out, I tightened my fingers in the heavy silk of his episcopal cloak. 'You are placing a potent symbol of power into Woodville hands.'

'Yet I will do it. Kneel, my lady, and I will bless you.'

Smoothly, he detached himself from me. Elizabeth knelt as the Archbishop took the Seal in its velvet pouch from the purse at his belt. He placed it into her hands, folding her fingers over it, his head bowed in prayer.

'God bless you and your children, my lady.'

I knew Gloucester would disapprove, but short of snatching it back I could do nothing but accept.

'I think you have shown ill judgement here today,' I remarked.

Bishop Lionel was expressionless; Dorset could only be described as smirkingly content; Elizabeth's face, head still bent, was hidden in her veils.

As I turned to go, leaving them to their achievement, anger hot in my throat, the little girls took my eye, pretty things with the fair colouring of Edward and his wife, sitting together on a window seat. Silent, too young to know the full portent of what was unfolding around them. I had nothing to say to them, even though I stood godmother to more than one. My battle was not with them. I knew not what their future would be.

Elizabeth's voice followed me as the door was almost closed behind me.

'I hoped for some level of understanding from you, but you will do whatever your son Gloucester asks of you. He is clever and manipulative. He will have his own way and you will allow it.'

I looked over my shoulder. 'I will not, I will support justice. I think, madam, that you might regret opposing my son in this manner.'

I believed what I had said. Justice was everything.

Cecily, Dowager Duchess of York, to Thomas Rotherham, Archbishop of York and Lord Chancellor of England

Written from Baynard's Castle

Your Grace,

Here is a matter for you to consider. When my son the Duke of Gloucester is once more in London, he will advise the young Prince, when he is crowned King, whether to leave that post of Keeper of the Privy Seal in your hands, or not. He may very well choose not to do so, if he feels you have been perfunctory in your task. I made my thoughts plain enough yesterday, in the absence of the Lord Protector and the Prince, but you chose to reject my advice. If you value your position you may wish to reconsider.

I understand the conflict between your past and present allegiances, but it was imprudent of you to give the Great Seal into the hands of the Dowager Queen. Particularly as it might well now fall into the hands of the Marquess of Dorset, her son. That would not be a popular move to many who despise the ambitions of the Woodville family. I suggest a night of reflection, your grace. Send one of your household with a suitable letter and request that the Seal be restored to you, as Keeper of the Privy Seal, appointed by my son the previous King. Send your apologies that you made an error which you must remedy.

Furthermore I advise you to remain open in your loyalties. The young Prince is under no threat. Nor is the Dowager Queen, however persuasive her fears might be. The Duke of Gloucester is merely fulfilling the last wishes of his brother, King Edward the Fourth.

Cecily, Dowager Duchess of York

**Thomas Rotherham, Archbishop of York,
to Cecily, Dowager Duchess of York**

Written from the Palace of Westminster

Madam,

I now see the error of my ways. Such dismay and desolation at the death of the old King quite undermined my good sense. I was wrong.

I have duly requested that the Privy Seal be restored to me.

I trust that the Duke of Gloucester will approve, and you also, my lady.

York

Chapter Thirty-Three

The Wheel of Fortune Spins Again

England's Chronicle, *the fourth day of May 1483*

Rejoice and raise your voices in loud acclaim.

Our fears were premature. The rumours abounding in the City were indubitably false.

On this day, our young Prince of Wales, as yet uncrowned, has ridden into London to an outpouring of public acclaim. At his side, his uncle the Duke of Gloucester. Our Prince was clad in rich blue velvet, bidding to become as tall and fair and as gracious as his father our late King. The bells rang, an oath of loyalty was taken. We are pleased to announce to all loyal subjects that a new coronation date has been set for the twenty-second day of June.

We see nothing but good in the arrival of our young Prince with his highly esteemed royal uncle.

We believe that the Dowager Queen, anticipating her role as the new King's Mother, should emerge from sanctuary and take her place in the celebrations. There is no threat to her or her children. The Duke of Gloucester is equable enough to settle the ongoing clash of will and temperament between Lord Hastings and the Woodvilles over who should guide the new King. We believe that the new King's reign will be a time of great blessing for England, and that the Duke of Gloucester will guide him effectively into adulthood.

One question that we would ask the Duke of Gloucester:

What is to be the fate of Earl Rivers and Sir Richard Grey and Sir Thomas Vaughan? Are they guilty? Would they have used their heavily armed escort to gain control of London in the young King's name, to rule for their own benefit?

The Duke of Gloucester is not saying.

We hope to hear of their release. Clemency for any past treachery, which may or may not exist, will provide an excellent start to the new reign of King Edward the Fifth. Or does the Duke of Gloucester not believe in clemency, when its name is Woodville?

England's Chronicle, *the seventh day of May 1483*

A meeting of some importance.

Held at Baynard's Castle, and not one of the powerful men there present bearing the name Woodville.

The Duke of Gloucester, his firm ally and friend Lord Hastings, his cousin the Duke of Buckingham, Lord Stanley, Bishop Morton of Ely. Nine bishops all told. All executors of the late King Edward's will.

But not the Dowager Queen, the principal executor.

What will be the outcome? Can they execute the will of the late King if the Queen is not present? It seems that they can. Gloucester has already confiscated all the goods, seals and jewels of his brother.

Since Gloucester has made his base at Baynard's Castle, and since we understand that Duchess Cecily is in residence, we can only presume that she is in agreement with whatever policy is decided for the new King. Gloucester could equally have remained at his own impressive house of Crosby Place on Bishopsgate. Instead he has chosen the traditional base of the House of York.

Do we read something into this?

The young King, for his own safety, is now lodged in the Tower of London until his coronation because the Bishop of London's Palace is far too unaccommodating for a full royal retinue. It is thought that the Queen will be persuaded to allow her younger son, Richard, Duke of York, to join his brother there. And perhaps also the son of the late Duke of Clarence, Edward of Warwick, who is now eight years old, might join them.

All the younger generation of the House of York together under one roof.

What will Gloucester do next? Here's what we predict:

★

Seize the title Protector of the Realm for himself, as his late father had done.

Confiscate the lands and offices of the Woodvilles and their friends.

Employ the servants of his brother, the late King, to serve him.

Dismiss Rotherham, Archbishop of York, from his post as Chancellor of England.

★

The fate of Earl Rivers and his son is still unknown.

Cecily, Dowager Duchess of York, to
Katherine, Dowager Duchess of Norfolk
Written from Baynard's Castle

My dear sister,

I think that I have been appallingly, unforgivably, naive.

What do I make of my son, Richard of Gloucester?

In all his life Gloucester was a loyal brother to Edward. He stood by him in the difficult years, joining him in exile, remaining a formidable support in the north to rule England in the King's name with a fair and stalwart right arm. When Clarence turned against Edward, Gloucester remained true.

I thought that I knew him well. I thought that as Protector of the Realm he would fulfil Edward's wishes and ensure the tranquil passing of power from father to son.

Yet now I sense in my son an antagonism. A hardness. An ambition that is as firmly engrained, if not more so, than that of his father. From where did this emerge? Perhaps it is always a truth that a mother underestimates the abilities and ambition of her youngest son.

Why should it surprise you? you would say. Why would he not have ambition?

And it should not surprise me. A young man of no more than thirty years who has been a successful Constable of England must have a will of iron. It is just the direction of his ambition that worries me enough to send me to my knees at my prie-dieu.

It was always Buckingham who disliked the Woodvilles worse than death itself, from so many years ago when he was forced into marriage with the Woodville girl. And so does Lord Hastings despise them. Perhaps this deep-seated hatred is the source of Gloucester's unease, that the Woodvilles will grasp ultimate power unless he takes steps to stop them.

What has he done?

Nothing that I would not support wholeheartedly, securing the right to act as Protector of the Realm from the Council, punishing the Woodvilles by confiscating their lands. Oh, I have no fears for Elizabeth or her children behind locked doors in the care of the clergy at Westminster Abbey, but there are rumours that render me restless and unsettled. If Gloucester will make his permanent headquarters at Baynard's Castle, I might glean more than common gossip. All I can trust is that the Prince will be crowned as planned on the twenty-second day of June. Then the country may breathe easily and return to celebrating the joyous occasion with a surfeit of ale and food.

But I may never breathe easily again. I have to say, there is always an anxiety attached to a realm under a child King. Am I foolish to be concerned about this? You will probably say that I am, but it niggles like a summer fever which cannot be dislodged by frequent and unpleasant dosings of Devil's Bit.

Rivers and Sir Richard Grey will be released, the Dowager Queen will come out of sanctuary for the coronation, and the fifth King Edward will, in the fullness of time, take command.

Gloucester does not seek my opinion. Nor do I think he would accept it if I offered it. It is a lowering thought. But sons grow up and take their own path in life. I trust Gloucester's path is the right one, the honest one. He assuredly made an impressive entry with the Prince. When all was festive around them, the Prince clad in vivid blue to draw every eye, Gloucester was clad in severe and funereal black velvet, in severe mourning for his dead brother. Was this clever strategy, or honest grief? I no longer know.

I will do all that I can to bring my grandson to the throne that is his by right. Which sadly is very little. I sense that the future is held firmly in Gloucester's powerful and clever hands.

Cecily

Cecily, Dowager Duchess of York, to Elizabeth, Dowager Queen

Written from Baynard's Castle

Madam,

I do not hesitate to admonish you. You are guilty of grave misjudgement.

You are misguided in withdrawing your visible support from the heir to the throne. Nor have you enhanced your reputation to any degree by pitting yourself against my son Gloucester. Do you suppose that your absence will undermine his role at your son's side? Gloucester does not need you to gild his public face. You persist in portraying him as your worst enemy, for which there is no evidence.

All will go ahead as planned by my son the late King, with Gloucester as Lord Protector. It has been decided. Gloucester will hold authority as Lord Protector until King Edward is of an age to assume power in his own right. The transition from one King to the next runs smoothly, in spite of your remaining maliciously shut away in Westminster Abbey. The coronation date is set.

If you have a concern for Earl Rivers and Sir Richard Grey, they are still in Sheriff Hutton where I understand they will be tried for treason. The Earl of Northumberland will oversee the final decision-making.

Allow your younger son to join the Prince in the Tower. Time must hang heavily for him. He will enjoy his brother's company.

Elizabeth, I urge you most strongly to emerge for the coronation. Family unity is so important on these occasions. We must be seen to be as one. If you hear rumours that Gloucester and I are at odds, they are false. It is mere troublemaking by those who would sow dissention.

Gloucester holds nothing but good for the House of York.

Cecily, Dowager Duchess of York

Chapter Thirty-Four

*An Old Scandal Resurrected
and a New One Born*

Cecily, Dowager Duchess of York, to
Katherine, Dowager Duchess of Norfolk
Written from Baynard's Castle, June 1483

Kat,

I have inadvertently discovered a document, carelessly left with a pile of tenancy agreements. It is written by a clerk but is signed in Gloucester's hand. Since reading it I have been unable to sleep. My appetite has fled. It is not a document that Gloucester would wish me to read.

Or perhaps he does not care.

Or perhaps he wished me to do so.

In my darkest of moments, when I suspect my son of deep dealings, I think that it was left deliberately for me to read.

The years rolled back to my finding that altered family tree in Hereford, when Richard began to consider the throne to be his. The raw reek of fresh ink and paint. There it was again. The planning, the black writing, plotting a dangerous path for our family.

Oh, Katherine, the worst of it all is that I fear I can do nothing to deflect what is to come. I remember so long ago, when the children were still young, showing Margaret and George and Diccon the painted depiction of the House of Lancaster, in which we had no part.

Gloucester is about to put this hand to a re-spinning of the fatal Wheel of Fortune. My reputation is once more to be trampled in the political dust, and I know nothing about a contract with Eleanor Butler, the Earl of Shrewsbury's daughter. A lady I believe is now dead. Did Edward marry her? Did he promise her marriage? I should be shocked at the possibility of such duplicity, but these days I am beyond shock. Edward proved himself quite capable of such momentous deceit.

I thought of sending you a copy but it is not a document I would wish to fall into hostile hands. Except that I fear that Gloucester proposes to make it all public anyway.

The hurt is beyond bearing.

Why has he done it? Are his ambitions so grandiose? Does he believe that he is being excluded from his birthright? Yet I would say that it was never his birthright to take.

Pray for me, Katherine. I need consolation and strength of will.

Another question. Will Hastings and Buckingham support him in this risky venture? He has worked hard to shackle them to his side in this new reign.

Your sister, whom it seems will once more, for the sake of the political repercussions, be humiliated in the eyes of the world,

Cecily

Written at the direction of the Duke of Gloucester: the case for the barring of Edward of York, Prince of Wales, from the throne

This is based on the following two premises, both appertaining to the fact that illegitimacy is a bar to inheritance.

The rumours, that have never died away, that Cecily, Duchess of York, committed adultery during her marriage to Richard, Duke of York. While in Rouen, as a young woman in her husband's absence on military matters, she had an affair with one of the archers of the Duke's household, a man named Blaybourne. Given the timing of this birth and the Duke's absence, it would seem a fair premise. It has been much the talk of the French Court for years. It was believed by the Earl of Warwick and the Duchess's own son George, Duke of Clarence, that the Duchess was not chaste within her marriage.

If King Edward the Fourth was thus baseborn, he should never have been King. Nor, then, does his son, King Edward the Fifth, have that right.

It is now widely believed that the Duke of Clarence was also baseborn, as well as his brother King Edward the Fourth. Neither resembled Richard, Duke of York, both being tall and fair, broadly built and well favoured. The Duke of York was smaller of stature, more finely made and conspicuously dark of hair.

It should be noted that Richard, Duke of Gloucester, much resembles his father.

The second premise is more substantial in our eyes.

We hold to the evidence that the marriage of Edward the Fourth to Elizabeth Woodville was invalid from its conception.

King Edward had been contracted to another woman, Eleanor Butler, daughter of John Talbot, Earl of Shrewsbury. Contractual alliances are a lawful agreement. The witness to this legal pre-contract is Robert Stillington, Bishop of Bath and Wells. He was present, as were two other witnesses. Such a pre-contract is as binding as a marriage ceremony. Thus the marriage between King Edward and Elizabeth Woodville was bigamous.

Since this marriage between the King and Elizabeth Woodville was not legal, the children of that marriage have no claim to legitimacy. The child Edward, who many regard as the future King Edward the Fifth, has thus no claim to the crown of England.

It is therefore presented herein that the legitimate ruler of England is Richard, Duke of Gloucester, legitimately born of the marriage of Richard Duke of York and his wife Cecily.

Katherine, Dowager Duchess of Norfolk,
to Cecily, Dowager Duchess of York
Written from Epworth

Sister,

You need to talk to him.

Only you know the truth of his claim. Only you know your honesty and chastity within your marriage. Only you know where your loyalty in the future might lie.

I am presuming that Gloucester cannot be dissuaded from making use of this inflammatory information.

I note that you have accepted that he is no longer the youthful Diccon. Nor even the more dignified Richard. He is Duke of Gloucester, and his own man. You must perforce accept it.

Katherine

Cecily, Dowager Duchess of York, to Richard, Duke of Gloucester

Written from Baynard's Castle, the thirteenth day June 1483

Gloucester,

Do we live in the same household? I find it impossible to meet with you. Our paths never appear to cross, not even at Mass, which I have noted. I wish to speak with you. Since you live in my house, I expect you to at least break your fast with me.

Is the news from the Tower true? It is beyond my belief. Lord Hastings was the most loyal friend that Edward ever had. And yours, too, I would have surmised.

Your mother,

Cecily

Richard, Duke of Gloucester, to Cecily, Dowager Duchess of York

Written from the Palace of Westminster

Madam,

With utmost regrets I am unable to be at Baynard's Castle today. There are perilous matters of state that must be dealt with.

The recent disaffection of Hastings is true, as is his punishment.

I know that you will understand the need for my precipitate action against him.

Your most humble son,

Gloucester

Blood and drama.

We cannot believe our ears. Or our eyes. We would deny it, but have witnesses to this astonishing deed.

Lord Hastings, that most prestigious of men, a man of repute in his loyalty to the House of York, arrived at the Tower of London for a Council meeting. Wherein he was charged with treason and summarily executed, without trial or legal judgement. The execution was at the will of the Lord Protector.

Never was there so loyal a man, so staunch a friend to the late King as Lord Hastings. Never was there such benevolent support for the young King Edward the Fifth, or we had presumed for the Lord Protector himself.

Who would seek his death?

Who would benefit most?

There is one, who we will not yet name, who might fear that Hastings's fealty to King Edward the Fourth, and so to his son the young King, would cause him to be an uncomfortable bedfellow in the present circumstances.

We await events. We still do not yet know the fate of Earl Rivers and Sir Richard Grey, incarcerated in a Yorkist fortress in the north. We do know, however, that Bishop Morton of Ely has been arrested for treason.

The Queen remains in Westminster Abbey with her younger children. In the circumstances it might be difficult to find fault with her choice.

Duchess Cecily is remaining ominously silent. We hear that the Duke of Gloucester has sent, as a gift to his Lady Mother, a basket of strawberries, grown by the apparently treacherous

Bishop Morton who is famous for such delicacies. Do we detect the hint of a guilty conscience in this gift from her son?

We understand that Duchess Cecily spends much time on her knees in her chapel. Some would agree with her that there are a multitude of souls that need praying for.

Richard, Duke of Gloucester, to Cecily, Dowager Duchess of York

Written from the Palace of Westminster

Madam,

I understand your grief at Hastings's betrayal of our family.

A plot has been discovered to have me killed. Hastings was named as the perpetrator of the plot. The penalty of treason is death. As I am Constable of England as well as Protector of the Realm, I have the power to so condemn him and oversee the execution.

I know that you will be as sorrowful as I at this harsh evidence of perfidy.

Your humble son,

Gloucester

By an anonymous hand, sent to the Dowager Duchess of York at Baynard's Castle

This is what you should know about your only living son.

He seeks the throne for himself.

Lord Hastings was executed because he would never countenance the deposition of the young King. Lord Stanley, Bishop Morton and Archbishop Rotherham, previously Lord Chancellor, are all under arrest. What would you wager on their continuing existence? All were known for their fidelity to the late King. Earl Rivers (a Woodville) remains in captivity but still, for now, owning his head.

Where is the evidence of Lord Hastings's treason?

Perhaps you should ask your son.

Will you expect him to offer you veracity or falsehoods?

As for the young King, not yet crowned: 'Bastard slips shall not take deep root.'

A forceful sermon to be preached at this dangerous time, denying the boy his birthright.

Look to see your son Gloucester seize the crown for himself. We doubt you have any influence to deflect his intentions. What will become of the young King, your grandson, then?

Fall on your knees, Duchess of York, and pray most heartily.

Duchess Cecily's intercession to the Blessed Virgin Mary

Hail Mary, full of Grace, Our Lord is with thee.

Blessed art thou among women, and blessed is the fruit of thy womb Jesus.

Holy Mary, Mother of God,

Pray for us sinners, now and at the hour of our death.

Is my son of Gloucester guilty as charged?

Chapter Thirty-Five

A Political Necessity

Duchess Cecily interviews the Duke of Gloucester in Baynard's Castle, June 1483

My son. Diccon, my child. Richard, my son. Now outgrown them all to be Duke of Gloucester, Lord Protector, Constable of England, accused of murder and a plotted usurpation.

My son, entering my chamber with quiet authority, awarded me a full Court obeisance, hand on heart, a flamboyant sweep to his arm. I wondered if it was to impress me with his new status as Lord Protector, or to discourage me from asking questions. His garments, austerely dark with slashed sleeves, were certainly as imposing as the gold chain that rested on his shoulders. If that was his plan, he would fail. I had brought him into this world. I had watched him grow. I had seen him in fear and in boyish pleasures. I had sent him into exile to save his life. I would not be deterred from my questioning, from my need for the truth.

I wished I had brought the clerk's document with me, but I had not. It had fouled my fingertips. I had no wish to handle it further. Yet I had the anonymous note tucked in my sleeve. Even more foul in its implications, but my son must see it.

I waited until he rose to his full height, took my hand and led me to a cushioned seat. It might be my own home, but he dominated the space. He might not be as tall and well favoured as his brothers, but there was an aura of power about him. Was it stronger today, or was it merely my imagination?

What sort of man had Gloucester become over the years since the child I had given into Warwick's keeping? Not the fair, engaging Prince such as Edward had been, but those who recalled the Duke of York, his father, would see a resemblance in the slight build, the darkness of hair and eye, the starkness of features. Not unhandsome but his face encompassed a severity that did not always encourage intimacies.

It struck me that he had lost the lightness of spirit of his youth. Instead, here was a man of authority, on the battlefield and in the Council chamber. A man who could win great loyalty as well as distrust.

'They said that you were unwell,' he observed, his eyes searching my face.

'Which is palpably untrue.' I sat, releasing my hand from his. 'I needed a reason to get you here, one that I knew that you would not ignore. You may be driven by ambitions, but you were never without compassion.'

He stood before me.

'What is so urgent? You, more than any woman I know, understand the demands of affairs of state.'

'The rumours are that there is discord between us,' I said as the most benign introduction I could think of.

'There are always rumours, my lady.'

So he would continue to be formal today.

'Mayhap there will be a truth in them before the end of this conversation. Tell me about Hastings's death.'

There was no hesitation. 'He was discovered to be guilty of treason. It is my duty to remove treason from this realm.'

'Did he threaten your life?'

'So it seems.'

'Do you have evidence?'

'Enough to prove his guilt.'

'Will you tell me?'

'It is not necessary.'

I was no more effective than if I had been assaulting a curtain wall with a handful of pebbles.

'I dislike your dissembling, Gloucester,' I said.

'There is no purpose to your questioning, madam. You must excuse my necessity to be elsewhere. And you must trust me. Do you need me further? I have much to occupy me.'

'Five more minutes of your precious time.' I could almost taste the irritation in the clipped responses, the rigid shoulders, the stern features. I would not be hurried. I stood and poured wine, handing him a cup.

'Drink with me.' And when, surprisingly obedient, he took the cup: 'Will my reputation be dragged once more through the ruinous mud of adultery, to support your claim to England's throne?'

His silence was stark. His hand, about to raise the cup to his lips, froze, before moving steadily on its path, and he drank.

'Would you destroy your mother's dignity, her reputation, her honour? I had thought you better than Clarence, my son.'

His eyes held mine, but I could not read the expression.

I returned to my cushioned chair, even though I must look up into his face.

'I advise you not to deny it,' I continued. 'I have read the document that would bar your nephew from the throne on the grounds of illegitimacy. You should be more careful with such dangerous arguments. It is unwise to leave them where others can read them. Or perhaps you no longer care. Hastings's death was all part of the well-planned strategy.'

The faint colour along his cheekbones faded. His control was perfect.

'If you accuse me of deliberately leaving it for you to read, then you misjudge me. I would rather have told you myself than have you read it, but I will not deny my purpose.'

'Then I will ask again. Will you slander me, as your brother and Warwick were prepared to do, to achieve power in this realm?'

'No.' He contemplated the enamelled cup, running his finger around the rim so that his rings glinted in the light, a little groove appearing between his brows. 'Only if it becomes necessary.'

I felt the colour flood my own cheeks at the callous implication. 'You have a choice?' I asked.

'Yes, I do. It is not my wish to smear your good name. I believe that I can achieve what I most desire by using the existence of Ned's pre-contract instead.'

What I most desire. A phrase to answer all my questions about Gloucester's aspirations.

'Poor Eleanor Butler,' was all I said. 'A woman who is conveniently dead, so nothing can be proved. Did Edward lure her into his bed with a promise that he would wed her? We know he used the same empty words with other women, not least Elizabeth Woodville. Do you suppose that he ever intended to marry Elizabeth? Perhaps it was Jacquetta who spurred it on, and trapped him. Perhaps he planned to slide out of that responsibility, as he did with Mistress Butler.'

'Perhaps.'

He was still watching me, silent and careful, as a cat overlooking a mouse-hole, waiting for the mouse to emerge.

'How fortunate for you, to discover so strong an argument for Edward's illegal marriage. Should I be grateful that you will spare me? Of course you have no proof of my infidelities either. There has never been any proof. Nor will there ever be. Only your father and I will ever know the truth and, since he is dead, it is my word and your belief in it.'

He bowed in acknowledgement.

'For that reason I will not willingly impugn your dignity,' he replied.

How cool and calm. How superbly confident he was. Or if not, he was expert at cloaking his thoughts. For a moment he reminded me of his father; the naked ambition that flared like a beacon to warn of invading forces. I was forced to acknowledge that he would undermine Edward's reputation; he would just as readily destroy mine.

'Do you accept that Edward made that contract with the Butler girl?' I asked.

'Yes.'

'But we have no proof of that.'

'It was in his character to woo a woman to his bed with promises, as you have said. Edward's indulgent immorality was a byword. Can you deny it? And who is to say that I do not hold the proof?'

At which I stood. I could no longer sit, fear making me restless.

'I don't like it, Gloucester. It is a useful ploy but smacks of self-interest.'

'Nor do I like it. I would rather I had your support than your condemnation.'

'Then make a case for me to believe,' I challenged him.

'You have read the document. If Edward's marriage was illegal, if there is even a pinch of doubt of it, then his children are illegitimate. Bishop Stillington will stand by his claim that he witnessed the alliance between my brother and Eleanor Butler. If that is so, the two Princes cannot make a claim on the royal inheritance. If it is true, then there is only one claimant to the throne.'

'There is Clarence's son.'

'Was Clarence illegitimate, too, as well as being a traitor?'

I had to breathe slowly, to swallow hard. It was as if I swam through a vat of honey, facing one accusation after another, delivered without mercy from my own blood.

'Would you ask me that?'

'Others will. But listen to my reasoning. Clarence's birth aside, there are dangers to having a child King. If you would fight for the strength of the realm, as you have done all your life, you have to support me in this. I am the only legitimate blood of the House of York. I will rule well and restore the realm to stability. I have earned my reputation in Scotland and the north. I have a son to follow me. My right cannot be questioned.'

'Yet many will.'

He turned away, for the first time a disquiet in him.

'Do you truly seek a restoration of the Woodvilles, madam?' he asked, studying the holy icon with its gilded Madonna and child, as if she would give him a response. 'You know what will happen. Once declared to be of age to assume the power for himself, the young King will recall his mother and brothers and cousins to his side. They will dominate all gifts of land and power, as they did in my brother's reign. Do you approve of that?'

I looked away when he swung round, his robes swirling in heavy folds of expensive cloth, releasing a faint aroma of orris root. His arguments had an undeniable strength, more discernible than the perfume of violets.

'Do you support me, my Lady Mother?' Gloucester continued when I remained taken up with my thoughts. 'Or will you work against me? I know the power of your connections. And your persuasion.'

'I have grown too old to be persuasive.' My response was flat and dry, a statement of unacceptable fact.

'Do you need my flattery? You have been involved in the cut and thrust of politics for your whole life. It will not stop now.'

I felt a ripple of what could only have been panic. 'It is too much to decide. You must await my reply on this.'

'I will wait. But not for long. Will you denounce me as a liar, or stand beside me? Are you my enemy or my friend?'

'I am your mother, Diccon. Your mother.'

For a moment, at my use of his childhood name, his features softened into a vestige of a smile.

'And I revere you for it. You were always my rock, the one solid foundation of my life. I recall so little of my father, only brief memories and the tales you told of his bravery in battle, his fight to remove those who sought their own power in England. You told me of his careful strategy to seize power for himself. You told me of his death on the battlefield at Wakefield, a martyr dying for the Yorkist cause. Now I know the truth. I will be wiser, more careful in my planning. I will not make the same mistake that he did, of underestimating those who call themselves my friends.'

The smile had faded.

'I remember your telling me how much I resembled my father, that I bore his name and his features, but, as the youngest son, I would not inherit his land or his titles. Today I will put my own seal on this kingdom. I am the last of his direct male blood of the House of York. And you, my Lady Mother, should be proud of me.'

I handed him the anonymous letter, which he barely read. With distaste, striding across the room, he cast it into the fire.

'It is true, isn't it?' I suggested. 'I no longer have the power to influence you, do I?'

'No, my Lady Mother. You do not.'

'Does it matter what I think?'

'Yes.' His mouth twisted in what was not a smile. 'Yes, I think that it does.'

Duchess Cecily's intercession to the Blessed Virgin Mary

Hail Mary, full of Grace, Our Lord is with thee.

Never have I been faced with such a conflict of conscience.

My son demands too much of me. My honour is once more undermined. My lord Richard's reputation resurrected for common folk to grin over as a cuckold. Edward's reputation further stained with his promises to Eleanor Butler, if there is truth in it. In any of it.

Do I acknowledge Gloucester's claim?

My sister spoke the truth.

Only you know the truth of his claim. Only you know your honesty and chastity within your marriage. Only you know where your loyalty in the future might lie.

Blessed Virgin. Sons are not easy creatures to deal with. I must make my decision and live with the consequences.

Duchess Cecily makes her decision in Baynard's Castle, June 1483

We met before Mass as arranged and walked together into the chapel where we knelt, side by side. I was aware of him, his every movement as he sank to his knees, head bent.

Concentration on the religious office for once was beyond me. My thoughts, regardless of the priest's guidance, ran along one difficult stream with its endless possibilities. The turbulence of more warfare, engendered by a child with the reins in his insecure and inexperienced hand. The Woodvilles returning to power in the King's counsels.

Or a series of placid eddies with Gloucester as the new King, already wed with an heir. A new reign with a proven man at the helm. Proven in battle and in government.

Would I risk an illegitimate claim through my grandson, if Eleanor Butler had indeed given her promise, or would I support the true York blood of my son?

Who was I, in this fateful decision-making?

Dowager Duchess, wife of Richard, Duke of York. Cecily Neville with royal blood in her veins. Once King's Mother and might be so again. Keeper of the flame for the House of York. Holder of bright memories. There were so few left to do so now.

And whatever I might decide, would it have any bearing at all on the mind of the man at my side as we participated in the High Mass?

Afterwards, alone in the holy atmosphere of incense and gilded saints, 'I promised you an answer, Gloucester. You were gracious enough to say that it mattered to you, even if you will reject what I have to say.'

He waited, chin lifted a little.

'I will support you,' I said. 'I will not work against you.'

I thought he might have sighed softly, but the candle-flame at my shoulder burned steadily, untroubled by any movement of air.

'You will give me your blessing?' he asked.

'I will. I promise. A sacred oath, if you wish.'

Upon which he raised my hand and kissed it.

'I will support you in your claim that the Woodville marriage was false and so the young King illegitimate,' I continued. 'At the same time I hold you to your promise of filial reverence. That you do not hold up my name for public ignominy.'

'I will be silent.'

'Then I can accept that you will take the throne as King Richard. It is what your father would have wanted.'

With a sweep of his palm, he doused the candle, but still I saw the crease in his brow.

'Was Edward a bastard? And Clarence?' he asked.

It was the last thing that I had expected, that he would question me so directly.

'You will never know.'

'It is between you and God.'

'And I will not make confession to you.'

He bowed in acknowledgement, making the shadows shimmer. 'Age has not weakened your mind or your heart.'

No, it had not. I might have sixty-eight years to my name but I was as clear-thinking as I had ever been.

'Will you have Rivers executed?' I asked.

'Yes.'

'I doubt he will be the last.'

'No. There will be those who oppose me, who must be silenced.'

He turned to lead me to the door, collecting hat and gloves from where he had left them.

'What of the boys?' I asked. 'The Princes? And Clarence's son?'

His hand closed warmly around my fingers. 'They will be raised gently, as sons of my brothers. The illegality of their parents' marriage is not their fault. Is that acceptable to you?'

'And Elizabeth?'

'Woodville powers are at an end, but she will not be harmed. She may remain in sanctuary if she so wishes. Do you not trust me?'

'I must. I'll hold you to your promises. But don't break your word to me.' I gripped his hand hard. There was no smile now, no persuasion, only the implacable will that had been mine all the years of my life. 'But I warn you, my son. If you do, if you impugn my honour again, I will complain loud and long before anyone who will hear me, of the injury you have done to me.'

'I have no doubt that you will.' We were outside in the warmth of the day captured within the high walls of my home, the sun on my shoulders a blessing. 'Meanwhile we will work together to bring my father's dreams to fulfilment. I will take on the inheritance of the House of York. I will be crowned and Anne will be crowned as my Queen. You should rejoice. At last the union of Plantagenet and Neville, as you and my father should have been King and Queen.'

It was difficult, but perhaps I should rejoice.

You might regret clashing with my son, I had warned Elizabeth Woodville. Now the threat of his power was levelled at me. There were so many reasons why I must not oppose him. If I did, what would I achieve other than my own unhappiness?

'Will you, as the new King, take some advice from an experienced woman?' I asked, exhibiting none of my inner turmoil.

'Of course.'

'Send north to the centre of your power, to York and to your Neville family at Raby, to bring troops to aid and assist against Elizabeth Woodville, who will assuredly plot to murder you and your cousin Buckingham.'

'The extent of your knowledge never fails to amaze me. Excellent advice.'

He kissed my cheek. I saluted his.

The kiss of Judas. The kiss of betrayal. The kiss of hope for the future. The House of York would remain and prosper.

England's Chronicle, *the twenty-fifth day of June 1483*

We hear that on this day the Duke of Buckingham has been seen to visit his cousin of Gloucester at Baynard's Castle. He has asked him to take the crown and rule England as King.

It does not take any intelligence to assume Gloucester's acceptance. We expect a joint crowning since his wife, Anne, Duchess of Gloucester, is also resident in London. The two illegitimate Princes keep no state, but live most comfortably in the Tower of London under the care of their own household, appointed by their concerned uncle of Gloucester.

Sir Anthony Woodville, Earl Rivers, is dead. Executed for treason in the company of his nephew, Sir Richard Grey.

The Woodville rule is over.

The Plantagenets are returned.

The House of York is in the ascendant.

The Duchess, as custom dictates, will not be present at Gloucester's coronation. Despite her age, she remains in active and fervent support of her only surviving son, travelling frequently in her barge along the Thames between Baynard's Castle and the Palace of Westminster. Head held high, back straight, she must reminisce on the events that have fashioned the direction of her life.

It is thought that she will retire to Berkhamsted again, now that Gloucester's position is secure, but whether she will remain there, we would think not. The lure of government is too heady for a woman raised from the cradle surrounded by power and intrigue. We would miss her imposing figure and dark veils, her imperious nose, the priceless reliquary gleaming with religious power on her breast.

We wish her well and a long life.

The Duchess is a woman of much honour, we suggest, in spite of circulating stories to the contrary. To which no one gives any credence whatsoever.

**From Cecily, Dowager Duchess of York, to
Katherine, Dowager Duchess of Norfolk**
Written from Baynard's Castle

My well-beloved sister,

I have spoken with Gloucester, with all the authority that a mother can command. I fear that it is too little now, but I will hold him to his word, accepting that the stability of the realm desires a man full grown, not a child. I have to trust that Gloucester will rule fairly and justly. This is cruel pragmatism, a necessary gift to all who will dabble in power and politics.

Gloucester will make use of the Eleanor Butler scandal if he must, but will leave my honour intact. I do not know whether he believes in my supposed infidelity. All I know is that it is a keen political weapon to use against the Woodvilles if all else fails. The vicious scandal, stirred up by my own family in their battle for power, will hang over me until the day of my death.

Gloucester has shown his gratitude. He has promised that next year my manors and lands of Berkhamsted will be confirmed in my name. He also gave me a basket of strawberries. Is my alliance so easily bought? I could not eat them.

For the sake of the kingdom I have accepted my own adultery and the bigamous marriage of my son. Can a mother do more? I think not. I will find it difficult to write to Elizabeth, to commiserate with her that her son will never rule. I do not have the fortitude to visit her.

It is my plan to return to Berkhamsted, weep my tears, and live a life of righteousness and dedication. My loyalty now, and in the future, will lie with my son Richard, King Richard the Third.

Your infinitely weary sister, yet still clinging to hope for the House of York. How can I turn my back on all we have striven for?

Cecily, King's Mother

Why Write about Cecily Neville?

Cecily Neville, Duchess of York, is one of the most appealing women of English medieval history. How could I not choose to write about her, despite the obvious challenge? The Wars of the Roses are both vast in scope and complex in the range of family connections. It was a challenge that enticed me.

Cecily, mother of two kings, lived to the great age of eighty years, through five reigns, interacting with such a *dramatis personae* of famous, infamous, and influential characters. Where to start and where to finish?

Some hard decisions had to be made, based on Cecily's direct involvement in the events and their consequences. Thus *The Queen's Rival* begins in 1459 in Ludlow, with Cecily facing a Lancastrian army, and ends with the coronation of King Richard III. After that her role became more onlooker than participant. It was quite deliberate to omit the Princes in the Tower and the death of Richard III at Bosworth. Cecily's acceptance of Richard's claim to the throne provided a natural ending.

There are some characters who, although essential to the outcome of the Wars of the Roses, had little direct impact on Cecily's life during these years. My apologies to all who would have liked more than a mention for Margaret Beaufort and Henry Tudor; I was not unaware of them, but these people are for another time and place. In *The Queen's Rival*, they are dispatched to the periphery.

I acknowledge that the name Wars of the Roses was not con-temporary with the events, nor were the emblems of white and red roses widely used. They are, however, evocative names and symbols and I make no apology in using them.

Cecily, Duchess of York, was the doyenne of late medieval history. What a marvellous life she led through the whole span of the fifteenth century, the Queen who was never crowned. Cecily is not one of the 'forgotten women of medieval history', but she insisted that I write about her. And rightly so.

And Afterwards

Cecily, Dowager Duchess of York, lived on into the reign of King Henry VII, to see her last son Richard die on a battlefield and her granddaughter Elizabeth become Queen of England as wife of Henry VII. She lived a life of piety in these years, rarely travelling from Berkhamsted. She died on 31 May 1495 after signing her detailed will, and was buried beside her husband Richard in the Church of St Mary and All Angels at Fotheringhay. Around her neck on a silk ribbon was tied a papal indulgence. When Elizabeth I visited Fotheringhay she was made aware of the ruinous state of these tombs after the ravages of the Reformation, and arranged for their renewal. The bodies of Cecily and Richard were reburied together in new tomb.

King Richard III reigned until 1485 when he was killed at the Battle of Bosworth, the last of the Yorkist kings. His son Edward had already died in 1484 at the age of ten years, and his wife Anne earlier in 1485. Richard's crown was taken by Henry Tudor as King Henry VII, the first Tudor monarch. Richard's body was famously discovered in 2012 in a crude grave under a car park in Leicester, near the site of the Greyfriars Priory Church. He was reinterred in regal splendour in Leicester Cathedral in 2015.

Elizabeth Woodville lived a comfortable life in Bermondsey Abbey, and died there on 8 June 1492. Her funeral was at Windsor

Castle and she was laid to rest in a simple ceremony beside her husband King Edward IV in St George's Chapel.

Elizabeth of York, daughter of Edward IV and Elizabeth Woodville, married Henry Tudor, becoming Queen Elizabeth and uniting the York and Tudor families. She was mother to Prince Arthur and also the future King Henry VIII.

Edward, Prince of Wales, and Richard, Duke of York, the sons of Edward IV and Elizabeth Woodville, known to history as the Princes in the Tower, have been the subject of much speculation since they vanished from the public eye. Their ultimate end is unknown, or who might have been responsible. Whatever happened, their claim to the English throne was destroyed. A subject for a novel all on its own.

Margaret, Dowager Duchess of Burgundy, had no children of her own. She remained unmarried after the death of Charles the Bold, giving skilful and far-sighted advice to her step-daughter Mary of Burgundy until Mary's death after a fall from her horse. Margaret continued to support the Yorkist challenges to the House of Tudor from Lambert Simnel and Perkin Warbeck. Margaret died in 1503 at the age of fifty-seven years.

Margaret, Countess of Salisbury, and Edward Plantagenet, Earl of Warwick, the children of the Duke of Clarence and Isabel Neville, paid a heavy penalty for their family connections with the Yorkist claim to the English throne. Margaret was executed in 1541 in the reign of King Henry VIII on the charge of treason. Edward was executed in 1499 for treason in the reign of Henry VII.

Travels with Cecily Neville, Duchess of York

For those of you who might enjoy following in the footsteps of Duchess Cecily: in person, by travel guide and history book, or by internet...

Palace of Westminster, London

The royal palace which Cecily would have known was sadly a victim of fire and no longer exists. What a loss to lovers of medieval history it is, particularly St Stephen's Chapel which was the creation of the best artisans of the day. Today we have only the Jewel Tower and of course Westminster Hall. This is impressive enough, constructed by Richard II, showing us what the rest must have been like if we could only imagine it.

Raby Castle, County Durham

The magnificent castle in County Durham, a truly northern stronghold, home of the powerful Neville family and where Cecily Neville was born. She was to be known, but not in her own time, as the Rose of Raby.

Baynard's Castle, London

The centre of operations for the House of York in London, an impressive structure, so we are told, with walls and gardens and its own wharf on the north bank of the Thames. Sadly it no longer exists, but a blue plaque marks the spot on Paul's Walk almost opposite Tate Modern. Imagination needed but its position was supreme.

Palace of Berkhamsted, Hertfordshire

A royal palace much enjoyed by Edward III was originally a motte-and-bailey castle but was greatly added to as an important centre throughout the medieval period. Joan of Kent and the Black Prince spent some time there and it was where Cecily lived through her final years in strict piety. There are remains, but not nearly enough to do justice to the castle where Cecily lived and prayed and kept in touch with her extensive family. After her death, becoming unfashionable, the palace gradually fell into ruin and was only saved from extinction by English Heritage. It is still possible to imagine Cecily there in quiet retreat.

Tonbridge Castle, Kent

Very little remains of this home of the Stafford family where Cecily spent her imprisonment with her sister, but it does have a most impressive gateway and the remnants of the original motte and bailey. The castle was slighted during the English Civil War and was ruinous before being rescued by new owners in the eighteenth century. Now a picturesque spot on the Medway.

Sandal Castle, West Yorkshire

Considerably ruined today, the remains of the motte and bailey give a sense of what was one of the Yorkist strongholds in the north. From here Richard of York chose to lead his troops out to face a much greater army at the Battle of Wakefield where he and his son Edmund of Rutland met their death. There are no battlefield remains to appreciate.

Canterbury Cathedral, Kent
A solemn place for you to make your own pilgrimage, where Cecily visited to pray at the tomb of Thomas Becket when her family was falling to pieces around her with Warwick and Clarence defying King Edward. Such a wealth of history and connection in this formidable centre of history and worship.

Ludlow and Ludlow Castle, Shropshire
A superb castle in the Welsh Marches, and a little town that has preserved its medieval structure. Definitely a 'must-see' place, where Cecily stood in the market place and surveyed the ravaged town after the Lancastrian army ran amok. The castle is a gem, with much extant stonework from the period and before (as well as enough Tudor rooms to keep Tudor fans happy).

Ludford Bridge, Shropshire
The battlefield is not marked but you can stand on picturesque Ludford Bridge and admire the River Teme as you imagine the Lancastrian troops, with both King Henry VI and Queen Margaret in attendance, gathering to the west.

Hereford Castle, Herefordshire

This is where Cecily was reunited with Richard. Today there is no stonework remaining, although the flat site is still there to the east of the cathedral above the River Wye, called Castle Green. With a short stretch of banks and ditches and part of the moat now called Castle Pool, you will need your imagination to 'see' the medieval fortification, but Hereford is worth a visit in its own right, particularly the cathedral.

Fotheringhay, Northamptonshire

Once a large motte and bailey with a stone keep, there is little left of the castle which was the most favoured of Richard Duke of York, but the Church of St Mary and All Saints is a place of pilgrimage for those whose loyalty is captured by the House of York. Here you will find the tomb of Richard, Duke of York, and his wife Cecily Neville. Sadly it is not the original from when Richard's body was reinterred from Pontefract. There was much damage done during the Reformation and the Yorkist tombs were smashed. Queen Elizabeth I ordered the removal of the remnants and the creation of the present monuments to Richard and Cecily that we see today.

Micklegate Bar, York

The tragic place for so many heads to be exhibited over the years. Hotspur's of course. But also the heads of the Duke of York, Earl of Salisbury and Earl of Rutland. Any visitor to York will find their way around the superb walls to Micklegate Bar.

Acknowledgements

My thanks to my editor Finn Cotton, and the whole team at HQ Stories, who launched *The Queen's Rival* into the world. I value his dedication, expertise and professionalism. And not least his enthusiasm for the characters and events that fill *The Queen's Rival*. I am grateful for his tolerance in allowing them to say what I wish them to say.

My perennial thanks to my agent Jane Judd, whose continuing support and friendship are both beyond price. Her advice on reading my first complete draft is of inestimable value. I know that we have both enjoyed the exploits of Cecily Neville.

For all things technical and for the creation and care of my website I must thank Helen Bowden and all her IT experts at Orphans Press. I am constantly in debt to their technical know-how.

ONE PLACE. MANY STORIES

Bold, innovative and
empowering publishing.

FOLLOW US ON:

@HQStories